VIVA PUCCINI!

MEL WEISER

outskirts press

Based on actual characters, events, and historical facts, this book is, nevertheless, a work of fiction. Dialogue and certain scenes were created for the purpose of dramatization.

Outskirts Press, Inc.
http://www.outskirtspress.com

ISBN: 978-1-9772-4256-3

PRINTED IN THE UNITED STATES OF AMERICA

For my wife Joni,
who is love, laughter
and all things wonderful in my life.

- 1 -

She opened the front door of their house and found him slumped on a kitchen chair. She rushed to him, dropping her packages carelessly on the table.

He was nine years old, and he was crying as if someone had broken his heart.

“What is the matter, my darling boy?” she asked. “What happened? Why are you home so early?”

“The...the teacher...said...said...I am sick,” he sobbed.

“What? Why did he say that? Does something hurt you?”

“No.”

Anxiously, she felt his forehead. “You do not feel warm to me. Are you weak? Do you want to sleep?”

“No.”

“Why did your teacher say you are sick? What did he say?”

“He said to tell you I have a genius inside me.”

“What?”

“I have a genius inside me,” he repeated and burst into tears again.

The concern gave way instantly to a radiant smile, and she broke into happy laughter. “He said that? He said you have genius inside you?”

“Yes. Why are you laughing?”

“Oh, my dear, dear boy...you are wonderful! You are not sick. Genius is good.”

“Do you have a genius?”

She could hardly stop laughing. “No...no, I do not.”

“Does Ramelde have it?

"No. None of your sisters has it."

"I do not want it! Take it out of me!" Tears ran down his cheeks.

She wiped them lovingly. "Do not cry, my darling boy. Your genius will bring much happiness into your life."

"No! Take it out. It will make me sad!"

Both mother and son would prove to be disastrously accurate in their predictions.

- 2 -

If fate ordains a young boy's future, family will direct his course. Giacomo Puccini, Italy's great composer, was born into a family of musicians. His great-great grandfather, Jacopo Puccini, was a composer and the San Martino Cathedral organist; his great-grandfather, Antonio Puccini, was a Cappella Master and, like his father, organist in the San Martino Cathedral; his grandfather, Domenico Puccini, wrote operas and chamber music; and his father, Michele Puccini, was a highly respected composer of religious and secular music. Michele was also a very potent man who kept his wife, Albina, almost constantly pregnant in their thirteen years of marriage.

Giacomo was born in Tuscany's City of Lucca on December 22, 1858. He was baptized Giacomo Antonio Domenico Michele Secondo Maria Puccini, a mouthful of names only the first and last of which he ever acknowledged. When his father died, Giacomo Puccini had seven sisters and a soon-to-be born brother.

His father Michele believed a classical education was even more important to life than music. But his mother emphatically disagreed. To Albina, a classical education was valuable, but it could never be as important as music. She decided at his birth that Giacomo would continue the Puccini music legacy and be the greatest of all composers. There was no way the little boy could escape that decision. Consequently, at six years of age, he was enrolled at the Pacini School of Music, where he studied with Albina's brother, Fortunato Magi. Yes, it was troubling that Giacomo had little interest in his academic studies. But what was *more* distressing, what was impossible to accept, was his lack of interest in music.

Giacomo's Uncle Fortunato quickly lost patience with his student.

"I am sending my nephew back to you," he told Albina. "I have never had a lazier student. Furthermore, he is without talent, and I predict nothing good will ever come of him."

"What did you learn?" Albina questioned sternly on her son's arrival home.

"Nothing," he whimpered. "Uncle Fortunato is too strict."

'That is how you learn, silly boy. Discipline. There is no learning without discipline."

"He kicks me."

"Then you deserve it."

"Every time I sing a bad note or play a wrong note on the organ, he kicks me."

"Where?"

"In my shins. It hurts."

"Then do not sing or play false notes. You must go back to Uncle Fortunato and tell him you are sorry, and that you will try harder."

"No, he is mean!" The young boy began to cry.

Albina was firm, but she was also a caring mother. Love as well as determination lived in her heart. Though she was adamant about Giacomo's future, her son's tears were needles that pierced her being and penetrated her resolve. She drew him close. She embraced him and wiped his tears. Holding his face gently in her hands, she looked into his dark, sad eyes and asked softly, "Do you like music?"

He nodded.

"Do you not want to learn music?"

He sniffled and nodded again.

"What does that mean? You do *not* want to learn music?"

"I want to learn."

"You want to learn piano?"

"Uh huh."

"Good." She dabbed a handkerchief gently over his wet cheeks. "It will not come to you without study and practice. You *must* study and practice."

"Not with Uncle Fortunato." Tears began to form again.

"All right...all right...do not cry, my sweet Giacomino, do not cry. Will you be a good boy and study hard if you have another teacher?"

He nodded his head.

"Very well." She grinned at her son. "We shall find another teacher for you."

Giacomo broke into a huge smile. He lunged at his mother and embraced her fiercely.

The next day, Albina Puccini began her search for a teacher to whom her son could relate, someone who would instruct her little boy with kindness and consideration. It wasn't easy to find the perfect music teacher, but she would settle for nothing less. She attacked her problem with the passion of a treasure hunter in search of a lost and precious gem. Eventually, she found her jewel in Carlo Angeloni, who was also a teacher at the music school.

When he was introduced to little Giacomo, Angeloni greeted him with a gentle handshake. "I believe you and I are going to be great friends," he said, looking directly into the boy's eyes and smiling warmly. Then, from the very start of their relationship, he instructed his student with patience, understanding and rich compliments. In no time, Giacomo loved him. Also, the fact that his teacher told him about the joys of hunting added another dimension to the student's admiration. It was the perfect match.

"Are you happy with your teacher?" Albina asked her son.

"Oh, yes, Mama," he answered. "Maestro Angeloni laughs. And he makes jokes. He is not like Uncle Fortunato."

Now his music instruction went well, and he progressed to everyone's satisfaction. But academic subjects were still a problem. He absolutely hated mathematics, and everything else bored him senseless. "He is impossible," his mother Albina heard teachers say repeatedly. "He does not pay attention to what is being taught, and he drums his fingers on his desk as though he is tapping piano keys."

When she wasn't pleading with him to be more attentive, Albina was pleading *for* him – to be readmitted to classes each time he was expelled for bad behavior. "He refuses to read," she was told. "He is in school only to wear out the seat of his pants!"

Years later nothing changed during his secondary school studies. Then, Giacomo proved even less interested in books. Then, he excelled in pranks and practical jokes.

"Zizzi," he asked his close friend Zizzania, "what can we do to enliven our lives?"

"Read a book."

"This is not funny. Lucca is so dull during the summer months; I cannot stand it."

"Giaco, relax. It is too hot to do anything."

"How can you accept that? We should be doing something and not just sitting around like frogs waiting to croak."

"If we do anything in this weather, we will surely croak."

"That would be better than nothing. Think of something, Zizzi. What can we do? Something to wake up this city."

"I could kill you."

"I am serious."

"All right, you could kill me."

"Zizzi...."

"Or I could kill myself...."

Now that was a thought. "Yes!"

"Yes, what?"

"You can kill yourself."

"Thank you."

"Not really. I mean we can make it appear as though you have killed yourself. The city is dead now. We could cause a stir and bring Lucca back to life."

"I like that." Zizzania became interested. "I truly like it. Giaco, you are a genius! How shall we do it?"

The prospect of executing a hoax on the citizens of Lucca was too enticing to let it slip away in laughter. This had to be done. Imaginations flared. Energies were fired. They started immediately, and worked long and hard to prepare a dummy that could be mistaken for Zizzania. Facial features, hair, hands, body size. Finally they dressed it in his clothes and hung it by the neck in the cellar of the building in which Zizzania lived with his parents. With light coming only from a stairway and a sidewalk grating it was easy for them to hide and wait for the dummy to be discovered. They didn't have to wait long. An elderly woman who had an apartment in the cellar came home from her morning shopping. The sight of a "body" swinging scarily in the dim light and shadows shocked her with the force of a lightning bolt. Dropping her packages she staggered into the street screaming madly all the way and fainting on the sidewalk in a dead heap.

Giacomo and his friend Zizzi thought that was hysterical. They laughed so hard they could barely breathe. The prank made the local newspapers. Everyone talked about it. And the city did, indeed, come to life. Some called it another example of Lucca depravity; others laughed at its ingenuity. However the authorities didn't think it was funny. The old woman recovered, but when it was discovered who had been responsible for her trauma both boys were brought before a local judge.

"You," the judge said ominously, pointing a finger at Zizzania, "you are found guilty of faking a suicide. And you, young man," his finger went to Giacomo, "are guilty of helping him."

They stood with heads bowed. Neither said a word.

The judge didn't see their smiles. If he had they would surely have received a harsher punishment than reprimands and a few months of supervision. Albina Puccini, however, was furious with her son. In the street outside the courtroom she made her anger with Giacomo clearly known. "I do not understand you. You are like a wild dog. You run about looking to bite innocent people. When are you going to stop your nonsense? When are you going to apply yourself to becoming what you are meant to be? Your ancestors are watching you. I hear them. They are crying in their graves."

Giacomo loved his mother dearly. He couldn't ignore her distress. It pained him, and he had no wish to hurt her. "I am sorry, Mama," he said. "Please do not be angry with me. I will try to make my ancestors happy. I promise you, I will try."

And he was good to his word. He began to apply himself more diligently to his piano skills and to his composition studies. He improved his keyboard fingering. He wrote short pieces that pleased his teacher. In time Albina smiled her forgiveness. She embraced him, and all was right again between mother and son. However, though his remorse was like a boulder on his back, it didn't keep him from seeing his close friends, fellow pranksters who offered a present to lighten his burden. With the assistance of a cooperative young lady, they removed the considerably heavy weight of virginity from his youthful loins. Awakening his sexuality, it was a gift that altered his very life.

Puccini's music skills continued to develop. He had been responding so well to Angeloni's guidance that by the time he reached fourteen years of age, he was skilled enough to assume the traditional family position of organist at Duomo di San Martino, his city's ancient and widely renowned cathedral. This was particularly gratifying to Albina. Her brother Fortunato, who was presently the church organist, was now being replaced by her son. How wonderful! How just! Remembering Fortunato's detrimental pronouncement about Giacomo's future, Albina grinned and gloated.

The magnificent Cathedral of San Martino had been consecrated by Pope Alexander II in 1070. However, it had taken 400 more years to complete the huge structure. Often called the Marble Cathedral because of its extensive use of pink, green and white stone, it is an architectural wonder. To be an organist there was, and still is, a great honor. A fourteen-year-old boy in that position was an accomplishment beyond measure. Giacomo was rightly proud – especially when he brought home his first salary and placed it in his mother's hands.

Albina looked at her son's shining face. Tears came to her eyes. Smiling through them she touched his black, curly hair. "Thank you, my darling son," she whispered. "Now you are truly the man of this family."

Life was a daily struggle. But somehow Albina had held the

family together. Giacomo's earnings, though not enough to end her struggle, eased his mother's burden considerably. Being anointed "Man of the Family" with such loving, tearful appreciation meant more to the boy than a papal blessing.

"There will be more, Mama," he promised.

As he grew older young Puccini's organ skills approached mastery. San Martino worshippers marveled at the full, rich sound that swelled through the cathedral nave. Each Sunday Giacomo swept into hymns and other religious works with a verve that made listener spirit soar. Occasionally he even inserted a bouncy secular passage into his playing. This upset his sister Iginia terribly; Iginia was studying to be a nun.

"Secular music in church is a sin," she complained.

"There is nothing wrong with it," he defended himself. "I use secular music only at the end of service as everyone is leaving. Seriousness during service; smiles after."

Iginia compressed her lips, but disapproval still shouted in her silence.

Church attendance improved. His reputation spread through the city. In time he added Choirmaster to his musical title. This, of course, increased his salary and helped the family further. It even allowed him to keep a little for himself. He was only in his teens but with money in his pocket he started to smoke. Albina did not object. Smoking was common among young Lucca boys in the 1800s. With a cigarette or one of the popular, crooked little Italian cigars dangling from a corner of his mouth Giacomo puffed and swaggered like a man.

Sometimes, though, smoking could lead to desperate behavior.

"Carlo Carignani," he said, "if I do not have a smoke right now, my lungs will collapse and I shall die at your feet. Give me a cig... please." He was sixteen at the time.

"Impossible."

"Stop being cheap."

"If I had one I would certainly give it to you, Giaco."

"Then lend me some money so I can buy some."

"And if I had money I would lend it to you."

"No money?"

"Not a *centesimo*."

"We have to find money. I need a smoke!"

Giacomo thought hard. An idea came to him. It would be dangerous, but desperation made danger meaningless. He told Carignani his idea and led him to the cathedral. It was a late, weekday afternoon, and only a few worshippers were there. The boys entered through the apse door and wormed their way into the organ loft. Quietly, and with infinite care, they removed two of the smallest pipes from the organ. Each boy hid one under his jacket. Then, like thieves in the night, they slipped from the church and made a fast and successful escape.

The stolen organ pipes were sold to a junk dealer, and the ill-gotten "loot" went for cigarettes. Certain notes in the Sunday hymns were never missed. Knowing what they would be Puccini always avoided them, deftly supplying different phrases whenever they were supposed to be played. When a priest finally noticed spaces where the missing pipes had been the ensuing disturbance swirled around Giacomo like a desert sandstorm, but it never touched him. Who could ever believe that the organist himself would be the culprit responsible for this confounding mystery?

The organ thieves were never discovered, and Cathedral San Martino's Great Organ Whodunit was solved only when Puccini laughingly confessed the episode much later in life as a glaring example of youthful irresponsibility.

Meanwhile as part of his music studies with Maestro Angeloni, Giacomo was introduced to opera. It interested him. It moved him. Angeloni gave him a deeper appreciation of its loveliness and how it related to life. Opera made him sing. It made him think. One day, feeling particularly happy, he thought: *Life is beautiful. It gives me everything. I am admired; I am helping my family; I have friends; I have a marvelous teacher, with whom I even go hunting; this wonderful city of Lucca offers me many opportunities for diversion; and I have my health and my work. It can offer me nothing more*.

There was more, though. It was 1874 and something was about

to happen in the neighboring town of Pisa, something so important it would shatter his contentment and change the entire course of his life.

The genius of Italian opera then was Giuseppe Verdi. His compositions – *La Traviata, Rigoletto, Macbeth* and a host of others - had stunned and charmed the music-loving Italians since 1839. When *Aida* premièred in 1871 it played for almost five years to packed houses in city after city. Now Giacomo learned it was going to be presented in Pisa. How could he remain in Lucca when Verdi's *Aida* was going to be performed in Pisa? Miss this opportunity? Regret his failure for the rest of his life? Never! With the eagerness of a hunting dog after a rabbit he raced to his two closest friends Carlo Carignani and Giuseppe Papeshi.

"Carlo, Giuseppe" he gushed, "I have just learned that Verdi will be in Pisa! I am going. Come with me!"

"Verdi? In Pisa?" Excitement gripped his friends.

"When will he be there?" They asked together.

"Not the Maestro, you damned fools, *Aida*!"

"Ohhh...."

"What do you mean '*Ohhh*'? When will we have another chance to see *Aida*?"

"Is she coming alone?" Carlo asked.

"What?"

"Will she dance with me?" Giuseppe wanted to know.

Puccini realized he was being played. He grinned sheepishly and shook his head.

Pointing a finger at him, Carlo said, "Now who is the damned fool, Giaco?"

All three laughed at Puccini's embarrassment.

"We know about *Aida*," Giuseppe said. "We were going to tell *you*."

"Then you will go with me?"

"No."

"*No*?"

"No..."

"But...."

"You will go with *us*."

There was more shoving, more laughter, more warm roughhouse friendship.

The trio set off for Pisa early in the morning of March 11, 1876. Pisa is 18.5 miles from Lucca. They had no money. They had no transportation. All they had was their youth, their enthusiasm and good shoes. Helped once by a farmer and his wagon, they made it to Pisa in seven hours. Luckily they arrived at the theater just before the curtain rose. Now the problem became entrance. How were they going to see *Aida* with no money for tickets? Whom did they know to help them? No one. It should have been impossible. But Puccini hadn't traveled eighteen miles to miss this opportunity. He was prepared. The trio waited until the last moment. Then Giacomo led his friends to the stage door.

"Signor," he said urgently and respectfully to the ancient doorman, "We have come all the way from Lucca with an important letter for the stage manager that *must* be delivered before the opera begins." He waved an envelope he'd put in his pocket before leaving Lucca.

"Give it to me," the doorman said. "I will see that he gets it."

"No, no, no. We have been ordered to deliver it to him personally. We were told if he does not receive it before the curtains part, something terrible will happen during the performance."

The doorman studied the three earnest faces. He frowned.

"Please, Signor..." Giacomo begged.

"For the good of the opera..." Carlo added.

"There isn't much time!" Giuseppe urged.

It will never be known if the doorman knew he was being duped or if he allowed three young music lovers to enter out of the goodness of his heart. Telling the story years later Puccini laughed and said, "I believe I saw the old man smile as we charged past him." It makes no difference. What is important is that the boys raced into the 1100 seat Teatro Nuovo, sneaked quickly up to the balcony, where the seats were not reserved, and settled down for a performance that utterly overwhelmed them.

"Hearing *Aida* in Pisa," Puccini is reported to have said, "It opened a musical window for me."

Verdi had touched his soul.

All the way back to Lucca, he relived the opera with his friends. Their arms waved, their voices rose in snatches of melody, their faces glowed with excitement.

Puccini was seventeen at the time, and back in Lucca the indelible memory of that experience haunted him. Until then he'd only dabbled in composition, turning out a few short, religious pieces or some light things that he and the five-piece dance band he'd helped to form often played. But now it was different. Now his interests took a more serious turn. And they didn't start in a small way.

The first significant work he tried was a grand symphony to which he gave the pompous title: *A Preludio Sinfonico in A Principali* (A Symphonic Prelude in A Major). It was meant for a large orchestra, and it was much too dramatic and complicated to be well received. But it was enough to stoke his fire. Quickly he composed another big orchestral piece: *Preludio Sinfonico.* But this, like the first prelude, did absolutely nothing to enhance his reputation. It didn't matter. *Aida* had ignited him. "God," he said, "has touched me with His little finger. I cannot deny what is stirring within me."

Ideas now raced through his head like a forest fire. He couldn't stop them. Consequently, when teacher Carlo Angeloni gave him an important graduation assignment, he attacked it with the full power of his imagination.

"I gave Giacomo an assignment," Angeloni later told Albina. "He was to compose a Mass for the Festival of San Paolino."

Paolino was a 4th century poet-priest who became Lucca's patron saint.

"He did not do it?" Albina asked.

"Oh, yes, Donna Puccini. He completed it. That is why I am here."

"It is not good enough?"

"On the contrary, it is excellent. I will miss him sadly, but I am convinced now that he must go on without me. He must have instruction beyond my abilities."

Albina was overcome with emotion. She had feared bad news from Angeloni, but her fears had been groundless. Her dreams for her son were being realized. "What do you suggest, Maestro?" she asked eagerly.

"After he receives his graduation certificate from our institute, he must go to Milan and enter the Conservatorio."

This was more than Albina had expected. Carlo Angeloni had suggested Milan's Conservatorio. *Milan!*

Working feverishly, Giacomo had completed his Mass soon after his teacher gave him the assignment. He called it: *Mass for Four Voices and Orchestra,* and it premièred at the San Paolino festival on July 12, 1880. Almost an hour long, the composition was played beautifully. The music critic of Lucca's leading newspaper praised Puccini, saying: "This Mass is exceptional in its construction, melodies and harmony." That and the enthusiastic audience reaction sent Giacomo's spirit flying. What was more important, though, was Carlo Angeloni's critical and emotional reaction. Hearing it performed by a full orchestra, Angeloni declared, "A promising young artist has given us a musical composition that reveals talent for which all of Italy will one day cheer!"

- 3 -

Giacomo sat with his mother in the kitchen of their modest home. Dishes had been cleared away. The table separated them. With forearms on the table and fingers interlaced, Albina looked solemnly at her son. She had told him there was an extremely serious matter to be discussed. He couldn't imagine what it would be. Was his mother ill? Had he done something wrong? Did she need more money? Was one of his sisters or his younger brother Michele in trouble? As the man of the family was he going to be asked to protect someone's honor?

"We must consider your future," Albina said.

"My future, Mama?"

"Yes." She studied his puzzled expression. "Your Mass was well received. Your teacher has spoken about it with me. Now Maestro Angeloni believes you must leave Lucca when you are graduated from the Pacini Institute."

"*Leave Lucca?* But..."

"You must study at the Milan Conservatorio."

"But I am doing so well with Maestro Angeloni." Giacomo saw himself separated from friends, family, work, and the comfortable life he was presently enjoying. He saw himself being thrust into the turmoil of a major city, alone, struggling with the multitudinous problems of survival. The possibility shook him. It was not something he wanted. He had to resist. However, knowing his mother's strength, his objections were devious. "I cannot go to Milan, Mama. How will you and the family survive? You will lose my salary. There will be no money."

"That is not a problem for you to solve. You will go to Milan."

"But there will be fees...and monthly expenses...and –"

"We will find a way," Albina cut him short.

"I may not be accepted –"

"We must try."

The finality in those words ended all further discussion.

Giacomo's reluctance to leave Lucca should have been strong enough to reject his mother's insistence. But in Italy, especially 19th century Italy, the first son in a family was almost always the parents' favorite. He was pampered, spoiled, given special attention and considerations beyond those of his siblings. Usually, he grew into a *Mammoni*, a "Mama's Boy." So it was with Giacomo Puccini. And in that role he could never consider disobedience to the wishes of his mother. If Albina said: "We will find a way," he knew the matter was settled. He would eventually be in Milan studying at a highly respected conservatory where he would be expected to bring honor to his family and his ancestors. How this would be accomplished rested now entirely with Albina Puccini, and he was certain that his mother would explore every conceivable avenue to make it happen.

Giacomo's grandmother was Angela Ceru, and one of Angela's brothers was Dr. Nicalao Ceru. When Giacomo's father died, Ceru became the self-appointed protector of the Puccini family. He was a successful doctor, he wrote articles for *Il Moccolino,* a local newspaper, and he was quite wealthy. Exceptionally tall and somewhat imperious looking, he appeared a little formidable, especially while curling one end of his full mustache during serious contemplation. However, that was only appearance. Though he could, at times, be gruff and insistent, he had a gentle disposition.

Uncle Nicalao Ceru became the first stop in Albina's crusade for assistance. She knew he was aware of Giacomo's efforts, and that he'd heard her son's Mass at the Festival of San Paolino. It had even moved him enough to praise Giacomo in one of his *Il Moccolino* articles, connecting him glowingly to his musical lineage with the aphorism: *"I figli dei gatti pigiliano itopi."* ("The children of cats will catch the mice" ...or, in more colloquial terms: "The apple doesn't fall far from the tree.")

Albina sat before him now in his well-furnished comfortable home. She was forty-seven and beginning to show signs of aging. Her hair was long, graying, parted down the middle and coiffed somewhat severely in a tight bun at the nape of her neck. Her once-sweet features were slightly blurred by added weight, her ample figure hidden in a plain black dress. And, except for the wedding ring she still wore, her hands and wrists were free of jewelry ornamentation. Sitting sedately, erectly, and holding a large, black purse on her lap she was the picture of maternal rectitude. She may have been surrounded by taste and wealth, but Albina Puccini was not a woman to be intimidated, or swayed from purpose.

She gazed at her husband's uncle.

"Uncle Nicalao," Albina began, "I come to you because you are an important man in a position to make a grand contribution to the glory of our city."

Nicalao Ceru smiled at her and nodded his head slightly in appreciation of her opening gambit.

"Everything of importance that happens in Lucca interests you," she continued.

He nodded again.

"And nothing escapes you."

A third nod.

With her introduction over Albina took a deep breath and attacked directly. "My son Giacomo is in need of your munificence. Assistance is sure to bring honor to both Lucca and to you, Uncle."

Nicalao grinned broadly. *Munificence? Hmmm. A lovely word. Impressive.*

He liked that. *She has prepared herself well.* "Albina," he said, "I am delighted to have you in my home. May I offer you coffee? Some crackers?"

"That would please me."

Having been informed of her intention to visit Nicalao was ready. He went to a credenza and returned shortly with a cup of rich, black, Italian coffee and a small plate of crackers that were topped with thin slices of cheese.

"You must join me," Albina insisted.

"I intend to," he answered, going to the credenza to pour coffee for himself.

There was a slight formality in this meeting. Though related by marriage Albina never felt truly close to Dr. Ceru. He functioned on an entirely different level of society, a much higher level. Caring for her eight children had kept her too occupied to approach Ceru for social reasons. However, despite the formality, she felt things were going exactly as she had hoped.

After a sip of coffee, the good doctor put his porcelain cup on the small, damask-covered table between them. He crossed his legs and looked kindly at her. "And how may I help my charming niece?" he asked.

Albina relaxed perceptibly. There had been such warmth and gentleness in his question that she smiled broadly for the first time. Yes, this was going to turn out well, easier than she had feared. Giacomo would be going to Milan. He would not want for money. He would devote himself fully to his music, and Uncle Ceru would be his generous *mecenate*, his patron.

"My son Giacomo," she began earnestly, "is the organist of the Duomo."

"I know."

"He has composed impressive works."

"I know."

He is also a fervent admirer of our beloved Maestro Guiseppi Verdi."

"As am I."

"One day, he will equal Maestro Verdi with music that will live in eternity...if given the opportunity."

First, "munificence" ...now, "live in eternity"....a good phrase. There is more in this woman than most people would suspect. Doctor Ceru smiled. His interest in Albina's petition grew. "And what may I ask would be the nature of this opportunity?"

"Schooling. He must go to Milan. He must study at the Conservatorio."

"Then he should go."

Albina's heart beat faster. He had agreed! It had been simple. Her son's future was assured. She was tempted to reach and grasp her uncle's hand in gratitude. But the last step remained to be taken. She sat straighter. She smiled. "We do not have money for such schooling. Will you be kind enough to be his patron, dear Uncle Nicalao?"

The answer came quickly. "No."

Albina's heart stopped. "No?"

"No, Albina...no," Ceru answered quietly. "I know of Giacomo's musical achievements. They are exceptional. I know also of his pranks and escapades, and I am not convinced of his eagerness to succeed in Milan. He is frivolous. He and his friends are too wild. They drink too much; they are more interested in playing dance music in cafes than truly appreciating the magnificence of Verdi and Rossini. And I have heard many disturbing stories of their behavior with innocent young women. If I were certain of my nephew's determination, I would agree to your request in a moment...but I am not. So, unfortunately, I must say, 'No.' And I am very sorry to have to say it."

Another mother might have been crushed by this rejection. Not Albina Puccini. She gathered her wits quickly. She placed her cup gently on the small table between them. She retrieved her large black purse and smiled at him. "Some of what you say is true, Uncle Nicalao," she said evenly, "which means, also, some is not. It is true that Giacomo has been a little wild at times and that he and his friends have engaged in some objectionable activities. But it is also true that his musical gifts are beyond question. The wildness will disappear with age, as it did with you and most other mature men of accomplishment. The musical gift will remain and flourish, as it did with Maestros Verdi and Rossini. I am sorry that you cannot see this truth of life. However, I wish to thank you for your time, your patience and your coffee. Good day, Uncle."

She moved to stand.

Truth of Life...hmmm....another unexpected phrase.... Dr. Ceru raised a hand.

"Please, Albina," he said. "A moment."

Albina hesitated. At another slight, gentle gesture of his hand she settled back on her chair again.

Ceru looked steadily into her eyes.

Albina matched his gaze.

He raised a thumb and forefinger and began slowly to twist the right end of his white mustache. "Though you speak quietly, there is passion in your words," he said softly. "And you are correct in what you say: All men with vibrant lives do things in their youth that they are embarrassed to admit in their maturity." He paused and smiled. "I am one, of that you may be certain. Sometimes, as you say, we forget this *truth of life* as we age, and we look upon our young with unrealistic expectations. I do not know if I have misjudged Giacomo, but I am willing to admit that possibility. If he truly possesses the genius and desire you see in him, and you are not simply being swayed by the love and faith of motherhood, I will be there for him."

Albina's spirit soared again. "You desire proof?"

"Yes."

"How may he prove this to you?"

"First, he must be superior in his entrance examination to the Conservatorio."

"And second?"

"Let us be concerned with the first. If he does not satisfy that requirement, there may be no second."

Albina Puccini stood quickly. She wore a wide, satisfied smile. "He will not disappoint us, Uncle Nicalao," she said with conviction, and then repeated softly, "Be assured, he will not disappoint us."

Albina was pleased with Nicalao's proposal. It was fair and not a difficult requirement to satisfy. As far as she was concerned, the meeting had ended positively. But, still, something troubled her. Yes, there was hope. But hope was not enough. As she walked to her home, she considered her position carefully. She needed something else. But what could it be? *What*...? And then it came to her. By the time she entered her simple apartment on Lucca's Via di Poggio, Albina Puccini had her next move fixed firmly in her mind.

Given Dr. Ceru's hesitancy Albina suspected her uncle might be unwilling to meet all of Giacomo's financial needs regardless of a superior examination grade. She had no specific reason to believe this. It was only a feeling. But it was strong enough to make her believe she would have to be secure. She needed *certainty.* There would have to be a guarantee of additional support. But from whom? Her friends were in no better financial position than she. All had responsibilities that precluded the kind of generosity that Giacomo's education would require. Friends were limited, but... *acquaintances*? Yes, acquaintances. There the picture assumed another coloration. Some people she had met through her husband's church affiliation were well-to-do. Some were even extremely wealthy. At least one in that group might help.

One did.

The Duchessa Caraffa di Noia.

The duchess was acquainted with Albina. Her two daughters Mimi and Nini had attended seminary school with Albina's daughter Iginia. As soon as she could, Albina corresponded with her. She requested and was granted an audience. On the appointed afternoon, Duchessa Caraffa greeted her warmly and graciously. She led Albina into her lavish greeting room and showed her to an ornate armchair. "Would you care for refreshment?" she asked.

"Perhaps," Albina answered. "After I have described the reason for my visit."

The duchess smiled and nodded. They settled back in their chairs for a convivial afternoon. It didn't take long. The meeting quickly became a collaboration of two women who shared a visceral need for female unity in a world dominated by men. "We must seek assistance on a high level of authority," Duchessa Caraffa suggested enthusiastically.

"Do you have someone in mind?" Albina asked.

"I am familiar with the Marchesa Pallavicini. She is Lady-in-Waiting to Queen Margherita. We shall request a royal scholarship from Her Majesty for Giacomo's education at the Conservatorio."

The suggestion made Albina's head spin. The *Queen*? Did she dare to petition the pinnacle of royalty? Yes, she dared. For Giacomo's future she would dare anything. With the Duchess of Caraffa's guidance Albina Puccini drafted a letter for her son, a letter that was brief in form but replete with a mother's hopes and dreams.

"Dearest Majesty," she began, and then she continued by acknowledging the Duchess of Caraffa's suggestion to write this letter. Quickly she established Giacomo's musical promise and the fact that he had completed his studies satisfactorily in Lucca. Then, going directly to her point with mention of the queen's patronage of artists, she requested royal assistance for her son's attendance at the *Milan Conservatorio*.

The letter was delivered quickly into Queen Margherita's hand by her lady-in-waiting, the Marchesa Pallavacini. The queen's reply didn't come, however, for many weeks, during which time Albina worried and waited impatiently. She said absolutely nothing to Giacomo about what she had done. She did however tell him of his great uncle's reaction to her request, adding at the close of her narration, "I have said you will pass the test, Giacomino, and now you must not make my words a lie. Good will not be enough; only excellence will do."

Doctor Ceru knew nothing of Albina's letter to the queen. However, he felt and understood her anxiety. It had taken fortitude for her to come to him with this request. Well, he had made his offer and stated his condition. To question her further about Giacomo or the impending conservatory examination would only have added to her distress. Considerately he waited in silence for the approaching day and its results.

Giacomo, meanwhile, became a jumble of exposed nerves. He worried. He doubted his abilities. He imagined terrible consequences if he disappointed his dearest Mama. After graduating from Instituto

Pacini he'd enjoyed a period of delicious freedom. He taught music, he worked in the cathedral, and he spent enjoyable time with close friends. But he was no longer a carefree child. Out of his teens now, he was a twenty-two-year-old man with the additional concern that, irrespective of his test result, his age might negatively influence an admission decision.

The fateful day arrived. It was Monday November 1, 1880.

- 4 -

On Italy's 19th century tortuous roads Milan was almost 300 miles from Lucca. Unlike Giacomo's earlier Pisa adventure this could not be a simple excursion. This would require special transportation. A carriage? No, that would take forever. It would have to be by train the speed of which was from twelve to twenty-five miles per hour. Fare for the faster train was beyond Albina's resources. Giacomo would have to travel at the crawling pace of twelve miles an hour.

Preparation for his departure took place all through Tuesday. Classes were to begin in a few days, actually the first week of November. It was understood that he would return to Lucca if he were not accepted for study. But it was also understood that he might have to remain in Milan indefinitely if he should pass the examination. Albina's feelings were mixed. She began to miss her precious Giacomino even before he was to board the train, but simultaneously she hoped desperately that he would be able to remain in Milan. She had cleaned, folded and lovingly packed the clothes he would need for the trip, and she had cooked enough food for the day of travel. Discussing the examination carefully with her Puccini felt the weight of her concern. "Take care my dear Giacomino," she whispered looking steadily into his eyes. "And remember to write as soon as you have results." Then kissing his cheeks she freed him so he could take care of two important personal matters. First he spent some hours with his dearest friends Zizzania, Carignani and Papeshi. They joked outrageously with him but wished him a safe and successful trip. Next he visited his teacher Carlo Angeloni and welcomed his informative and reassuring words. Finally he returned home, and he relaxed with his family. He held Albina's hand and laughed at the excitement of his sisters and his young brother Michele who wished fervently he were able to go with him.

Now sitting at a train window and watching the countryside of Tuscany pass by slowly Puccini had an opportunity to consider what lay before him. He would have to find a room, someplace inexpensive that offered board as well as accommodation. It would have to be close to the Conservatorio. He would also want to visit the institution, test a piano, practice, keep his fingers limber. He had received a letter in Lucca informing him that his examination was scheduled for that Thursday. He had to be ready. Maestro Angeloni had told him what to expect. He would be asked to demonstrate something in harmony. Then he might have to develop a melody. There would also be questions about music to test his knowledge and understanding. The examination would be difficult, perhaps hours long, and it would be in the tradition of both audition and written test. Furthermore this would be only the beginning of his difficulties. The Conservatorio's curriculum would last a minimum of three demanding years and include classical and cultural subjects – drama, literature, logic, aesthetics, philosophy – as well as music theory, composition and history. Should he pass and be accepted he would be admitted for only the first year during which time he would still have to prove himself for the remaining two years.

As he considered everything Giacomo now felt his doubts returning with each passing mile, and he cursed himself. *You are such a fool. Your days are always peaks and valleys. Happiness cannot survive long in you. It must always be killed by worry.* The thought did nothing to ease his anxiety. It only intensified it. He drew within himself. He slouched in his seat and spoke to no one during the entire trip. He'd left Lucca in the late afternoon. With many stops along the way the train delivered him to Milan the next morning. He had slept fitfully through the night, and now he awoke with aching, tired muscles and engine soot all over his clean clothes. The train jerked to an unsteady stop. He looked bleary-eyed at the few disheveled passengers in the car. They had fared no better than he. Gathering his heavy, canvas travel bag Giacomo stumbled from the train. He looked about. He took a deep breath and then strode toward the street uncertainly wondering where and how quickly he'd be able to locate a suitable room for his stay in Milan.

Knowing little about Milan Puccini went directly to the stationmaster's office for information and assistance. The room was small, cold, and crowded. The man was large, warm, and expansive. "Come in, come in," he invited with a huge smile and a wave of his beefy hand. "The end of October in Milan can be a most uninviting time of year. Cold snaps are to be expected. You should come here when the air is gentle and the flowers are in bloom. Stand near the stove. Warm yourself. You came from Lucca?"

"Yes."

"Your first time in Milan?"

"Yes."

"I could tell. You look lost."

"I am." Giacomo smiled at the man's ebullience. No matter how dismayed or depressed he might be, friendliness always made him smile.

"We must not allow you to remain lost," the stationmaster said. "Let us see if we can find you. Where do you want to go?"

"I do not know. I am in the city for an examination, and –"

"What kind of examination? Are you ill?" he asked with concern.

"No. I am hoping to attend the Conservatorio and –"

"You are a *musician*?" His voice rose in pleasure and excitement.

"Yes."

"What instrument?"

"Piano."

"My favorite instrument! And you are going to study opera?"

"If I pass the examination."

"Wonderful! Milan is mad for music, and I am mad for musicians. How may I help you, my lost young friend?" His exuberance charged the office air.

Giacomo's uncertainty and anxiety vanished as swiftly as odors in a fresh breeze. He straightened and broke into an even broader grin. "Thank you, sir," he said. "Do you know where I can find a room until I finish my examination? Someplace inexpensive?"

"You have no place to stay while you are in Milan?"

"Not as yet."

"I imagine you are not the first musician to come to our Conservatorio without a place to stay."

"I imagine you are right," Giacomo agreed. He wondered if this jovial, pudgy person were about to offer him a room.

"I imagine the Conservatorio has considered this problem."

"I imagine you are right again." He was enjoying this man.

"Then they will have the solution for you. My advice: Do not go around the city looking for a room. Go directly to the school's main office. They should have a listing of available places for lost musicians like yourself."

Giacomo shook his head in embarrassment and mumbled, "I should have thought of that."

"You're not supposed to think of those things, my young friend. You are a musician. You think of beautiful things. Music. *Opera!*"

"You are very kind, sir."

"You will find the building on Via Conservatorio. Go with God, young friend, go with God."

"Thank you, sir." Giacomo turned to leave.

"Wait!"

Giacomo stopped.

"Your name...what is your name? I want to write it down. I shall go to your opera when I see it advertised on a poster."

At that moment Puccini couldn't have received a better gift. "Giacomo Puccini," he said with a proud ring in his voice.

"Good luck to you, Giacomo Puccini," the stationmaster called as Puccini left the office. "I shall not forget you."

"Nor I you," Puccini called back. Was this a portent of how everything was going to be in Milan? Was he going to enjoy success? Was God smiling at him? He closed his eyes and said a quick, silent prayer.

Walking now became a pleasant stroll. Warmed by the office stove and the stationmaster's kind words he smiled, pulled his shoulders back, lifted his head, hummed a remembered passage from *Aida* and headed for his future on Via Conservatorio. The day had suddenly become brighter, the city more attractive. Gone were his self-doubts and his other uncertainties. He was ready for his examination. And it never occurred to him that failure was a strong possibility.

- 5 -

In 1807, the French Viceroy of Italy had established the Conservatorio di Milano in the Church of Santa Maria della Passione. It was accomplished through a Royal Napoleonic Decree. From its inception this conservatorio dominated the musical scene. By the time Giacomo appeared there seventy-three years later it had grown to be the center of all major Italian opera activity. Its instructors were respected composers; its academic staff, equally admired.

He was greeted by an office receptionist. "When we opened our doors at the beginning of the century," he was told, "we had only eighteen students, and all boarded on the premises. Today we have too many for that. However we have arranged for our students to live elsewhere near the Conservatorio. You have nothing about which to be concerned. There will be comfortable accommodations for you on Via Passione while you are here for your examination."

Relieved of that concern Giacomo felt more buoyant than ever. He left his canvas bag in the office and spent the next hour becoming acquainted with the school's rooms. He looked into a rehearsal hall where he suspected he would be performing for the examiners. He tried the piano rapidly running the keyboard in flourishing arpeggios and scales, and he was satisfied with the sound. He walked into another room where he suspected lecturers presented the curriculum's required classical subjects. He shuddered at the prospect of sitting through dull lectures, but knew he'd have to change that attitude if he expected to receive a certificate from this august institution. No one interrupted him. No one challenged him.

Outside the rooms in the piazza he saw four students walking, laughing, and chatting animatedly. *They are all so young,* he thought. *No one is as old as I.* Concern about age shook his equanimity again. However it didn't last long. The stationmaster's words suddenly flashed in his mind: *I shall go to your opera when I see your name advertised on a poster.* And he murmured, "It is going to be all right...it is going to be all right."

Satisfied with what he'd seen of the schoolrooms, Giacomo retrieved his travel bag from the front office and made his way to Via Passione. There just as he'd been told by the receptionist he found a room. It was a small room, but it was clean and comfortable. If he should pass the examination and remain in Milan, it would cost him with board only thirty lire a month. *Yes,* he thought happily, *God is still smiling at me.*

Night had not yet arrived. He'd had nothing to eat since finishing Albina's last sandwich on the train, so he left his room and made his way to Milan's main shopping area. There he found a small restaurant where he wolfed down three bowls of Milanese minestrone soup and beans. Then he strolled about the area gawking at its modern designs and its swirling activity. He felt the magic of Milan working on him, and he wished friends were with him to share his excitement. Milan was certainly not Lucca. Being there was an extraordinary experience for a small-town boy.

As darkness crept over the city and shadows sneaked into its crevices Puccini returned to his room. He unpacked his few belongings and relaxed. It had been a turbulent day, one that had battered his senses and shaken his emotions. He wrote a brief letter to Albina telling her he had arrived safely, had visited Milan's Galleria, was impressed with the city, and was now exhausted. He sent her kisses and told her, "I shall write tomorrow, dearest Mama." Then he slipped into his comfortable bed and fell quickly into a deep and much-needed sleep.

The first phase of Puccini's examination was scheduled for 10:00 am.

He'd been correct in assuming it would take place in the

rehearsal hall where yesterday he'd tested the piano. He smiled as he entered the room. He felt confident...a trifle nervous but still confident.

An examiner greeted him. "You are Giacomo Puccini?"

"Yes."

"Good. Thank you for being on time. You will have to go to another room for the next phase of your examination, and others will be waiting for you there. We are grateful for your promptness."

Giacomo smiled and nodded appreciation of the compliment.

"I am Maestro Bazzini," the examiner said. "Let us begin."

Puccini went to the piano. He settled on the seat. His heart beat faster. He flexed his fingers and ran the keyboard. *What will they ask me to play?* This was the moment his mother had cautioned him about. This was the moment he dreaded. He closed his eyes and hoped quickly he would be up to the challenge.

"Are you ready?" Maestro Bazzini asked.

"Yes."

"Very well. You will find one line of a bass passage before you on the piano stand. Take a moment to study it."

Giacomo glanced at the line. "What do you want me to do with it?" he asked.

"Please play the harmony for it."

Puccini couldn't believe his ears. *Harmony for a single bass line?* That's what he had been so anxious about? Did they think he was a novice at the piano? Or were other applicants for admission to this prestigious music school all beginners? He smiled, nodded, took a deep breath of relief and supplied harmony for the assigned line. Somehow, though, that harmony didn't seem to be sufficient for an examination. Quickly and without being asked to do more, he switched the bass line into a half dozen other keys and segued smoothly into glittering harmony for all of them. Then he stopped and looked at his examiner. Maestro Bazzini's face was blank. Giacomo's heart dropped. He'd hoped to impress him. But had he erred in doing more than he'd been asked to do? Had he been pretentious? Stamped himself an exhibitionist? He wondered, *Have*

I failed the examination already? He didn't know what to think. As always, when he was uncertain about anything, self-doubt returned and shook him to his core.

"Now," Bazzini said solemnly, "you will find a melody in D Major on the music stand under the bass line you have just harmonized. Kindly give me additional melody to that D Major passage."

Believing he may have already ruined his chance to study at the Conservatorio, Puccini's confidence returned with a vengeance. Bazzini wanted melody? All right, melody is what he'd get. With nothing more to lose he would give this examiner melodic passages he'd remember long after he, Puccini, was gone. He straightened on the piano bench, squared his shoulders and plunged into the D Major melody with masterful finesse. First he played it as written. Then he reprised it in the styles of Bach, Mozart and Wagner. Finally he offered his own improvisations of the passage. Song filled the hall. It swelled forcefully and whispered sweetly. Delightful music rippled from his fingertips. He played as if he were at his organ in the great Duomo di San Martino filling its nave with blissful hymns. He swept into the reprises with verve, with passion, and when he played the final notes he looked up almost defiantly. This time, the face of examiner Antonio Bazzini was not blank. This time it wore a faint, enigmatic smile. And Giacomo wondered: *Is he smiling for me or sneering at me?*

Maestro Bazzini gathered the pages of notes that lay before him on the desk. He said nothing about Puccini's performance. Instead, coolly and simply, he instructed him to "proceed now to classrooms at the end of the corridor, where you will, with other applicants, undertake the written portion of your examination."

There was something a bit forbidding about Maestro Antonio Bazzini. Sixty-two years of age, with a high, broad forehead, piercing eyes and a full, graying beard and mustache, he exuded the authority of a no-nonsense instructor who would be sure to demand unwavering effort. Unsmiling and a bit brusque he was a virtuoso violinist who had composed enduring chamber music, and he carried himself like a man who expected respect. Giacomo didn't know what to make of Bazzini, but he feared the worst. *Another tyrant like my Uncle Fortunato,* he thought. *Dearest Mother, why have you forced me to do this?* Troubled again he stood, nodded to his examiner, mumbled, "Thank you," and left the hall for the second part of his examination.

The room at the end of the corridor contained only ten student chairs and desks. When Puccini entered, he found seven of them already occupied with other aspiring applicants all looking anxious and expectant. Five were male; two were young women. No one spoke. No one moved. All looked ahead at the large desk before them where two instructors consulted each other in hushed tones. Giacomo settled behind one of the empty desks and, as he did, the instructors ended their muted discussion. "Giacomo Puccini?" one asked.

"Yes," he answered.

"Good," the instructor said. "You complete our roster. Let us begin. Each of you will find the examination before you on your desk. You are to answer all questions. Do not leave any question unanswered. That is very important. I repeat: *All* questions *must* be answered. The examination will end in precisely one hour. Good luck. Begin now."

The pages were face down. Puccini turned them over and felt his stomach flip. He'd believed this written portion of his examination would pertain to music. But he was shaken by what he saw. The very first question asked him to explain the principal objectives of ancient Greek dramatic literature. *Ancient Greek dramatic literature?* His brain rattled. His breath caught. *Greek literature? Dio! Dio! What am I doing here? I do not belong in Milan. I want to go back to Lucca.*

Giacomo looked at the second question. It was no better. Asking him to explain why the Sistine Chapel is a masterpiece of Renaissance painting it swung another powerful blow at his already crumbling confidence. *Literature...art... are they all like that?* He glanced quickly at the three remaining questions. *Yes...yes...yes... they are all like that, all about art, all about culture.* He didn't know what to do. He remembered the proctor's instruction: *"All* questions *must* be answered!" and dismay overwhelmed him.

For a moment Puccini thought of getting up, returning to his small room, packing his belongings, and fleeing back to Lucca. But the face of his mother flashed in his mind, and with it came all the belief and hope Albina had in him. He was to be the continuation of the Puccini legacy, the scion of musical masters. Time and again she'd made that clear to him. Running back to her without even trying to answer these questions would be a disgrace from which he would never recover. He had to try. He had to summon whatever academic knowledge he'd absorbed from discussions around the family dinner table and from his teacher Carlo Angeloni. He remembered his father's belief in a rounded education: *"Puro musico, puro asino"* (Pure music, pure jackass). And he wished he'd been more attentive to the lectures of his Pacini school instructors. But wishing was not going to lift the burden of these five questions, and running away wouldn't do that either. The solution to a problem he learned then and there was to face it.

He attacked the first question with renewed determination. *The principal objectives of ancient Greek dramatic literature?* He thought hard. He saw his mother and sisters around the dinner table. He pictured Carlo Angeloni in their classroom. At first nothing happened. His frustrations intensified. His patience wavered. But he persisted, and soon words floated up from the depths of his subconscious. Isolated words. Lonely words. *Hubris. Fatal flaws.* He reached for them desperately. Wrote them down and stared at them. Then satisfied he had something to hold onto, he expanded them and wove them into a brief, coherent essay that, somehow, addressed the question. Reading his paragraphs he wasn't sure they would satisfy the examiners, but he felt better about having supplied something. *This is no different from music composition,* he told himself. *Words are the notes, sentences are the melodic measures, and paragraphs are my themes and emotions. I can do this.*

Puccini completed the written part of the examination with five minutes of the allotted hour to spare. He rose from his seat and walked to the front of the room with his papers in hand. An instructor accepted them and looked at him strangely. "You are the oldest candidate in the room," he said softly. "What took you so long to apply?"

The question surprised him. He had no answer. All he could say was: "I hope I am not too late."

"We shall see," the instructor said unsmilingly. "Tomorrow morning, ten o'clock, this room for your interview."

The abruptness of the direction unsettled Giacomo even more and stayed with him for the rest of that day. He had intended to write to his mother and Angeloni to tell them of the ordeal, but his thoughts were too garbled. Instead he went to a cafe where he sat in a corner, nibbled on some gorgonzola cheese, and fretted.

The next morning in the classroom he waited for the arrival of his interviewers. Who would they be? New examiners? What would they ask?

They appeared precisely at ten, Maestro Bazzini, and the two instructors who had proctored the previous day's written portion of the examination. They sat behind the table at the front of the room. Giacomo sat before them. "Good morning, Signor Puccini," greeted the instructor who had asked him the unsettling question at the close of yesterday's meeting. "Let us get right to the point. I am Maestro Magliani. I teach the humanities here at the Conservatorio. My associate Maestro Panichi and I have read the essays you submitted, and we must say they present a disappointing understanding of Western culture. Yes, they show knowledge but only superficially so. Why is that?"

Puccini suddenly felt a boulder had been dropped on him. He opened his mouth to speak, but nothing came out. He was at a total loss for words. The examiners waited, faces blank, eyes peering at him. Finally, Giacomo found his voice. "Why were my essays unsatisfactory?" he asked rhetorically, and then he quickly answered his own question. "Because I have been a fool, Maestros...because I allowed the selfishness of youth to keep me from appreciating the beauty and significance of other art forms. I am older now. I know better now. And if I am admitted to the Conservatorio, what you will impart to me from your wealth of knowledge will not fall upon deaf ears."

He didn't know where the answered had come from. It was as though someone were speaking through him, speaking for him. Maestro Magliani nodded slightly. Apparently the answer pleased him. But Puccini saw a smile flicker on the faces of the other two instructors, and he wondered again: *Are they smiling for me or laughing at me?*

He didn't have time to worry about that any further. What followed was a stream of challenging questions from all three examiners. They probed his youthful escapades, his family background, his age, his interest in opera, his musical compositions, his Cathedral San Martino organist position, even his feelings about the recent unification of Italy. They were relentless. Nothing escaped them. Though the interview lasted only a half-hour, it was intense and long enough to leave him exhausted and bewildered when it was over.

"Thank you, Signor Puccini," Maestro Magliani said at its conclusion. "The council will meet tomorrow to make its final determinations. Results will be posted outside the main office the following day at one o'clock. We wish you well."

They filed from the classroom quickly, leaving him alone to gather his wits. He sat in a daze for the next twenty minutes searching for meaning in the broad, sweeping scope of the interview. It seemed to him it had been about everything in general and nothing in particular. Where had they been leading him? What were they looking for? And whatever it was, had he given it to them? Once again he was certain he'd failed his examination and would be returning to Lucca.

The rest of that day and the morning of the following day became a blur to Giacomo Puccini. He could think only of the council's final decisions. Exactly at one o'clock on the afternoon of the posting he stood at the main office door anxiously, even shyly, like a child not knowing if it would be petted or spanked. He was not alone. The other seven applicants crowded around him murmuring their concerns to each other.

"I heard they will be accepting only four of us," one of the two young women offered.

That prompted some babble.

Feeling like an old man within this cluster of young students Puccini said nothing. But he thought: *Only four?*

The office door opened, and a secretary appeared with papers in hand. The group fell silent. She said nothing, but she smiled at them after tacking the papers to the hall bulletin board and then disappeared quickly back into the office. Like locusts in a wheat field the applicants swarmed toward the board.

There were two sheets of paper in the posting, one atop the other. The top sheet explained the examination saying it was designed to see who would benefit most from a Conservatorio education. It added that only four students would be accepted, and that a formal letter of acceptance or rejection would be mailed to all applicants in three days. Registration for classes would be on November 21, with classes to begin on the following day, November 22, 1880. The final sentences noted coldly:

THE VALUE OF YOUR ENTIRE EXAMINATION IS 200 POINTS. THE FOUR HIGHEST SCORES ARE OF APPLICANTS WHO HAVE BEEN ACCEPTED. THEIR NAMES ARE ON THE ACCOMPANYING PAGE.

"Turn the page, turn the page" one of the boys urged excitedly. And the others exploded in a burst of noisy agreement.

Since he was standing before the notice, Giacomo reached quickly and lifted the top sheet of paper. Groans of disappointment and cheers of excitement battered his eardrums. But only a long, deep sigh came from *his* mouth.

There he was!

And not only there, but at the top of the short list of names:

GIACOMO PUCCINI

He couldn't believe his eyes. He stared. He touched his name. He whispered it almost reverentially. Then grinning as if he'd just been honored with a royal title he turned and joined the other three celebrants in raucous congratulations while the four rejected young applicants drifted away confused, tearful, devastated.

Puccini was asked to join his fellow victors for a celebratory drink at a nearby cafe. Though he wanted to be with them he knew it was impossible. *Money.* He didn't have enough in his pockets for even one small glass of wine.

Money...money. His time in Milan would always be about money.

It saddened him to refuse, but he apologized without explanation and rushed back to his room on Via Passione where he wrote a jubilant letter to his mother.

- 6 -

Receipt of Giacomo's letter produced a rush of relief through Albina so intense she believed for a moment she would cry. She wanted to laugh, to shake the walls with her happiness, but her upbringing was too restrictive to permit that kind of emotional display. Albina Puccini was a woman of deep feeling but limited demonstrativeness. Instead she simply clutched her son's report to her breast. She closed her eyes and grinned silently like the happy winner of a national lottery. Then as quickly as possible she gathered her family together and read Giacomino's letter to all. The Puccini family was a tight knit, loving clan, with all sibling members distinctly interested in each other's accomplishments. Their brother's success in Milan brought great joy to all, especially to the youngest member of the family, Michele.

"Mama, I want to go to Milan," he announced. "I want to be with Giacomo. I want to study at the Conservatorio too."

"You will, Michelino," Albina responded lovingly. "You will, when you finish your school studies."

"I want to go now!"

"Be patient and work hard, my son. It will be only two more years, and they will pass quickly. You will see."

What followed this gathering added immensely to Albina's happiness. The next morning she dressed with particular care. She was going to present herself to someone unannounced, and she wanted everything about her appearance to be especially appropriate. This was going to be a meeting about which she had thought carefully.

She was going to see Uncle Nicalao Ceru.

Help and vindication were her objectives. Dr. Ceru had promised monetary assistance if Giacomo could prove himself by passing the entrance examination. Well her son had not only passed, he had achieved the highest score of all applicants. What would Uncle Nicalao have to say about *that*? Would he abandon his reservations about Giacomo now? Or would he insist upon yet another test before helping him?

She stood before the door of Dr. Ceru's home and nervously adjusted her coat.

Dr. Ceru's servant admitted and announced her, and Ceru appeared immediately with a questioning smile on his face. "Albina," he said. "Indeed, a pleasure. Come in, come in. I am having my breakfast. Please join me."

"Thank you, Uncle Nicalao," she said. She followed him into the breakfast room. "I do not wish to disturb you. I am here only to show you this." She offered Giacomo's letter.

Puzzled, Ceru accepted the letter. "Please," he said motioning her to be seated.

She sat stiffly on a high-backed chair her hands folded primly on her lap, and she watched him as he opened her son's letter. She wondered what he was thinking as he read: *"...My entrance grade is the highest of all...Please tell Maestro Angeloni I found the examination surprisingly easy...."* Would Ceru be pleased? Annoyed? It made no difference. However he would react, she was ready for him.

Uncle Nicalao lowered the letter and looked at his niece. He smiled. "Well," he said, "I have always said Giacomo is an intelligent boy. It is his character that concerns me. The question is – yes, he has been admitted, but will his character allow him to *complete* his studies?"

Albina had feared this. Her response came quickly and with her own confident smile. "We shall never know if he is not given the opportunity to try. That is true, no?"

Dr. Ceru clapped his hands and laughed appreciatively. "Yes, that is true, Albina. Very true. And he is going to need some assistance along the way, is he not?"

"That is why I am here now."

"I understand." He looked admiringly at her. "I did say I would help. Well, Giacomo can count on me. Perhaps one day he will be successor to our Giuseppe Verdi. Let us hope so. I will be pleased to contribute to his success. I shall send him thirty lire a month, as long as he remains at the Conservatorio. How is that?"

Albina beamed. "That is most generous of you, Uncle Nicalao. I thank you...for my son and for myself. Now I shall be happy to join you at breakfast."

Later at home again, Albina's happiness was short-lived. Reality seeped into her thoughts. Thirty lire a month for three years was, indeed, a generous gesture, but Giacomo's monthly rent alone would be thirty lire. Where would the necessary additional money come from? Money for food, for the incidentals of a student's life?

Her answer came in a few weeks' time when a stranger appeared at her front door. Albina was puzzled. The stranger introduced herself as Marchesa Pallavicino. She handed Albina a sealed letter. Albina looked at the seal. Her heart beat furiously. The stranger had identified herself as a lady-in-waiting, and the letter was from the Queen of Italy! She tore the seal and read the letter's contents. She sighed. She smiled. She wanted to laugh and dance. Her efforts had not been in vain. *Giacomo has been granted a one hundred lire monthly scholarship for the first year of his studies at the Milan Conservatorio!* Her dreams for her son were being realized. First, Uncle Nicalao's assistance, and now a royal scholarship. Her Giacomino's studies were guaranteed. He was safe!

Life in Milan during that first year of Conservatorio study proved to be hugely exciting for Puccini. In 1880, Milan was the center of Italy's cultural life. It had the great La Scala opera house, it breathed theater, avant-garde music filled the air, progressive thinking dominated conversations, sophisticated fashion and manners prevailed, and the city's physical character blossomed everywhere in the construction of new and wondrous buildings. There were parades, exhibits, races, and all forms of entertaining activities. Milan was alive. It vibrated infectiously with promise and enthusiasm!

And Puccini loved it.

This was Giacomo's first time away from his loving family. But he adapted to his new life quickly and eagerly. He went to see operas at the Teatro Manzoni and the Teatro Dal Verme spending only a few *centesimi* for gallery seats in the highest reaches of the theaters. Or he cadged free tickets from friends. He visited cafes and enjoyed Milanese soups. He window-shopped for hours in Milan's famous Galleria Vittorio Emanuele. He wandered the streets and inhaled the spirit of the city.

Often he did this alone. Sometimes with new friends. One such friend was Pietro Mascagni, who went on later to compose the enormously successful opera *Cavalleria Rusticana*. Puccini and Mascagni shared a room and rent expenses for a year, avoiding their creditors with ruses that could have been hilarious operetta librettos.

"Hide, Giaco, hide!" Mascagni would scream. "He's coming... he's coming."

And Puccini would dive into a closet and wait there until Mascagni dealt with some businessman who demanded payment of a long-overdue bill.

"He's not here, Signor," Mascagni would say sympathetically.

"He owes me money! Where is he? "

"I wish I knew, sir. He owes me money, too."

"He is a scalawag!"

"No, sir...he is worse than a scalawag."

"I will report him to the authorities!"

"Do so, sir. Report him! Would you like me to go with you?"

"He owes me money! He is a thief!"

"Of the worst kind! He stole my lady friend."

"What?"

"Yes, he seduced her, ran away with her, and left me all alone to cry over my loss." And here, Mascagni would fake weeping, blow his nose loudly and wipe away non-existent tears. "I don't know where he is, sir, or if he will ever return. But if you find him will you tell me, please? I have a score to settle with that scoundrel."

At other times, Mascagni would cook in their room on a tiny alcohol stove – something strictly forbidden – while Giacomo banged away on the piano covering the clatter of plates, pans and food preparation with loud scherzos and rondos *con tutta forza*.

Theirs was a warm and close friendship. However Mascagni, five years younger than Giacomo, was still filled with adolescent impatience. Formal education didn't suit his musical goals. It was all too slow, too restrictive. Consequently, after one brief year he left the Milan Conservatorio and became the conductor of a touring opera company. This gave him the freedom he needed to create and to test his own compositions. Though he and Puccini parted, their friendship remained strong through the years. A binding force of their friendship may have been their mutual poverty. They shared what they had, but neither one ever had enough money to live without worry. This became particularly true for Puccini when Queen Margherita's scholarship ended, and Dr. Ceru's thirty lire became Puccini's sole source of support. Letters to Albina constantly wailed about deprivation:

"Dear Mother...I need beans.... but I have no money...."

and

"Dearest Mother...There is no money even for a glass of wine, so I remain in my room and sleep..."

and

"My Darling Mother...I loathe poverty! Yesterday I had to sneak into the theater to hear Carmen....Tonight, however, I am fortunate... I shall eat beans...!"

Hardly a letter went to his mother or his favorite sister Ramelde that didn't mention some financial difficulty: The stove in his room needed repair; his clothes were threadbare; he'd just pawned his coat; there were no *centesimi* for cigarettes or cigars; he was smoking cocoa leaves; he'd sold his watch and tie pin; he needed new pants; he had no money for coal; it was winter and he was freezing!

Academically Puccini wasn't faring much better. In his studies with Antonio Bazzini he was exposed to musical intricacies that confounded and distressed him. Bazzini demanded that he learn fugues and string quartet pieces, that he should become familiar with music theory and the complexities of classical composition. This was not what Giacomo wanted. Back in Lucca his teacher Angeloni had introduced him to opera, and his Pisa experience with Verdi's *Aida* had made him say: "God touched me with his little finger." Formal composition didn't interest him. It was too bland, too mechanical. He needed excitement, passion. He wrote to his mother:

"Everyone writes opera here...I do nothing but rage!"

By constantly complaining Puccini kept his family's concerns at a constant boil. His mother and sisters did everything to make him happy. In true Italian fashion they continued to treat him as their "Mama's Boy." Sister Ramelde sent him a new suit, though the cost of it was a terrible financial strain. Albina sent him small amounts of money from the meager, municipal pension she had been granted when her husband died. She even petitioned the city council for a scholarship when Queen Margherita's monthly stipend expired, and she was devastated when it was refused. No one in the family thought of telling him to stop feeling sorry for himself. No one thought of telling him to find some means of augmenting his income. In Lucca he'd found income-producing occupations: he'd been an organist and a member of a cafe band. Certainly Milan offered him similar opportunities. He had free evenings. Instead of wandering around the Galleria Vittorio Emanuele until it closed, or sitting in a cafe, or wasting time reading novels, he could have helped himself and eased the burden on his mother and sisters.

But he never thought of that. Nor did his family. Giacomo was their hope. Giacomo was their shining promise. If her son needed assistance, Albina Puccini would search everywhere for a way to provide it.

In addition to the pain of poverty, Puccini suffered terribly from homesickness. He had Milanese friends, and he dined with them and enjoyed the exciting activities of the city with them. But they were not enough. He still pined for Lucca. Lucca was where he had always been protected. Lucca was where living had been easy. In Lucca he'd never worried about food or staying warm. In Lucca his studies with Angeloni had never been as demanding as they were at the Conservatorio. He missed his city. He missed his home. Pampered since the day he was born Giacomo Puccini, now a young man in his twenties, was unable to manage the vicissitudes of life on his own. He wanted his Mama. He was dependent and childish in many ways Nevertheless, he persevered through his first year at the Conservatorio – erratically, complainingly, but with surprising success.

Lessons with Maestro Bazzini were more rewarding than Giacomo was willing to admit. Antonio Bazzini was a gifted teacher and recognized as such throughout the musical world. Despite his resistance Puccini benefited greatly from his instruction. He learned about musical aesthetics, about dramatic theory, about the importance of self-discipline, all of which played mightily in the creation of his future work.

Maestro Bazzini recognized and appreciated the progress his student was making. "Signor Puccini, your *Quartet for Strings* is very good," he offered in one of their teacher-student meetings. "It is sensitive, imaginative, and it reflects the Baroque influence of Antonio Vivaldi very well. I am pleased."

"Thank you, Maestro," Puccini replied. "I was hoping my changes from major to minor keys would not offend you."

"On the contrary, I found them stimulating. Baroque skills will contribute to your compositions next year when you enter your opera classes."

"Maestro Bazzini, may I ask a question?"

"By all means."

"I am also interested in the German composer Richard Wagner. His operas move me. They are muscular. They breathe fire."

"What is your question?"

"Oh, yes, my question...do you believe Maestro Wagner is changing the face of Italian opera?"

"Why do you ask?"

"Because I will be composing operas, and I will want my work to be as strong and dramatic as his. Like Vivaldi, Wagner is changing me, and I should not like to include influences in my work that are not as deeply effective and lastingly significant as his. Do you believe Maestro Wagner is changing the face of Italian opera?"

"That is a pretentious question, Signor Puccini."

"Pretentious?"

"It presumes too much. You are in your first year at the Conservatorio. You are many years from learning enough to compose successful operas, and now at this early stage of your education you are presuming 'deeply effective and lastingly significant' work. Do not be impatient, Signor Puccini. There is much to learn, and there are many obstacles to overcome. Great ambition is admirable, but perspective is necessary if you are to avoid the pain of great disappointment. I sincerely hope you will thrill the music world someday. I see that possibility in you, but I urge you to keep your eyes and your heart on the present and not to be anxious about the future. Allow yourself to be influenced, avoid imitation. Your music must be yours and yours alone. Good things may happen to you, Signor Puccini, but they will require great effort on your part...effort I should add that I am detecting in the compositions you have been submitting to me in our class. I particularly like your *Quartet for Strings* and the influence of Vivaldi in this work. If you will demonstrate equal imagination, understanding and skill under Wagnerian influence I will be equally pleased, especially since I do believe that the German Richard Wagner is surely changing the face of Italian opera."

Then Maestro Antonio Bazzini smiled benignly at his dazzled student.

It was the longest speech Bazzini had ever made to him. Ordinarily his answers to Giacomo's questions were succinct. But this time he had not only answered the question, he had also offered sound advice, a warm evaluation of Puccini's work, and belief in Giacomo's potential.

"I sincerely hope you will thrill the music world someday. I see that possibility in you...."

The words rang in Puccini's head. He'd always needed emotional stroking. Now, for the first time, this stern disciplinarian was offering him a gentle hand. In that moment, he began to see Maestro Antonio Bazzini in a new light. He smiled gratefully. "Thank you, Maestro," he said enthusiastically. "I thank you for your time and your interest." He offered a hand.

Bazzini took the extended hand in both of his. "Remember my words," he said with a smile.

"I shall," Puccini responded. "Indeed, I shall."

After this meeting, Giacomo Puccini felt honored to be studying with Maestro Antonio Bazzini. Of course this didn't stop him from whining about assignments and wailing about the difficulties he faced. Nothing could change that. But thereafter he did feel more comfortable in Bazzini's classes.

It was then that another extraordinary instructor entered Giacomo Puccini's life and paved his way to the fame and fortune that Albina Puccini had envisioned so fervidly for her darling son.

- 7 -

It came on the heels of death. The Conservatorio's director, Stefano Ronchetti-Monteviti, died suddenly in November of 1882 at the age of sixty-eight. His replacement became Maestro Antonio Bazzini. This created a teacher opening. It was filled quickly, and the new instructor proved to be much more than a tutor. He soon became Giacomo Puccini's godsend.

Maestro Amilcare Ponchielli was sixteen years younger than Bazzini. His opera, *La Gioconda,* had thrilled Milan and established him as a composer of admirable talent. Though fierce in appearance – bulky, with deep set eyes, a bushy beard and sloping shoulders that caused him to lean forward almost aggressively – in manner he projected calmness and surprising affability. He listened attentively. He laughed and engaged warmly. Giacomo loved him instantly. And when he discovered Maestro Ponchielli's principal interest was opera, Puccini believed he had once again been "touched by the little finger of God."

He wrote and told his mother all about this marvelous man, and he assured her that his progress would be rapid and promising because of him.

Albina was thrilled. She wrote to his teachers. She thanked them for their guidance. And then brazenly she begged their help in finding work for her son after he would receive his graduation certificate. Both maestros responded in writing to her plea.

Bazzini's words were polite and sharp. He told her he was pleased to have Giacomo in his classes, and that Giacomo was doing well and progressing satisfactorily. He added that finding him employment was something he could not grant, that Giacomo had to make useful contacts, to be disciplined, and to continue working diligently.

Unlike Bazzini, Ponchielli responded with kind and gentle assurances. He told her how delighted he was that Giacomo was one of his best students. And he assured her that he would help Giacomo to secure a position once her son had completed his studies at the Conservatorio. Then he thanked her for her motherly interest.

The letter thrilled Albina. She was now satisfied that her Giacomino was in the hands of a teacher with almost paternal feelings. That he was still a lazy student unwilling to apply himself to anything that didn't stir his interests still bothered her deeply. But encouraged by Ponchielli's gentle words she hoped her son's ways would be changed.

They were.

Motivated by Ponchielli's steady encouragement Puccini threw himself into his assignments. He still found aesthetics sheer torture. In his notebooks he scribbled: *"Help me, God!!...I cannot stand any more of this!!...I am in pain!!...Will it never end? This is killing me!... Help!"* But his steady string of assignment compositions impressed and pleased both Bazzini and Ponchielli. In 1882 and 1883 he wrote no fewer than *fourteen* fascinating pieces – suites, adagios, scherzos, fugues, preludes, trios for violins and piano, orchestral symphonies and vocals for baritones, tenors, and sopranos.

His relationship with Maestro Ponchielli deepened steadily and meaningfully.

"Signor Puccini, I should like you to visit with my wife and me at our summer villa," Ponchielli said at the beginning of 1883. It was Giacomo's final year at the Conservatorio.

Puccini was thrilled. "Maestro, you honor me."

"You will end your studies soon, and when you do I shall want you to meet some people whom you should find most interesting."

Puccini smiled sheepishly. "My studies will not be over until I complete my final examination satisfactorily."

Ponchielli grinned. "Yes," he agreed, "but neither of us is truly anxious about that, am I correct?"

Puccini nodded. "I thank you for your confidence, Maestro."

"It is well deserved. And since we shall no longer be student and teacher, when you receive your certificate of graduation I should like us to use our Christian names. You will be Giacomo to me, and I will be Ami to you. Will that be acceptable to you?"

Puccini was speechless. "I...I... Maestro, I... I do not know what to say. It will be difficult for me to address you as...as...Ami."

"We will become friends, and my friends will be yours...unless of course you prefer not to be my friend?"

Puccini was breathless. "Nothing would please me more...*Ami.*"

"No, no," Ponchielli said quickly with a smile. "Maestro...until you have been graduated. Ami *after* that."

Before graduating, though, Puccini had to pass his final academic examination and to compose a symphonic piece that would be presented by the student orchestra. Realizing how much this could mean to him he set himself to both tasks and became an ardent and uncompromising student.

The written graduation examination took place on June 24, 1883. Grades were posted two days later. He rushed to the front office. Standing before the bulletin board he held his breath as he scanned the notice for his name. When he saw it, his heart leaped to his throat. He had achieved a score of 163 points out of a possible 200 and was well within the passing range! The academic burden had been lifted from his back.

All that remained for graduation and the start of a professional career was the performance of his musical composition. He had titled his piece *Capriccio Sinfonico.* And he had put his soul into the effort. He needed this to be well-received. True to form he worried. Since it was to be played by the Conservatorio's amateur student orchestra Giacomo feared his *Sinfonico* would not be presented well.

On July 14th, 1883 he paced outside the school's auditorium smoking one cigarette after another. He was neatly dressed in the suit his sister Ramelde had sent him. His jet-black hair was combed at the sides leaving a slightly tousled curl over his forehead, and his mustache was trimmed neatly above his wide, full-lipped mouth. He was a handsome young man with an attractiveness that immediately intrigued many women. At this moment, though, women and seduction were the farthest subjects from his mind.

Maestro Ponchielli approached him and noted his nervousness. "Are you ready for this?" he asked quietly.

"Is one ever ready for this?" he asked, grinding the butt of his cigarette into the cobblestone pavement with the toe of a polished shoe.

His teacher smiled. "I believe you will have many opportunities to discover the answer to that question."

Puccini smiled weakly in return. "Thank you, Maestro. And I hope you will be at my side for all of them."

"Your *Capriccio* will be the fourth composition in tonight's program. Try not to be anxious. I am confident it will be well-received."

"I wish I were as confident. The orchestra needs more rehearsing."

"No. It is in good hands."

"Good hands? The conductor is only a student."

"Not tonight. Tonight all compositions will be conducted by Maestro Faccio."

Puccini's eyes widened. "M... Maestro *Franco Faccio?*" he stammered.

Ponchielli smiled and simply tilted his head in a slow nod.

"But...but...I witnessed the rehearsals...the conductor was...."

"A student? Yes. For rehearsals. Music reviewers are in the audience. The Conservatorio wants only the best for them."

"Maestro Franco Faccio...." Puccini breathed in amazement.

Franco Faccio was Italy's most admired conductor. He was a composer of operas, a former Conservatorio student of Stefano Ronchetti-Monteviti (the school director who preceded Bazzini) and the famed conductor of La Scala opera house's 110-piece orchestra. Faccio brought countless operas to scintillating life with the magic of his baton. Musicians practiced assiduously in the hope of one day playing for *Il Maestro*.

"Come," Ponchielli said. "Let us take our places. The program will be starting soon."

Puccini, dazed, allowed himself to be led to his seat.

Once his student had been seated, Amilcare Ponchielli left him to join his lovely wife, opera singer Teresina Brambilla.

Puccini sat through the first three compositions like a man in a trance. He heard nothing. He saw nothing. He barely moved. But when *Capriccio Sinfonico* and his name were announced as the next presentation, he jerked as if he had received an electric shock. Every nerve, every cell in his body became instantly alert. He sat erect. He clasped his hands across his chest. He stared at the stage. He held his breath as Faccio waited for total musician attention. Then, sharply, down came *Il Maestro's* baton.

The first blast of drums and brass filled the auditorium. It was followed quickly by the gentle and easy *andante moderato* of strings and woodwinds. Giacomo couldn't believe his ears. His music swelled to stirring passages and segued smoothly to soft, romantic melody. He closed his eyes. His fingers relaxed across his chest. He exhaled a long, deep sigh. All his apprehensions dissolved instantly in the fullness and richness of the student orchestra's skills. He smiled. He almost laughed aloud. *I must never again doubt my beloved teacher,* he thought. Ponchielli knew. Ponchielli understood. *Capriccio Sinfonico* was indeed in good hands.

The piece lasted only fourteen minutes. However, at its conclusion it received resounding audience approval in continuous applause. Puccini looked around. Everyone was smiling and responding enthusiastically. He thought his heart would burst with pride and happiness. He had done it. He had worked hard for many hours, even capturing snatches of melody on scraps of paper as they exploded in his head while he was eating, walking or reading. And it had all been worthwhile. *They like it,* he thought. The *Sinfonico*'s reception was an unqualified success, a prodigious validation.

He glanced to his right. Across the aisle Maestro Ponchielli applauded and looked his way with a wide smile. Puccini grinned and nodded vigorously in return. He could barely sit through the remainder of the program.

But what he felt that evening was mild compared to the joy that overwhelmed him the next morning.

Filippo Filippi was Italy's most important music critic. He wrote for the prestigious *La Perseveranza,* and he had been in the audience. After hearing Puccini's *Sinfonico* he believed young Giacomo possessed a gifted musical talent. He wrote: *"Signor Puccini demonstrates a rare blending of style, personality and character. More experienced composers have not done as well."* Then he concluded his review with this sentence: *"He has created something genuinely inspiring, something truly fresh and engaging."*

The critic's words sent Puccini immediately to his desk. There he wrote a jubilant letter to his mother. For the first time he truly saw a future in music. Before the graduation concert he had spoken of music as his life. But that was more from Albina's persistent insistence than deep and genuine conviction. Now his struggles had been justified. Angeloni...Bazzini... Ponchielli...all had struck sparks in him. Finally, *finally,* these small flashes had merged, fused and flared into an all-consuming blaze of passion. *Yes, he was going to be a composer.* There was no question, no hesitation. *He would create great works.* But he would not create orchestral music, despite his *Capriccio Sinfonico*'s success. No, no...his efforts would be for the stage.

They would be for opera!

- 8 -

Maestro Amilcare Ponchielli's summer villa was located in the small village of Maggianico near wide and serene Lake Como. Lovely homes dotted the lake's hillsides. Exquisite gardens and vineyards could be found everywhere. Thick forests surrounded the blue waters. And like stage scenery the awe-inspiring Alps towered over everything. No wonder Maggianico attracted the sensitive and creative minds of the age. Musicians, novelists, composers, painters...all congregated in local cafes nightly generating an aesthetic vibrancy so strong it was a palpable entity in itself.

In the 1880s an intellectual movement began that ultimately altered Italy's entire artistic and cultural character. It was called *Scapigliatura Milanese* which translated roughly means: "The Disorderly People of Milan." The community around Lake Como was decidedly *Scapigliatura Milanese.*

This was the aesthetic and creative environment into which Ponchielli now brought Puccini.

"I have told you, Giacomo, there are some people I should like you to meet," he said soon after Puccini arrived. "One in particular is Ferdinando Fontana."

"The poet?"

"You know of him; that is good."

Ferdinando Fontana was no ordinary writer. Unusually versatile he authored plays, poems, newspaper articles, opera libretti... whatever literary form struck his fancy. Born in Milan on January 30, 1850 he was only eight years older than Puccini. However he had authored a prodigious body of work by the time Poncielli intended to bring him and Puccini together.

"I am excited to meet him, Maestro."

"No, no. You have been graduated. Henceforth you must call me *Ami.*"

Giacomo shook his head slowly. "It will feel strange on my tongue."

"I will be introducing you as my friend. *Maestro* will not serve my purpose."

"Very well..." He took a deep breath. "Ami." He smiled and grunted.

Ponchielli grinned at his discomfort. "The more you use it, the easier it will become."

"I will try, M... *Ami.*"

"Good. See? That was not difficult. Now...I want you to meet Ferdinando because I spoke to him about you only two weeks ago. We are both very friendly with Antonio Ghizlanzoni."

The name took Puccini's breath away. "*Aida*'s librettist...." he whispered.

"Yes. Antonio invited us to *Il Barco,* his family's hotel near Milan. Ferdi and I spent three days there, during which time I told him you were in need of his assistance."

"His...his assistance...?"

"Exactly. You say you want to compose for opera. I believe you should. The Sonzogno Competition is where I believe you should start."

Edoardo Sonzogno, owner of the newspaper *Il Secolo* and Milan's Teatro Lirico, had established an annual opera competition for new Italian opera talent. The Sonzogno Prize for one-act operas quickly became the most important and valued means of gaining recognition and entrée into the operatic world.

Giacomo's head was spinning. "The...the Sonzogno Competition?"

"If you are willing."

"Yes...yes...I am more than willing."

"Good."

"But...but...I will need a libretto...I have no libretto."

"That is why I spoke about you to Fontana, and that is why I want you to meet him. He is eager to help."

During their three days together at Ghizlanzoni's *Il Barco* hotel Ponchielli had praised his protégé enthusiastically to Fontana. He'd even extracted from him an interest in authoring a one-act libretto for the Sonzogno Competition. Of course there was a matter of fee, which Ponchielli negotiated down to 100 lire upon completion of the libretto and 200 lire more if Giacomo should win the Grand Prize. All that remained was for the participants to meet and to see if their personalities could effect a harmonious collaboration.

"He will be here tonight," Ponchielli continued. "My wife is preparing an excellent dinner for all of us. Do you like *Anitra al Cognac*?"

"I have never tasted it."

Ponchielli grinned. "Then I predict – after your first mouthful you will become as enamored with it as I."

Puccini grinned with him. "I am always receptive to an experience of love, Ami," he said quickly with a playful bow.

Ponchielli laughed. The reply pleased him in two ways: One for its wit and the other for the easy use of his Christian name.

Fontana arrived at the Ponchielli cottage at seven o'clock. He took one step into the house. Then he stopped, closed his eyes and inhaled deeply. *"Anitra al Cognac!"* he exclaimed loudly enough to be heard in the village piazza. "Ahhhh...I smell the duck...I smell the garlic, the mushrooms, the onions, the cognac...I smell the claret... ahhhh...I am in heaven."

Mrs. Ponchielli came from the kitchen grinning like a child on Christmas day.

"With a nose like that," she said, "you should be in a museum instead of wasting your time writing drivel."

Fontana threw his arms wide. "Teresina," he cried, "you are not only a great opera singer, you are also Queen of the Kitchen and Empress of My Heart. Come to your servant, come to your slave."

Laughing all the way Teresina Ponchielli walked into his arms for an exaggerated *abbraccio* and a peck on both cheeks.

"I am starving," Fontana told her. "I will have three servings of your superb anitra tonight...one for my appetizer, one for my entree, and one for my dessert."

"You will have only what I give you, and that will be: Lobster Marsala for your appetizer, Anitra al Cognac and pasta for your entree, and peaches with burgundy and almonds for your dessert." And she tapped him once playfully on his chin as she stepped away from him.

"Excellent," Fontana replied happily. "I shall have three servings of each."

So began a four-day vacation for Giacomo Puccini that would live vividly in his memory forever. There was laughter. There was rich conversation. There was the endearing warmth of camaraderie. By the end of his time in Maggianico, Puccini had not only reached a new level of friendship and conviviality with his former teacher, he had won for himself as well a collaborator of outstanding accomplishment. Ferdinando Fontana's exuberance and intellectual acuity ideally matched Puccini's respect and creativity. The two men blended perfectly.

After dinner everyone retired to the cottage's sitting-room for wine, while the young family maid cleaned and rearranged the kitchen. Giacomo, Fontana and Teresina lit cigarettes; Ponchielli enjoyed a cigar. The small room was comfortably and charmingly furnished. Gentle and colorful pictures decorated the walls, a few chairs of attractive design faced each other around an oval short-legged table, and an upright piano occupied a corner. Ponchielli and Teresina sat together on a blue patterned, camelback sofa. Fontana and Giacomo settled onto cushioned straight-backed armchairs.

"Teresina...Teresina," Fontana sighed with his customary ebullience, "your dinner was magnificent... *you* are magnificent."

She smiled. "And *you* are a shameless master of flattery."

"Yes, yes, that is true," he responded, "but my flattery is always couched in truth."

Everyone laughed. It was impossible not to. He was an infectiously charming young man.

Then Fontana stretched contentedly and asked. "Now, what shall be the subject of our conversation?"

"What are you writing now?" Teresina asked.

"Something for our young friend here."

Giacomo grinned in anticipation.

Fontana and Ponchielli had agreed earlier that something in the vein of the macabre would be appropriate for the contest and compatible with Giacomo's talent. Fontana was aware of the success Puccini had enjoyed with his *Capriccio Sinfonico,* but he understood also that he was dealing with someone who was yet to achieve mastery of the opera form, and he knew there were limitations to Puccini's composer skills at this time in his development. Therefore he felt they would need something that would provide ample challenge for Giacomo while exciting the sensibilities of the Sonzogno Competition judges. A story of the macabre, of the supernatural...that was the answer!

"I have begun a libretto for another composer that I believe will suit your purpose far better than his," Fontana said looking at Puccini.

Giacomo asked excitedly, "And you call it?"

"*Le Villi*. Actually it is from a German story called *Le Willis*, but I have Italianized it."

Fontana had not informed Ponchielli earlier of this decision. "Hmm," Ponchielli murmured now, "*Le Villi...*a she-devil, a fairy of malevolence. Yes...yes...that will be good for you Giacomo."

Fontana leaned forward eagerly, his forearms resting on his knees and fingers curled into tight fists. "No, no, it will not be good for you, Giacomo. It will be *perfect."* Then he launched into a passionate description of the libretto's plot. "The setting will be the Black Forest of Germany. The story begins happily: A young village girl is preparing to be wed to her young lover. She is dancing joyously in the forest with friends. However the wedding must be postponed when the young lover is called away to the bedside of a rich and dying uncle. On seeing him the old man is revived. In good health once more he keeps his nephew from returning quickly to the Black Forest. The young man meets his uncle's winsome ward, who is heiress to the uncle's wealth. She falls desperately in love with him, and at the insistence of her guardian the young man and she are married. Back in the Black Forest the forsaken maiden, whom I shall call Anna, and her brother, who will be named Konrad, learn of the wedding. Outraged, Konrad goes to confront the young man."

"And what is his name?" Giacomo asked hungrily. "The young man's."

"Since this takes place in Germany it is Heinrich, but I am partial to Roberto."

"An appropriate name," Ponchielli said. "Go on, please."

"Konrad and Roberto argue heatedly, almost violently. Konrad challenges Roberto a duel, in which Konrad is seriously wounded. Barely alive he returns home to the forest and to his sister, where he soon dies."

"How sad," Teresina murmured.

"It becomes sadder," Fontana continued. "With the loss of her lover and the death of her brother Anna's heart is irreparably broken. She pines. She grieves. She despairs. And soon she, too, dies."

"Oh, my...." Teresina gasped. "You make me want to weep."

The story was affecting Puccini deeply, too. He'd begun to hear music in Fontana's words.

"Mourning over her grave Anna's father calls upon the gods to avenge the suffering and death of his son and daughter. A year later, Roberto visits the place of his childhood. While walking through the forest he hears music. He follows the sound, and in a clearing he sees women dancing. He draws closer. He is intrigued. *Then*...the face of one dancer astounds him. She is Anna! She beckons him, and he is drawn irresistibly to her and into the dance. He cannot escape. The dance becomes wild, insane. Anna holds him captive. She keeps him dancing, dancing, *dancing*. He becomes frantic.

He tries to break away, but it is impossible. The music quickens. It becomes wilder, madder. And he dances with her...dances and dances...until his heart explodes in utter exhaustion and he, too, dies. The music softens to a sonorous conclusion. The curtains close. Silence reigns. Anna the she-devil has been avenged."

Fontana's voice had risen and fallen dramatically. His hands had waved and stabbed expressively. His face had contorted emotionally. But after his final words he sat motionless and watched his audience for reactions.

All three listeners sank back on their chairs thrilled and breathless.

"Excellent," Ponchielli murmured.

"I must be Anna," Teresina breathed. "If you select anyone else to sing Anna, *I* shall die!"

All eyes went to Puccini.

"I will compose music for this libretto that will have the judges cheering," he said softly.

Fontana clapped his hands and leaped to his feet. "Good. My libretto will be yours, Giacomo."

Puccini stood and extended a hand. "Thank you, Ferdinando," he said. "My gratitude is greater than words."

They shook hands vigorously, sealing the agreement.

"We are now friends," Fontana said. "You *must* call me Ferdi."

"And you *must* call me Giaco."

"And we *mus*t toast this auspicious moment with a glass of my favorite sherry," Teresina proposed.

Which they did.

Many times.

Happily.

- 9 -

The Sonzogno Competition had already begun to accept submissions. Though its main office was in Milan, the competition was open to young artists from all of Italy, from every province, every village and hamlet. And midnight of December 31, 1883 was established as the final moment of submission acceptance.

When asked how long it would take to complete his libretto, Fontana committed himself to the beginning of October. But he added, "I shall send you scenes as I finish them."

"Excellent," Puccini said. "That will give me more than enough time to compose a score worthy of your story."

Giacomo returned to Milan with his mind swirling in wonderful memories. He was now close to Ponchielli and his wife, and he had become the friend of a gifted collaborator. Also he had an exciting libretto for his first opera, and he had met, in addition to Fontana, some of the most exceptional opera artists of the day. Now he could look forward to bringing honor and happiness to his mother with the competition's grand prize of 2,000 lire.

Life cannot be better, he thought. *I am on my way.*

As soon as he reached his apartment, even before he unpacked his little travel bag, he sat at his desk and wrote to Albina, telling her of his vacation and his good fortune.

His letter, however, would never be complete if it didn't include his usual request for money:

> *"...Of course, dearest Mama, I shall return to Lucca while I wait for Fontana's libretto. Consequently, I will need money for a train ticket...."*

Somehow, Albina found the money to bring him home to his family. He had been away from Lucca for three years. The reunion was thrilling. Albina, his sisters, and his brother Michele greeted him with laughter, with cheers and loving embraces. Giacomo's heart swelled with happiness. He looked at their smiling faces. *This is where I am happiest,* he thought. *I can compose my music from here as well as Milan. All I need is a piano, paper and pen. And here there are no food and money concerns to intrude upon my concentration.*

Seated around the kitchen table, he gave Albina the bronze medal Maestro Bazzini had presented to him when he received his graduation certificate. She was overcome. The family applauded. He bowed comically. Then he regaled everyone with stories of his Milan adventures. He had them laughing, gasping, eager to hear the smallest details. He was the center of attention. He was home, and he loved being there.

"Will you be returning to Milan?" Michele asked.

"I will have to, if I am to accept the competition prize."

They laughed at his little joke.

"I know," Michele said. "But *when* will you return?"

"Why do you ask? Would you rather I stay here forever?"

"No. I want to go to Milan with you, and I must earn my train fare before you leave."

"It is much nicer here in Lucca, little brother. Do you really want to go to Milan?"

"Yes, oh yes. I want to study singing at the conservatorio. I want to sing in your operas."

The family laughed at his ardor.

"First I must compose them," Giacomo said grinning.

"You will, my darling Giacomino," Albina said with deep conviction. "The libretto you described is wonderful. You will write enchanting music for it. Victory in this Sonzogno Competition is assured, and it will be the start of your wonderful career."

Puccini took his mother's hand and kissed it gratefully. Tears filled his eyes.

Indeed, Lucca is where I belong, he thought, *and I can barely wait to read Fontana's first scenes.*

Only one thing darkened the brilliance of his homecoming. It was Albina's appearance. When he left she had been a full-bodied woman, robust and clear-complexioned. Now she seemed thinner to him. Her skin had lost some of its clarity. It had become somewhat sallow, and her eyes had lost their luster. She was still vigorous and assertive, but she was not the same mother who had tended him and led him to this stage of his life.

I must talk with her about this, he told himself. He was deeply troubled.

The next morning after a restful night's sleep Giacomo awoke to the aroma of freshly baked bread, and he stretched luxuriously in his old bed. He smiled and stretched once more. Yes, Lucca was not like Milan. Lucca was comfort. Lucca was safety. Lucca was love. After relieving himself he washed his hands and face. Then he dressed quickly, and he dashed like a teenager down the flight of stairs from his bedroom.

Albina was awake and waiting. She smiled happily on seeing him. "You slept well?" she asked.

"Marvelously, Mama. And you?"

"As well as can be expected." She had tried to be flippant, but he heard a note of anxiety in her voice.

"You are not well, Mama?"

"Oh, it is nothing. As I told you in my letters, there is some stomach discomfort. That is all."

"Is it getting worse?"

"No. But it inconveniences me and keeps me close to my chamber pot." She raised her eyebrows and chuckled at her little witticism. "Only that could keep me from your graduation, my Giacomino. But I was with you in spirit."

"I know, Mama. I felt your presence."

They were on the sofa in the family sitting room. Sisters and brother had all left for the day to address their respective obligations. Albina took her son's hand. Changing the subject, she said, "Yesterday you mentioned your need of 100 lire for Signor Fontana."

"Yes. I will need that amount when he completes the libretto. However you are not to worry, Mama. Understand? The sum is large, but I know where to find it."

Given Albina's condition Puccini didn't want his mother to know how worried he was about meeting the financial obligation of his agreement with Fontana. Though he sounded bold and confident, in reality he had no idea where the 100 lire could be found. There were some slim possibilities – like requesting a grant from the City Council or asking some of his Lucca friends for loans. He would pursue these of course, but his natural inclination to doubt made him expect failure even before trying them.

After enjoying his first home-cooked breakfast in years Giacomo prepared to eliminate this obstacle to his peace of mind. The City Council would be his destination that morning. *They must see the benefit in granting my petition*, he speculated. *The Grand Prize of the Sonzogno Competition will bring honor to the city.*

He could have saved himself the trouble. Appearing at the Municipal Office he stated his name, the fact that he had been the organist for San Martino Cathedral and the reason for his visit. His name brought a sign of recognition, and the reason for his visit produced an enigmatic smile. "Unfortunately, Signor Puccini," he was told, "the Council is not honoring such petitions at this time."

He left the Municipal Office disappointed and wondering about that strange smile. Puccini never understood that leaving his position as San Martino organist abruptly with no advance notice and no attempt on his part to find a replacement had displeased Lucca's authorities and placed them in a difficult position that generated lasting resentment. As he left the City Council building he could feel a little knot of desperation tightening in his stomach.

He spent the rest of that day searching for old Lucca friends. Zizzi Zizzania...Carlo Carignani...Giuseppe Papeshi. When he located them, each reunion was joyous, uplifting, and memorable. But none eased that tightening knot. Though his friends were delighted to see him again and eager to learn of his Milan experiences, all were as destitute as he.

Quietly nursing the day's failures Puccini tried to keep his anxiety from Albina with smiles and animation. However he failed there too.

"What is wrong, Giacomino?" she asked.

"It is nothing, Mama."

"It is something. What is it?"

She sees into me as if I were glass. He sighed. "A bad day that is all."

"Tell me."

Puccini studied his mother and once again saw the changes that had come over her in the three years he'd been gone.

"Have you been seen by a doctor, Mama?" he asked.

"Do not change the subject Giacomo. Why was this day bad for you?"

"I will tell you after you answer my question."

Albina smiled. "Do not concern yourself, my son. Yes I have been examined by *two* doctors, one of whom is your Uncle Nicalao. Both have said it is a slight indisposition for which I am now taking their prescribed medication."

Her explanation did nothing to alleviate Giacomo's concern. But it satisfied her part of their agreement, and it compelled him to describe his day.

Albina listened attentively. And after his final, sad words she said with fierce determination, "Do not despair. You will have your one hundred lire. I will see to that."

The next morning Albina Puccini placed Fontana's 100 lire into her son's hand. "Now," she declared, "you *must* win the Sonzogno Competition to repay your kind Uncle Nicalao."

With Fontana's fee in his hand Puccini felt the weight of one obligation lifted from his shoulders. But a more onerous one had dropped heavily upon his back. Now Dr. Ceru's help made winning the Sonzogno 2,000 lire Grand Prize an absolute necessity.

That afternoon Giacomo visited his Uncle Nicalao and thanked him for his generosity. Dr. Ceru made light of his gift. "Your gratitude is appreciated, Giacomo," he said, "but unnecessary. Only your success and happiness matter. I predict great fame for you and this competition will prove me correct. Go with God, my nephew, and make all of us proud."

- 10 -

With each passing day the Sonzogno Competition grew increasingly fateful. Puccini became restive. How long would he have to wait? His future lay in the hands of Ferdinando Fontana. Was it safe, or had his collaborator returned the story to the composer for whom it had been originally intended? If it was still his, how far had the librettist progressed? Where were the first scenes? Fontana's dramatic performance in the Ponchielli sitting room danced in his mind. Time was torturing him.

Albina observed these moments. They made her feel helpless. Like her son she could only wait, and waiting with him in the house made her insides ache.

"You do nothing," she chided him. "You have not touched the piano since you played your *Capriccio* for us on the first day of your arrival. Practice, Giacomino. You must practice or your fingers will die."

"My fingers are not dying, Mama. See?" He wiggled them at her.

In exasperation Albina threw up her hands. "Have you visited your teacher, Maestro Angeloni?"

"Not yet, but I intend to see him when the libretto arrives."

"Why are you waiting?"

"I want him to see what I will be working on."

"You can always show him the libretto. Go now. Tell him about it. Speak with him. He will be as happy to see you again as you will be to see him."

"Maybe it will come today."

"Go! Leave the house. Now!"

Giacomo knew that tone. Growing up he'd heard it as often as he had heard endearments, and it had never failed to bring chastisement when it was ignored. Though he was now a man, his reaction was the conditioned response of the obedient son. "All right, Mama. Be calm. I am leaving now to see Maestro Angeloni. See?"

He left the house quickly hoping that his behavior hadn't contributed in any way to her illness.

Maestro Carlo Angeloni was overjoyed to see his former student. He threw his arms around Giacomo and almost kissed him. "Come in, Giacomo. Come in... come in," he shouted, pulling Puccini into his small apartment.

Puccini had written to him a few times during his Conservatorio education, and Angeloni had asked Albina often about his favorite pupil's progress. Their reunion was more like the embrace of father and son than teacher and pupil. Giacomo glowed in the warmth of his teacher's greeting.

He was given Angeloni's favorite chair. When he objected and attempted to leave it, Angeloni stood over him and pressed his shoulders. "Stay where you are. You are my guest, Giacomo. I want you to be comfortable in my home."

Puccini smiled and acquiesced. Settling into the plush cushions he accepted a large glass of wine and relaxed into the best afternoon he had ever enjoyed with his former teacher.

On a less comfortable chair Angeloni faced him and leaned forward. "You must tell me all that you have done in Milan. Who were your teachers? What did you learn? Where did you go? What operas did you see?" His enthusiasm poured out in a torrent of questions.

Giacomo laughed. "If I answer all your questions, I shall be talking forever."

"Good. Begin."

That brought another laugh. Puccini took a long draft of wine. He squished it around in his mouth, he swallowed contentedly, and he began.

He started with a description of the school and the apprehensions he'd suffered facing his entrance examination. He described Bazzini and Ponchielli, and he thanked Angeloni for the preparation he'd received in Lucca that allowed him to benefit from their excellent instruction. He told him about some of his roommates and the escapades in which they had indulged themselves. He recited famous names – members of the *Scapigliatura Milanese* whom he had met during his four days with Ponchielli on Lake Como: *Boito, Cameroni, Arrighi, Catalani, Petrella, Mascagni*. Angeloni asked questions endlessly. Giacomo had more answers. And the more he talked, the closer he and his listener were bound in the warmth of hearty camaraderie.

When all questions had been answered to his satisfaction, Angeloni sat back with a wide grin. "All right," he asked, "where do you go now? Will you stay in Lucca? Your diploma qualifies you for a position at the Instituto Pacini your old school. Would you like to teach there?"

"No, no, no, no....classrooms give me claustrophobia. I suffer in them like a chained gorilla struggling to break his bonds and race for the freedom of his jungle."

They laughed like children at a party.

"I like your simile. You should put it to music."

"Perhaps someday I will." And, ape-like, Puccini grunted a few melodic notes.

That brought even more laughter.

"You will want to earn money, will you not?"

"Always."

"You could teach privately."

"A student or two just for cigarettes and train fare."

"Then you will go back to Milan?"

"Yes. I have an excellent librettist there for my first opera."

Angeloni's eyes widened; his jaw dropped. "A librettist? An opera?" He leaped to his feet. "That is *marvelous*, Giacomo! You should have told me this *immediately.* Why did you make me wait for this wonderful news?"

"I was saving the best for last."

Puccini's grin spread even wider. Angeloni's reaction was perfect. Here were support and faith all wrapped in one outburst of pure excitement and joy. "And I shall be entering the Sonzogno Competition with a wonderful libretto," he added.

What followed was the best part of the day for Giacomo Puccini.

Angeloni couldn't learn enough about the upcoming project. He questioned. He exclaimed. He advised. His heart was clearly with Puccini. And when everything had been explained, he relaxed on his chair and said: "If you need me, Giacomo...in *any* way ...I am here for you. Remember you may count on my help always."

He extended his hand, and Puccini gripped it tightly. "You have helped me more than you will ever know," he said emotionally. "And I *will* come to you if I should ever need more of your guidance and assistance."

Walking home Giacomo Puccini relived every moment, every word, of this remarkable day. He and Carlo Angeloni had been together for *six* hours. Six hours of continuous conversation. Normally soft-spoken and relatively subdued, Puccini had been stimulated by something his personality needed and would continue to need all his life: *passionate encouragement*.

He hummed a strain from Bizet's *Carmen,* and he strode happily to its rhythm: *Yes...yes...*he thought...*give me my libretto, Ferdi Fontana, and you will hear music to make the angels sing!*

Giacomo went to the train station every day to see if anything had come from Fontana. And every day he returned home disappointed. However on the ninth day after he'd left Milan, the first scenes of *Le Villi* reached Lucca, and they made him gasp.

- 11 -

Puccini trembled as he tore open the large envelope. When he tossed it aside, he held ten pages of neatly written script in his hands. He scanned each page hungrily. He was in the Black Forest of Germany. Sunshine filled a small clearing through the lacy leaves of tall, silver birch trees. Delicate shadows shimmered in a summer breeze, and a graceful ballet was in progress, with sweet, flowing movements of love and promise.

Yes...symphonic...I can do that, Giacomo thought. He leafed through the ten pages, devouring the dialogue. It was rich. It was real. He had been praying for this, scenes that could evoke emotion, feelings that he could translate into stirring musical passages. *Yes... yes... action...passion...exactly what I need.*

Confidence raced through him. *I must work...yes...immediately.* There was no fear that this feeling would leave him. He was in command of his creative faculties. He heard Fontana's words, and musical chords reverberated in his head. He saw ballet movement as musical notes danced before his eyes.

He went directly to the small, upright piano that stood against the living room wall. He arranged blank music paper and pencils on the little table near his leg. He placed Fontana's pages on the music rack. He looked at them for a few seconds. He raised his hands. He hunched his shoulders, and....

Nothing happened.

His hands hovered above the piano keys. His brows creased. He bit his bottom lip. Consternation replaced anticipation. His fingers clenched slowly into fists and then dropped to his lap. He couldn't play what had been whirling in his head. It had been exciting there, but now it seemed wrong. Suddenly he understood: The music he'd been hearing had been sporadic flashes of inspiration. It had lacked continuity. Fontana was presenting him a full story, and these were the first steps in the opera's journey. They would have to be taken carefully, sequentially, not in flashes of inspired moments.

He'd never composed for opera. How was it done? Maestro Ponchielli had discussed the required approaches in his composition lectures. But he, Puccini, had been too busy feeling claustrophobic and sorry for himself to appreciate what he was being given. Now he regretted his inattentiveness. He realized that though he'd waited impatiently for Fontana's scenes, he had never really considered them equally important to music. Librettists? Yes, they were necessary. They were the story tellers. But it was the music that made opera, not the story.

Staring at the pages before him Puccini had a shattering epiphany: *Opera was not a patchwork of melodious arias and dull recitative. It was a slow, steady progression of meaningful dramatic and emotional moments, all conveyed through the perfect marriage of words and music. And without a complete understanding of the nuances inherent in the opera's dialogue that marriage would inevitably disintegrate and leave its music on a mound of contempt.*

He saw it now. He would have to approach this from the very beginning. He would have to study the words carefully and not believe his music alone would be the beauty of the piece. He took Fontana's pages from the music rack and went to the room's most comfortable chair. There he slouched and read them repeatedly. He struggled to uncover the mysteries within librettist language, the deeper meanings that could awaken their musical mates lying dormant in his heart.

Two hours later Giacomo Puccini closed his eyes. *I see it now...I understand it...I feel it...I am ready.* He leaped from his chair and walked quickly to the piano. Sitting before the keyboard he raised his arms. There was no hesitation this time. No doubt, no confusion. His hands came down confidently. His fingers caressed the keys. And the ballet music of his first opera was born. It flowed from his heart and soul and filled the room. It was love. It was elegant. And it was right.

Before he could forget what he had played he scribbled the notes on the music sheets at his side. Quarter notes...eighths... sixteenths...thirty-seconds...they cluttered the pages. From time to time he replayed phrases, polishing, improving them. He was indefatigable. He worked for hours filling sheet after sheet. A wave of creativity had crashed over him pounding him with its energy and rushing him through Fontana's first scenes like a cork riding the tide. Everything in his past paled in the enormity of what he was feeling. This was the most exhilarating experience he'd ever had. And what he was writing was good, exceptionally good. He knew it. His soul had been released. It had truly found its niche. It would live and thrive in opera. And he, Giacomo Puccini, would devote himself religiously to it and be a happy man.

No one could interrupt him. He was alone in the house. He wrote like a man possessed, and he completed all three of Fontana's scenes that very afternoon. After he made final corrections that now looked like disorderly chicken tracks, he played through everything one last time, smiling and glowing with satisfaction through every measure. *Ferdi, my new friend,* he thought confidently, *give me more scenes like these and the Sonzogno Grand Prize will be ours.*

Albina returned just as he played the final notes. Hearing them, she cocked her head and smiled. *He is at the piano...thank you, Jesus, he is at the piano.* She went to the family living room expecting to find him relaxed and toying with the keys. Instead, she was surprised to see him leap to his feet at the sound of her steps.

He grabbed both her hands.

"Mama," he said softly, "they have arrived...the scenes. Sit down. Sit down, Mama, and listen...listen to what I have written."

Albina Puccini had not been schooled in music. However immersed in it from her earliest days with father and husband she possessed a natural and uncanny sensitivity to its phrasings. She remembered vividly his earlier description of *Le Villi*'s story line. She had clapped her hands appreciatively when he'd narrated it for the family. Now she allowed herself to be seated in the armchair Giacomo had occupied earlier. And with arms crossed over her ample bosom she settled back to hear what was exciting her darling Giacomino.

Giacomo began to play. Before each of the three scenes he offered a dramatic explanation of what he believed he'd achieve emotionally for its words and action.

Albina listened silently and carefully. Occasionally she signaled him to proceed when he turned to face her for a sign of approval. His presentation took only ten minutes, but those ten minutes filled Albina with all the joy he'd hoped would be on her face. After playing everything, he sat facing the scrawled music on the piano rack, hands on thighs, his head slightly bowed, and he waited for her to say something. All he heard was a slight rustle. It was the sound of Albina's clothing as she rose from the armchair. She walked to his side. She turned his head and took his face in her hands. Looking down at him she whispered with deep emotion, "You are going to be a great composer, my son." Tears of happiness danced on the rim of her eyes as she kissed him lightly on his forehead, almost like a blessing.

The following morning Carlo Angeloni had no classes at the *Instituto Pacini.* Giacomo knocked on the door of his apartment and almost bowled him over as he rushed into the tiny sitting room. "Good morning, Carlo, good morning. I have something you must hear. I need your expert, unequivocal reaction."

He went directly to the room's piano before Angeloni could even greet him.

Carlo followed him, smiling with interest.

"They came yesterday," Giacomo blurted. "The libretto scenes. I worked all afternoon on them. Listen...listen...tell me what you think." Then as he did with his mother, he explained and played.

Like Albina, Angeloni sat silently and listened. However, unlike Albina, when Giacomo's final notes trailed into a gentle lull, he had much to say. "You have given the scenes grace, tenderness and the excitement of impending conflict. I hear a trace of Bizet in the love scene, but not enough to keep the moment from being entirely yours. It is interestingly imaginative, and its sweetness touches the heart. The departure scene, when Roberto leaves Anna to visit his dying uncle, is a delicate moment. It must express the uncertainty of separation, the love of reunion, and the mystery of possible death. I am pleased to say, Giacomo, you have provided all of that. I find all three scenes exciting and original."

It was as if God had spoken to him. Puccini went to Angeloni and grasped his arms. "Thank you, Carlo," he said throatily. "Thank you...thank you...thank you."

"No," Angeloni replied. "It is I who should be thanking *you*. Thank you, Giacomo, for starting my day so wonderfully."

They both laughed heartily.

"When can you expect the next scenes?" Angeloni asked.

"Soon I hope."

"Until then we must celebrate what you have already accomplished."

"What do you propose?"

"Winter will soon arrive, but the weather is still good for hunting."

The proposal pleased Giacomo immensely. Hunting fowl had been one of his favorite pastimes while growing up in Lucca. As one of his students he had already enjoyed days in the field with Angeloni. Eager to celebrate with him now as a respected composer he agreed to the suggestion with the alacrity of an explorer eager to visit a new land.

He didn't send his music to Fontana. He believed another pianist would not do it justice. He preferred instead to wait until the entire opera would be completed, at which time he'd return to Milan and present it most effectively himself. So in a warm, friendly letter he complimented Fontana, informed him of his progress, and urged him to send more scenes as quickly as possible.

Fontana sent additional scenes regularly, and by October 6th he'd honored his promise with a complete opera. The final day for

Sonzogno Competition submission was December 31st. Composing as the scenes arrived would have given Puccini ample time to meet the contest's deadline.

But he didn't compose.

Instead, the comforts and pleasures of home drew Giacomo into the crippling trap of satisfaction. His initial enthusiasm faded in the easy pace of Lucca life. The scenes arrived and sat on the piano. He looked at them daily. He read and reread them, and he longed to feel that thrilling communion of words and music again. But it didn't happen. Then to quell his growing self-doubts he'd leave the house for lengthy visits to Angeloni and other friends, who always tried to bolster his sagging spirit with encouragement and praise.

His dawdling weighed heavily upon his suffering mother. Albina watched him closely, her dismay growing every day as she saw him leave the house. "You must work, Giacomo," she insisted. "The competition will end shortly. You will lose your opportunity and disappoint everyone. You *must* work."

"I shall, Mama, I shall. There is still time. I have weeks yet... *weeks*."

But the weeks passed. December 31st drew closer. And the prospect of Sonzogno success grew frighteningly dimmer.

Albina's desperation made her ill. In addition to her stomach pain she began to suffer headaches. She tried frantically to move him. If he didn't take command of himself, she scolded, if he didn't force *Le Villi* from his soul, everything he had accomplished up to that point – his Lucca Festival mass, his conservatorio studies, his *Capriccio Sinfonico*, his friendships with Ponchielli and Ponchielli's Milanese contacts – everything would disappear in self-loathing. He could no longer wait for inspiration to lead him. He could no longer waste precious days enjoying friends and excusing laziness. He had to sit at his piano and work...yes, *work,* until with his music, Fontana's fine libretto would blossom into the fullness of the sublime opera it was meant to be.

Puccini understood her concern, and it pained him deeply.

But he couldn't seem to address the problem. In his torment he wondered: *Is music still within me? Why is it not showing itself? The first scenes exploded like a divine cloudburst. Why am I failing now? Where is my music?*

He could see the anguish he was causing Albina. It was in her posture, her movements, her face. And the love he felt welled into choking pain. "I will finish the opera, Mama. I promise you. Do not make yourself sick over this. I love you, dear Mama. I would never do anything to disappoint you. I *will* complete the opera."

Albina's distress became his stimulant. When she failed to leave her bed one morning at her customary 5:00 am, he drove himself in guilt to face Fontana's pages. He sat at the piano and stared at them for almost an hour hoping another cloudburst would happen. When it didn't, he inhaled deeply in desperation and finally plunged into the words.

He struggled as if he were drowning. He played new phrases again and again, but he was dissatisfied with everything he was hearing. The notes on his music sheets jumbled like footprints stumbling on pristine snow. Despite the torture, though, he made progress. Slowly, some passages took shape. Slowly, words and music blended. Slowly, action and melody fused into moments of vibrancy, excitement and life.

After hours of deep concentration and endless repetition, Puccini finally relaxed on the piano seat.

"Mama," he called going to her bedroom, "Come...I want you to hear what I have written."

Albina rose from her bed. And with strength she hadn't shown in weeks, she followed her son into the sitting room.

He played for her.

She closed her eyes and absorbed the scene. It was Roberto's introduction to his uncle's ward. The girl was ravishing, intelligent, charming; the uncle was sickly but recovering in the possibilities of this meeting.

Giacomo's music gave special meaning to Fontana's words. It filled them with a stronger emotion than they'd previously suggested. It enriched them. It brought the dramatic essence of the scene into focus, and it filled the room with heart-warming truth.

Albina felt it. She bowed her head.

He finished playing and turned for her reaction. "What do you think, Mama?" he asked. "Is it disappointing?"

Mama was smiling through tears. "You will not disappoint a soul with what you are doing, Giacomino," she said earnestly. "Now you must continue. Success is in your hand. Close your fingers. Make it yours."

Giacomo was deeply moved. "I will, Mama," he whispered. "I swear to you, I will."

That day Giacomo Puccini learned another simple truth that became the foundation of all his future success: *Creativity may sometimes be that divine cloudburst, but more often it is a slumbering giant who is awakened only by insistent prodding and effort.*

Only one week remained before the Sonzogno Competition would end. December 31st hurtled toward Puccini. He could feel the seconds ticking. He worried constantly that he would not meet the deadline. With Albina's steady encouragement, though, he became obsessed. He sat at his piano day after day and composed painstakingly for hours. It seemed impossible, but he completed his music for the entire libretto on December 31st, just in time to be placed on the afternoon train and to reach Milan only minutes before the midnight deadline.

Now Giacomo Puccini entered a period of intolerable uncertainty. He'd have to wait two interminable months for the decision of the Sonzogno judges.

- 12 -

The day after sending *Le Villi* to the Sonzogno offices Puccini visited Carlo Angeloni and played the entire one-act opera for him from memory. Listening intently Angeloni grunted and murmured approvingly at various times, but he never interrupted his presentation. However, when the crescendos of the last scene crashed to their final thundering chords and then segued into softness and silence, when Roberto lay dead at the feet of Anna's revenged spirit, Angeloni rose from his chair. He walked slowly to Giacomo, placed hands on his shoulders, and solemnly pronounced, "The prize will be yours."

Nothing could have meant more to Puccini in that moment than those five words. "It is truly that good?" he asked almost timidly.

"No," Angeloni replied. "It is better than good. It is splendid."

Spirit strengthened, Giacomo watched time slide by now with greater equanimity and growing hope. He imagined what the Grand Prize could mean for him. Recognition. Publication. Money. Work. Doors would open for him, and he would have access to the stars of opera... maybe even to the great Verdi himself.

He exchanged letters regularly with Ponchielli and Fontana. From Ponchielli he learned that twenty-eight operas had been submitted to the competition from all over Italy. From Fontana he learned that four judges would name the contest winner and other operas worthy of Honorable Mention. Ponchielli advised him to be patient, to engage in activities that would occupy his attention. Fontana informed him that Ponchielli and Franco Faccio (who had successfully conducted Puccini's *Capriccio Sinfonico*) were two of the judges, and that he, Fontana, was confident of *Le Villi*'s chances.

Puccini took Ponchielli's advice. Since he had sent his only copy to the contest judges, he wrote a fresh copy for himself in which he strengthened the score further with little passionate changes and additions. Also, he accepted a few students for voice and piano instruction. He didn't particularly care for teaching, but it occupied his mind and allowed him a small income for his cherished cigarettes and an occasional wine with friends.

With little else to do he accepted an invitation from Fontana without hesitation. He left Lucca at once to visit the librettist and to play the music of *Le Villi* for him.

Fontana greeted him like a brother. "It is so good to see you again, Giaco. You look well, a little tired, from the trip no doubt, but well. I have a good dinner prepared for us and a soft bed waiting for you. How long can you stay?"

"Not long. I have students waiting for my return. But you and I will surely enjoy our days until then. I am eager to play *Le Villi* for you."

"And I am equally eager to hear it."

That evening after dinner Puccini and Fontana visited Teresina and Amilcare Ponchielli in their home. "I have no piano," Fontana announced grandly from the doorway, "but you do. So we three will sit quietly and listen to Giaco play what he has written for my libretto...unless of course you would prefer not to have two poor struggling artists in your clean and lovely home."

The Ponchiellis laughed and pulled him into the house.

Puccini received an especially warm welcome, and no time was wasted in getting him to the piano.

Unlike Carlo Angeloni these listeners responded immediately to everything they were hearing. They applauded dramatic sections. They cheered melodic moments. They were entranced by symphonic strains. At the conclusion of the opera Teresina proposed a toast to Puccini's artistry, and Giacomo flushed in everyone's praise.

He returned to Lucca after four happy days with Fontana. Soon after arriving he resumed his teaching and met with friends again for drinks, cigarettes and lively conversation. Then one evening upon returning home from one of his cafe respites, he found his mother Albina at the kitchen table with a pencil and newspaper in her hands. She didn't say anything. She merely handed him the newspaper and pointed.

He looked at the page and saw the article she had circled with her pencil. It announced the results of the great Sonzogno Competition.

Puccini's heart beat faster as his eyes scoured the article column.

And the winner was.... Where was his name? *Where?* He read the article again. *My name.... Where am I?* He wasn't there. Instead he saw the names of two other composers: Guglielmo Zuelli and Luigi Mapelli, whose operas *La Fata del Nord* and *Anna e Gualberto* would be given full productions at Milan's Teatro Manzoni in addition to winning the Grand Prize of 2,000 lire.

The news staggered Puccini. Disappointment crushed his dreams into a quivering mass of disbelief. *How could that be?* His opera hadn't been deemed good enough even for honorable mention. *Not even honorable mention?* He felt his failure deeply. Everyone would laugh at him now. He was lost.

But that wasn't the way his collaborator viewed their loss.

Ferdinando Fontana was not a man to be so easily daunted. He had heard Puccini's music. He believed it was equal in every way to the words of his libretto. He had no doubt it was better than the two operas that had won the Grand Prize. While Puccini moped after the decision, Fontana boiled. He couldn't understand the decision. He couldn't accept it. *This must not be allowed to go unchallenged,* he told himself.

He visited Ponchielli who agreed wholeheartedly with him.

"How could *Le Villi* not have won?" he asked Ponchielli. "You and Faccio were judges. Why was it rejected?"

Ponchielli shrugged and replied simply, "We were only two of four votes, Ferdi."

"And you could not sway one of the other two?"

"A third was brought in, and we were outvoted."

Albina, however, had a more pointed explanation: "You waited too long," she told her disconsolate son. "You wasted time, and then you hurried. Your pages were scrawled and impossible for the judges to understand."

Whatever the true reason, disappointment turned Giacomo Puccini into a drifting soul that stagnated through days of despair. He drew into himself. He sulked. He avoided friends and ignored his students.

Fontana, on the other hand, was not a man to nurse wounds. Instead, he leaped into action. He contacted his *Scapigliatura* friends. And one in particular liked what he said so much he proved to be singularly important to Fontana's plans. That was Marco Sala.

Marco Sala came from an immensely wealthy family of amateur musicians. His entire family sang or played instruments. Music was the source of life to them; they ate and breathed it. He played violin in minor orchestras and wrote articles for music periodicals. But all music didn't appeal to him. He and his two brothers were ardent supporters of modernism, vociferously challenging the period's beloved traditionalists. Marco's access to Milan's journals allowed him to preach his gospel of revolution freely. *"Verdi is an old man,"* he wrote. *"Italy needs new blood, new voices to drown out the filth of the past!"*

This call for modernism was not peculiar to Italy. It was the bell of change ringing throughout western civilization. In literature, painting, theater, music – in all the arts – romantic depictions of life and love were under attack. Reality had become the heat of cultural passion. According to Sala and his compatriots it promised freedom from the stultifying past. In opera that freedom existed in Wagnerian imagination, in dissonance, in soaring melody. These were the sounds that were favored by the *Scapigliatura Milanese,* and Marco Sala was a leading member of the group.

"He is with us," Fontana pressed Sala. "Puccini will refresh all of opera. He will be our new voice, bringing the magic of fresh ideas to the opera stage. You must help."

Sala needed little coaxing after Fontana's strong endorsement.

"Yes," he agreed, "we must listen. We shall have a private presentation of *Le Villi* at my palace as you wish."

Fontana clapped Sala's back. "Excellent, Marco!" he exclaimed. "I shall arrange everything."

With Ponchielli's help Fontana stirred interest quickly within the *Scapigliatura*, and a small group of extremely influential opera lovers agreed to attend the meeting. Then in a briefly worded letter he notified Puccini of the impending gathering and urged him excitedly to return to Milan.

Told he would be expected to play his score for this esteemed audience, the shaken composer balked.

Fontana was shocked by his reaction. This was unacceptable. He went to the train station and wired a blistering telegram:

NO INVITATION. STOP. I ORDER. STOP. RETURN IMMEDIATELY OR ELSE.

FERDI

Telegrams were messages of great importance in 1884. Receipt of one meant good fortune or calamity. Fontana's telegram sounded calamitous. It sent shock waves through the Puccini household.

"You must go," Albina insisted, and her words were echoed by Michele and all of his sisters.

"But –" he began an objection.

Albina stopped him: "There can be no hesitation."

The eternal Sisyphus, she would push her son up the hill of musical success with the last spark of life in her body.

"The fare will be –"

"Found!"

Her firmness told Giacomo he'd lost this contest too. He closed his eyes and nodded silent agreement.

Train fare for the trip to Milan posed no problem. With words of encouragement generous Doctor Ceru rescued his nephew again. This time with forty lire. A telegram was sent to Fontana confirming

Giacomo's departure, and the next day the composer was met by his librettist with open arms. Almost six weeks had passed since the Sonzogno decision and a few days more since they had last seen each other.

"Our opera," Fontana said, "is too good to wither in the decision of blind judges. We will show them the error of their way. Welcome, Giaco. We have work to do."

He didn't stay with Fontana this time. Not knowing how long he'd have to remain in Milan, Puccini spent his first day, Monday, April 7th, locating and settling into a small, fifteen lire room on Via Monforte, where he hoped to relax for Marco Sala's salon gathering. But sleep was impossible that night. Anxiety shook him awake every time he closed his eyes.

He spent the next two days with Fontana formulating and rehearsing the program they planned to present.

Then on Thursday, April 10th, 1884 the invited luminaries assembled in Sala's family palazzo. Among other notables in attendance were Arrigo Boito, leader of the *Scapigliatura;* the Ponchiellis; Alfredo Catalani, who was a respected opera and symphony composer; and Giavannia Lucca, head of the firm that had full Italian publishing rights to Richard Wagner operas.

Entering Sala Palazzo, Giacomo Puccini couldn't stop the quivering of his stomach. He'd never been invited to a palace. Its opulence overwhelmed him. The rooms were enormous. Portraits of imposing ancestors and huge Renaissance paintings with lush, semi-nude figures covered the walls. Roman and Greek statuary stood everywhere in ancient splendor. Pink and gold marble framed huge doorways. Crystal chandeliers hung from red, silk sashes. Chairs of the richest fabrics and woods waited on highly polished intricately designed floors. Ushered through these rooms by immaculately liveried servants, Puccini, in the one suit he owned, gawked at everything and immediately felt indigent and insignificant.

Marco Sala, however, welcomed him as if he were royalty. "Welcome...welcome, Maestro Puccini. How kind of you to grace my home with your presence. We are so looking forward to your presentation tonight."

Giacomo offered a hand and said a bit formally, "Signor Sala, I am honored to be here."

Sala took the extended hand and pumped it in a firm, hearty shake. "Please, please...tonight no signor. Tonight I am Marco."

The warmth of that greeting quelled the quivers. Puccini joined Fontana and the other guests, sufficiently relaxed to enjoy the gathering's witty conversation. Soon he was eased even further by an exceptional dinner, fine wine, and an assortment of especially delicious desserts. After this, holding a delicate glass of wine, he moved with everyone to the palazzo's music room. Once everyone was seated, Sala stood before the group and welcomed one and all amiably again. "I am happy to see your expectant faces," he said. "Before this evening ends, I am confident you will believe tonight's music to be the best ever offered in the Sala salon...at least, that is what its librettist has assured me."

That brought the laughter he wanted. He motioned toward Fontana who took the gesture as his cue and stood to introduce the entertainment.

"As you know," he said, "Giacomo Puccini and I entered our litte opera, *Le Villi,* in the recent Sonzogno Competition. Sadly, three judges – not our own Ponchielli and Faccio – failed to appreciate it as we do. Tonight we ask for *your* judgment. I shall narrate from the libretto while Maestro Puccini will play the opera's music for your enjoyment and consideration."

Giacomo placed his wine glass on a small table near the grand piano. He nodded acknowledgment, the audience applauded politely, and the program began.

Approval was heard quickly in murmurs and occasional applause. Puccini's enthusiasm grew. Soon he was playing his score with a heat of passion that brought shouts of approval.

At the concludion of their presentation Fontana and Puccini stood and bowed to vigorous applause. They basked in the *Bravo! Bravisimo!* exclamations and then embraced happily like schoolboys in athletic victory. They had been right; the judges had been wrong. All was good in the world again.

Well not quite. One more step had to be taken in Fontana's plan if the evening were to be a complete success.

Arrigo Boito was the first to take that step. "We must arrange a production of this little gem," he said.

"Yes," publisher Giovannina Lucca agreed. "It should be done at La Scala after the Sonzogno productions are presented. Everyone must see the superiority of *Le Villi* and the fallibility of contest judgments."

"What do you estimate would be the cost?" Ponchielli asked Boito.

"I do not know. But I should prefer to see it première at Teatro Dal Verme, instead of La Scala. I know Count Dal Verme. He will be kind to us," Boito said. "Four performances, on consecutive evenings. Whatever the cost we shall arrange the production. To which I hereby pledge the first hundred lire!"

"And I another hundred," Sala quickly shouted.

"It will need additional funds for costumes and posters," Fontana added. "As much as 350 or 400 lire, would you say?"

Laughing and clapping his hands Sala ended all concerns: "I have friends who will be quite angry if they miss this opportunity. This is exciting!"

When they left the palace that evening Giacomo and Fontana could barely contain their happiness. The sky was clear. The air was brisk. They lit cigars and blew huge clouds of smoke. They waved their arms and giggled in bursts of memory. "Now," Fontana said, "are you not happy you have returned to Milan?"

Puccini grinned. "I can only say you must command me any time I become obstinate again."

"I shall, my friend. Be assured I shall."

Giacomo could have written to his mother immediately upon arriving at his little room. He could have eased Albina's anxiety as she waited for word of what had prompted Fontana's startling telegram. But he didn't. Days passed. He waited, hoping to learn more of how Fontana's plan was progressing. He fretted that the enthusiasm exhibited at Sala's soiree might have been a demonstration of conviviality rather than a sincere desire to produce his opera. "Should we not have a contract, something in writing to guarantee everyone's participation?" he pressured Fontana.

"With these people," Fontana responded, "a contract is unnecessary. Their word is guarantee enough. Think only of your music and the staging of our 'little gem,' as Boito calls it. Stop worrying. Everything is in my hands and, modesty aside, my hands are very capable hands, indeed."

It didn't help. Puccini continued to fret until...

At the end of April, Fontana informed him that sketches for the set had been completed and 530 lire had already been collected. "Think only of music," he told his anxious composer. "I have said, and I repeat: I take responsibility for all else."

It wasn't until two weeks before rehearsals were to begin that Puccini informed Albina of the progress he was making. On May 13th, 1884, he wrote:

Dearest Mother,

It fills me with joy to tell you of my opera's success. It will soon be presented at Teatro Dal Verme. Costs are enormous. However, they are being shared by friends of a wealthy patron. Copies of the music are my responsibility. Please send 200 lire. I shall write more, my dear Mama, when I have time. I send you grateful kisses.

Your Giacomino.

His mother's health concerned him, and so did his sister Nitteti's impending wedding. But Puccini was an artist, and the personal needs of artists usually take precedence over the cares of other people, even those they dearly loved.

Receiving his letter, Albina sighed with great relief. It was not enough, however, to suppress a sudden pain in her stomach. She winced and thought: *It is becoming more intense with each passing day*. Thankfully, she was not alone during these trying moments. Though Otila had a husband and her own family obligations, and Iginia was restricted by her duties as a nun, the other three of her five daughters, Tomaide, Nettiti and Ramelde, were always at her side. They comforted her. They took excellent care of household needs. And they kept their brother Giacomo apprised of their mother's condition.

Unlike their brother, though, they worried more about Albina than about their own problems. And they feared. They saw her decline a little more each day. Despite Albina's constant assurances that she was suffering only slight periodic inconveniences, they believed the end of their dear mother's life was steadily and rapidly approaching.

Giacomo was conflicted. He wanted to return to Lucca. At the same time, *Le Villi*'s opening night had him and Fontana in a frenzy of activity. Score and libretto improvements, role casting, set construction supervision, costume approval, conductor conferences – all these and more demanded Puccini's presence in Milan. Return to Lucca at this time appeared to be impossible. He hoped his mother would understand and insist that he remain in Milan to make their dream of success a reality.

But a particularly dark letter arrived from Ramelde. It described their mother's condition in shocking detail, and It could not be ignored. He returned to Lucca on May 14th to see Albina before she would die. The days he spent at her bedside were days of anguish. He brought in a highly respected stomach specialist from Pisa. The doctor's report wasn't promising. Albina had become a shadow of her former self. She was semi-comatose, unable to respond fully to his comforting words or the loving touch of his hand. Death sat on the edge of her bed. Puccini could feel its presence. How long it would take to claim Albina remained a mystery. It could be a day. It could be a month. It could be more. Her demise, however, was a certainty.

Meanwhile, in Milan the *Le Villi* date had been set. The Puccini-Fontana opera would be tested on May 31, 1884, before a discriminating audience of critics, friends of the *Scapigliatura* backers and all the teachers at the Milan Conservatorio. He had to be there for the final rehearsals, he simply *had* to. Only ten days remained until opening night. He left Lucca with a broken heart, wondering all the way back to Milan if he would ever see his mother alive again.

He learned immediately that Amilcare Ponchielli had achieved something wonderful. He'd convinced Giulio Ricordi of Casa Ricordi, Milan's most prestigious music publishing house, to print the production posters at no cost to the opera's participants. The announcement featured an ethereal semi-nude woman and two smiling female heads floating mysteriously in space. An attractive poster, it produced strong interest everywhere it appeared.

Tickets were available at Teatro Dal Verme's box office.

"Are they selling well?" Fontana asked Boito.

"Better than well," came Boito's encouraging answer. "You may find every seat occupied."

Every seat would be an amazing accomplishment for a one act opera. Dal Verme was a huge theater. Its horseshoe-shaped orchestra section could accommodate 2,000 attendees, and two elegant tiers of boxes plus a large gallery could seat over a thousand more.

Boito's optimism stemmed from the musical feud that press releases were generating. *Le Villi* was being presented as an opera that had been ignored by the Sonzogno judges, but one that was far, far superior to the mediocrity of the competition's winners. To miss it would be to miss something of rare excellence and a lost opportunity to judge for oneself. Milan's opera fanatics devoured every word. Discussions and arguments raged throughout the city. Judges were praised; judges were condemned. Sides were taken. Tempers flared. And on opening night Teatro Dal Verme was, indeed, packed.

Outside the theater, watching thousands of richly attired

audience members arrive, Fontana and Puccini had different reactions to the crowd's enthusiasm. "Look at them," Fontana whispered happily. "They are like hungry dogs sighting a hare, eager to tear it apart if given the chance. But we shall not give them that opportunity, right? Tonight, they will dine on luscious *Coniglo Dulce* and go home with a taste of rabbit so wonderfully sweet it will last for weeks."

"I wish I could be as hopeful as you, Ferdi. What will happen if they think the rabbit is overcooked or seasoned poorly?"

"Cheer up, Giaco. They will love it."

Puccini could not be cheered. He always feared consequences. Failure would be painful for Fontana, but he would recover. He had already achieved respect and recognition. He would simply go on to his next project. *But for me,* Puccini thought, *there will be no "next project." For me, there will be only artistic oblivion, and then what shall I do?*

He had a certificate of graduation from the Milan Conservatorio... but, so what? The only thing left to him at twenty-six years of age would be a teacher's position in one of the Lucca institutes, and he would never be happy doing that for the rest of his life. Fontana's enthusiasm only magnified the danger he was facing.

They took their seats in the seventh row of the orchestra. Fontana sat erect boldly, daring the audience to dislike *Le Villi*. Puccini slouched in his seat, unable to look to his right or his left.

Ordinarily, operas could be as long as four or five acts in length. Since *Le Villi* was only one act, two other short productions had been added to the bill to fill the evening hours. To add to Giacomo's agony, both preceded his work. They were of no special consequence, and they had him and some audience members fidgeting with impatience.

Finally, the orchestra struck its opening chords of *Le Villi*.

Talking throughout the theater dribbled to silence.

The heavy curtains parted, and everyone was transported in flickering lights to the Black Forest of Germany.

Puccini drew a deep breath and held it as long as he could.

Fontana heard the sharp intake of air. He patted his composer's arm.

The first sign of audience approval came in applause as the opening ballet moved gracefully to the symphonic sweep of Puccini's elegant passages.

Giacomo sat up a little straighter.

More applause followed when singers added their expertly trained voices to his rich orchestration.

Giacomo began to look around and to enjoy his audience's reactions. He looked at Fontana. Fontana grinned and nodded his head approvingly.

The performance continued to even greater acclaim. The musical end of the first part brought the audience to its feet with demands strong enough to force three reprises. And before the final curtain closed, *Le Villi*'s duets had to be encored again and again to thunderous acclaim.

Puccini and Fontana were ecstatic. Friends and strangers swarmed about them, touching them, shaking their hands, expressing excitement in exclamatory terms.

"Magnifico!"

"Sbalorditivo!" Astounding!

"Congratulazioni, Maestro, congratulazioni!"

What had begun in the fear of failure ended in the supreme happiness of success.

Giacomo couldn't wait to tell Albina. Besides wanting to share his joy, he prayed his good news would help her to a miraculous recovery. With only forty *centesimi* in his pocket, he borrowed money from Fontana once again and sent this short but jubilant telegram:

DEAREST MOTHER STOP ENORMOUS SUCCESS STOP ENDLESS CURTAIN CALLS STOP FINALE REPEATED THREE TIMES.

- 13 -

Critical reactions confirmed the evening's success. Praise cascaded from the pens of reviewers like a thundering waterfall: *"...a precious masterpiece..." "...brilliant acoustic colors..." "...harmonic richness and bold imagination..." "...elegant..." "...refined..." "...freshness of fantasy..." "...phrases from the heart..." "...a true composer..." "Puccini to the stars!"*

Tickets for the remaining performances were unobtainable. Everybody in the opera community wanted to see *Le Villi,* and Puccini's name was on everyone's lips. How the Sonzogno judges could have ignored this "brilliant work of musical art" became the subject of serious discussion, and ribald jokes about critics raced through the city.

Giacomo Puccini had become an opera giant in one production.

Giulio Ricordi was in that May 31st audience, and he had been deeply moved. The following afternoon he sat in his office and waited for Amilcare Ponchielli to appear. Ricordi was a determined man. Forty-four years old in 1884 he had entered the family firm when he was twenty-three. With tireless perseverance he soon became one of the leading figures in Milan's music world. He was admired for his uncanny ability to discover and champion young aspiring artists. Among them Amilcare Ponchielli had long ago won his special favor.

Ponchielli arrived for their meeting promptly at 1:00 pm.

Ricordi rose from behind his ornate desk and greeted him warmly.

"Amilcare," he said. His voice was as gentle as his facial features.

He was a well- proportioned man with kind eyes, a high forehead, neatly trimmed hair, a prominent nose, and closely cropped beard and mustache. "I delight in seeing you, my friend."

"And I, you," Ponchielli responded in their embrace. "I saw you at the theater last night. You enjoyed Puccini's music. I could tell."

"Oh, yes. It was a most satisfying evening."

They sank into comfortable armchairs in the conversation area of the large office.

"Everyone seems to agree with you," Ponchielli stated. "Have you read this morning's reviews?"

"Indeed. He appears to be 'a new sun rising in the heavens of opera,' as one critic wrote. But I detected touches of Wagner in his score."

"I knew you would, and that is why I am here. Please, Giulio, do not allow your detestation of German opera to color an appreciation of Puccini's promise."

"I cannot deny his talent...but *Wagner*...why Wagner?"

"He is young and finding his way. You would be wise to sign *Le Villi* to a contract and, to paraphrase one reviewer's metaphor, 'to guide our sun to his place among the stars.' "

A staunch traditionalist Giulio Ricordi loathed the work of Richard Wagner. "It is an abomination," he had been heard to say. "It is an earthquake that will destroy Italian culture."

"I know Puccini was one of your students," Ricordi said, "but that should not cloud your judgment."

"Believe me, it does not. What we experienced last night was more than even I expected."

From there Ricordi listened to Ponchielli's careful analysis of *Le Villi*, of its weaknesses as well as its strengths. "If he is given opportunity and your guidance," Ponchielli concluded, "I see in Puccini a fresh voice. I see an heir to our immortal Verdi. Meet with him. Talk to him, Giulio. Please. See for yourself."

The music publisher replied softly, "I make no promises, Ami. But you offer a compelling argument, and I shall consider what you have said."

Strengthened by the glowing reviews and wild audience acclaim *Le Villi*'s singers and orchestra made the opera's final performance the most memorable of all. Puccini was called to the stage amid booming applause, and he was ceremoniously crowned with a silver laurel wreath of victory.

The excitement, the cheers were more than he could endure. Tears filled his eyes and emotion choked him speechless. He could only bow repeatedly to the demanding acclaim. If life had ended then and there he would have died the happiest of men. But to die then would have been terrible, for it would have deprived him of the even greater joy that was to embrace him.

On June 4, 1884, the day after the production closed, Giulio Ricordi invited Puccini and Fontana to his mansion on Lake Como. "I should like to discuss your future in more convivial surroundings than my office," he said. "Will you come?"

Would they come?

It was as if God himself had opened the gates of heaven. Fontana and Puccini wondered what Ricordi could possibly have in mind. The next afternoon they arrived at the publisher's villa. There they enjoyed three days of exquisite relaxation and unexpected career planning.

"Then the terms are satisfactory?" Ricordi asked on the final day.

"Wholly," Fontana responded.

"And to you, Giacomo?"

"I am speechless with anticipation."

"Excellent. Let us seal our agreement for now with a handshake and a special wine I reserve for occasions such as this."

Twenty-four hours later the team of Fontana and Puccini signed a publishing contract that guaranteed productions of *Le Villi* throughout Italy and Europe. In addition to that each received an advance of 1,000 lire for a full-length, two-act expansion of the opera. Then, to assure uninterrupted work on the expanded version, a monthly stipend of 300 lire was assigned for one year to support Giacomo Puccini, the ever-poor composer.

On June 8th the agreement was publicized in the company's *Gazzetta Musicale.* It informed the entire music world that Signor Giulio Ricordi of The House of Ricordi had obtained world rights for the translation and production of *Le Villi,* and that another new opera would soon be presented by its outstanding artists in the very near future.

Giacomo Puccini was ecstatic. With success, recognition, and the prospect of relief from suffocating poverty his position was now a dream come true. He left Milan for Lucca the very next day, where he found Uncle Nicalao, sisters, brother, and a huge contingent of friends waiting for him at the train station. Critical reviews of *Le Villi* had reached the local newspapers. He was now more than a family hero; he was a municipal hero as well.

"Welcome, Giacomo, welcome!" Dr Ceru shouted, throwing his arms around him as he stepped from the train. "You are everything we hoped you would become. You have made all of Lucca proud of you, my boy, deeply, deeply proud!"

Glowing sentiments came from everyone on the station platform. They overwhelmed Puccini. He felt love for family and city welling within his chest. "*Grazie...grazie...*," he kept repeating as he embraced his family and friends.

"Come," his sister Ramelde whispered in his ear. "Mother is waiting for you."

"Yes," he said, sobered by the reminder, "how is she?"

"You shall see."

What he saw as he entered Albina's bedroom wrenched his heart. On his last visit she had been wasting in her cancer. Now she appeared almost skeletal. Her eyes had sunk into her face. Her mouth was now a thin bloodless line. Her skin hung in loose folds around her neck and arms. She lay on her back seemingly asleep, with her long grey hair fanned over a white pillow. But when she heard his voice whispering, "I am home Mama, your Giacomino is home," she opened her eyes and with tremendous effort managed a weak smile.

He took one of her hands and held it in both of his. He felt the bones of her fingers and forced back tears. Where had his mother gone? This was not the robust woman who had dressed him and fed him when he was a child. This was not the sturdy woman who strode with confidence and energy through Lucca marketplaces. This was a stranger who could only squeeze his hand feebly as he recited the details of his Milan success, a wasted figure in whose weak responses he felt the love of a lifetime.

Puccini remained at Albina's bedside throughout the week watching her, talking to her soothingly.

But the man's artistic hungers superseded everything, even grief. When he learned that his *Capriccio Sinfonico* was to be conducted more than 200 miles away, he left his dying mother to attend the performance. He still worried about what was happening at home, but critical raves for the *Sinfonico* and predictions of a wonderful future for him mitigated his anxiety. Later he was forced to leave Albina again. This time, however, it was to meet with Giulio Ricordi.

Ricordi had scheduled the two-act version of *Le Villi* to première in Turin's Teatro Regio, after which it would move into Milan's splendid La Scala opera house. It was on June 13, 1884 that Puccini and Fontana learned of these plans. They threw themselves into a new *Le Villi* immediately. However, Puccini received word that he was needed in Lucca, and once again he rushed back to his mother's bedside.

On July 17, 1884, Albina Puccini died peacefully, surrounded by daughters, her sons, Dr. Nicalao Ceru, and a few of her closest friends.

Though he had expected her death, Puccini felt his life had been shattered. He'd lost his foundation, his bearing, the indefatigable strength that had believed constantly in him. How would he get along without his Mama? To whom could he turn now? Placing a hand upon Albina's coffin, Giacomo wept like a lost child. Grief had sunk its fangs into him deeper than ever, and it would not let go.

Important work called to him from Milan. Fontana and *Le Villi* were waiting. Should he remain longer in Lucca? Should he leave? He didn't know what to do. But his future pulled at him and forced him to a painful decision. As head of the family he addressed some of the many responsibilities that accompany death and burial. And that done he left Lucca for Milan.

Once he was there, he wallowed in his misery. He simply could not think about music. Grieving continued deep in his bones. He felt empty, and he expressed this emptiness in a letter to his sister Ramelde with words that made her weep: *"She fills my mind, dear sister. I dream of her. I miss our mother. I miss her terribly, Ramelde. I pray you are not suffering as I am...."*

Fontana didn't know what to do with him. He tried consoling words. He tried gentle persuasion. He tried cheerful friendship. Nothing worked.

"I know you mean well, Ferdi," Puccini told his librettist, "but your efforts are not rescuing me. They only remind me of my loss and push me deeper into my grief."

"Work is the only balm for great sorrow," Fontana advised.

This was reinforced later by Ponchielli, who reached him finally by saying, "Your mother dedicated her life to your success, Giacomo. Failure to work now when everything is at your fingertips is a denial of her great love. Your success will bring peace to her eternal soul."

With those words constantly in mind Puccini forced himself back to his piano. To Fontana's great relief progress on *Le Villi* continued – very slowly but nevertheless steadily. However, Puccini was not the amiable person everyone remembered. He seldom smiled. He withdrew and went nowhere. He described his state of mind to Dr. Ceru in a plaintive note: *"My life is empty. I eat. I work. I smoke. I look out my window. I lead a hermit's life, a prisoner of my loss."*

Only four weeks remained to complete *Le Villi* for the Turin opening. An immutable deadline had been set for November 2nd, and time was now pressing him.

Goaded by Ricordi's inquiries about his progress, Giacomo Puccini struggled desperately with his muse and ultimately forced the expanded *Le Villi* score from his troubled soul. Revision of the one-act opera was completed on October 28th and delivered to Casa Ricordi on November 2nd, the day of the deadline. Rehearsals for Teatro Regio began at once. Fontana pulled Puccini to all of them, hoping to engage him and to drag him back into reality. "This new aria troubles me," he said.

"Why?"

"It is not the music. A romantic expression of love is exactly what the words require.

"The soprano's voice?"

"No."

"What are you suggesting?"

"Anna should have her aria in the second act, and Roberto should sing his in the first. A masculine voice at the start will establish strength and give impetus to the action."

"Our tenor could not give anything impetus if it meant his life."

"It is the theater's acoustics."

"No, it is the orchestra. It believes it is a marching band."

Endless piddling concerns brought Puccini back to life, but they stretched an original thirty-four-minute masterpiece into a gross distortion of its former self. Fear then made Fontana and Puccini believe Turin would fail and be a terrible omen of what awaited them in La Scala.

Once more *Le Villi* stirred its audiences to rapturous applause. The Turin version promised to be La Scala's hit of the opera season. Its composer and librettist were ecstatic. They returned to Milan, and apologized for the mountain of complaints they had piled on their publisher. Giulio Ricordi smiled at them kindly and said, "I understand artistic temperament. Anxiety is endemic to the creative process. I have had no doubts about your genius, and you have proved me correct once again. I should like you to begin thinking about another opera, a new one that will surpass the beauty of your present success. Now let us anticipate an equally satisfying reception of *Le Villi* at La Scala."

Production values in Milan were far better than those at Teatro Regio. Acoustics, singers, orchestra, ballet dancers – all were superior to those of the Turin production, but audience and critical reactions were shockingly inferior. At La Scala, applause was tepid at best. There were no lengthy curtain calls, no prolonged cheers, and no spontaneous outbursts of appreciation.

Puccini and Fontana were stunned. What had gone wrong? Bewildered, they slipped from the theater before the final curtain closed and nursed their wounds at Casa Ricordi.

"Let us not despair," Giulio cautioned. "This was only one audience. We have yet to see tomorrow's critical reviews."

No reviewer raved. Some found parts of the new version melodic and interesting, some enjoyed the symphonic ballet extensions, some its fresh arias. In the main, though, all criticisms were caustic and brutal. *"I'd hoped to find something new, something refreshing and exciting,"* one of the most important reviewers in Milan wrote, *"but instead I found it heavy and cold."*

Another extremely influential voice opined: *"The score is ponderous with melody and orchestration so thick it sometimes drowned out a singer's voice."*

Despite these reactions Ricordi kept the production running through thirteen performances. Attendance shrank every night. "I still have faith in *Le Villi*," he said. However his loyalty was shattered four months later when another production, this time in Naples, had its disgusted audience hurling boos, hisses, catcalls and everything but rotten tomatoes at the performers.

The experience made one thing clear to the opera's creators and producer: *Some stories must remain what they are meant to be.* As a one act opera, *Le Villi* had been true to its original intent, true to its form and its structure. Expansion had violated its integrity. It was a lesson that Giacomo Puccini carried with him for the rest of his life: *Find the truth in a creation and adhere to it always. Tampering with truth can lead only to disillusionment and defeat.*

- 14 -

"We must put *Le Villi* behind us," Giulio Ricordi finally advised his woeful clients. "Disappointment is the child of failed expectation. We expected too much. We should have been satisfied with our one act *Le Villi* and attempted something new and different. That is what we shall do now."

Puccini and Fontana were in Ricordi's office, slouched in armchairs.

"I have said," Ricordi looked at Puccini, "that we must talk about your next opera. The time has arrived." He turned and addressed Fontana. "What ideas do you have for another libretto, may I ask?"

Fontana looked at him blankly.

"Come, man, you must have *some*thing. *Le Villi* was not an aberration. What else is in your mind?"

Fontana fidgeted. He didn't like the tone of Ricordi's voice. It wasn't harsh, but it was insistent. "I have not given it much thought," he said.

Ricordi hadn't expected that. "No?" he asked. "Is it not odd to have only one libretto idea in a repertoire?"

Puccini watched the exchange. Though the question had been asked softly, it seemed challenging. He wondered what was happening.

"I have ideas," Fontana replied. "It is that I have not given a new libretto for Giacomo much thought. Considering the demands of *Le Villi*, I hope you understand why."

"I understand. Will you do it now?"

"This minute?"

"Certainly not. But soon? I should like to produce a new opera for you at La Scala within a year. Do you believe that will be possible?"

"I am sure it will be. Just allow me a little time to recover from our present debacle."

"Whatever you need. I am certain you will think of something extraordinary."

Puccini was puzzled. Were Fontana and Ricordi at odds? If so, why?

Actually, friction had begun in the signing of their *Le Villi* contract. Though they had shaken hands and toasted their future, Giulio Ricordi was taken aback when, in private, Fontana expressed disappointment about the 1,000 lire he had been given. When Ricordi asked what he thought should be a reasonable advance, Fontana startled him with an outlandish figure. Ricordi immediately and emphatically refused to comply. Nothing more had been said about the incident. It had been left to die. But like all disagreements it festered below their smiles and amiability.

"How soon will you be able to begin work on a new opera?" Ricordi asked.

Puccini realized the question had been directed at him. "Uh...I... I am unable to say," he stammered.

"Let it be soon, Giacomo." Ricordi's voice became gentle, solicitous. "Recovery from your loss may require more time. I understand that. But it has been months since your dear mother's passing, and you must not allow your talent to wither. Please think of work."

"I shall try." Giacomo knew he was being evasive.

Fontana saw his discomfort. He rescued his friend. "Work is impossible," he said, "until I provide him with a satisfactory libretto."

Ricordi smiled. "Exactly. Then we are all in your hands, are we not? Remember, La Scala in one year, or...well, we shall see."

It was not the most satisfying meeting they'd ever had with Giulio Ricordi. Far from it. It left Fontana annoyed and Puccini disoriented.

"Do not worry, Giaco," Fontana comforted his friend after they left Ricordi's office. "He was being difficult. It means nothing. I shall think of something, and you will shake the entire Milanese world again with the beauty of your music. I promise you."

However, Fontana couldn't honor his promise. He tried, but that magic story, the golden idea that would excite in character and action and, most important, suggest heavenly sounds to his waiting composer evaded him. This was not because he was incapable of creating an exciting story. Fontana was an erudite man with an active and imaginative mind. He could have conceived a story of beauty, love, danger, lust, murder and revenge. But he was a nineteenth century librettist, and librettists of that period rarely, if ever, created their own stories. They preferred, instead, to find a tale elsewhere that they could adapt to the operatic stage. *Carmen, Otello, Cavalleria Rusticana, The Barber of Seville, Lohengrin* and many more– all came from short stories, legends, novels, poetry or stage plays. These were the feeding grounds for librettists, whose names eventually faded into obscurity.

In the world of opera it was clearly understood that words preceded music. There could be no opera without a story. Consequently, the composer could only wait and hope while his librettist searched feverishly for that shadowy, gripping tale.

"I believe I have something," Fontana finally wrote from his home. *"I shall be in Milan in four days. Let us meet at Ricordi's."*

Upon being notified, Giulio Ricordi immediately cleared his afternoon schedule for this meeting. Now he and Giacomo sat in Ricordi's spacious office and watched Fontana go into another of his masterful, animated presentations.

"I found our story in a little-known play by the French poet Alfred de Musset," he began. "It is titled *La Coupe et les Lèvres*, The Cup and the Lips, but we shall name it *Edgar.*"

Puccini and Ricordi looked at each other and smiled expectantly. "Go on," Ricordi said. "You have our attention."

Fontana grinned. "We are in a Flemish village," he continued. "It is dawn. Villagers are going to the fields. But Edgar, our tenor, has fallen asleep in the local tavern and has to be awakened by soprano Fidelia, while fiery Tigrana, the mezzo, is watching and waiting to be alone with him. When Fidelia leaves, Tigrana attempts to seduce Edgar, and then ridicules him mercilessly when she is rejected. However, when the villagers later scorn and curse Tigrana for her immoral ways, Edgar comes angrily to her defense. His fury causes him to set fire to his own house after which he threatens to leave the village and take Tigrana with him. But Fidelia has a baritone brother, who is desperately in love with Tigrana, and when he learns what Edgar has done and said, he confronts Edgar and challenges him to a duel. Edgar wounds him, after which Edgar and Tigrana escape from the village with an angry mob at their heels.

"That is Act One. The opera will be in four acts. Each is filled with drama and action. Edgar tires of Tigrana in Act Two. They argue. They fight. He joins the army to escape her, and she swears revenge on his faithless soul.

"In Act Three, we see Edgar's funeral, with Fidelia's brother singing of Edgar's death in battle. The villagers wail and mourn, but then are awed when the coffin is opened and they find it...*empty*!

"In Act Four, Edgar appears. He had arranged the mock funeral to disgrace Tigrana and to drive her from the village. Fidelia is filled with relief and happiness. She rushes to embrace him, but she is stopped by an enraged Tigrana, who draws a wicked knife from her skirt and stabs her repeatedly to death. Edgar is overcome with grief. He collapses at Fidelia's feet. Whereupon the villagers pounce upon Tigrana and drag her to some soldiers who, as she screams and curses everyone, carry her away to be executed."

Fontana stopped abruptly. His narration had been impassioned. His eyes darted now from Puccini to Ricordi to Puccini and back to Ricordi. His facial expression became his voice; it asked: "What do you think? Is it exciting enough? Do you like it?"

Puccini responded first. His head bobbed slowly. "Yes," he said softly. "It has scenes. Intensity. Variety. Sensitivity. I hear arias, duets, choral possibilities. I like it."

Fontana grinned. His attention snapped toward Ricordi, and relief exploded from him in a raucous laugh. The publisher was also smiling and nodding agreement. "When may we expect the first draft of your libretto, sir?" he asked, putting his approval into words.

"I shall start on it immediately." He turned to Puccini. "As we did with *Le Villi,* I shall send scenes to you as I complete them. You will not have to wait long for them."

Two weeks later, still in Milan, Puccini received the first scenes of their new opera, and more followed with appreciated regularity. By May of 1885, Giacomo had the full libretto of *Edgar* in his hands. He read the pages repeatedly. Something was wrong. They didn't move him. They had sounded exciting in Fontana's dynamic presentation. They had stimulated musical ideas. But somehow on paper they seemed to have lost their charm. It couldn't be the words. No. They were better than those he'd heard in Ricordi's office, more incisive, descriptively fuller, sharper in dialogue. *It must be me*, he thought. *I have become dull and insensitive.*

While he'd waited for the full libretto, his depression had returned. He had tried to work on libretto segments, but no music would come from him. Now he stared at Fontana's words as if in a trance. Only something unusual, something wonderful and totally unexpected could pull him from such debilitation.

That came in the form of his younger brother Michele.

"Michelino, *Michelino*!" he cried when he saw him. "Oh, I am so happy to see you!" He embraced his brother fiercely. "What are you doing in Milan? When did you get here? How long are you going to stay? Are you alone? "

Michele was thrilled by this reception. He loved his brother. He admired and respected him. Now he laughed and glowed in Giacomo's excitement. "I told you in my letters I would come to Milan someday," he said. "Now I am here."

"Yes...I see, I see.... Are you alone?"

"Of course. Who else should be with me?"

"Ramelde? Nettiti?"

Michele laughed. "They have husbands now and no time for their little brother. Besides, I am no longer a child, and I am quite capable of traveling by myself."

"Of course, of course...forgive me...I am so happy to see you I am not thinking clearly... forgive me, my dear brother, forgive me...." For the first time in months, Giacomo Puccini laughed with pure pleasure, enfolding Michele in another joyous embrace. Words poured from him. "Are you well? You will stay with me. How are our sisters? Who paid for your train fare? Uncle Nicalao? "

"I have been working and saving for this day ever since you first left us, Giaco."

"Good for you! Do you have extra? We can always use money."

"I want to study music. Like you, I am here for the Conservatorio...."

"You have been accepted?"

"Only for the examination. But you said that was easy."

"It is...it was...and I shall help you. You will be accepted. I am certain of that."

"And I can help with money. There must be work in Milan."

"Yes, of course, of course...oh, Michele, I have missed you. Welcome to Milan... welcome, welcome."

Michele settled quickly into Giacomo's apartment, and for a while, his presence brightened Puccini's days. Under Giacomo's guidance, he passed his entrance examinations. They laughed and celebrated together. They dined together. They saw Milan together. However, Giacomo soon discovered that little brother Michelino had grown into a rather shiftless, aimless young man. Michele preferred sleeping to working, playing to studying, eating to cleaning, indifference to care. Soon he pushed Giacomo to impatience. Irritation became a wedge in their relationship. "Michele, your clothes are everywhere. On the floor. The kitchen table. In the sink. I gave you a dresser drawer. You have my permission to use it."

"I will, Giaco, I will. My, my...you become upset so easily."

"Not easily, Michele; with reason. Spilling food over the dampers and strings of our piano is no small thing."

"I said I was sorry for that."

"Apologies never repair damage, Michele, never."

"If I had money, I would repair the piano, Giaco."

"If you would work, you would have money."

"There is no time for work. I am a student, remember?"

"But you are not studying. You will fail your courses."

"They are boring. You said so yourself when you were a student."

Living together became impossible. Eventually, Michele decided to leave, and Puccini was happy to see him go. "I am not meant to live with family," Michele said as they parted. "I will always love you, Giaco. Believe me that is true, but I must go my own way."

Michele found an apartment with other Conservatorio students. Then once he was satisfied that his brother was safely settled, Giacomo Puccini hurried from Milan for Lucca to recover from the months of disappointment through which Michele had put him.

It was the first week of November. Temperatures danced around freezing. Breathing sent wisps of vapor into the air. The luscious verdure of Tuscany gasped in the tightening embrace of autumn. Trees were shedding desiccated leaves in final blasts of breathtaking beauty. Wildflowers struggled for life, with weaker plants losing the fight and leaving swaths of bare spots that would widen with each passing day. A hint of snow was in the air, and winter panted eagerly for its cue to color the entire landscape white.

Giacomo huddled in his seat as the afternoon train chugged its way to Lucca. He was chilled. His arms hugged his chest. His shoulders hunched. His head bent forward as if he were sleeping. He didn't see the changing countryside. He didn't notice his fellow passengers. He was thinking *Lucca...Lucca...that is where I belong... not Milan...it is in Lucca that I shall find myself again.*

Once there Puccini found no comfort in his Lucca. Memories flooded and almost drowned him. Everywhere he went, he saw Albina's face. In every sound, he heard her voice. His sisters were gone, fulfilling their own destinies. His two favorites were married and living in other towns. Another was in a convent. His home was gone. Friends had dispersed. Though he visited Carlo Angeloni and his Uncle Nicalao, their obligations kept them too busy to see him often. He was alone.

Dr. Ceru and Puccini's sisters had disposed of the family domicile and all its furnishings, with the proviso that he could reclaim particular items within a year if he could find enough money to repurchase them. Income from the sales was divided evenly amongst the Puccini siblings, with Michele's portion attached to a note urging him not to spend it foolishly, advice he quickly ignored.

The little windfall helped Giacomo to find an inexpensive, furnished apartment with a piano, two rooms where he could recover in quiet, relative comfort. But Lucca was not meant to be his salvation. Everything he saw there only intensified his loneliness. "Why do you make me suffer so?" he asked God one day with arms spread and face turned upward to an overcast sky. "If I had courage, I would join you and end my pain. Why do you not take me now, while I am facing you, wanting to leave this world?"

It was one of the many times that Giacomo Puccini would wish to die.

He saw no future for himself. Money problems continued to plague him. He lived frugally, but he was in debt to his Uncle Nicalao, to Fontana, to everyone. If Giulio Ricordi had discontinued his monthly support, his situation would have been utterly untenable. *"What is wrong with you?"* Puccini snarled, staring into a mirror. *"Are you going mad?"*

He tried to lose himself in books. He struggled with cheap, contemporary novels, smoking absently as he did, his cigarette butts filling a nearby ashtray. Or he wandered aimlessly around piazzas looking through store windows, seeing nothing. To fight insanity he gave singing and piano lessons to a few students. Occasionally, just to activate his lethargic creative juices, he forced himself to his piano. By sheer will power, he actually wrote a piano piece, which he titled: *Three Minuets for String Quartets* and believed it was totally worthless. In the main, his days and nights were empty... until the end of November 1885. It was then that he experienced something so cataclysmic it not only brightened his life, it changed it forever.

- 15 -

"Signor Puccini," she said softly extending her hand, "we met briefly last year in Milan. Do you remember me?"

He took the hand. It was slim and soft. How could he forget her? She had flirted with him while her husband sat by smiling insipidly. "Yes, I remember you," he said. "I even remember your name. Signora Gemignani. Am I correct?"

"*Esatto.*" Her smile was sly and enchanting. "My husband has insisted I see you to further my music education. Please say you will help me."

Her husband was Narciso Gemignani, a prosperous grocer and successful wine salesman. He was tall, broad shouldered and handsome, with a high forehead and black hair neatly barbered and parted on the left. He had intelligent brown eyes, a prominent nose, and a strong chin. And he was only twenty-nine years old. Clean shaven, except for a mustache that curled upward expertly at its tips, Narciso was always conscious of his appearance. He wore expensive suits with satin lapels, small wing-collars attached to his immaculate shirts, and a diamond stickpin in his carefully knotted tie. He was an out-going young man who conversed smoothly, enjoyed women and loved music. Also, like most successful Italians of the period, he sang and performed with family and friends in private concerts and salon gatherings. Naturally, living in Lucca all his life, Narciso was aware of the Puccini family's musical history. Having attended the same school as Giacomo, he knew of Puccini's position in the San Martino Cathedral and of his leaving it for the promise of Milan. And when the enormous success of *Le Villi* at La Scala raised Puccini to heroic standing in Lucca, Gemignani thought of him with an admiration that bordered on adoration. He hoped fervently that one day he would see him again, and that he, Narciso, would enjoy an electrifying discussion with *Il Maestro* about, "the infinite beauty of operatic music."

The opportunity to meet Puccini arose when Narciso had to be in Milan on urgent business matters. Ordinarily, he undertook such trips alone. But this time, acceding to his wife's insistent argument for a needed vacation, he brought Elvira along, promising her a memorable dinner with their Lucca celebrity.

Determined to keep that promise, Narciso inquired within his business circle and discovered where Puccini often dined. Then visiting the cafe he learned which evening of the week his prey would most likely be present. Puccini loved the soup and beans at that particular restaurant, and he tried to eat there every Tuesday evening. Narciso Gemignani reserved a table for that same evening, and he arrived early with Elvira and waited for Puccini to appear.

This carefully plotted meeting occurred in September of 1884, only two months after Albina's death, when Giacomo was struggling with both enervating depression and the difficult expansion of *Le Villi* into a two-act opera.

Puccini entered the cafe at 8:00 pm and went directly to his usual table in a corner of the room.

Narciso brightened on seeing him. He nudged his wife. "There he is," he whispered excitedly. "It is he!"

"Invite him. Quickly. Go to him and invite him to our table."

Narciso didn't need coaxing. He rose – a bit too eagerly, spilling some red wine on the white tablecloth – and crossed the room. "Maestro Puccini," he said softly, looking down and smiling at his Lucca hero, "how wonderful to see you."

Puccini looked up at him with a puzzled expression.

Gemignani hurried to explain. "I am Narciso Gemignani. Like you, my wife and I are from Lucca."

Now, Puccini understood. "Oh, yes, I remember you," he said. "We went to school together. You were two years ahead of me."

Narciso brightened in this recognition like a sputtering ember suddenly bursting into flame. “Yes, I was,” he agreed happily.

Puccini glanced across the half-empty room where Elvira sat stately, nodding in his direction.

“We would be honored if you will join us for dinner,” Gemignani begged. “Please, Maestro, be my guest.”

Puccini was in no condition to be congenial. Gracious, yes, but definitely not congenial. However poverty had made refusal of a full dinner unthinkable. He considered the invitation, but just for a moment, and then he smiled despite himself and said, “Thank you. I should like that.”

He rose and followed Gemignani to his table. Introduction to Elvira completed, Puccini took a seat opposite his hosts. Discussion began immediately on inane but mutually familiar points of interest: school days in Lucca; people in Lucca; places in Lucca; weather in Lucca; events in Lucca. Narciso dominated the conversation, while Elvira, his lovely wife, watched Giacomo steadily, smiling a few times and occasionally directing a flattering observation his way.

It had turned into an unexpectedly pleasant and satisfying evening for Puccini.

But his pleasure ended abruptly as he cleared his plate of an exquisite steak dinner, and swallowed his last glass of Chianti. “What do you believe is the future of Italian opera, Maestro?” Gemignani asked suddenly and with intense earnestness. “I have read of what is called the `*Scapigliatura Revolution*.’ Will you please explain that to me?”

A simpler question would have elicited a more likable response. After all, Giacomo hadn’t found his generous host and wife disagreeable, and the superb dinner had dispelled his despondency. But the difficulties in addressing a subject so ponderous suddenly overwhelmed him. In a mood only for light banter, he was definitely not ready to expound upon *Scapigliatura* and the current generational war raging in operatic music. His smile disappeared.

“You pose a serious question,” he said quietly. “A very important one, too. But the future of Italian opera and the place of *Scapigliatura* in that future are not topics that can be discussed lightly over dinner. Let us reserve them for another time, shall we? When I am back in Lucca and can relax with you in an environment more conducive to the subject?"

By offering the possibility of another meeting, his reply satisfied and excited Gemignani. "Will you be returning to Lucca soon?" he asked eagerly.

"I hope to."

"And we hope you will allow us the pleasure of knowing when you are there."

"Yes, please," Elvira added quickly. "We should so like to see you again."

"I shall certainly let you know when I am in Lucca again," Puccini replied smoothly. With that, he thanked them for their hospitality and excused himself for the solitude of his apartment.

Now, a little more than one year after that dinner, Puccini looked at Elvira Gemignani and smiled in the memory of it. "Yes, I remember you," he repeated. "Clearly. And your gracious husband. How is Narciso? That is his name, is it not?"

Her smile broadened. "*Esatto*, again. Is your memory always so correct?"

"Only with charming people."

She liked that. "*Grazie*, Maestro," she said warmly. "I am going to enjoy studying with you...if you will accept me as a student."

Born on the 13th of June 1860, Elvira Gemignani was twenty-five years old when she stood before Puccini in his Lucca studio-apartment. He was twenty-seven. She smiled and moved with a silky grace. Having mothered two children, a daughter Fosca and a younger son Renato, she exuded the confidence of maturity. She was taller than most women, and her posture was straight and sure. She wore her long dark hair twisted and piled high on the top of her head. Except for a wedding ring, tiny pearls in the lobes of her pierced ears, and a small cameo brooch hanging from her neck on a long, thin chain, she wore no jewelry. She was modestly but fashionably attired, in a high-necked print dress that reached down to and covered her shoes. She was strikingly attractive, and her friendly demeanor pleased immediately.

Giacomo wanted to smile, but he forced a slight, thoughtful frown instead. He believed that made him appear more authoritative and businesslike. "And what does your husband have in mind for your musical education, Signora Gemignani?"

"Whatever I want, Maestro."

"All right, what do *you* have in mind?"

"Voice. I love to sing. Do you teach singing or only piano?"

"Both. But I instruct only those students who will benefit from my instruction. Time is extremely precious to me, Signora. I cannot waste it."

"I understand, Maestro. And how shall we determine if I am worthy of your time?"

The question nipped with an edge of sarcasm, but the twinkle in her eyes made it all playful and delightful.

"Why, we shall have to hear you sing. Is that not so?" Giacomo couldn't help himself; he grinned.

She grinned in return. "I should say that is a most appropriate solution to our problem, Maestro."

It hadn't taken long. He was snared. Banter, wit, charm, strong femininity may have been exactly what Giacomo Puccini needed at that time. He chuckled, and his gloom evaporated as quickly as a film of alcohol in the burning sun. Tilting his head slightly, he gestured toward the piano. She preceded him. Then, as she stood at the side of the instrument waiting for him to settle on the piano stool, she seemed slightly unsure of herself.

"Let us first relax the vocal cords with scales."

"Very well."

His hands ran over the piano keys, and she followed with tight-throated notes.

"No... no... open the throat. Louder...louder."

They tried again, and she improved.

"Better...once more."

Her third run of scales was fully confident.

"Excellent. Now, what would you like to sing for me, Signora?" he asked.

He expected a romantic ballad or a light and simple aria from some opera, but she intrigued him by naming a rollicking, popular song of the day. "Do you know it?"

"I do. And the key you prefer?"

She sang a few notes.

He found her range quickly and then said, "All right, let us see if you can benefit from instruction." He began the song's introduction.

When it was time for her to join him, her voice quavered and faltered. She stopped and apologized. "I am nervous, Maestro."

He was gentle with her. "That is understandable. My studio is new and cold to you. Familiarity is reassuring, and heat is comforting. Take a moment. Think. Imagine yourself someplace where you are alone, a warm, quiet environment where you feel relaxed and safe. Close your eyes."

She closed her eyes.

"Think. Do you see yourself there?"

"Yes."

"Are you happy there?"

She smiled. "Very."

"Good. Now open your eyes and sing your happiness."

He struck an opening chord. Her eyes snapped open. He rolled into the song's introduction once more, and this time her voice leaped into the chorus strongly and surely.

They ran through the song and slipped into an even more dauntless reprise. After a bright flourish and one final chord, Giacomo showed approval with short jerking nods of his head. "Yes," he said, "I think you will not be a waste of my valuable time."

Elvira burst into a happy laugh. "Thank you, Maestro, thank you. I shall not disappoint you."

"I expect you will be an exemplary student."

"Yes...*yes.*"

They agreed that her lessons should start the following Monday, and that they would meet twice a week with more meetings to be scheduled if necessary. She left his studio in high spirits, laughing, waving an arm and singing the last strains of her audition song with raucous vigor.

When she was gone, her presence lingered in the room. Giacomo couldn't stop thinking of her – her appearance, her laughter, her voice. She had enchanted him. Then he considered the money that two and possibly three vocal sessions a week would add to his dwindling resources, and he felt so good he actually shouted, "A superb meeting!" It was a feeling he hadn't experienced since the astonishing audience reaction to his one act version of *Le Villi.*

- 16 -

Returning to her house, Elvira Gemignani was a new woman. She had left to escape her mother-in-law, a dour, demanding harridan who guarded her grown son like a hawk protecting its young. Elvira had just turned eighteen when she married Narciso. She was a child, naive, virginal, and thrilled to be a married woman. The prospect of having her own house, raising children, and engaging in pleasant social activities had been her girlish dream.

But Elvira's fantasy died quickly. Proximity killed it. She'd never considered the presence of a coddling parent whose son had no desire to shed his *ragazzo di Mama* (Mama's Boy) chains. After a brief honeymoon in Rome, she and Narciso lived with his mother in her small house. Mama watched everything, and everything her new daughter-in-law attempted was never good enough for her precious son:

"No, no... this is how Narciso likes his breakfast."

"No! You are not folding his laundry correctly."

"The way you make the bed is not to his liking."

"How could you not remember to buy his favorite olives?"

A year later, Elvira's daughter Fosca was born, and matters worsened. Now she was seen also as an incompetent parent, a mother who did not understand the needs of her suffering child.

"She is the product of my son's seed. You must hold her gently."

"Your breasts are too small to produce sufficient milk."

"She cries because she does not feel love from you."

Elvira complained to her husband. "Your mother will destroy our marriage," she warned. She begged him to intercede, to tell his mother that she, Elvira, was the woman of the house now, and that she knew how to care for him and their child.

Of course, Narciso would never do that. The mere thought sent shivers through him. "She is trying to help, *amore*," he said. "Allow her to be part of our life."

"No!" Elvira snapped in the first of their many arguments. "She does not wish to be part of our lives. She wants to *own* our lives! I cannot bear this any longer. I must have my own house. Find a house!"

As soon as finances permitted, Narciso did just that. But it was around the corner from where his mother lived, and mother walked the short distance every day to make sure her son's needs were being adequately attended.

By the time Elvira's son Renato came into the world, she could no longer tolerate the sight of this carping watchdog. "Tell her I do not want her coming here every day," she ordered Narciso.

"Are you insane? She is my mother!"

Mother's criticisms now brought sharp retorts from Elvira. Each was quickly reported to the son as gross disrespect from a strong-willed and ungrateful snipe.

Away often on lengthy business trips, Narciso feared what might occur in his absence. "You must avoid confrontation," he told Elvira sternly.

The suggestion infuriated her, and it precipitated another stormy quarrel. She tried to stay out of her mother-in-law's sight. She took to long walks with her children and longer talks with friends. The tactic brought temporary relief. But *le nemica* (the enemy) continued to appear in Narciso's absence to make certain his children were being cared for properly. Elvira felt vulnerable and alone. She believed her home life was troubled and unsatisfying. She needed more. Something strong to ground her, to give her a sense of her own worth again, and she had no idea what that could be.

One night, when she cried her anguish in a rage, Narciso provided the solution to their problem: "Your concerns are only of the children, the house, and my mother," he said. "You are bored. Find an activity that will occupy your mind, something interesting and challenging."

She thought about that all through the following day. *Yes,* she agreed, *I need an activity, something different that will be mine and only mine.* By nightfall she knew exactly what that would be. "I am going to take singing lessons," she announced to her husband. "It will be as you said, interesting and challenging."

She expected resistance. Instead she was delighted when he immediately said, "Excellent! A fine activity. You have a lovely singing voice, and lessons will keep you occupied and happy. I approve wholeheartedly."

"I shall find a good teacher."

"Maestro Puccini is in Lucca. I read that recently in a newspaper. We had dinner with him last year in Milan, remember? If he is accepting students while here, he would be a marvelous teacher for you. Do you want me to find him and ask for you?"

"No, I can do that myself."

Though Puccini had seen Elvira Gemignani to the door of his studio, smiling and anticipating her next appearance, he wasn't allowed to remain that enthusiastic very long.

The next day, he received a letter from Fontana. It wasn't sharp, but it conveyed in clear terms a deep concern about their opera *Edgar*. That it came in the form of dialogue made it even more pointed. Fontana wrote:

> *Signor Ricordi asked me to visit him at his office. Our conversation lasted almost an hour. I shall reproduce some of its more pertinent words.*
>
> *"Have you heard from him?" he asked, clearly troubled.*
>
> *"Not recently," I answered.*
>
> *"Nor I," he replied.*
>
> *I defended you. I said, "In his last letter, he told me he is working."*

"If he is working," he said, "he is producing. If he is producing, there must be music. I have seen no evidence of that. He should be keeping us abreast of Edgar's progress. I have nothing to tell investors when they ask questions."

Giaco, my friend, you must send us music! I gave you the libretto in May. It is now March of another year! If you are not composing, my god, what are you doing with your time?

Prior to Elvira Gemignani's audition, Giacomo's depression had stifled all desire to compose. Now, it was no longer depression that prevented him from working. It was pleasure.

In the first lesson after her audition, he saw the possibility of future progress. She came to that lesson excitedly, like a young girl about to attend a royal ball. This was going to be her opportunity to develop something entirely and solely hers. It was to be her liberation. She appeared in brightly colored clothes with a tiny hat perched precariously on top of her carefully coiffed hair.

"May I comment on your attire?" Puccini asked after greeting her.

"If you choose."

"It is quite cheerful."

She grinned "It expresses my hopes, Maestro."

"Good. Let us begin. We shall not be singing today. There is more to singing than song."

"Yes, Maestro."

Patiently, he took her through scales, and then through relaxation, breathing and lip exercises. She responded with enthusiasm and was thrilled with what she perceived to be immediate improvement.

When the hour ended, Elvira was so stimulated, her elation was almost a palpable entity. She pouted charmingly and objected: "The hour has gone too quickly. May we not continue?"

Puccini grinned. "No, Signora. Now you must practice these exercises every day for an hour until we meet again."

"I shall. Yes, I shall."

It was agreed that they would meet every Monday and Thursday, and that his fee would be paid on the second session of the week. At the door, Elvira extended a hand. Puccini took it and held it a little longer than he had intended. "Music," he said, "can be like the scent of a favorite perfume. It awakens one's soul. These exercises are to be your perfume. The more you practice them, the more intense will become its scent, and the more your soul will be awakened."

Her eyes widened. She hadn't expected such poetic advice. She smiled. "And what is *your* favorite perfume, Maestro?"

"Lavender. Like music, it has always awakened my soul."

Something was happening to Giacomo Puccini. Whereas his mornings usually began dismally with a heaviness of spirit that made each movement an effort, he awoke this day thinking of Elvira and looking forward to their meeting. He leaped from his bed. He bolted a fast breakfast. Then hurriedly, he brought order and neatness to his cluttered studio. He made his bed. He emptied ashtrays. He straightened piles of novels. Finally, putting sheets of music out of sight, he surveyed the room and exhaled a satisfied breath that sounded almost like a musical note. She would be arriving in forty-five minutes. He wondered what she would be wearing, and what she was doing at that moment.

As infatuated as Puccini, Elvira prepared herself with equal attention to detail. She bathed. She selected an attractive dress. She combed her hair with particular care and applied a subtle shade of makeup to accentuate her cheeks and lips. Studying herself in a full-length mirror, she was pleased enough with her appearance to smile and whisper," *Buona, Elvira, buona."*

It was a good job. She looked alluring and happy. She told the children to be kind to their nanny. Then she kissed them and, humming a tune, she left the house for another step into her new and exciting musical adventure.

He heard the light tap of the rapper and opened the door

immediately. He smiled appreciatively at her appearance. As she brushed past him to enter the studio, his breath caught in the unexpected and heady scent of lavender.

"I am happy to see you again," he said.

"And I, you."

"Let us begin immediately. Have you practiced your exercises?"

"All week, Maestro."

"We shall see." He ran her through their last meeting's work. Her improvement was impressive, and he told her so. "Yes, you have been practicing. I thank you. It makes me feel our efforts are not being wasted."

The hour had passed too quickly for Elvira. Then in its final minutes something provocative occurred that instantly changed their teacher-student relationship to that of man and woman.

"Your tones have improved remarkably in one week," he said. "Continue with the exercises. I should like you to sing next time."

'Thank you, Maestro, thank you."

"There is one thing more before you leave: We must strengthen your breathing. Singing requires diaphragmatic breathing. Let me show you. Stand here."

She did as told.

"It begins with posture. Straight. Head up. Excellent. May I touch you?"

"Of course."

Tentatively, he placed a palm over her abdomen. He didn't feel the expected rigidness of undergarment support. Then the scent of her lavender touched him like a tantalizing feather, and he struggled to control a desire to embrace her.

Elvira saw him fluster. She bowed her head in embarrassment. "One needs freedom to breathe," she explained demurely.

"Indeed," was all he could say. He went through a demonstration of diaphragmatic breathing, after which he led her to the studio door urging her, "Continue to practice, Signora. In three months, your husband and friends will marvel at the beauty of your voice." He fumbled slightly with the door handle.

Looking straight into his eyes, she offered a hand. "Until next time, Maestro."

He took the hand. "Yes...yes...until next time...practice... remember, practice...." The words were unusually throaty.

She squeezed his fingers and left him with a slight, enigmatic smile on her lips.

That smile, that squeeze of fingers puzzled and teased Giacomo Puccini every day and every night until he saw Elvira Gemignani again. What had they meant? Why did they sneak into his thoughts so disturbingly? They brought images to mind. He couldn't forget the feel of her body, the scent of her perfume. Everything about her now intoxicated him, and he stumbled through his hours like an alcoholic searching for another drink of her wine.

At home again, Elvira was in no better condition than Giacomo. The pressure of his hand upon her abdomen had sent shivers through her. Her breath had caught. Her eyes had closed. And now she waited for their fourth meeting, more excited by anticipation than she believed she ever could be. She didn't understand fully what was happening. All she knew was that this dark, handsome, soft-spoken, brilliant composer was bringing something into her life that made her feel especially alive and happy. And after all, isn't that exactly what her husband Narciso wanted for her?

It took only three more weeks for Elvira and Giacomo to meet in their first kiss.

Though desire for it had been building with each lesson, they had with herculean control restrained their growing passion until it became an explosive force that could no longer be contained. The kiss happened quite unexpectedly and with a gentleness that left both of them breathless and confused.

She was standing at his side near the piano. They had just completed a song, a phrase of which Puccini identified as needing special attention.

"Here," he said, "you must be *molto affettuoso*, very tender, soft, gentle. See?" His index finger touched the direction on the music sheet.

She bent down and leaned forward to see the direction. Her perfume worked its magic. He inhaled deeply. She turned her head to look at him and saw longing in his eyes. Her heart pounded. Their mouths were inches apart. Slowly, Elvira moved her head closer until their lips met, lightly, gently, and they knew their first moment of bliss.

Each meeting after that began with a kiss and ended with an embrace and a kiss, and each kiss led them more deeply into the pit of passion. It was at the start of their seventh week together that Elvira excused herself and disappeared into the kitchen. When she didn't return in ten minutes, Puccini became concerned. They had dispensed with Signora and Maestro immediately after that first intimacy. Now they addressed each other by their Christian names. He went to the kitchen to see what had detained her. She wasn't there. Puzzled, he called for her: "Elvira? Elvira? Where are you?"

"Here, Giacomo. Come, help me. I need you. Help me."

He followed her voice. It led him from the kitchen to his tiny bedroom. The door was closed. "Elvira?" He tapped on the door.

"I am here. Help me."

He opened the door and saw her standing near his bed. She wore nothing but a tremulous, inviting smile. In that moment, Giacomo Puccini thought he would choke on his heart.

She extended her arms, and he went to her.

Their lovemaking became a weekly ritual. What had started as a leap into lust grew quickly into what they believed to be deep and eternal love. They began to see each other three and four times a week, even daring to stroll the piazzas or to meet foolishly and recklessly in Lucca cafes where, unconcerned, they could be seen by friends.

Back from a long, eight-week business trip, Narciso noticed changes in his wife's behavior. She smiled more often, and she was more attentive to the children and to his needs. What pleased him most was the absence of angry arguments and scathing comments about his dear mother. He attributed it all to the singing lessons he had urged her to have with his idol, and he felt gratifyingly responsible for her new-found happiness.

"Your wife is being unfaithful to you, and you are a fool," his mother scolded.

"What?"

"She is having an affair with Giacomo Puccini!"

"What are you saying?"

"I saw them walking together on the *Via Fillungo*.

"Do not make something out of nothing, Mama. He is her teacher."

"Teachers and students do not walk arm-in-arm as husband and wife!"

Narciso's head snapped to watch his mother snort and leave him with a knowing sneer.

Is Mama correct? Am I blind? Is my wife making a fool of me? Doubt and suspicion had been planted. Mama was pleased. And Narciso would not know a moment of security and marital peace ever again. Aware of Elvira's propensity for violent reaction, he refrained from direct confrontation until he could be certain of her infidelity. However, since business took him away from home frequently, he had little opportunity to watch her closely. He suffered.

Meanwhile, Giacomo Puccini became obsessed with the ecstasy of love. His agreement with Fontana and Ricordi to complete *Edgar* in time for a December La Scala opening vanished from his mind. He could think only of Elvira. Letters from Fontana went unanswered for weeks. When he did respond, he explained his tardiness with fabrications and promises to send *Edgar* the moment it was finished. But months flew by, and he composed nothing.

Giulio Ricordi considered terminating Puccini's 300 lire monthly stipend. He told Amilcare Ponchielli that he, Ricordi, no longer had faith in their protégé. That sadly, like many young aspiring artists, Giacomo was just another one-success composer.

Only a defense by Ponchielli saved Giacomo. "Please, Giulio," he begged, "be patient with him. He has genius in him. I see it. Do not allow momentary disappointment to destroy a budding Verdi. He needs you."

"For you, Ami, I shall wait a little longer before severing my relationship with him. I pray you are right in your assessment."

Puccini continued his affair blissfully oblivious to the possibility of discovery. However, in April of 1886, Elvira's attitude toward him began to change. She was no longer the free, responsive lover. Occasionally, she carped at things he said or did. She cancelled lessons. Once, she avoided him for two straight weeks, and when she saw him again, she refused to respond to his questions and concern.

Puccini became distraught. What was happening? Had he done something to offend her? Had her husband discovered their love? Giacomo lived his days in a daze. Elvira. Elvira. He wanted only to see Elvira. Then one weekend he did see her, and his romantic escapade came crashing down burying him in an avalanche of confusion and fear.

It was in June of 1886. Elvira stood before Puccini with tears blurring her features, hands wringing, and voice barely intelligible. "I am pregnant, Giacomo," she babbled. "I am pregnant."

- 17 -

A novice in affairs of the heart, Puccini didn't question Elvira's revelation. He never doubted his responsibility. It was to be his child, and he would soon become a father. Tearfully, desperately, she had said the child was his. That was enough. Her anguish was indisputable confirmation of her words.

"How long have you known?" he asked.

"Three months."

Now he understood her recent change in behavior. He took her in his arms. "Do not cry," he whispered. "We shall face this together."

They kept the pregnancy from Narciso until it was impossible to hide the fact any longer. When it became obvious, when she bulged and her breasts swelled, Narciso had his evidence. Mother had identified the father. Confession was all he needed. That his own infidelities failed to mitigate his fury was an expression of 19th century culture. Italian husbands were allowed their mistress peccadilloes, but wives their extra-marital men? *Never.* Thereafter, Narciso and his mother turned every moment with Elvira into a flaming hell.

"Who is the father?!" he demanded each time he looked at her. "Who is the father? *Who is the father?!*"

Living together became impossible. Fighting flared at a glance. And in one stormy argument Elvira finally screamed the answer he wanted: "GIACOMO! MY TEACHER! MY LOVE! ARE YOU SATISFIED? YOU THREW ME INTO HIS ARMS! YOU SENT ME TO HIM! *YOU ARE TO BLAME! IT IS YOU! YOU! DO NOT BLAME ME!*"

Unable to endure another moment with her husband, and not

knowing where else she could go, she ran from her house without her children and moved into Puccini's small apartment. He wiped her tears with kisses. "It is all right, *mi amore.* Do not cry...do not cry...we are together now...we are together."

Living together openly now they quickly became the all-consuming scandal of their Lucca community. Family, friends, strangers...*everyone* was outraged and seemed to have no other subject to discuss.

"What have you done?" Giacomo's sister Ramelde cried. *What have you done?!* It was not a question. It was the demand of disbelief and dismay.

"You have shamed the family!" his sister Iginia pronounced from her nunnery.

"You have made a mistake. Let us hope it will not destroy your career," Fontana warned.

"He has brought dishonor to all of Lucca!" the city's influential Del Fiorentino family declared in a newspaper article.

Puccini and Elvira now tried to avoid attention. But it was impossible. The scandal followed them everywhere they went. Fearful that Narciso might attack him in the rage of cuckoldry and humiliation, Puccini rented a dilapidated house in the small town of Monza, 180 miles away. It was all he could afford.

The move didn't bring the forlorn lovers comfort. Elvira wept constantly. She tore at her hair. "My children...my children...what have I done? They will miss me. I miss them. They will become ill, and I will not be there to help them. My God, what have I done?"

Giacomo felt helpless. All efforts to comfort her failed. They were isolated in Monza, she was pregnant, and regret was tearing their love apart.

Eventually, a faint ray of moderation brightened their lives. Narciso Gemignani agreed to share his children with their mother. He sent their daughter Fosca to Elvira and kept their son Renato to himself. The agreement didn't satisfy Elvira, but it was all that her husband would allow. She had lost her son. She might never see him again. Misery continued to twist her soul.

Puccini accepted Fosca immediately. She was his stepdaughter, and he tried earnestly to create a family of his own. However, as a Catholic, Elvira could not obtain a divorce, and marriage never became a consideration. More months passed. Entangled in this net of pain, Giacomo could not give *Edgar* a moment of the attention it needed. Letters continued to come from Fontana and Giulio Ricordi. Then when all seemed as hopeless and as dark as it could possibly be, Uncle Nicalao Ceru plunged a knife even deeper into Puccini's troubled life.

"You are a grave disappointment. You have failed everyone," he wrote sternly. *"I am finished with you.* Le Villi *has brought you 40,000 lire. I demand repayment of my loan to you at once with interest!"*

The demand jolted Puccini. Even Uncle Nicalao had turned against him. Good, kind, generous Uncle Nicalao. But he'd believed the doctor's money had always been a gift, not a loan. And 40,000 lire from *Le Villi*? Where did he get that figure? *I have earned only 6,500 lire, and every centesimi of that has gone to repay debts,* he agonized. Quickly, he collected all Casa Ricordi royalty statements. He studied them. Yes, he was correct. He had received only 6,500 lire. To prove he was still a poor desperate artist with barely enough money to support his new family, he sent the statements to Dr. Ceru and begged for understanding. It didn't help. Uncle Nicolao continued to demand his money.

Then on December 23, 1886 what should have been a happy event became the cause of additional angst. Elvira delivered a healthy baby boy, soon to be christened Antonio. He was another child to be raised, another mouth to feed, another responsibility to tax their almost non-existent income.

"You must write," Ricordi insisted when Giacomo requested further advances on royalties. "We are waiting for *Edgar.* You *must* write!"

And Elvira nagged constantly, "We have no money. We will starve. You must do something."

He forced himself to face Fontana's libretto. He sat at his piano and struggled. But his efforts were devoid of the enthusiasm so essential to his creativity. What emerged was bland and stripped of passion. Nevertheless some passages did coalesce and assume the shape of an opera. He wasn't satisfied with them, but he sent his efforts to Fontana and Ricordi only to make them believe he was hard at work and to keep his 300 lire stipend flowing. His ploy worked. It appeased his librettist, and it persuaded Ricordi to continue sending him the money he so desperately needed.

However, Giulio Ricordi was not entirely satisfied. Yes, Puccini was working, but he was working much too slowly. They had to talk. Ricordi sent Giacomo train fare and forced him to appear in Milan for discussions on *Edgar*'s progress. These sessions lasted hours. They became frustrating and debilitating confrontations. Puccini sank ever deeper into his wish to be free of this burden. He brooded. He dallied. He shirked. He believed he was losing his mind. It is amazing that Ricordi didn't abandon the entire undertaking, because it took Puccini almost *four years* to compose the entire score and orchestration for *Edgar*!

In those four years poverty turned Elvira into a harpy with a tongue that sliced ugly pieces almost daily from Giacomo's self-image. "So you completed your opera. Congratulations. Verdi could have composed *three* operas in that time!" Anger and accusations became her modus operandi. Puccini was no longer the great Maestro in her eyes. He had become a lazy incompetent, the source of all her unhappiness.

To escape her venom Puccini fled to Caprino Bergamasco, Fontana's home, and stayed with his friend for weeks at a time.

"Unhappiness is killing you. Leave her," Fontana advised.

"I cannot."

"Why not?"

"She is my wife."

"That is foolish. You are not married."

"In my eyes we are. And Tonio is my son."

Discussions like this gave him no relief. They drove him instead to Milan to be with his brother Michele, who was too troubled with his own life to give him much care and attention. Then he would flee to Lake Como to be with the Ponchiellis, where he would receive the compassion and understanding he so sorely needed. However, grief strangled him once again when these visits ended on January 16, 1886. On that day his dearest friend, Amilcare Ponchielli, died of pneumonia, a victim of the year's severe winter. He was interred in *Cimitero Monumentale,* Milan's Monumental Cemetery, the principal burial ground of Italy's 19th century artists. His passing was an insuperable loss. Giacomo attended the funeral and wept uncontrollably.

There were times when Puccini sneaked into Lucca to see friends and family. But barbed comments from his sisters and their husbands about his illicit lifestyle made him too uncomfortable to remain there long. Distress and loss seemed to face him at every turn.

Even his brother Michele brought him pain: "I am leaving Italy," he announced. "I am going to Argentina where opportunities are greater than here in Milan."

"Argentina?!"

"I am told there are many people there from Lucca. They will help me."

Nothing Puccini said could dissuade Michele. He had made his decision. He would be leaving for Buenos Aires soon, but he would write often and send Giacomo expensive mementoes as soon as he became an envied, wealthy man in the New World.

Michele's actual departure wounded Giacomo deeply. Now he felt totally alone. His dear mother was gone, he had lost Ponchielli, his sisters didn't was to see him, Elvira made his days unbearable, and now his brother had abandoned him for a frivolous dream. All he had was a questionable career and a very uncertain opera.

Edgar finally opened at the La Scala opera house in Milan with the great Franco Faccio conducting the orchestra. Puccini waited nervously outside the theatre. Only thunderous applause could be his salvation. He clasped his palms to his lips and prayed.

But God was not listening to Giacomo Puccini's prayers that night.

There was applause, but fervor was clearly missing. The next morning, Milan's newspapers offered inconsequential criticisms. They recognized some musical growth, and they noted a few inspired moments. In general, though, the reviewers and audiences were not at all pleased with *Edgar.* Ticket sales plummeted. Despite his genius, Giulio Ricordi could not save this production. He closed the opera and immediately cancelled a planned second production. A disaster of monumental proportions, *Edgar* unsettled Ricordi so alarmingly it ended the publisher's association with Ferdinando Fontana forever.

"It is the libretto," Ricordi told Puccini. "Signor Fontana consistently rejected suggestions for its improvement. Understand this: Great music can never succeed from a weak story! I still believe in your genius. We shall work together. We shall strive to revive *Edgar* after I have settled matters with its librettist!"

The attack surprised Puccini. He believed *he* had been the cause of *Edgar*'s failure, but now Ricordi was relieving him of this burden. Was the fault really Fontana's, or was his publisher expressing resentment of the librettist for other more personal reasons? He didn't know. Regardless of the true motive, it was clear that Giulio Ricordi was suggesting an end to the Puccini/Fontana collaboration.

But Fontana had been his creative mainstay. How could he compose without Fontana? He bowed his head and closed his eyes. Deeply troubled by the position in which he now found himself, Puccini made an instantaneous and life-altering decision.

"Be assured, Signor Giulio," he said, "I shall do everything in my power to work with you for the great success we have both envisioned for *Edgar*."

Ricordi smiled his satisfaction.

Giacomo worried about his next meeting with his dear friend Ferdi.

His fears about Fontana's reaction were groundless. "Do not worry about this," *Edgar's* librettist said when they met again. "Signor Gulio's separation agreement is quite satisfactory. He has paid me well. It is the way of theater, Giaco. Move forward, my friend. Move upward, onward, and be successful."

Enormously relieved, Puccini now applied himself feverishly to his moribund opera. *Edgar* became his *raison d'être*. He met with Giulio Ricordi and listened to his suggestions. He composed one new musical passage after another. There was no more procrastination. Composition obsessed him. And finally, after weeks of arduous application, he sat back and told himself: *It is good now. It has been rescued.*

Such satisfaction wasn't to comfort him very long.

He hadn't received a letter from his brother Michele in two months. "Why does he not write? How busy can he be that he does not answer my letters?" And quite unexpectedly, he found his questions answered in a brief *Corriere della Sera* newspaper article.

"On March 22, 1891," it said, *"Dominico Michele Puccini, younger brother of opera composer Maestro Giacomo Puccini, died of yellow fever in Rio de Janeiro, Brazil. He was twenty-seven years-old."*

The news of Michele's death was a lightning bolt. It stabbed into Puccini's skull and immobilized him. It drove him into a depression so deep that sisters and friends feared he might never emerge. He wept. He would not eat. He told his sister Ramelde that Michele's death was a tragedy that affected him even more deeply than Albina's, and that he wished to die and to join his brother. *"Life is too much to bear,"* he wrote. *"Only death is its relief."* And he was very close to committing suicide. However, questions chewed on him like voracious worms, and they kept him alive: What was Michele doing in Brazil? He had been living in Argentina. Buenos Aires was his home. Why was he in Brazil? *Why?* The questions pulled him from his stupor. He had to know the answers, and he wouldn't rest until he found them. He searched everywhere. He read papers. He asked officials. He questioned friends. Finally, he learned the full story:

Michele Puccini found feminine charms irresistible. And like his brother he fell in love with and seduced a married woman. This woman, though, was not the wife of an itinerant wine salesman. This woman was the wife of an Argentine senator. When Senator

Perez, an extremely powerful and influential man, discovered his wife's infidelity, he raged and challenged Michele to a duel. Foolishly, young Puccini accepted the challenge. They met on a grey Monday morning. With seconds and officials observing they took their positions as directed and raised their guns. Michele fired first. The bullet found its mark, and his opponent fell to the ground. Michele left the scene quickly, believing he had slain him on "the field of honor." But the senator did not die. And he did not accept the honorable conclusion of his challenge. Recovering from his wound, he swore he would find and kill his wife's seducer as soon as he was well. Fearing the threat and the power of the senator's position, Michele fled the country to Rio de Janeiro, Brazil. And there, only a few months later, his skin turned yellow, he suffered seizures, fell into a coma and died quickly of malaria – poor, all alone, a sad and broken dreamer.

Oddly, the facts behind Michele's death became Puccini's release. He no longer thrashed about in the pain of ignorance. He continued to mourn the loss of his brother, but slowly he returned to the world, to his work and to the House of Ricordi.

Giulio Ricordi had been wonderfully patient and compassionate during Giacomo's travail. He had tried to comfort him, always maintaining gently that work was the only unguent for a wounded soul. Now the kind publisher greeted his protégé with warmth and encouragement. "I am so happy you are well enough to work again," he said. "We had accomplished much before your terrible loss, and we shall complete our opera now in little time. You are a brave man, Giacomo, a brave and brilliant artist."

Before learning the bizarre circumstances of Michele's death they had disposed of the entire fourth act. They had shifted its prelude to Act I. They had shortened one and eliminated two major arias in Acts II and III. And they had dramatically altered a significant banquet scene. *Edgar* was clearly tighter, faster, and musically more dramatic. "I am eager now to proceed," Ricordi told Puccini.

Edgar's second opening took place on January 28, 1892, in Ferrara, Italy. Difficulty in finding a Milan theater was the given reason. But, in truth, Ricordi didn't trust the objectivity of his city's audience and critics. He wanted a less jaded reaction. After Ferrara it went on to Turin, Madrid and Buenos Aires, and in all four presentations it was received well...not wildly, but well.

Puccini modified the libretto after each production; but he succeeded only in mangling it further. He was simply not a librettist. His limited knowledge of dramatic structure dragged him into irremediable error. *Edgar* became a disjointed mess, more like a patchwork of scenes than a smooth, flowing story. Extensive revisions mutilated the plot and weakened its characters. And by the time *Edgar* closed its South American productions, Puccini was so bewildered and disgusted with his work that he called the opera "a defective organism," "...the most horrible thing ever written!" Thereafter, he swore he would have nothing more to do with this blight upon his reputation.

Giulio Ricordi, however, had been impressed by Puccini's dedication and commitment.

"As you, I am disappointed in *Edgar*," he said. "But we must not permit this *cantonata,* this blunder, to divert you from your destiny. We must find another libretto for you quickly. One with dramatic intensity, sympathetic characters and continuity, from all of which your music will emerge naturally like the dawn of a resplendent day."

This amazing support heartened Giacomo. It gave him the will to continue. It was backed also with money. At this stage of their relationship Puccini had received more than 16,000 lire from the House of Ricordi, a sum that deeply distressed its board of directors. Its members urged Giulio to separate the company from this composer who had nothing to offer, for whom continued aid could only be a drain on their treasury. "He is a leech; he is sucking our company's blood," one member complained.

But Ricordi resisted all objections with passionate, adamant proclamations. "I tell you, he will do justice to the House of Ricordi! His operas will swell our treasury. I know genius when I see it. You must trust me when I say this. You *must!*"

The board retreated in the heat of his demand.

To Puccini, Ricordi said, "Nothing will stand in our way. We shall find the perfect libretto for you, and you will honor the memory of Amilcare Ponchielli. That is as it is meant to be. That is as it *will* be!"

"My thanks to you come from every cell in my body, dear Signor Giulio," Giacomo answered. "I shall not disappoint you again. On my mother's grave, I swear it."

Ricordi was deeply touched. "I believe you, my boy. We shall find your libretto, we shall."

"I have been thinking of a possible story."

Ricordi was pleased. "And it is?"

"It is a thin novel over 100 years old. I read it some time ago, and the tale has never left me."

"I am intrigued."

Puccini jumped ahead enthusiastically. "It is by a French priest named Abbé Prévost, and its title, *L'Histoire de Manon Lescaut et du Chevalier des Grieux*, is almost as long as the book."

His levity failed to produce its intended pleasure. Ricordi was visibly troubled. "I know it well. No! You need something fresh, something different. *Manon* is already on the stage. Why in heaven's name do you wish to compose music for an opera that already exists, one that has been presented successfully more than two hundred times at the Opéra-Comique?"

"Because I can make it better. It will be different. Now it is a comedy, but I see drama. Massenet wrote with French lightness. I can give it Italian passion."

Ricordi had to smile at his intensity. It screamed commitment. He closed his eyes and thought: *Should such resolve ever be denied?* He didn't like the idea of *Manon* as drama, but he nodded slowly. "All right, Giacomo," he agreed, "let us see where this will take us."

Heartened by Ricordi's approval and by his promise to find "the best librettist in Milan" for a serious version of *Manon Lescaut*, Puccini returned to Elvira, Fosca and their little boy Tonio. He hoped for a happy reunion, but his hopes were crushed quickly. Elvira's resentments had only deepened in his absence. Left alone with two children and not knowing how she would pay the rent on their shabby house or from where their next meal would come, she had struggled desperately to survive on the few lire he had been able to send her each month.

Facing her mate, she greeted his smile with coldness and recrimination. "So here you are. You left us to starve, and you return with nothing. Are you going to sleep your life away again, or are you going to apply yourself to another opera which, like your *Edgar*, is certain to fail?"

Puccini's smile disappeared. He took a deep breath and sighed. "A cold and biting welcome, Elvira. Strangely, I had hoped for more but expected nothing less."

He stared at her.

"Do not look at me that way!" she flared.

"I am beginning to understand something." He sighed once more and turned away. He was certain now their love was gone, dissolved completely in the acid of poverty and regret. Passion had caused their disgrace. Now, only obligation kept him from leaving her immediately.

- 18 -

Manon Lescaut possessed Puccini. It became his escape from Elvira. Peace lay in their efforts to avoid each other. She would disappear for hours, leaving him with the children, rarely revealing where she was going. He would wander the countryside, enjoying the quiet, thinking only of *Manon*. He hungered for Giulio Ricordi to find "the best librettist in Milan." Who would that be? The question nagged. Weeks passed and his impatience grew. He wrote to Ricordi, telling him of his eagerness to work. *"I hear music in everything I see. Please, Signor Giulio, find my librettist."*

And one afternoon he received train fare, a letter from Ricordi, and the long-awaited: *"I have found our poet!"*

Giacomo was thrilled. He planned to leave home the next day, but Elvira had a plan of her own.

"I will not remain here like a rag while you enjoy yourself in Milan. I am taking Fosca and going away for a week."

"And Tonio?" he asked. "Will you not take him?"

"He is your son. Care for him."

She had created a problem. Tonio was now six years-old, a sweet, handsome boy who laughed loudly and ran about with the energy of a young bull. How could he, Puccini, care for him while he was meeting with Ricordi and his new librettist? "You must take Tonio with you," he insisted. "He is your son."

And Elvira answered emphatically, "Assume the responsibility of fatherhood, will you? He is yours as well!"

There was no persuading her. In desperation, he went to Lucca with Tonio and begged his sister Ramelde for help. "Watch your nephew. Please. I shall come for him as soon as I return from Milan."

Ramelde and his other sisters still deplored his fathering an illegitimate child and living in sin. They wanted nothing to do with their brother's situation. He had brought it upon himself. He must bear the burden of his folly alone. However, the sweetness and innocence in Tonio's eyes quickly melted Ramelde's resistance. Looking into them, she smiled and stroked the boy's head. "But only until you return," she said. "And you must return quickly."

"My promise," he said with a hand over his heart.

He left Tonio with Ramelde and went directly from Lucca to Milan.

Giulio Ricordi was waiting for Puccini in his office. With him was a full-bodied, chunky young man with lazy eyes and an indifferent air. He was dressed neatly in black shoes, a dark suit, white shirt, tie and tie pin. He had a bushy mustache with long, upward twisting ends, a full head of black hair, and a charming curl that he had carefully arranged to hang above his left eyebrow.

"Signor Puccini," Ricordi said happily when Giacomo arrived, "I should like you to meet Signor Ruggero Leoncavallo. Signor Leoncavallo, this is Signor Giacomo Puccini."

Ruggero Leoncavallo! Puccini couldn't have been more delighted. He extended a hand, grinning broadly. "Signor Leoncavallo, I am extremely happy to finally meet you."

Leoncavallo offered a limp handshake. "As I am you." His smile lacked warmth.

Next to Arrigo Boito, Leoncavallo was the most admired librettist in all of Italy. His exquisite sense of drama was evident in the many librettos he wrote for composers. But it was particularly evident in the exciting two act opera *Pagliacci,* for which he had also composed the music. Opening at Teatro Dal Verme on May 21, five months after Puccini's *Edgar* had closed in Ferrara, *Pagliacci* brought instant fame and status to its creator. It caused him also to believe he was an artist of incomparable talent.

"I saw *Pagliacci,*" Puccini said. "It is a magnificent achievement."

"Thank you. I saw *Edgar.* It showed some promise."

Giacomo didn't know what had been exchanged in that greeting. He had been sincere in his praise of *Pagliacci.* But what had Leoncavallo meant? He could have referred to *Le Villi.* Why had he chosen *Edgar*?

The innuendo and its ensuing silence were not lost on Giulio Ricordi. Sensing the possibility of artistic friction, he said quickly, "I am always amazed by our community. Though it is not large, many of its artists, sadly, have not yet met. It pleases me enormously now to bring two of my favorites together. Come, let us sit and discuss a new version of *Manon Lescaut,* which in its brilliance will astound the entire opera world."

The slight chill vanished in the warmth of Ricordi's deft touch.

They sat on the comfortable armchairs in the spacious room. Ricordi offered Puccini and Leoncavallo cigars. They accepted with expressions of pleasure. Then after lighting his own cigar, he said, "Let us enjoy ourselves," and all three sat back and puffed contentedly like old friends after a hearty meal.

Leoncavallo was the first to speak about *Manon Lescaut*. "I must admit, what you are proposing interests me greatly," he said, billowing smoke into the air. "I have always believed *Manon* to be more than lighthearted fare. I do not see sentimentality in De Grieux's love for Manon. I see passion, the desperate conflict of reason and need."

Hearing this, Puccini sat up straighter. His eyes widened. He leaned slightly forward. Interest sharpened his voice. "Exactly," he said. "This is not merriment. Manon must be won by the intensity of hunger. Go on. Please. Continue."

Ricordi smiled and nodded.

Stroked by this encouragement, Leoncavallo swelled and expounded further. "The students and townspeople are not frivolous accessories to De Grieux's behavior. Their laughter must not be pleasure. It must be mockery. It must hurt. It must goad De Grieux and drive him deeper into his pain."

"Yes," Puccini agreed. "That is exactly how I see it."

"Cogent argumentation, fiery passion, explosive conflict, tragic consequences – these are the elements of effective drama. These are the devices to render audiences helpless, to bring them to tears, and to leave them cathartically limp and happy," Leoncavallo concluded firmly. "Our *Manon* should be a statement of human truth, a *verismo* opera."

Verismo! It was precisely the word Puccini had been hoping to hear. It meant *truth* - life as it is, not as we should like it to be.

Ordinary people, common locales, everyday struggles were replacing the gods, kings, queens, and mythological figures of 19th century Romanticism. Audiences wanted something different, something *real.* This was happening not only in Milan but everywhere in western culture. In literature, England had its Charles Dickens, France its Emil Zola, Russia its Fyodor Dostoevsky, America its Theodore Dreiser.

In opera, Italy had its *Scapigliatura,* its Arrigo Boito, Franco Faccio and Ruggero Leoncavallo.

Verismo. A magic word to Puccini. And here he was with the librettist of *Pagliacci,* one of the strongest proponents of *verismo* truth. He was thrilled. He was speechless. In this collaboration, *Manon* could not fail to be a great success.

He glanced at Giulio Ricordi. His grin told the publisher how pleased he was with his new librettist. He looked at Leoncavallo, agreement shining in his eyes. "Signor Leoncavallo," he said, "it will be both pleasure and honor to create with you. I am so eager to see what you will do with *Manon*. I am speechless with anticipation."

Never losing his supercilious air, Leoncavallo smiled faintly and said in return, "Be assured, sir, I shall resurrect your ability to speak."

Personalities of the 1800s often engaged in ridiculous ego skirmishes. Wit and biting observations became their weapons of self-defense. Apparently, Leoncavallo's armament included a stiletto of condescension. Puccini felt the prick of it. He had been cordial and honest. He had done nothing to warrant belittling. But Leoncavallo had found it necessary to minimize him. Puccini found this unsettling. However, he didn't respond in kind. Instead, he merely smiled, and all three men then puffed elaborately on their cigars with different views of their meeting. Ricordi saw progress. Leoncavallo saw success. Puccini saw trouble.

As soon as he was free, Giacomo kept the promise he'd made to his sister, and he returned immediately to Lucca for his son Tonio. Ramelde met him with smiles as Tonio raced to his father and greeted him with hugs and shouts of joy. Giacomo dropped to a knee before the boy. He looked lovingly into his limpid eyes. "And were you a good boy while I was away?" he asked. "Did you do everything *Zia* Ramelde asked you to do?"

"Yes, he did," Aunt Ramelde answered happily for Tonio. "He is an angel. You do not deserve him." There was no rancor in her speech, no judgment. Evidently Tonio had won his aunt's heart and altered feelings about her brother's mistakes.

Giacomo felt his own heart pulse with gratitude. He looked at his sister. "Thank you, Ramelde," was all he could say. He sensed he was no longer an outcast. Thanks to Tonio's childish charm, a turning point had been reached in his family ties.

He went home with Tonio a much happier man than when he'd left. He had his librettist, his son, and one of his sisters again. Now if he could settle matters with Elvira, he might find the contentment that seemed always to be beyond his reach. He doubted their love could ever be recaptured. Once doused by a wave of contempt, the flame of love can rarely be revived. But if he could reach some kind of accord with her, a simple armistice that would bring peace and quiet into their lives again, that would be enough. On the way home, Giacomo hugged his son and hummed as they sat on the rocking seat of the Lucca train. *What we need*, he thought, *is a new start. Perhaps even a new place... somewhere peaceful, away from everything that reminds us of the past, away from taunting relatives, away from creditors, away from the threat of Narciso... a place where a vengeful husband will never think of looking for us and where I can work in peace.*

Yes...yes. He knew exactly where that would be. He had stumbled across it on one of his escapes from Elvira's railing. Torre del Lago.

It was a tiny old village on the edge of small Lake Massaciuccoli. It had pine forests, birds, and flowers hugging a pristine beach. And there were enough hunting and fishing opportunities to satisfy all of Puccini's needs for relaxation. He had fallen in love with Torre del Lago the moment he saw it, and he had resolved to live there one day, away from all his troubles. *It is time now,* he told himself. *We shall move to the lake and hopefully find there some of the joy we once had.*

Five days later, returning from a stay in Florence, Elvira placed her travel bag on a chair and removed her hat. Then she greeted Puccini and Tonio with a gentle smile and totally unexpected welcoming words. "Ahhh, here is my sweet Antonino. Come and give Mama a big hug and kiss."

Tonio ran into Elvira's waiting arms. After covering his face with kisses she turned to her daughter, who had been standing silently at her side. "Fosca, dear," she said, "take your little brother into the courtyard and see that he is happy. I must talk with his father."

Fosca, now a sweet, twelve-year-old, smiled and obediently took Tonio's hand. Then in a gabbling explosion of words, the children ran loudly and happily from the house.

Puccini was baffled. Elvira looked at him calmly, a gentle smile pulling her lips. "We were in Florence visiting my sister," she said.

Now he feared bitterness. After all, her sister had often said he was responsible for Elvira's unhappiness. He had seduced her, hadn't he? He had destroyed her marriage and ruined her life. He and Elvira were now godless in the eyes of the Catholic Church, and were raising their children in unpardonable sin. She had even gone a step further than his sisters by declaring Puccini an agent of the devil. How could Elvira have returned from a week in that environment without having her own despair reinforced?

"What did you do with Tonio while you were in Milan?" she asked.

"I did not take him. I was gone but one day. My sister Ramelde watched him."

Elvira nodded. "I feared you would leave him unattended while you had your meetings."

"I would never do that."

"So you say. And how was your day in Milan? Did you accomplish anything?"

Now he understood. Something snide coated the questions, faintly but indisputably there. This was the same Elvira. Nothing had changed. It was simply a new attack strategy. Beneath the smiling, controlled exterior, anger still boiled in her cauldron of regret. It would never be any different but perhaps one day it could be made only to simmer. He could live with that.

"My day in Milan," Puccini said, "was quite satisfactory. A libretto will arrive soon and require my full attention."

"And the librettist is...?"

"The genius of *Pagliacci.*"

Elvira raised her eyebrows. "Truly?"

"Yes."

"I am impressed. Perhaps, after all, there is hope for you."

"For us, if you are willing to remain with me. I shall be moving to another city."

"I understand you, Giacomo. I am not stupid. You know I shall not take Tonio if you leave me, and he will be your responsibility completely. You do not want *me*. You want only to have someone care for him while you work." She had accurately read his mind. And she had stated her understanding quietly, with the certitude of a woman in command of a difficult situation.

Truth was his only recourse. "You understand me, Elvira, as I understand you. Come with me to Torre del Lago, care for Tonio, give me the quiet I shall require, and your comfort will be assured when my new opera is a great success."

"*If* it will be a great success."

"*When* it will be a great success. I have Leoncavallo as my librettist. Only success can be the fate of *Manon Lescaut.*"

- 19 -

He moved to Torre del Lago, and Elvira moved with him. There was nothing else she could do. She had no friends, no money, and no welcoming siblings. Her sister in Florence tolerated only an occasional, short visit. Elvira saw no escape. She longed to be free, but she was inseparably tied to a man who, in her mind, offered no promise of relief. The most she could hope for was freedom from persistent poverty, and that would come only if his current project should succeed. She had to follow him.

In Torre del Lago, they found another run-down dwelling. It was a furnished cottage near the water, the rent for which was within their meager means. Besides clothes and a few personal things, Puccini had brought only his piano and a mound of opera manuscripts. Then he'd waited impatiently for Leoncavallo's *Manon* libretto. When it finally arrived, he was distraught by what he read. "He promised me *verismo,*" he muttered, "and he sends me *sciocchezze,* this nonsense!"

Everything in the libretto was nonsense to him. Characters, action, even dialogue seemed artificial. Giacomo wanted to hear music as he read. All he heard was the insipid whimper of artificiality. He wrote immediately to Leoncavallo, a long letter in which he described his concerns. He made specific recommendations for *Manon's* improvement. In return, he received a fatuous defense of the libretto with an irritating suggestion that being a composer Puccini did not know how to read words. After three more distasteful exchanges, Puccini raced to Milan and met with Giulio Ricordi.

Now Ricordi tried to calm him. "*Calmati, calmati,* you will injure yourself. He cannot be that bad. I shall talk with him."

"He will never give me what I need! I must have another librettist!"

"We cannot discard him as if his work is inconsequential."

"It is not inconsequential, Signor Giulio," Puccini fumed. "It is fatuous and uninspiring! He is an arrogant fool who will never give me what I need! Please, Signor Giulio, *please,* I *must* have another librettist!"

To mollify his desperate protégé Giulio Ricordi promised to search for another librettist, one who "will fire your creative imagination."

Giacomo returned to Torre del Lago. Weeks passed and he heard nothing from Ricordi. His anxiety intensified.

Actually, Ricordi had hoped that time would smooth the differences between *Manon*'s composer and librettist. But it had only exacerbated them. Fearing the possible disintegration of this project, Ricordi relented and met with Leoncavallo. He explained Giacomo's concerns and proposed the inclusion of another librettist "to assist you in your association with Signor Puccini."

Leoncavallo found the suggestion utterly demeaning. "You insult me, Signor Ricordi!" he stormed. "It is not I who needs assistance; it is your despicable composer! Satisfying him is an impossibility! *I demand release from my contract!*"

Hiding great relief, Ricordi accepted the demand. Then free of Leoncavallo, he quickly informed Puccini, "I shall have a new librettist for you in one week's time."

That became Marco Praga.

Praga was a popular Italian playwright who had achieved national recognition with two fast-paced comedies about women and sex, *Le Vergini* (The Virgin) and *La Moglie Ideale* (The Ideal Wife). Within strong plot lines and crisp dialogue, his characters behaved realistically and convincingly. Giacomo hadn't seen his plays, but he knew of Praga's successes. And though they did not suggest the dramatic intensity he needed for *Manon*, their other structural strengths encouraged him to meet with Praga. Unlike his meeting with Leoncavallo, this one did not arouse doubt or hesitation.

Praga was a charming man, intelligent, articulate and forthcoming. He spoke gently. He listened. He answered all questions without condescension. In agreeing with all of Puccini's objectives, he won the composer's heart. Then he sealed their collaboration with a firm handshake and his promise to have their libretto ready in a matter of weeks. Ricordi was happy. Puccini was ecstatic.

Marco Praga lasted two months. He had tried, but as a writer of light comedy he could not adjust to the demands of dramatic opera. Some of his ideas were sound, though, and they were retained. *Manon Lescaut* moved forward, but as slowly and erratically as a bewildered snail.

After Marco Praga came Domenico Oliva and, finally, Luigi Illica. Each of them disappointed Puccini and drove him to distraction. However, all of them had offered something to the final manuscript. Because Luigi Illica had contributed the most, he was asked to continue with the project, while the others were paid handsomely and released from their contracts.

At first, fearing discord between himself and his two dear friends, Praga and Oliva, Illica was reluctant to accept the assignment. But after obtaining assurances of endless friendship, he jumped into *Manon Lescaut* with an enthusiasm as intense as that of Puccini and Giulio Ricordi.

It was not an easy task to collaborate with Giacomo Puccini. He scrutinized every line of dialogue, every nuance of character, every aspect of set description. He demanded so many changes that volcanic disagreements erupted with Illica:

"Why are you incapable of understanding me? It must convey sweetness, gentleness and love!"

"I need an entirely new ending for Act Two!"

"Power! Strength! *Do you not have any for me?*"

"Give me something different, something I have never before seen!"

"No! No! No! There is not enough romance between Des Grieux and Manon! Remember they are deeply in love now!"

"What you have written is more operetta than opera!"

Only one year older than Puccini, Illica was not about to accept the composer's attitude and demands subserviently. He fought back. He defended his ideas and words with the same vehemence he was facing. This was going to be his opera as well as Puccini's, and he would not be governed by his collaborator's inconsistencies!

"He vacillates. He demands. He has no understanding of what he wants," Illica complained fiercely to Ricordi. "He will compose music for a scene and then refuse to strike it when it proves to be unnecessary. He believes his music is more important than the opera's story. He does not realize it must emerge *from* the story, from its words, its characters, its actions. If I am ever again to work with Puccini, he must see clearly what he desires. He must communicate it fully, and then accept the completed libretto as it is given to him!"

Ricordi became the project's mediator, but forcefully he injected ideas of his own: "There are too many verses for the tenor in Act Three....For God's sake, Giacomo, your music is beautiful, do not destroy it with excessiveness....Shorten things! Dispense with uselessness, Illica!...And, above all, remove the kiss in the finale. It is unrealistic and supremely unnecessary!"

So many of Ricordi's suggestions were incorporated, he could have taken credit with Illica for the finished libretto. Actually, no one received credit. Ricordi believed all names would be too long for the opera's poster. Since Leoncavallo insisted on credit, saying: "All or no one!" it became no one. Posters and other promotional material announced the production solely with a reference to Puccini. Thereafter, opera lovers believed that Giacomo Puccini had been responsible for both the music and the libretto of *Manon Lescaut*. Despite all creative differences, though, Puccini, Illica, and Giulio Ricordi managed to achieve sufficient harmony to complete *Manon Lescaut* in December of 1892. That was nine frantic months after Puccini first met Ruggero Leoncavallo in Giulio Ricordi's office.

Was Giacomo pleased with the finished product? Not entirely. Yes, moments had stirred his creative juices, and he'd composed sweeping arias for them. Others had offered recitative opportunities, and he'd flowed passionately with them. However, questions still plagued him. Had he composed a cohesive opera, one that would sweep its audience smoothly to a dynamic finale? Or had he written music that would produce some pattering applause but mainly yawns and groans? However, to offset Elvira's endless doubt, he told her, "Regardless of what others may think, I have composed a satisfying and beautiful opera."

As *Manon Lescaut*'s première drew near, thirty-four-year-old Puccini once again prayed for success but feared failure.

Giulio Ricordi chose Turin again over Milan, and February 1, 1893 was set for the opera's opening. After two months of promotion and rehearsals, the night finally arrived. Ricordi had done his work well. Turin's Teatro Regio was filled to capacity. Music critics from every publication of worth were there. And doubt hung overhead like a threatening cloud. Puccini had failed to meet expectations twice. Would *Manon* be a third time? Whispers floated about:

"I heard Cesira Ferrani sing Elsa in Wagner's *Lohengrin*. I thought her voice too thin."

"I do not care for Giuseppe Cremonini; his tenor quavers in the high notes."

"Let us hope the conductor knows how to compensate for performer weakness."

"Pomé is conducting? Oh, my, his baton is so uncertain."

Eyes turned upward toward the royal box. There Princess Letizia sat in gown and tiara, surveying through small binoculars the jeweled and richly attired members below, many of whom were gazing at her through their own opera glasses.

Conductor Alessandro Pomé appeared and strode to his place in the music pit. A light applause followed him. Conversations trickled to silence. The baton rose, held for a moment, and then stabbed the air.

Giacomo Puccini's music filled the theater.

In a wing offstage, head bowed, chewing a fingernail, Giacomo listened to every note. Was that a false one? Were the violins strong enough for the distant rows? Murmurs could be heard. What did they mean? The orchestra swept into the heart of *Manon*'s overture. The murmurs became a soft rumble. What was happening? Puccini had never heard a sound like this, not at *Le Villi,* not at *Edgar*. Was there a disturbance somewhere in the theater? The curtains parted. He heard gasps. Students and townspeople filled the village scene. The rumble swelled and underscored the opening choral. *Oh, God*, Puccini thought, *there is a fire somewhere! Am going to die before I succeed?* The answer to his question came even as the tenor Giuseppe Cremonini sang the final notes of *Manon Lescaut*'s first aria. No longer a murmur, no longer a rumble, the underscoring rose and exploded into a roar of approval so loud and prolonged that stage action stopped and performers were compelled to stand in silence. The applause continued. Shouts of *Bravo!* filled the theater. *Composer! Composer! Maestro! Maestro! Bravo!*

Puccini could not believe what he was hearing. His heart pounded. Tears came to his eyes. He fumbled and bit his lip. The calls continued, and he was forced to appear onstage before his opera could continue. Bowing to the applause and cheers, he could barely breathe in his joy. And this was after the *first* aria! What did the rest of *Manon* hold in store for him? *Please, God, do not let this end.*

It did not end.

This time, God was listening, and God must have been cheering with the audience. Performances were halted repeatedly with calls for aria encores, for ensemble encores, even for conductor bows. And Giacomo found himself drawn to the stage some twenty-five times, bowing, smiling, and mouthing his thanks. *Grazie! Grazie! Mille grazie! Grazie a tutti!* At the end of the third act, Princess Letizia was so moved she called Puccini to the royal box. She thanked him passionately and told him his music was affecting her deeply. "You are bringing me a joy I rarely feel in theater," she said, grasping his hand. "I thank you, Maestro, I thank you."

The fourth act sent shock waves through the audience and prompted the strongest reaction of all. At its conclusion, as *Manon* lay dying in a barren desert of America, exiled, broken, and begging forgiveness for her sins, every member of that audience stood, applauded, wept, or shouted Puccini's name without restraint.

In that moment, Giacomo Puccini felt an emotion that transcended ecstasy. It filled his entire being. It gorged his chest. It rushed into his throat and brought tears to his eyes. He felt as if he were ascending to heaven. It was the soaring of his soul in the bewildering realization of enormous success. At long last, he had found it – he had found and captured that rare theatrical beast, the Hysterical Ovation.

Manon Lescaut turned Puccini overnight into a national treasure. Unanimously, critics proclaimed him Italy's true voice, an artist who expressed the country's heart and soul better than any other young composer in the land. He became a new leader of modern opera, the musical spokesperson of the future, a hero of the *Scapigliatura*.

The following day, he wrote jubilantly to Elvira and told her of the opera's reception. *"Audience enthusiasm transcended appreciation. No one would leave the theater. I have never heard or seen anything like it!"*

His words surprised Elvira, but they also brought her relief. Though she had come to doubt his brilliance, she never stopped hungering for his success. Now she saw the promise of easier times ahead. There would be no more scrambling for food and clothing, no more anxiety over creditors, no more fear of eviction. If Giacomo was being honest with her, if he was not exaggerating, their lives might once again assume a semblance of sanity and purpose. She could only hope it was all true. In addition to her relief she felt an old and familiar flush of warmth for him, and wanting to protect the splendor of this feeling, she wrote and told him, *"I could not be happier for you, Giacomo. I send you my heartfelt congratulations."*

She became impatient for his return to Torre del Lago. She had to know more about the première of *Manon Lescaut* and to discuss with him what it could mean to their lives.

While Elvira considered the uncertainty of their future, Giulio Ricordi was busy assuring it. Requests for the opera's production rights poured into the office of Casa Ricordi as soon as critical reviews appeared in the nation's publications. Eventually they came from every opera house in Italy, they came from theaters in England, from France, from Germany, Spain, Hungary, Russia, and as far away as Brazil and Argentina. And each contract put more money into Giacomo Puccini's empty pockets. In no time he repaid the House of Ricordi all he owed for its years of supportive advances and for the unfaltering faith that Giulio Ricordi had expressed in him. He erased all debt, including the money demanded by Uncle Nicalao Ceru.

He and Elvira found stability in their lives. With poverty behind them they fought less. They smiled and laughed more. They bought clothes for themselves and their children. They purchased needed food and dined well. He ordered a new bicycle, a new piano. And finally, they moved from their cramped and shabby quarters into a larger, more attractive, two-story house on the edge of Torre del Lago's inviting lake.

In Lucca, his sisters and boyhood friends rejoiced. Uncle Nicalao swelled with pride. Influential people thought of him again as a favorite son, his sexual indiscretion no longer a blot on the city's name. Even Narciso Gemignani, Elvira's husband, found something good to say about him: "I have always maintained his music will be of momentous importance to Italy. Now he proves I am prophetic!"

At a banquet honoring him in Turin's best hotel, Puccini was awarded the city's highest honor, the *Cavaliere dell'Ordine della Corona d'Italia.* It was a laurel to be cherished. With a friend's assistance, he had written and memorized a florid acceptance speech. Now he looked about the room. His audience of officials and society figures waited eagerly to hear his memorable words. He saw their expectant smiles, their attentive expressions. He was going to impress them. He breathed deeply. He smiled. He opened his mouth...and, as always, promptly forgot everything he had so assiduously prepared. Nervousness not only gripped him, it choked and almost strangled him. He fumbled with the award. He blinked in confusion. He coughed. And all he could offer was a barely whispered, "I...I... thank everyone."

But it didn't matter. He was cheered wildly, nevertheless.

In the streets, wherever he went, people recognized him. They spoke his name with respect and, at times, even adulation. It was all an affirmation of his worth, something about which he had never been sure and never would be sure. And though he was a shy man, he reveled in it, wishing only that his dear mother Albina and his beloved mentor Ponchielli were alive to enjoy the fruition of their faith. He was now to be known as Maestro, not the maestro of Conservatorio certification, but a Maestro of Opera! With *Manon Lescaut* drawing huge crowds, he walked confidently everywhere. He had arrived. There would be no more pain, no more suffering. Tomorrow was his.

Sadly, his view of the future could not have been more distorted.

- 20 -

On February 16, 1893 two days after *Manon Lescaut*'s successful Turin production closed, Giulio Ricordi greeted Puccini with a broad smile and hearty handshake. They were in Casa Ricordi's office. Once again they settled into its comfortable leather chairs. Once again they puffed contentedly on Giulio's thin Italian cigarillos and drank his expensive red wine.

"You are looking well," Ricordi observed.

"I am feeling well," Giacomo replied with a wide smile.

"Yes, success is the alchemy of life. It changes the lead of pain into the gold of happiness. I am certain your mother and Amilcare are happy for you, Giacomo, as am I."

"From my heart I thank you Signor Giulio for all you have done for me."

Ricordi waved his cigar, shook his head, and laughed. "No, no, you are making our investors wealthier and my solicitations easier. I thank *you*."

Both men chuckled at the retort.

"But now," Ricordi continued, "you must embrace your future. You must not wait. You must strike while *Manon Lescaut* still excites. People are eager to hear more of your music. Another success will secure your fame and fortune."

"I shall do whatever you say."

"We must speak to Illica right away. He must give us another libretto one as good as his *Manon*."

"Yes. I have thought carefully of this, and believe I have learned what that must include."

The response intrigued Ricordi. "Really? Elaborate."

Giacomo leaned forward, excitement touching his posture and words.

"*Verismo.* A libretto must have the purest elements of life: beauty; love; pain. It must concern ordinary people. It must have passion, conflict, and disappointment. And there should be the death of a beautiful woman in a foreign setting. I see these clearly now as the essentials of effective modern opera. *Manon* had them. All of them."

Ricordi smiled at his intensity. "You make it almost a formula."

"I had not thought of it that way, but one might say it *is* almost a formula."

"No, no, Giacomo. Opera is music and voice. These are what bring an audience to its feet and move it to tears and shouts of *Bravo!* "

"I agree. It is the music, always the music. But as you have said, a good story is necessary to stir the composer's musical instincts. *Manon* has taught me this truth. It has all the elements I have enumerated. And our next libretto must have them as well, Signor Giulio. It must."

With a tilt of his head and his cigar poised near his mouth, Ricordi considered what he'd just been told. Obviously, Puccini had given *Manon Lescaut*'s success deep and serious thought. He had not allowed euphoria to overwhelm him, to reduce him to a state of joyful inactivity. Clearly, success was important to him. He needed more of it. He was ready to work. Well, if his young composer chose to think of librettos in formulaic terms, if that would fire his creative imagination, then he, Giulio Ricordi, was not about to contest Puccini's conclusions in music debate. "Very well, Giacomo," he said, "your next libretto will have in it all the elements you desire. And if Illica cannot supply them to your satisfaction, then we shall simply find another librettist who can."

Beauty, pure love, pain, ordinary people, passion, disappointment, the death of a beautiful woman in a foreign setting...these became the thrust of Giacomo Puccini's quest. He had suffered through endless arguments in the past, passionate imbroglios over libretto changes, because he'd never seen clearly what it was he wanted. But that would not happen again. Now certitude had replaced uncertainty. Now he was sure of his needs, and Luigi Illica, or any other librettist, would never again be able to accuse him of vagueness and vacillation!

"I shall speak to Illica of this tomorrow," Ricordi promised. "We shall come to an accord quickly, because I should like to present your next opera at La Scala within the year."

Giacomo clapped his hands once happily. "Thank you, Signor Giulio. I am eager to work and ready to meet with him whenever you believe it is appropriate to do so."

But Luigi Illica wasn't eager to work with Puccini again, and he had no desire to meet with him. He'd had enough of Giacomo's diatribes, enough of his inconsistencies, and he reminded Ricordi of this when they met the following day. "I have told you," he said with a scowl, "never again. I do not need his stupidity and his insults. The man knows nothing about dramatic structure, and his ignorance causes him to make absurd demands."

Ricordi smiled his gentle smile and replied, "No one can dispute your words, dear Luigi. But we must look upon his temperament with kindness. He is still relatively new to opera. He does not have your experience or your wealth of dramatic knowledge. But he is learning, and you have been his teacher. He sees more clearly now what is required of him in the librettist-composer collaboration. He respects your skills and imagination immensely. Do be patient with him. I beg you."

Mollified by the praise, Illica softened his words. "Do not misunderstand, Signor Giulio. I have no wish to minimize his brilliance. Musically, he is everything you have said repeatedly of him. The success of *Manon* is ample proof of this, but –"

"Other successes await you," Ricordi tempted. "You are an extraordinary team. Together, you will become *il sole e le stelle d'Italia,* the sun and stars of Italy! It is your destiny, dear Luigi. Do not turn your back on it."

"If I could be certain –"

"You can be certain," Ricordi interrupted, "that you will always have me to moderate differences. You can be certain we shall all enjoy the rich rewards of breathtaking success. You do appreciate success, do you not?"

Illica had to smile. "You are most persuasive, Signor Giulio. Irresistibly so."

"Then you will meet with him?"

Illica's smile broadened. "Yes, I shall meet with him," he answered calmly.

"Excellent! You will see that Puccini has learned from *Manon,* and doubt no longer punctuates his artistic perceptions."

"I pray you are right, Signor Giulio, I pray you are right."

All three met the following day. Ricordi's calm demeanor controlled the entire discussion and the afternoon passed amiably and productively. Giacomo expressed admiration for Illica's contributions to *Manon Lescaut*'s success. Illica reciprocated with glowing praise for Puccini's music. And Giulio Ricordi chuckled inwardly at the juvenile sensibilities of artistic character.

"Please, Giacomo, enumerate for me again the dramatic elements you have detected in *Manon,*" Ricordi prompted Puccini, to which Giacomo responded with flashing eagerness, "Gladly." Then he launched into the list he had outlined earlier to his publisher.

Initially, Illica felt resistant to Puccini's intrusion into his domain. He was the librettist. He didn't need instruction from a musician about drama. After all, he would never presume to give Puccini advice about aria composition. Why should Puccini dare to tell him how to write stories? But to his credit, as Giacomo explained his insights and his needs for creative stimulation, Illica's resistance dissolved and he listened with increasing interested. When Puccini concluded his passionate presentation, Illica nodded slowly in agreement. "Yes," he said, "*Manon* does, indeed, have all you describe."

"And that is all I need," Giacomo asserted. "Give me that again and our next undertaking will be pure joy."

"No more vacillation?"

"Never."

"No more time-wasting demands?

"I shall be as straight as an arrow."

"No more insults?"

"My word on it."

Illica studied him.

Silence sizzled in the room's cigar smoke. Puccini waited. Would his hope be snuffed out in refusal, or would it explode like a beautiful firework blossom in acceptance? His answer came in the slow smile that lit Illica's face, and in his extended hand.

"Together," Illica said, "we shall make the success of *Manon Lescaut* dim in the beauty of our next endeavor."

Puccini shook his hand vigorously. "Yes, we shall," he agreed happily, "Yes, we shall."

Ricordi sank back into his armchair, breathing contentedly in the harmony he had created, a harmony that, despite all good intentions, was never meant to last.

- 21 -

Buoyed by the prospect of another great success, Giacomo Puccini left Milan the following morning and returned to Torre del Lago. He'd refrained from writing and informing Elvira of his meetings with Ricordi and Illica. Now he entered his home and experienced a warm flush of comfort and belonging. Everything was as it had been when he left: neat, clean and orderly. Chairs were in place around the kitchen table. An immaculate, flowered cloth covered the table's surface. And an Italian arum plant stood in its center, spreading green arrow-shaped leaves attractively. Though it was winter, the room's window was slightly open and a gentle breeze off the lake rippled its delicate curtains. He glanced at his cherished upright piano. Elvira had dusted and polished the mahogany wood. She had even stacked his composition papers neatly on the small table at its side. *If only she would treat me with the same attention and consideration....* He sighed and wondered where she and the children could be. Elvira would usually be home at this hour, preparing something in the kitchen. If not indoors, the children should be outside the house entertaining each other. Tonio had recently started his schooling; Fosca was well into her education. It was late afternoon, and classes had ended earlier. Where could all of them be?

As if on that thought, he heard Elvira's voice calling.

"Giacomo? Giacomo, are you home?"

He remained silent in their bedroom waiting for her to find him, not knowing what to expect.

She appeared at the room's doorway. Seeing him, her brows

creased, and her face broke into a quizzical smile. "You are here. You should have informed me you were returning."

"I would have arrived before the letter."

"You could have telegraphed. When did you arrive? Why were you silent when I called? Are you all right?"

He didn't know if he was being chastised or welcomed.

"Are you hungry? When did you eat last? You look thinner than when you left."

"I have been working hard."

"No excuse. Work demands food. I shall prepare a good dinner, and you will tell me all that happened with *Manon Lescaut*." Elvira approached him. Her eyes narrowed. Her lips were pulled into a faint smile.

He was standing with his hands clasped, unsure of himself and of the moment.

She stopped inches from him. She looked into his eyes, and then did something totally unexpected. She placed a hand gently on the back of his clasped hands and squeezed lightly. "Welcome home," she whispered. "It is good to see you here again, Giacomo. The children and I were shopping. They are outside now. They will be thrilled to know you are home."

Dinner that evening was one of the best he'd ever had with Elvira. He ate heartily, but he was so overwhelmed by the absence of acrimony, by the occasional smile that he barely tasted flavors. Elvira asked a stream of questions about *Manon*'s success and his meetings in Casa Ricordi. He answered all of them in detail and with increasing willingness. Occasionally, his reply brought laughter or a clap of hands. And once, she even reached across the table and touched his hand appreciatively. It was the second time she'd touched him since his arrival. He had no idea what to make of her sudden show of tenderness, but he knew he liked it.

Later, Elvira asked him to play something for her. With an alacrity born of acceptance he sat at the piano and played passages from *Manon* and *Le Villi,* while she listened with her eyes closed and nodded approval.

It was a perfect evening, a quiet one of peace and contentment... until it came time to retire. After kissing and hugging him, the children went noisily to their room. An air of uncertainty filled the vacuum. He hadn't shared a bed with Elvira in what seemed like ages. Did this wonderful welcome home imply a physical change in their relationship too?

Elvira stood. She approached him. Giacomo looked up at her. At thirty-three, Elvira had become a full-bodied woman, stern-looking but still pleasing to the eye. She looked down at him. "I am hopeful our lives together will now become more serene and conducive to your work," she said quietly. "I should like that."

"I, too," he answered.

"But we must be very careful," she continued. "We must do this slowly. At this point, I am not ready for more than talk. We shall continue to sleep apart until I am certain about you and your intentions. Good night, Giacomo."

There was no kiss, no further touch of hands. She turned quickly and left him alone in the room to ponder exactly what she'd meant by "...until I am certain about you and your intentions."

- 22 -

The following weeks continued to be everything Puccini had been hoping for. They were weeks of contentment and pleasure, weeks that extended into months, and months into a full year. Elvira had said his freedom was "conducive to work." But he didn't work. Instead, he enjoyed himself smoking, hunting, fishing, reading, loafing, and with sudden trips to Budapest and London to see productions of *Manon Lescaut*.

Elvira began to eye him suspiciously. Were these months of idleness a portent of things to come? Would she have to berate him repeatedly and force him to his piano? One day she hinted, "Your piano is gathering dust."

"I cannot compose without a libretto," he explained.

"And you will not have a libretto without complaining to Illica," she countered.

Subtle comments began to cloud the brightness of their home life. An edge of tension developed in their exchanges.

"Idleness is the parent of dullness," she would sing as she dusted his piano.

"I am not idle," he would say. "I am waiting."

"Without prodding, waiting is a weak excuse for inactivity."

"What would you have me do?"

"Write to him. Tell him how you are longing to work. Urge him to give you a libretto!"

Actually, Illica had made a number of suggestions to Puccini, every one of which had been summarily rejected. "The man does not know what he wants," the librettist fumed to Ricordi.

"Nothing pleases him. I suspect we shall never create another opera together, and I am entirely content with that!"

Believing Illica was not earnestly looking for a suitable story, Puccini intensified his own search. He read and discarded an endless assortment of publications. And finally, he found two books that piqued his imagination. One contained brief episodes about unconventional Parisians; the other was a short story called *La Lupa – the She-Wolf.* Of the two, a dangerous she-wolf interested him far more than dissolute French characters. It was another *verismo* tale, this time about Italian peasants. And it concerned a woman so inflamed with uncontrollable lusts she is led inexorably by them to her own brutal death.

Intrigued by the idea, he notified Ricordi about both discoveries. "But," he said, "I confess a preference for *La Lupa."*

"Are you certain of this?" the publisher asked. "The scenes of Parisian life seem equally promising."

"No, no. *La Lupa, La Lupa!* It has fire, passion, and a clearly defined story. If I had a libretto now, I would begin work on the score *immediately*."

Ricordi was elated. "I shall tell Illica at once of your discovery. I am excited for you, Giacomo."

Puccini decided he had to speak with *La Lupa*'s author. There was the matter of permission. Without approval there could be no opera. The fact that Giovanni Verga lived in Catania, over 700 miles from Torre del Lago, didn't matter. He had to go!

"I am going to Sicily," he announced to Elvira.

Her face darkened. "What is in Sicily?"

"My next opera. I have found a story, and I must speak to its author."

"I am not sure I believe you."

Carefully explaining his need for the trip, he attacked Elvira's doubts. He seemed eager to compose. But was this a ruse, another ploy to escape work? Given a choice, Puccini always selected the pleasure of idleness over the pain of composing.

Elvira may have been considering the money another successful opera would bring. Or, simply, she just might have wanted to get him out of her sight. Whatever the reason, she appeared to be satisfied with his explanation. "I understand," she said. "Do what you must."

Puccini had expected sourness, another heated quarrel. Now, her gentle approval sent a rush of relief through him.

"I shan't be long," he promised.

"Take as long as necessary."

The voyage to Sicily down the coastline of the Italian boot was long and uneventful. The ship was small but equipped with comfortable amenities. A dining room provided tasty cuisine. Three instrumentalists – pianist, violinist, and cellist – offered unobtrusive background music to dinner conversation. Puccini enjoyed everything. His thoughts, though, were entirely on *La Lupa* and Giovanni Verga.

He had never met Verga. But he'd telegraphed the author and asked for an appointment. He was thrilled to receive a subdued but positive response. He knew that Verga had written many *verismo* stories as well as the wonderful play *Cavalleria Rusticana*. He knew also that *La Lupa* was in play form being readied for stage production. But he didn't know what to expect of Verga the man. Would he be affable or abrupt? Would he consent to an opera based upon *La Lupa,* or would he believe his *She-Wolf* should remain a short, mysterious, theatrical drama?

At fifty-three, Giovanni Verga was a fit, strong-looking figure, with thick, closely cropped gray hair, black eyebrows and a full, salt-and-pepper mustache. Verga carried himself with a self-assurance that later led him into politics and a term in the Kingdom of Italy's senate. Giacomo was impressed from the moment he saw him and felt his firm handshake. In the days that followed they discussed *La Lupa* at length. Puccini was allowed to read the stage play. He asked numerous questions about dialogue, character, settings, and he received quick and strong answers to all of them. Verga liked him. Having heard of *Manon Lescaut*'s great success, Verga approved quickly of Puccini's desire to turn *La Lupa* into an opera.

Puccini was overjoyed. He left Sicily ten days later. He was so eager to begin work his cheeks ached from the broad grin of anticipation that brightened his face.

However, the return trip homeward soon changed everything.

Aboard the ship was the Contessa Blandine Gravina, daughter of Consima Wagner who was the second wife of Germany's august composer Richard Wagner. The Contessa was five years younger than Puccini, an attractive, vivacious woman. She always traveled with a young female companion, equally fashionable and animated. They seemed to enjoy everything they saw and touched. Men looked at them with interest; women, with envy.

When Giacomo learned of the Contessa's presence, he couldn't believe his good fortune. *Stepdaughter to Richard Wagner!* Richard Wagner, whose music he had devoured in his early years of Conservatorio instruction. Richard Wagner, idol of the *Scapigliatura*. Richard Wagner, composer of *Tristan and Isolde, Lohengrin, and Tannhauser.* And his stepdaughter was there on the ship? How wonderful! He had to meet her. He had to talk with her about her father and his music. But how should he accomplish this? He couldn't be gauche and simply introduce himself. Too many others were doing that. That approach would make him another intruder who would earn himself only a polite smile and indifference. He had to do something unusual, something that would attract special attention. He considered his problem and quickly devised a plan.

That evening, after dinner had been served and the instrumentalists were enjoying a break in their performance, Puccini excused himself to his table companions and went to the dining room's elegant Collard and Collard piano. Calmly, he raised and braced the top board. He slid the stool from beneath the key bed, then swiveled it to a satisfactory height and sat. No one noticed him. No one cared as he lifted the keyboard lid, as he looked down at the length of keys and smiled.

His thoughts had jumped to Albina, his dear mother, and how so many years ago she had urged him to love music. And here he was now on a ship hugging the Italian coastline about to surprise the Contessa Blandine Gravina. He smiled and shook his head slowly. How strange, how interesting life could be. A sense of well-being overtook Puccini. *I have been fortunate,* he thought. *No...I have been blessed.* It had taken time, but over the years, piano had become his soul mate. He felt a sudden, swelling tenderness for it. He touched the white keys so lightly their felt-covered hammers never struck the steel wires, never made a sound. It was the caressing introduction to an act of love. Then his smile softened. He inhaled deeply. He flexed his fingers, and he began to play. First he ran even, fluid arpeggios, with a softness that could barely be heard. He wanted nothing invasive, nothing disturbing. His notes melted into passenger voices. No one noticed them. After a few moments he segued artfully from his meaningless arpeggios into the soft and gentle opening of Shubert's *Sonata in G Major.* Peaceful and luminous, slightly louder, enough to have the piano's presence recognized. A few passengers looked his way. They smiled. All was calm. All was pleasant. And the hum of conversation continued. Then once the romantic strains of Shubert had been established to his satisfaction, Giacomo did the unthinkable. He shattered all complacency. Suddenly, abruptly, he cut the sonata in the middle of its sweetness and launched into a thunderous presentation of Richard Wagner's *Overture to Lohengrin.* The effect was startling. Dramatic. No longer subdued, music crashed and dominated the room. Wagner had leaped from the instrument. He was there. Larger than anything being discussed. Roaring. Declaring his genius to all. Conversation trickled to silence. Wine glasses were settled gently on tabletops. Full attention went to the pianist, who was sweeping into his performance as if he were at La Scala, playing before Italian royalty. Everyone listened respectfully. And when the final notes faded to rapturous silence, applause and unanimous shouts of approval erupted and shook the room.

Giacomo stood and acknowledged the acclaim with a smile and a slight bow. He looked towards the table at which the Contessa sat with her companion. He closed his eyes and slowly dipped his head in their direction. He couldn't miss the wide smiles of appreciation on their faces as they applauded with everyone else. He knew exactly what he was doing. This was the special attention he had hoped to achieve, the moment that would set him apart from everyone else. Confident now that he would not be treated with indifference, he walked straight to the women's table, bowed politely and said, "Good evening, Contessa Gravina. I am delighted you appreciate my playing even though it can never do justice to the magnificence of your father's music. My name is Giacomo Puccini and, like your illustrious father, I am in love with opera."

It had not occurred to Giacomo that Contessa Gravina might not understand him, but again he was in luck. The Contessa spoke Italian fluently.

"Your playing brought vivid images of my father to mind, Signor Puccini. For that I shall be eternally grateful. Will you join us, please?"

Giacomo smiled. "It will be my pleasure, Contessa."

Smoothly and with a touch of style, Puccini sat and crossed his legs. Then after being introduced to the Contessa's travel companion and graciously acknowledging her kind words about his playing, he began a conversation about Wagner and contemporary music.

"Your father," he said, "is placing all of Italy in a quandary."

"How is that so?" Contessa Gravina asked with great interest.

"One faction of our opera-loving community finds his music irresistible. Another, the more traditional, believes it is abominable."

The women laughed. "That is as it should be," Contessa Gravina said. "Anything that pleases everyone is certain to be meaningless. And what is your position, if I may ask?"

"Mine? Oh, I am decidedly among those who find it irresistible, and I hope my playing of *Lohengrin* was a testament to that." He had said it playfully, with a charming lilt in his voice.

"More than a simple testament, Signor Puccini," the Contessa replied happily. "It knighted you."

"You play so well, Signor Puccini. Do you play in an orchestra?" the travel companion asked innocently.

Contessa Gravina chuckled and tapped her lightly with her

fan. "No, dear," she corrected, "Signor Puccini does not play in an orchestra. Orchestras play for *him*. I asked you to accompany me to the production of his opera *Manon Lescaut* in Hamburg, but you preferred to be with your lover. That was an unfortunate choice. You missed something more extraordinary than the momentary pleasure of a few kisses."

Giacomo grinned at the gentle reproach. It was not only puckish and clever, it was an indication that his music had reached Germany successfully, perhaps even the ears of Richard Wagner himself. *Yes, the evening is progressing as planned*, he thought.

And it was...until the companion's next question.

"I am sorry I missed your opera," she said. "I shall be certain not to make that mistake again. Are you composing another now?"

Giacomo could not resist admitting: "I shall be soon. I have just discovered a story to which I shall very eagerly apply my music."

Contessa Gravina's eyes flashed interest. "Really? How exciting. I hope you will honor us with a description of this story."

And Puccini did.

He uncrossed his legs. He leaned forward. And with the dramatic flair of his good friend Ferdinando Fontana, he told them of *La Lupa,* the evil she-wolf, the demonically lustful woman who seduces her daughter's lover, destroys her family, and is savagely murdered during a solemn religious procession. Ending his narration with lurid details of the murder, Puccini sat back and waited for his listeners' approval.

The first to speak was the travel companion. With a look of horror, she whispered, "That is a *terrible* story."

Puccini blinked and turned to the Contessa, who stared directly into his eyes and said, "No, it is not terrible. It is beyond terrible. To make an opera of such a tale would be unforgivable. I do hope, Signor Puccini, that you will abandon this monstrosity for another more suitable subject, one in harmony with your enormous talent."

Giacomo was speechless. He could not believe what he'd just heard. Terrible? Monstrosity? What were they talking about? *La Lupa* was dynamic. It was meaningful, graphic, gripping. With his music it would have audiences gasping and cowering in their seats. It would bring them to their feet, cheering wildly in another hysterical ovation.

Contessa Gravina saw his confusion. “Surely, Signor Puccini,” she said, “you cannot be blind to the appalling nature of the story’s protagonist. She is evil. A shameless savage who willfully destroys her own family to satisfy her unbridled passions.”

“But she dies for her sins,” Puccini offered weakly.

“Yes...against the beauty of a religious procession...another sin. But this one committed by the librettist and composer. I implore you, do not subject your audiences to this horror. If you do, I predict failure and serious repercussions.”

There was nothing more to be said. His head reeling, Giacomo Puccini excused himself and went unsteadily to his stateroom.

After this intense exchange, Contessa Blandine Gravina and her travel companion seemed to avoid Puccini. He looked for them on the small ship, but proximity did not help. It was as if they had dropped into the water and would never be heard from again. But their words remained – like a maelstrom in his brain and a dagger in his heart. He had been so sure of *La Lupa.* He had seen the action and the drama in his mind’s eye. He had heard passionate music for the conflict, for the procession. Could he have been so wrong? Could he have mistaken lust for love, evil for drama? He had no answers. But he *did* know his original certainty had been shaken badly, and he wrestled with this new perspective through the remainder of the voyage.

Back in Torre del Lago again, Puccini continued to be assailed by doubt. And Elvira’s questions did not help him. “What happened in Catania?” she asked as soon as he entered the house. There was no welcome, no greeting acknowledging his arrival. Just the cold question, “What happened in Catania?”

“It went well,” he said.

“Then why are you looking sad?”

“It is not sadness. I am tired and troubled.”

“Why should you be troubled if it went well?”

"Something happened on the return trip that was unsettling."

Her voice had become sharper with each question. He didn't care to discuss his problem just then, and her tone only hardened him further.

"You will answer me," she insisted. "I am not a servant in this household to be treated as you wish. What could possibly have turned a successful trip into something unsettling?"

There was no escape. He knew days of anger would follow if he did not respond. That would be considerably more painful than talking about his problem now. He surrendered. "Sit down," he said. "This will take some time."

They sat at the kitchen table. For the next half-hour, Puccini related all the details of his trip to Sicily. When he was through, he asked her quietly, "What are your thoughts?"

Elvira shook her head slowly and seemed to sneer. "Truthfully, I did not expect anything else of you, Giacomo," she said. "You have been sitting here a full year, bemoaning the lack of a libretto, blaming Signor Illica for your indolence. Now you have permission from Giovanni Verga to transform *La Lupa* into an opera, and you are hesitating? You will allow the opinion of two giddy women to make you doubt your own belief in the story? What is wrong with you? You ask my thoughts? All right...I think, as always, you are searching for another way to avoid work!"

With that, Elvira rose from the table, glared at him and stamped from the room.

They didn't speak for two days. During that time, Giacomo Puccini struggled with uncertainty. True, he had been enthusiastic about *La Lupa*. True, he had been thrilled by Verga's approval. True, he had been eager to begin composing. But *La Lupa* now troubled him, and he would never again feel comfortable about shaping it into a successful opera. It had to be abandoned. With that decision set firmly in mind, Puccini wrote to Giulio Ricordi. He explained his new reservations about the *La Lupa* story, and he begged for understanding. To mitigate Ricordi's disappointment, he suggested an alternate idea – the book of Parisian sketches. And he swore to start on it as soon as Luigi Illica could provide him with the first scenes of a libretto.

Giulio Ricordi accepted his explanation, but not without sadness. So many months had been wasted. If Puccini had accepted the book about Parisian artists long ago, they would have had a full opera and been half-way into production by now! But remorse could not change anything, and scolding would only worsen a difficult situation. Calmly, Ricordi congratulated Puccini on his painful decision. He wrote, *"I wish you a ticket for the most direct train to station Bohème."*

And thus began the tortuous and torturous journey into *La Bohème*, the most successful opera of Giacomo Puccini's entire career.

- 23 -

From the very start, Giulio Ricordi's metaphoric train tracks to *Bohème* were repeatedly upended or strewn with enormous boulders of discord.

Wanting to cement Puccini's commitment, Ricordi printed a brief announcement in his company's opera magazine: *"Signors Giacomo Puccini and Luigi Illica have once more joined their impressive talents. This time it is for an opera to be titled* La Bohème. *A production date will be announced as soon as particulars have been finalized."*

Ricordi hoped *La Bohème* would now be completed without contention or delay.

However, he hadn't contended with another librettist. Ruggero Leoncavallo came back into their lives with a vengeance. After reading Giulio Ricordi's announcement, Leoncavallo made a public proclamation of his own: *"An opera from Henri Mürger's book,* Scènes de la Vie de Bohème, *was originally my idea! It is one for which I am presently preparing a libretto, the title to be* La Bohème. *Many months ago, I casually mentioned my intention to composer Giacomo Puccini. It amazes and pains me that he would steal my idea and use it as his own!"*

The Milan opera community went wild. It usually laughed at artistic conflict. Artists accused each other of everything from inconsideration to misbehavior. But disputes usually centered on trivial matters. This was different. This was serious. Leoncavallo was announcing theft of the most personal and precious commodity in theatrical practice...an *idea.* Ideas were guarded as if they were government secrets. They were the essence of success, and success was the prize of honest effort. Puccini, Leoncavallo contended, had stolen something of infinite value, not from some newspaper article, but from his brain! The community buzzed. It was a direct challenge, an insult that could not be left to drown in the sea of gossip. It had to be answered.

Puccini sent his reply at once to *Corriere dells Sera,* Milan's most prominent newspaper. *"Maestro Leoncavallo's statement in yesterday's* Il Secolo *is in serious error. I do not need Maestro Leoncavallo to discover ideas for an opera. To accuse me of stealing an idea is as asinine as his name. He will write his music, and I shall write mine. The public will judge!"*

The exchange precipitated a feud, one that raced through Italian opera like a brushfire. It excited everyone. Here were two respected composers at odds about the serious questions of integrity and publishing rights.

Having died thirty-three years before this feud erupted, Henri Mürger, author of the book *Bohème,* couldn't settle the dispute. Production rights had become public domain. The matter of integrity is what caused both sides to bristle. Puccini even took to playing with Leoncavallo's name. In Italian, "Leone" means lion, and "cavallo" means horse. But Puccini chose the word "asino" after Leon. Since "asino" means "ass," thereafter, Leoncavallo became "Leonasino" –
a lion's ass.

The feud degenerated into squabble, and Ricordi relished every newspaper reference to it. It had become free advertising. It had stimulated debate about the anticipated merits of both *Bohèmes*. And to Giulio Ricordi, debate always generated ticket sales. All he needed was a completed opera. To that end, he urged Puccini and Illica to waste no time in bringing *La Bohème* to the stage.

"I imagine," he said, "all three of us are in accord on the matter of urgency."

"Now that we are finally agreed on *La Bohème* as our next endeavor, I shall do my best," Illica agreed, casting a derisive glance at Puccini.

"Of course, Signor Giulio," Giacomo replied, fixing a lazy stare on Illica. "But my music can only follow the libretto words of my esteemed collaborator. The responsibility for haste, he must agree, will primarily be his."

Giulio Ricordi rolled his eyes and shook his head at the twin barbs. "Harmony, gentlemen, harmony," he sighed. "Without it, I am afraid we shall never see the completion of our opera."

Illica grunted softly and turned his head away from Puccini.

Puccini smiled and said, "I shall be waiting for those words in Torre del Largo. Please, my dear Luigi, do not make me wait too long."

At home again, Giacomo waited impatiently for his librettist's words. He had returned expecting peace and quiet. But he received more of that than he wanted. Soon after arriving, he described his Milan discussions to Elvira in great detail. It was his hope that she would see *La Bohème*'s acceptance by both librettist and publisher as evidence of its superiority over *La Lupa*. Elvira was not to be so easily convinced. She continued to believe he hadn't been swayed by Contessa Gravina as much as he had by an ingrained reluctance to work. And until she would see him at his piano, she refused to speak to him at all. Fortunately, her silence did not apply to the children. With them, she remained voluble and loving, and for that Puccini was deeply grateful. So he accepted the status quo. He hunted fowl on his beautiful lake, and he wondered what could possibly be taking Illica so long.

If Giacomo knew more about the intricacies of dramatic construction, he'd have realized that adaptation of Henri Mürger's *Scènes de la vie de Bohème* to play form would not be a simple task. The book had no central story line, no identifiable plot. It was a series of loosely connected episodes, involving hundreds of people in Paris's Latin Quarter during the 1840s. To find a common thread of action in them and to develop that into a moving, dramatic story would require understanding far beyond that of a composer with limited theatrical experience. However, that didn't stop him from accusing Illica of dawdling. "I am waiting," he told Ricordi. "Where is my libretto? Does Illica believe other matters to be more important than our opera?"

He had accepted Elvira's silence, knowing work was what she demanded. Consequently, Puccini appeared to work. He read and re-read Mürger's book making copious notes. Occasionally, he raced to his piano to try a musical phrase or melody that came to him.

It pleased Elvira to see him scribbling and rushing to his piano. And she finally relented by offering a few words as she served him his breakfast.

"Are you making progress?"

"I believe so."

"I pray it continues."

"Thank you."

The atmosphere within the house improved slowly. There were even moments of cheer and happiness. Puccini smiled more. He felt increasingly comfortable. And he attacked his piano with greater enthusiasm, even sending some of his story ideas and music to Illica and Ricordi. However, by preempting Illica's role, he initiated creative clashes that taxed Ricordi's calming powers to their limit.

"Who is the librettist, he or I?" Illica raged. "He believes he knows how to structure a story. But he knows nothing! He believes he can paste together unrelated fragments of music into a cohesive opera, and that is impossible! You know as well as I, Signor Giulio, that music must flow from a logical continuum of character, action, and words. I cannot work this way. It saddens me because I respect you, sir. But I must divorce myself from this project! Find another librettist, one who, for your sake, will be more adaptable to the deplorable interventions of *La Bohème*'s composer than I."

"I beg you, Luigi, do not be precipitous," Ricordi reacted. "He is merely being impatient, and that is a good sign. You and I are in agreement: His music *must* come from your libretto and not Mürger's book. And it will. I shall speak with him, I promise you. Please continue with your libretto, and all will be well. You are the most brilliant librettist in all of Italy. With your genius we shall produce an opera that will live in eternity. I know that to be true."

The response was as soothing as ice on a troubling burn. Illica grumbled softly but only to indicate residual displeasure. Identifying him as the most brilliant librettist in Italy mollified him enough to say, "Very well, Signor Ricordi, I shall put my trust in you."

"Thank you, sir, I thank you." Success brought a smile to Ricordi's lips, but he knew that harmony between his two artists could never be sustained. More conflict lay ahead, and some of it when it arrived proved to be far more serious than anything Puccini's personal problems in Torre del Lago could create.

Luigi Illica was a fast writer. Despite his reservations he continued work. Three weeks later he sent the first two acts to Ricordi who, pleased with them, forwarded them to Puccini. However, Puccini's pleasure on receiving them didn't last very long. Both acts only deepened his despair. He needed words that would generate original musical instantly. He had no idea, though, what they should be. In attempting to communicate this need, he referred to them only as "something."

"Give me something else, something different, something that will transport me," he would tell Illica endlessly.

Illica, on the other hand, required specifics to guide him. He needed ideas he could see and understand. Puccini's vague and shadowy "something" left him confused and angry.

"I do not understand why he cannot grasp what I am saying," Puccini complained to Elvira. "I tell him what I want in every letter, and then he fails to send anything that can stimulate me."

Elvira listened with unusual patience. She heard his frustration, the hollow note of helplessness. She had watched him pore over Mürger's scenes for hours, and she was beginning to hope that somehow, miraculously, his work ethic was strengthening. She touched his arm. "More can always be accomplished in person than through letters," she said. "Go to Milan. See Illica. Talk to him. You will feel better. You will work better."

Was he hearing correctly? Was this permission to leave her alone with the children? She had always disapproved of his absences. And now she was telling him to go to Milan? "You will not mind being alone?" he asked.

She heard his uncertainty. She smiled. "I always mind being alone, but success with this opera will mean much to you. I shall bear the discomfort of loneliness. Go to Milan, Giacomo."

If he could have sprouted wings, Giacomo Puccini would have soared among the eagles. He wanted to embrace her. But all he did was cover her hand with his, the hand that still rested on his arm. "Thank you, Elvira," he said, his voice slightly hoarse from the heat of appreciation.

He left Torre del Lago for Milan the following morning. She made sandwiches for the trip, she wished him well, and she insisted he write to her often. He promised he would. There was no physical show of affection on either part. But her gentleness was pleasant enough to keep him warm through most of the 300-mile train ride.

- 24 -

Settled once more in his Milanese accommodations, Giacomo geared himself for battle. He had sent telegrams to both Ricordi and Illica. He had notified them of his desire to meet with them the following morning. Now he went directly to the Casa Ricordi offices. *We shall settle these matters once and for all,* he thought. His mind was charged with what he believed to be incontestable arguments. *I shall tell him his words mean nothing if they cannot inspire me. I shall tell him I need imagery that tantalizes like a beautiful dream, and passionate emotions that squeeze the heart until it weeps in blissful pain. I shall tell him he must give me flesh, and surprises, and a conclusion that will never be forgotten. The question will no longer be: Can you offer this? My position will be: You must!*

He considered his points again and again as he hurried along, replacing words, rearranging sentences, knowing that Luigi Illica was not a man who could be easily persuaded. *I shall be forceful, but careful not to offend.*

By the time he reached the Casa Ricordi offices, Puccini believed he'd honed his attack to perfection. He knew Giulio Ricordi would strive to sustain an air of cooperation and friendship. But he knew, also, he would not allow that to steer him from his purpose.

What he didn't know was that Luigi Illica had been thinking along similar lines.

Waiting with Ricordi for Puccini's arrival, Illica told their publisher, "I am happy for this opportunity to tell Giacomo to his face how impossible it is to work with a composer who does not know his own mind!"

"I sincerely hope you will not do that, Luigi," Ricordi replied. "Your relationship with Giacomo must not deteriorate into intemperate clashes. *La Bohème* must always be our principal concern, not victory in a conflict of personality and creative differences."

"Signor Giulio, I am as eager as you to complete *Bohème* and to see it succeed. I would not continue with the undertaking if this were not true."

"I know that –"

"But progress cannot take place in the darkness of ignorance. He must allow me to write my libretto without immersing me in his stupidity, or I shall surely leave this project for something more pleasant and promising. I am not without opportunity, as you well know."

His vehemence troubled Ricordi deeply. This meeting could be one of the rare times the publisher's ameliorating skills might fail him. He would have to be particularly attentive if he hoped to hold their collaboration together.

When Giacomo entered Casa Ricordi, he greeted the secretary and was told, "Signori Ricordi and Illica are waiting for you. Go right in, sir."

Puccini entered the large office. Ricordi rose from behind his desk, went to him, and greeted him with outstretched arms. "Giacomo, how good it is to see you again."

Illica remained seated, said nothing, and merely lifted a hand slightly in recognition.

Puccini nodded in return.

"Shall we go into the conference area?" Ricordi invited with all the conviviality he could muster.

Nothing more was said. They left the office for the comfort of the larger room. Their silence suggested a difficult time ahead. "Well," Ricordi said after they were seated and puffing on cigars, "this is good. Let us see if we can reach some understanding of the difficulties we are facing, and of the paths we must follow to bring us to a happy and successful production of our precious *La Bohème*. Which of you will offer his concerns first?"

"I defer to my eminent colleague," Illica said without a smile.

Puccini couldn't miss the taint of acrimony in the word "eminent." *He is going to be even more condescending and difficult than Leoncavallo,* he thought. *"This will not be pleasant or easy, but I must do it.* He'd always feared and hated direct confrontation. He was not by nature a fighter. But an image of Elvira flashed in his mind. She'd given her blessing to go to Milan to solve his problems. She was waiting for him to return. He could not go back to her without facing the source of his difficulties. If he did, he'd have to bear her disappointment and disdain all over again. He felt the same nervous flutter in his stomach that he'd experienced when addressing the large assembly of dignitaries in Turin. He cleared his throat.

"Signor Giulio," he began, preferring to direct his complaint to Ricordi. "I wish with all my being to bring to you and the House of Ricordi another enormously successful opera, and to that end I shall do everything of which I am capable. However, it must be understood that all musical effort is doomed to failure when a composer has nothing from which to work."

Illica grunted, so choked with exasperation it brought a raised hand from Ricordi. "Please allow him to complete his statement, dear Luigi," Ricordi asked.

Illica squirmed.

"I ask only for a libretto that transcends the mundane. Something that will inspire, something that will –"

"There it is again!" Illica exploded, leaping to his feet. "*Something...something*. It is always *something!* You use the word constantly and have absolutely no idea what you mean by it!"

"Whatever it is, I know you are not giving it to me," Puccini shot back.

"If you knew what it is, you would tell me, and I would be able to supply you with it!" His voice had risen.

Ricordi rose quickly from his seat and went to Illica, who turned away from Puccini in frustration. "Luigi, dear Luigi," he said softly, "let us discuss this like gentlemen."

"It is difficult to be a gentleman when I am challenged with vagueness." He rose from his seat abruptly and brushed past Ricordi. He looked down at Puccini in his leather chair. "Find the words," he spat. "Tell me what you mean by *something*. Be specific, Giacomo, for God's sake, honor me with something *specific*!"

Puccini was taken aback by Illica's attack. He recoiled. He floundered. "All...all right," he said. "It is your words."

"My *words?"* Illica throat bulged. His face darkened. "You say my words prevent you from composing your music? How *dare* you?" He turned quickly and faced Ricordi. "This is too much! You will have to find another librettist. I am finished, Signor Giulio, *finished*!"

He turned to leave, but Ricordi jumped before him and blocked his exit. "Luigi...a moment...please...calm yourself...let us talk calmly...please."

"I shall never again collaborate with that man," Illica said, struggling to control his voice. He looked directly into Ricordi's eyes but waved an index finger in Puccini's direction.

"I did not mean you write poorly," Puccini shouted, standing quickly, but keeping his distance. "Your words are excellent. They are simply not the words I need."

Luigi Illica inhaled deeply. He brushed past Ricordi. He walked deliberately toward Puccini and stopped one foot away. With head lowered, he growled only two words: "Explain that."

Puccini paused. This had not gone as he'd hoped. He had wanted to be firm, not destructive. He'd imagined a passionate discussion, not the end of *La Bohème*. But here he was, inches from the glaring eyes of his librettist, trying to find the words that would placate Illica and save the opera. "I...I am sorry, Luigi," he said. "I have offended you, and for that I offer my eternal regret. I apologize. Please...*please*...forgive me."

Illica's balloon of fury and frustration burst in the honesty of Puccini's apology. He didn't know how to react. Stripped so suddenly and unexpectedly of his anger, he was a gladiator who had lost his weapon.

"I am truly sorry, Luigi," Giacomo apologized throatily again. He extended a hand.

Illica hesitated, but after a few heartbeats, he relented. He took Giacomo's hand and shook it once in grudging acceptance. Tension between them eased.

Ricordi dispelled the remaining enmity with a single clap of his hands and a huge smile. "Yes," he exclaimed happily, "we are all sorry. Such passion as we have just witnessed must be reserved for the stage, am I not right?"

Illica grunted.

"Come." Ricordi waved a hand signaling a return to the wide, comfortable chairs. "We have still to solve this problem." And as soon as all three were seated, he addressed Puccini with avuncular gentleness. "Now, Giacomo, tell us what kind of words you would like from Luigi."

Giacomo clasped his hands and brought them to his lips. He thought very carefully. The last thing he wanted was to precipitate another Illica outburst. One more would mean the end of everything. "When I hear sound," he began, "I hear it as musical notes. It may be laughter, or the cry of a child at play, or the clop-clop of a horse's hooves on cobblestone streets, or voices in simple conversation. There are no differences. All sound becomes music in my ears. It is the same when I read your libretto, Luigi. I see the characters, I watch their actions, and I hear their words. But I do not hear the music of opera in them. Please, I mean no offense. You are doing masterful work in shaping our story from Mürger's jumble of scenes and people. In the two acts you have written thus far, I see *Bohème* emerging, I feel the joy and pain of its characters, but I cannot hear the music."

"What are you saying?" Illica asked, but now his voice conveyed troubled interest, not anger. "What do you need in my words that would suggest music to you?"

Puccini thought for a moment, and then said quietly, "Poetry, Luigi, I believe it would be poetry. Your dialogue now is strong and clear. It is the true language of *verismo.* It breathes life into your people. But for *Bohème,* I need more than that. I need rhythms. I need imagery. I need...poetry."

Puccini fell back in his chair. He felt slightly spent. He hadn't expected to be that articulate about inspiration. Actually, he had never formulated a cogent explanation of how sound and music infused his life. He'd always just accepted the existence of music. He would sit at his piano and struggle to compose. That's all. It was work. However, he now felt a strange and exhilarating sense of fulfillment, as if a gap in the circle of his being had been magically closed.

There was silence in the conference room of Casa Ricordi.

Luigi Illica's eyes had narrowed in concentration. His elbows rested on the wide armrests of his chair. The fingers of his right hand stroked his beard absently. He stared at his thoughts. How had this affected him? What was he thinking? The questions troubled both Ricordi and Puccini as they waited for Illica's reaction. Silence became unbearable. Unable to tolerate it any longer, Ricordi brought a hand to his lips and coughed politely onto his thumb and crooked forefinger. It pulled Illica back into the room.

"Luigi?" Ricordi said softly.

Illica looked at him. It was a sad look.

"Do you have more questions? Has Giacomo satisfied you?"

"Completely." Illica breathed deeply. "In light of what I have learned, I must, with deepest regret, remove myself from further work on *La Bohème*."

This wasn't what Puccini or Ricordi had expected.

"But...but why?" Puccini stammered.

"I understand your need now, Giacomo," Illica said quietly, "and I respect it. Unfortunately, I cannot satisfy it. I am a dramatist not a poet."

"What you have already contributed is extremely valuable, Luigi," Ricordi insisted. "*Bohème* must be completed."

"But not by me."

"I reject your resignation."

"I am sorry."

"There is another solution to our problem."

Puccini and Illica looked at each other first and then questioningly at Ricordi.

"Would either of you object to an expansion of our collaboration?"

"Meaning?" Illica asked.

"Another member...a poet, Luigi...to give *Bohème* that which you admit being unable to provide, and to give you, Giacomo, the rhythms and imagery for your music."

Another member?

Librettist and composer considered the suggestion. They had difficulty enough working with each other. What would another temperament do to an already tempestuous mix? They remembered the plethora of difficulties that Leoncavallo, Oliva, and the others had created in *Manon*'s group collaboration. It had been torture. Wouldn't this be more of the same?

Seeing their doubt, wily Giulio Ricordi played his winning card. "We are on the lip of an enormous achievement, gentlemen," he said. "*Manon Lescaut* is being produced throughout the opera world. As you know, revenues are quite satisfactory, and they will continue to grow. Another opera with *Manon* appeal will mean enviable financial rewards for both of you, perhaps even financial stability forever. *La Bohème* is that opera. I am certain of that. For Giacomo's sake, all it needs is poetry."

The reminder of royalties brought terrible memories to Puccini's mind. He had starved. He had worn threadbare clothes. He had begged his mother repeatedly for money. He had been hounded by creditors. *Poverty...poverty*. It had even made him wish for death. Another success like *Manon*'s would, indeed, keep the grim curse of poverty from his door for years to come. He looked at Illica. "If another author is acceptable to you, Luigi, he will be acceptable to me." It was said softly, almost like a plea.

As with so many artists of the period, Illica also struggled to survive. *Money...it is always money,* he thought. He looked doubtfully at Ricordi. "Who would our poet be?"

"Yes, who?" Puccini asked quickly.

Ricordi answered with a sly smile, "Let me surprise you, gentlemen. You will not be disappointed, I promise."

Giulio Ricordi appreciated the power of verse. He'd witnessed it in the work of Giuseppe Verdi and the poet Arrigo Boito. It was a collaboration he had put together, and one that had produced *Otello,* the immensely successful adaptation of Shakespeare's great tragedy. If Boito had been available, he would have gone directly to him. But Boito was working just then with Verdi on another Shakespeare play. Equal to all challenges, Ricordi requested a meeting instead with the next outstanding Italian poet on his list.

Giuseppe Giacosa.

They met at a small café on Milan's Via Manzoni. It was a day made for agreement. The air was fresh and invigorating, the sky cloudless. Pedestrians walked casually, their chatter accompanying the twitter of birds on the lush branches of Aleppo pine trees that lined the streets. Ricordi and Giacosa sat at a small sidewalk table sipping red Ruffino wine and puffing contentedly on their full-bodied cheroots. They were relaxed friends who shared a love of art and many of the intimate secrets of opera.

"You must have something in mind, Giulio," Giacosa said, after a healthy swallow of wine. "We have not enjoyed a moment like this for some months. Why did you wish to see me?"

"I have a problem no one can solve as well as you."

"It is good to be needed," Giacosa said, smiling.

"It is better not to have the problem."

They chuckled.

"All right, Giulio, and if I can help, you know I shall."

Ricordi uncrossed his legs, placed his cigar in the table ashtray, leaned slightly forward, and in broad, sweeping terms, explained his difficulty and Puccini's problem.

Giacosa said nothing as Ricordi spoke. He asked no questions. He offered no thoughts. But his expression clouded perceptibly, and he pinched his bottom lip in growing concern.

"I need you to put our libretto into clear and moving verse. I need your deft and lyrical touches, Giuseppe," Ricordi concluded. "Without you, I am afraid I shall have to terminate this undertaking."

Giacosa was troubled. "When I read Maestro Puccini's reply to Leoncavallo's improper accusation," he said, "I asked myself, 'Why should any artist attempt to create an opera from Mürger's chaotic scenes?' I have read the book, Giulio. Yes, some of the situations are interesting, and the characters charming, but there is no continuity, no central life. I am afraid, my friend, to find it may be impossible, and I should be more hindrance than asset in the solution of your problem."

Ricordi answered with a smile and confident tilt of his head, "Do not fear, my friend, we shall do the impossible. Thus far, Illica has provided us with the first and second acts. I see the outlines of a gripping story in them, and I am rarely wrong in such evaluations. Presently, the acts are bloodless without music. Allow Maestro Puccini to bring them to life with the beauty of your verse. Join us. Do not commit *La Bohème* to the grave. Be its salvation."

The plea worked. Giacosa agreed to read Illica's acts before committing himself, but Ricordi returned to his office with the firm belief that Giacosa would become the missing and integral part of the *La Bohème* team. Three days later, he had his conviction confirmed.

Giacosa told him, "I see poetic possibilities in your opera, Giulio, and they intrigue me. Yes, I should like to be part of your endeavor. But you must understand one thing: I shall need absolute patience from everyone. I am meticulous in what I do. I cannot be hurried."

Assuring him his needs would be respected, Ricordi quickly arranged for all four members of the *La Bohème* team to meet. The following day, waiting for Giacosa to arrive, the publisher revealed the identity of his secret poet. Puccini and Illica were stunned. Though they had never met Giacosa, both were well aware of his reputation. They had to be; it was known by everyone in the opera community.

Giuseppe Giacosa had written thirty-two tragedies and comedies, two of which were verse plays that won him international recognition. He had also written countless poems and many articles on the realism *vs.* romanticism debate that was shaking all of Western civilization. In addition to this, he was a Conservatorio lecturer on dramatic literature, and the editor of a highly respected poetry magazine. A sweet human being, someone who was pained by the suffering of others and uplifted by their happiness, Giacosa's poetry expressed the beauty of his gentle spirit. In Italy, he was recognized as one of the significant literary figures of the age.

Giacomo was thrilled.

Illica, on the other hand, was doubtful. "I hope we shall not allow him to corrupt my words with excessive, flowery language," he said. "*La Bohème* must remain the drama I envision."

"It will, Luigi," Ricordi promised. "On my honor, it will."

However, he had detected a troubling shade of warning in Illica's words, and he feared there would be difficult days ahead.

Giacosa attacked Act I immediately. He had not misstated his work habits. He *was* meticulous, and he was slow...distressingly, frustratingly, gallingly slow.

While they waited, Illica continued to write. Ricordi fretted. Puccini bit his nails.

"I am going home," Giacomo told Ricordi one day. "I can do nothing here while I wait. Will anything ever meet his stringent criteria? He writes and rewrites and rewrites. Every word must be perfect."

"As with you. Must not every note be perfect?" Ricordi responded a bit irritably. "Reward comes with patience, Giacomo. It is a fact of life. But you are right; you can do nothing here while you wait. Go home. Be with your family. Fish. Hunt. Relax. I shall send scenes to you as I receive them."

Puccini needed no further persuasion. He telegraphed Elvira at once to inform her of his plans, and he left Milan early the next morning for Torre del Lago.

This homecoming was far different from his last. Elvira greeted him with a gentle smile before touching her cheek to his. She wore a dress about which he'd once expressed special appreciation. And her long hair was neatly pinned in an attractive pile on top of her head. She didn't seem harried or threatening in the least. "Welcome home, Giacomo," she said. "I am impatient to hear what happened in Milan. You must tell me everything."

This was unexpected and wonderful. Puccini couldn't have been happier. He grinned like a child receiving a present. Elvira could be woefully unpredictable, a devastating force one minute and a comforting blanket the next. Apparently, it was a time for warmth. Why? He didn't know, and he wouldn't enquire. To be welcomed this way was something not to be tarnished with questions. "It is good to be home, Elvira," he said. "As soon as I wash the soot of travel from my hands and face, I shall tell you all that happened in Milan. You will be as fascinated and pleased as I."

Then he turned to the children, who were standing and watching their parents with gleeful smiles, and he wrapped them in loving embraces.

Dinner that evening was totally satisfying. He spoke enthusiastically about Giacosa.

"What is he like?" Elvira asked.

"He is as tall as I, and about ten or eleven years older, I should judge. He leans to the rotund, with a balding head, bushy eyebrows, a full mustache, and a beard that almost lies upon his chest. I like him. He seems to exude patience, gentleness, and understanding. It is easy to see why his intimate friends sometimes call him *Buddha*."

"*Buddha*?"

"Yes. He has something spiritual about him."

Elvira smiled. "He sounds delightful. I should like to meet him."

"Oh, you will...you will."

"And you feel confident he can provide you with what you need?"

"Infinitely confident."

Then Giacosa's achievements gushed from Puccini like water from a firehose, and they extinguished all doubt.

Elvira laughed. "That is wonderful! A poet of such distinction will surely contribute significantly to the success of your opera." But she wanted more. She posed a flurry of questions and appeared to be storing his answers in her memory bank for future withdrawal. "Then Milan was hugely successful," she said when she had all she needed to know. "Excellent. I look forward to seeing how Signor Giacosa inspires you."

"And I look forward to working again with a libretto that will evoke the best that is within me." He leaned back in his chair and spread his arms.

The children laughed at his expansiveness and clapped their hands.

Two weeks later, Puccini received the first act of *Bohème.* He read it hungrily. His heart beat faster. Illica's flat prose had been transformed into images of lyrical beauty.

The fun, the joking, the free spirit of Rodolfo and his friends leaped off the pages.

And Mimi's frailty had been changed from pitiable weakness to a sweet symbol of unsullied love. She and Rodolfo were no longer mere neighbors, but two young people who were finding themselves in finding each other. Rodolfo sings:

Just wait my dear young lady, and in a word,
I'll tell you who and what I am.

And a metaphoric aria follows, filled with hope, dreams, and the spirit of youth.

Mimi responds:

My real name is Lucia...
I love all things that have gentle magic,
that talk of love, of spring,
that talk of dreams and fancies –
the thing called poetry...

Giacomo became euphoric. Here were the musical words for which he had been searching. Here were truth and purity. Here was his *verismo.* He thought, *I have found my muse in Giuseppe Giacosa,* and he leaped from his chair and rushed to his piano. His fingers raced over the keys. Rodolfo's aria poured from the center of his soul like a gently flowing stream. It filled the room. It burst through the walls and poured its beauty into every crevice of the house.

In the kitchen, Elvira stopped what she was doing at the stove. She felt the rhapsodic melody penetrating her being. She clasped her hands and brought them to her lips. She closed her eyes. And then she smiled as tears edged the rim of her eyelids. A rush of love swept through her. She hadn't felt this way in years. What was happening? She opened her eyes and drifted to the living room on the musical current. She stood in the doorway and listened breathlessly.

Giacomo wasn't aware of her presence, and if he had been he would have ignored her completely. He was too impassioned with what he was creating to have cared. He stopped abruptly. His thoughts tumbled. He reached for pencil and composition paper. He wrote aria notes frantically, as if in a second's delay they would be lost forever. He hummed. He sang. A phrase here, a passage there. He made changes. Some he kept. Others he scratched out impatiently. He threw pages aside. He worked feverishly, sometimes with explosions of satisfaction, sometimes with painful displeasure.

La Bohème was being birthed in a frenzy of artistic spasms.

Elvira saw his concentration. She felt his urgency. And she smiled. Then she turned silently and returned to the kitchen, thinking: *At last, he is working. At last, he will find some peace and bring peace to me.*

Puccini worked all through that afternoon. Satisfied with the arias, he returned to the opening of Act I and dipped into the recitatives. Ordinary conversation now held special meaning for him. He laughed at trivialities and found bright notes to give the opening dialogue the uplifting verve it required. Finally, he was drained. He could continue no longer. He looked over what he had composed, and he hummed its passages softly. Yes, they seemed to be good. But he wasn't certain. He would play them again tomorrow. In the light of a new day after a good night's rest he would see them more clearly. Certainly they would need more work. Ponchielli had taught him "nothing will ever come out perfectly in its initial stage." But he was ready for that work, even eager to attack it.

"I was listening," Elvira said when he emerged from the living room and saw her again. She nodded approval. "You can be brilliant when you put your mind to it."

It was said pleasantly, a gentle stroke of acceptance, but he couldn't miss the whisper of reproach in it. It didn't matter. He was too filled with a sense of accomplishment to permit it to blemish this wonderful feeling. "I shall have to work on it further," he said happily. "However, I do believe it is coming along."

"Indeed, it is," she agreed with a warm smile.

That night, Elvira kissed him lightly on his lips before she left him to go to bed. "Good night, Giacomo," she said softly. "I am still not ready for more than this. But I thank you for a wonderful day."

The following week was almost as heavenly as their first days together so many years ago. They continued to sleep apart, but there was laughter and kindness in their lives again. They talked without rancor. They shared thoughts more easily. She asked to read the first act, and Giacomo handed it to her willingly. She liked it and told him his music had given the words new life. This stirred his energies further. And he continued to work on Act I of *Bohème,* polishing it, bringing every musical phrase to artistic perfection.

Meanwhile, Ricordi and Illica waited impatiently for an end to his silence.

"When will you send your music to Milan?" Elvira asked him.

"I should rather play it for Luigi and Signor Ricordi than have anyone do that for me," he said.

"An excellent decision. When will you leave?"

"I have been thinking...two days?"

"Good."

She'd been agreeable ever since his return. No frowns. No brusque responses. No biting innuendos. *Can our love be returning?* he asked himself hopefully. The thought made him hesitate. "I shall be coming and going to Milan many times with *Bohème.*"

"So?"

"I hope this will not make you unhappy."

"As I told you once before, do what you must."

Two days later, she went with him to the train station and sent him on his way with another light kiss and wishes for great success. Giacomo was so intensely happy he could have run all the way to Milan.

Ricordi, Illica, Giacosa, and Puccini met again in the Casa Ricordi offices immediately upon Giacomo's arrival in Milan. The publisher, librettist, and poet were too impatient to hear his music for time to be wasted in lighthearted banter. After a few friendly words of greeting, they hurried him to the piano and encouraged him...even *urged* him...to play what his composing had produced. All four men were extremely apprehensive, Giacomo most of all. He looked at Illica and Giacosa with a wan smile before starting, as if to say, "I believe I have written something to embrace your words. I pray you will agree." And then he began, singing the libretto with his music. At first, his voice was tentative, uncertain, but as he played and heard occasional mutterings of approval, it became stronger, braver, until he was performing all the parts as if he were on stage at La Scala. And when he struck the final notes of Act I and sang Rodolfo and Mimi's exhilarating exit line:

Beloved! My love! My love!

Giulio Ricordi actually applauded.

Grinning broadly, Puccini shyly accepted firm and vigorous slaps on his back and shoulders. The air became charged with congratulations and happy predictions. "We are on our way to a memorable success, gentlemen, perhaps a masterpiece," Ricordi said emphatically.

Everyone agreed.

Even Illica admitted grudgingly that Giacosa's poetry had raised their efforts to another level of beauty. In the days ahead, there would be nothing but collaborative cooperation and agreement that *La Bohème* should be completed in a matter of months.

However, from early in May of 1893 until December 10, 1895, almost three harrowing *years* passed. Why had it taken that long to complete the opera when work on it had begun so optimistically? The answer: *Contention*.

The first ugly weed of discord sprouted from the mud of a petty complaint.

- 25 -

Alone with Ricordi, Giacomo Puccini confessed he was not entirely satisfied. True, his music had pleased his associates, but it had been composed in the rush of inspiration when eagerness to begin blinded him to a particularly disturbing impediment. Oh, he was still eager to work, but he would be unable to continue confidently until that hindrance had been eliminated.

Puzzled, Ricordi asked, "To what specifically are you referring?"

"Illica must be made to see he is affecting my composition badly and unnecessarily."

Ricordi was shocked. "Illica? Affecting your music badly? In what way?"

"He supplies too many stage directions. I do not understand why he is trying to imitate French dramatists. Descriptions. Movements. Smiles. Glances. Twitches. It is too much. It muddles thinking and obstructs invention. For the future, please ask Illica to write his scenes without these troublesome notes. They are a stifling, unnecessary intrusion."

Giulio Ricordi was so astonished he could barely speak. Puccini had never indicated this was a problem. And now, mention it to Illica? Imply again his work was faulty? That it created difficulties for the composer? Impossible! Such a suggestion would end *La Bohème* forever. The publisher shook his head. "No, no, Giacomo," he said. "I must refuse your request. My position has always been that of mediator in artistic disputes. I refuse to initiate conflict, and mentioning your concern would certainly precipitate a violent reaction. You must ignore Illica's directions. They are not there for you. Go home to Torre del Lago. Work on Act II. Your can transcend such insignificant distractions, I am sure. And you must *never* mention this to Illica."

Puccini's jaw dropped in disbelief. Giulio Ricordi had always been receptive to his concerns, and he had never rejected a request so emphatically. Sensing further objection would only aggravate the issue, he let the subject rest. "Elvira is expecting me," he said quietly. "I shall be going home tomorrow. There is much work to be done on *Bohème.*"

"Yes, there is," Ricordi agreed with a fatherly hand on Puccini's shoulder, "and time will not wait for us. Work is the panacea for all artistic ailments, Giacomo. Work."

Giacomo Puccini returned to Torre del Lago a troubled man.

However, Giulio Ricordi was even more troubled. He had always feared incendiary conflict between Illica and Puccini, and this silly complaint did not auger well for the future. If Puccini could be disturbed by something as trivial as stage directions, what could he, Ricordi, expect when more serious disagreements should arise? And most assuredly, they would arise. He sighed deeply. *Artists...*he thought...*infants in adult garb.*

To Ricordi's surprise, however, the most threatening member of the creative triumvirate was not Giacomo Puccini. Nor was it the extremely volatile Luigi Illica. It became the spiritual, the aesthetic, the superbly calm and respectful Giuseppe Giacosa. The Buddha.

Giacosa had completed his work on Act I of *La Bohème* at the beginning of May 1893, but he did not send Act II to Torre del Lago until the middle of October. Five months would pass! And they would be particularly difficult months for Giulio Ricordi who nursed two prodigious fears. One: Theft was quite common in 19th century opera circles. Though Puccini and Leoncavallo had stopped airing their differences publicly, the press saw advantages in the feud and took pains to keep it very much alive. Consequently, Ricordi worried that Leoncavallo might discover how Mürger's diverse episodes were being shaped into a coherent story and then steal some of Illica's and Giacosa's ideas for his own *La Bohème*. And two: If that were to happen, and Leoncavallo's opera were to be produced before Casa

Ricordi should be able to mount its own production, all work and expenses would then have been for nothing. Deeply concerned about these possibilities, Ricordi worried and begged his writers to keep everything they were doing a closely guarded secret. At the same time, he attempted to hurry Giuseppe Giacosa with repeated requests for more scenes. Unfortunately, his predicament only compounded his own fears by distressing the Buddha into an ominous protest.

"I told you I am slow," Giacosa said. "Poetry is too important to be sacrificed to the dictates of speed. It is laborious work. It takes hour upon hour to find the exact phrase or image. And that is even truer when I must work upon another author's words without corrupting his intent. Also, as you know, I have other writing obligations that require my attention. I should be going soon to Paris for the opening of my play, but I shall have to cancel that plan to continue work on *La Bohème*. This does not make me happy. I have been giving serious thought to this and, perhaps, I should withdraw now from your project before I do more damage to myself."

Ricordi protested in return. He told Giacosa he must not think of leaving. He stressed how wonderful his first act was, how it had inspired Puccini to flights of imagination rarely expressed by a composer. He insisted that he, Giacosa, was helping to lift Italian opera to new heights of grandeur, of glory, of immortality. Could any poet resist such blandishments? Certainly not the Buddha. Soothed, he thanked Ricordi for the faith he was expressing in his work and promised he would remain with *La Bohème* until it had been completed to everyone's satisfaction. "I shall remain," he conceded. But then he cautioned once again, "Remember, I cannot be rushed. You must allow me to do this properly."

It was only the first of many times that Giuseppe Giacosa wanted desperately to escape the burden of *La Bohème*. And it was only the first of many times that Giulio Ricordi had to use his guile and ingenuity to hold this troubled collaboration together.

In Torre del Lago, Giacomo Puccini waited for *Bohème*'s Act II. Elvira watched him with growing suspicion. He had returned subdued. He seemed to be considering something he was reluctant to disclose. *What can it be?* she wondered. He'd told her about the warm reception his music had received for the opera's first act. However, he was still disconcerted by Ricordi's refusal to act upon his complaint, and he didn't know how he could proceed with Act II when it would arrive.

Weeks passed.

He said nothing. He did nothing.

One morning, unable to tolerate his inactivity any longer, she finally scolded, "You sit like a forlorn lover. Your misery is unbearable. Do something!"

"I am doing something. I am waiting."

"Wait somewhere else...away from the house."

"Does my presence annoy you?"

"No. Your idleness does."

Puccini left the room wishing Elvira could feel his pain. He had made many friends in Torre del Lago...neighbors, tradesmen, fishing and hunting companions... and he thought of visiting some now but, instead, he wandered aimlessly about the living room, touching objects. Books. Newspapers. The leaves of a plant. Elvira's sharp words wouldn't leave him: *"Wait somewhere else... away from the house."* He went outside and wandered to the rear of the house. And there – totally unrelated to anything he was thinking at the moment – a pleasing thought suddenly struck him. He smiled for the first time that day. The idea was galvanizing. His weariness disappeared. His back straightened with decision. And he calculated quickly what he would need in order to bring this brilliant thought to fruition. He couldn't do it there. Not in the rear of his house. It would be a home away from home. And it would be solely his, a peaceful, comfortable place where he could relax without intrusions or accusations.

He found it quickly, a decrepit shack owned and run as a "café" by a disreputable character known as "Blackbird Legs." Puccini began to frequent the café. And when the unsavory owner was forced to leave Italy for safety reasons, Puccini and some friends quickly bought the shack. What followed was a rowdy christening ceremony that went far into the night and didn't end until everyone was too drunk to continue. *Café Giovanni della Bande Nere* (Giovanni of the Black Band) became *Club La Bohème,* a hangout where he and friends met for drinking, smoking, card playing, singing, and ribald conversation. Ridiculous rules urged members to swear without restraint; since some forms of gambling were legal in Italy, only *illegal* forms were encouraged; silence was forbidden; serious subjects were never to be discussed; and all killjoys were to be immediately and forcibly ejected.

Tables and chairs were installed. Also plants, pictures and, finally, an old, upright piano. Everything was always festive. Puccini loved going there. *Club La Bohème* brought him many hours of great pleasure. It also provided him with another avenue down which he could run to avoid the difficulties of work.

And Elvira felt her Giacomo did that far, far too often. One day only to escape her baleful glances, he buried himself in Act I of *La Bohème.* All at once, he believed he saw unpardonable weaknesses. *How could I have missed them?!* he thought. They were like a glaring light; they could not be ignored. He rushed to his desk and wrote to Ricordi, identifying them and insisting upon changes. This, of course, drove his librettists to distraction.

"There is nothing wrong with Act I," Illica fumed. "You have said so yourself, Signor Giulio. But there is something wrong with that man! Has he nothing better to do than to pick at perfection like a mindless woodpecker digging holes in a healthy tree?"

In bewilderment, Giacosa agreed. "The act is cohesive, lyrical, and musically beautiful," he said. "Why should he demand alterations?"

"Please...let us never reject suggestions out-of-hand," Ricordi responded. "We must always be receptive to each other's perceptions. Puccini does have a proclivity to fault-finding, I admit, but I have found his instincts to be unerring."

Resistance was dispiriting to Puccini. It didn't take long for him to lose interest. "I am sick of *La Bohème,*" he wrote to Ricordi. "Perhaps we should abandon it and return to *La Lupa*."

"No, definitely no!" Ricordi shot back firmly. "Too much time has been lost already. We must move forward with *La Bohème!*"

While trying to satisfy Puccini with changes to Act I, the librettists proceeded with the rest of the opera. Giacosa grumbled as he handed Act II to Ricordi, "I hope Signor Puccini will find less fault with this than he did with Act I."

Ricordi read the act immediately and, with a smile, he judged it to be excellent. He forwarded the second act to Puccini with a plea to apply himself to the act before something disastrous could occur.

The third act came from Ricordi, and then the fourth. As far as the librettists were concerned, the opera was finished. It was now in the hands of the composer.

But nothing the librettists wrote for *La Bohème* satisfied Puccini. Scenes had to be rewritten. Conflicts sharpened. Acts shortened. Poetry revised. Endless objections and their subsequent delays became Ricordi's nightmare. He found himself unable to smooth the ruffled sensibilities of *Bohème*'s librettists by himself. "*You must come to Milan,*" he wrote to Puccini. "*You must be here to voice your thoughts. It is impossible to continue this by mail any longer.*"

He showed Ricordi's letter to Elvira. The less she had to endure his unproductive presence, the better she felt. "Go. Yes, go...by all means go," she told him irritably. "At least in Milan, with your librettists and Signor Ricordi to goad you, you may finish this opera someday."

He left the next day deeply troubled. This time, there were no kind words from Elvira, no prepared delectables to eat, no gentle looks or good wishes. It was a terrible train ride, ten hours of endless doubt. And in Milan it was no better. Proximity to Illica and Giacosa did not improve his state of mind. On the contrary, it produced disagreements so intense that Giulio Ricordi descended from the lofty heights of conciliator to the gutter ugliness of belligerent. Like Puccini he began to demand changes. He quibbled, he squabbled, and he threw his own barbs and accusations at Giacomo with telling accuracy.

Giacosa could stand it no longer. He had once threatened Ricordi with: "I swear to you that I shall never be caught writing another libretto as long as I live!" And now he told Ricordi, "I am tired to death of this constant re-making, re-touching, adding, correcting, piecing together, extending on the one hand, and reducing on the other." Adamantly, he declared, "My health is being endangered by this discord. I am desperately in need of a vacation. I am going."

No amount of pleading by Ricordi could change his mind. He disappeared.

With Giacosa gone, Illica saw no reason to remain in Milan. He, too, disappeared.

Ricordi then threw up his hands. He left for Paris to help Giuseppe Verdi with a production of *Otello.*

A wounded Puccini returned to Torre del Lago to face Elvira's fierce and hostile glances.

Months passed. Puccini traveled to various cities for productions of *Manon Lescaut,* where he was healed by audience cheers. Elvira barely spoke when he was in the house, and when he left Torre del Lago for his *Manon* excursions she was happy to be rid of him.

Eventually, the *La Bohème* team recovered sufficiently to meet again and to resume work on the opera. But nothing changed. However, despite the emotional bloodletting, somehow, magically, the collaboration held together. And late in the evening of December 19, 1895, alone in his Milan apartment, Giacomo Puccini wrote the final notes of *La Bohème.* He replayed the last moments of Act IV. Then overcome by his heroine's death, he slumped on his piano bench and broke into tears. He sat that way and wept for a full five minutes. "It was as if I had experienced the death of my own child," he said later. Brushing tears from his damp cheeks with the heels of his hands, he studied the opera's musical notes. There it was, *La Bohème...* finished. He shook his head. He couldn't believe it. With palms on his thighs, he closed his eyes and inhaled deeply like a swimmer surfacing for air. Then opening his eyes, he grinned. He felt alive again. A huge wave of satisfaction washed over him. Only the late hour prevented him from rushing to Casa Ricordi offices to play the entire opera for Giulio Ricordi and his collaborating librettists.

The next morning he played the entire *La Bohème* score for them, and their reactions were everything he could have wished. Overcome with emotion, Luigi Illica approached him silently, and with tears in his eyes he embraced him like a brother. Giacosa, wiping his own eyes, said, “Thank you, thank you. You have made all your objections meaningful.”

And Ricordi simply took him by the shoulders and whispered, “As I had hoped, Giacomo, you have given us a masterpiece.”

Puccini’s return to Torre del Lago was equally gratifying. After relating to Elvira all that had been said to him, he concluded his report solemnly with: “I do not know how audiences may react to *Bohème* but, as with *Manon,* I am happy with what I have composed, and I believe, with Signor Ricordi, that it may be my masterpiece.”

Seeing the depth of his happiness, and pleased that he had finished his opera, Elvira took his hands in hers. She looked steadily into his eyes and whispered gently, “I pray it is God’s wish, Giacomo. I devoutly pray it is God’s wish.”

- 26 -

Giulio Ricordi began immediately to arrange a production of *La Bohème*.

19th century opera publishers did more than sell the scores of their operas to music lovers. They were also the opera's producers. They found the project's investors. They rented the theatre. They helped in the casting of talent, supervised the design and construction of scenery, oversaw the show's costuming, wig, and make-up needs, and they managed all publicity and promotion. With so much to consider, Ricordi became annoyed with Puccini when the composer demanded things that intruded upon his responsibilities. "I shall always consider your suggestions," he snapped, "but such decisions, you must always understand, are mine to make. We shall not open *La Bohème* in Rome or Naples, no matter how badly you wish to avoid Turin."

Turin audiences had adored Puccini's *Le Villi* and *Manon Lescaut.* Turin had cheered him, feted him, given him the *Cavaliere dell'Ordine della Corona d'Italia*. Insistence upon Rome or Naples for *La Bohème*'s première seemed to Ricordi like utter idiocy. "Why are you doing this?" he demanded. "Why are you being obstinate?"

Giacomo couldn't respond. The answer to Ricordi's questions was too painful for him to admit even to himself. It was...*terror*.

Puccini could not deny all that Turin had done for him. He even thought Teatro Regio's importance to opera equaled that of the Vatican's to Catholicism. However, he suddenly feared the city's audiences would now be hyper-critical, finding fault in *La Bohème* where none existed. Completing the opera had brought him great relief; but that relief had become panic.

"Please, Signor Giulio," he begged, "if not Rome or Naples, then anywhere but Turin."

"That is not for you to decide," Ricordi said. "I know my skills as well as you know yours. You must trust me with this."

It was going to be Teatro Regio, and there was nothing he could do about that. Puccini's fear loomed over him like a threatening specter. He couldn't escape it. And it caused him to impose his troubled thoughts and feelings upon Ricordi about every other aspect of *La Bohème*'s production.

"We must have the most celebrated singers we can find," he insisted.

"On the contrary," Ricordi responded. "It is the opera itself, not the voice of an individual that will be the foundation of its success. *La Bohème* requires a homogeneous cast, not celebrities."

"Then I must have Leopoldo Magnune to conduct the orchestra."

"We shall have a younger conductor."

"Who?"

"Arturo Toscanini."

"*He is little known and inexperienced!*"

"Indeed, but he is sensitive and vigorous."

"Who will sing Mimi?"

"Cesira Feranni." Cesira Feranni had sung the title role in Turin's enormously successful production of *Manon Lescaut.*

"Thank you, Signor Giulio, oh, thank you," Puccini said.

However, his gratitude wasn't deep enough to keep him from making other demands that vexed Ricordi to the limits of his endurance. When rehearsals began, he was present every day. His anxiety made him unbearable. That Ricordi was able to maintain his usual equanimity is a testament to the man's superb character and business acumen.

In Torre del Lago, Elvira read Puccini's daily letters with growing fascination. They told her of production problems and of the progress *Bohème* was making as they were being solved. She could feel the growing excitement. She could also sense his angst in every word. "*I want to be with you,*" she wrote, hoping he would be pleased with her interest. *"I shall find someone to be with the children, and I shall remain with you through opening night."*

His reaction pained her. *"No! My life just now cannot give you the attention you require. We would not even be able to dine together. We rehearse all day, from eleven in the morning to four-thirty, and in the evening from eight-thirty to midnight. I would not have time to speak with you. Stay in del Lago! You will come here when the time is right."*

The days dragged on.

Illica arrived in Milan to attend rehearsals. Puccini complained to him about Tieste Wilmant, the baritone singing the role of Marcello. *"He is vile. His voice is coarse, he knows nothing about stage movement, and he takes direction badly. He must be replaced!"*

But Illica rejected Puccini's complaints. Instead, he gave Wilmant special attention. He explained character relationships; he showed him movement; he demonstrated posture; he relaxed the baritone with words of encouragement. And though the actor never erased Puccini's anxieties completely, he improved sufficiently for the composer to finally say, "You are a master, Illica. You give me hope that he will not destroy our opera."

Opening night seemed suddenly to be racing upon them. There didn't appear to be enough time for all the little things that still had to be accomplished. But one-by-one, they were addressed and eliminated. *"I was wrong about Toscanini,"* Giacomo wrote to Elvira. *"He is a sweet, gentle, young man, a conductor with uncanny sensitivity and knowledge. I am quite pleased with him. I should like you to be here with me. Come. I shall introduce you to Toscanini and everyone else."*

Elvira left Torre del Lago at once. Her thoughts tumbled: *I had to urge him every inch of his way, but he has at last achieved the masterwork of which he is proud. I can only pray he has not misjudged the result of his effort.*

February 1, 1896.

A wintry night. Flurries of snow and puffs of breath filled the chilling air. Nevertheless, opera lovers converged upon Teatro Regio in Turin.

Tickets cost sixty lire, an unheard-of price in that age, and almost everyone of any musical and social significance was at *La Bohème*'s opening night. Patron and composer Baron Alberto was there, as were many of Italy's royal families. The Count of Turin. The Duchess of Genoa. The Duke and Duchess of Aosta. The Princess Letizia, who had been so overwhelmed by *Manon Lescaut*. Musicians, librettists, and critics filled the seats. They came not only from Turin but from other cities, even Milan. Ricordi's new posters in color, the first of their kind, had excited all of opera. Everyone was in the Teatro Regio to witness the rise or fall of Italy's uncertain hero. Would *La Bohème* lift him to heavenly heights, or would it plunge him into the abyss of oblivion?

The orchestra was ready. Preliminary tuning had been completed. Maestro Toscanini strode to his place before the musicians. Applause greeted his appearance. He bowed to the audience, turned to the orchestra, tapped twice on the music stand, and raised his baton. Quiet settled over the house. The baton came down slowly, and the long-awaited première performance of *La Bohème* began.

The curtains parted and took the audience instantly into the dingy, cluttered garret of Parisian artists.

A murmur went through the audience.

Puccini, listening in the lobby with Illica and Giacosa, tensed. Was that interest? Approval? Puccini bowed his head and closed his eyes.

Marcello and Rodolfo began to sing. They complained about the cold weather, about freezing and being hungry.

More audience murmuring.

Now, the tension was too much for Giacomo Puccini to bear. He turned, retrieved his hat and overcoat from the cloakroom, and hurried from the theater to pace the sidewalk immediately outside its entrance doors. Illica and Giacosa followed and paced with him. There they were, three silent figures, walking with short, shuffling steps on a lonely street. Heads down, hands in coat pockets, and cigarettes dangling from loose lips. All were frowning and listening intently for that magnificent, initial explosion of approval with its cheers, its applause, its bravos.

It never came.

Puccini looked questioningly at his librettists. They looked blankly at him. All three stopped their pacing. They bent their heads and listened. Finally, ...aah, there it was...applause. But it was weak, halfhearted. What was happening? The trio hurried back into Teatro Regio and took places at the rear of the theater. They waited there and watched. Courteous and considerate would best describe the audience, but where was its spirit, its excitement? Where was its admiration, its acclaim? It had none to show.

At the end of Act I, the singers received some recognition, and Puccini was called to take one bow. He did it self-consciously, embarrassed by the absence of audience enthusiasm.

Act II was only slightly better. It progressed in long silences, with just one burst of interest as everyone onstage marched off noisily, following a host of soldiers and their strutting drum major.

During intermission Illica and Giacosa returned to their seats. Puccini remained in the theater's lobby, hiding in a corner, straining to catch snatches of conversation.

"Poor Puccini," he heard one woman say to her companion.

And another couple passed close enough for him to hear, "It will most likely be removed from the season's schedule."

Elvira joined him. She didn't smile. She looked at him consolingly and said, "It is enjoyable, Giacomo. Far better than this audience deserves."

Acts III and IV generated some enthusiasm, and everyone seemed to be moved by Mimi's death scene. But through the entire evening *La Bohème* drew only fifteen curtain calls, and only seven of them belonged to Puccini.

Giacomo was crushed. He wanted to rush from the theater. He wanted to cry. How could this be? He, Ricordi, Illica, Giacosa – all had been certain they had produced a masterpiece. Why had the audience been so indifferent? In two excruciating hours, the failure of *La Bohème* had shattered every tenuous shred of self-confidence

Giacomo Puccini still possessed. He looked about and saw nothing. He wanted to speak, but he said nothing. It was as if he'd been suddenly blinded and struck dumb.

Elvira, however, loved the performance. She offered kind, glowing words. "It is magic," she said. "Your music brings dead words to vibrant life. I laughed at the antics, cried at the sadness, and almost swooned in the beauty of your arias."

She was sincere, but he was inconsolable.

"We must speak tomorrow," Ricordi told him after everyone had left the theater. "In my hotel suite. Nine o'clock. Illica and Giacosa will be with us." The publisher's unsmiling face added to Puccini's despondency.

"I shall be there," Puccini croaked.

"Go back to your hotel. Try to sleep."

"That will be impossible."

Alone in their hotel room, Giacomo and Elvira said little to each other. He sat on the small couch. Ready to retire, Elvira approached and looked down at his slumped figure. "Do you intend to sit this way all night?" she asked quietly.

He inhaled, closed his eyes, and raised both hands in a gesture of helplessness.

"You will feel better in the morning."

"You sleep," he said. "I cannot."

She stood without moving. Finally, she shook her head and sighed. She spoke gently to him. "You have composed a magnificent opera, Giacomo, and because one blind audience cannot see its beauty, you flounder in self-pity."

"Please," he responded quickly, "if there is one thing I do not need now, Elvira, it is your absence of understanding."

Her eyes widened. "You blind fool," she spat. "You cannot see sympathy when it stands before you."

"Perhaps," he answered, "but I can see failure in audience response, and tomorrow's reviews will show you what I can see and you cannot."

That he was right became piercingly clear when reviews

appeared the following morning. All three of Turin's opera critics wrote devastating opinions. Carlo Bersenzio, the highly respected reviewer for *La Stampa,* believed it would be impossible to consider *La Bohème* anything but a failure. "*Maestro Puccini,*" he wrote, "*offers some invention, but no emotional pleasure. His opera is certain to be forgotten quickly.*"

L. A. Villanis of the *Gazzetta di Torino* thought there were some musical moments that would appeal to the general public but, he said, Puccini had pandered to the simplest of tastes and had abandoned art.

And the most damning review was written by E. A. Berta of the *Gazzetta del Popolo.* At the end of a long, blistering article, he wondered why Puccini had chosen to compose this bland, unimaginative score when *Manon Lescaut* had revealed an artist of creative genius. "*We ask ourselves,*" he wrote, "*what could have moved him along this lamentable path?*"

The next morning at nine o'clock, Ricordi's hotel suite was filled with smoke as Puccini, Illica, and Giacosa gulped coffee and puffed grimly on cigars. No one spoke. Newspapers cluttered the table around which they were seated. All were reading the reviews, exchanging pages and reacting in different ways. Illica grunted. Giacosa sighed. Puccini was too bewildered to feel anything. To Giacomo, the words were a maelstrom, sucking him into suffocating darkness.

Only Giulio Ricordi seemed above and unmoved by the critical reactions. He stood near a wide window, gazing silently at the morning activity below, waiting for the right moment to speak. When he sensed the other members of his *Bohème* team had had sufficient time to read everything, he blew a cloud of cigar smoke, turned casually to them and said with a faint smile, "Poison, gentlemen, poison. It is designed to kill for reasons too petty to be considered seriously. I spit it from my mind as I wish you, too, will do. Even our new colorful posters were rejected as being garish and obscene. We are offering the world something new, something different in *La Bohème*. That is difficult for most to accept. We must expect the effete mentality of reviewers to recoil and to spew venom."

"But as you say, Giulio," Giacosa said after a long sigh, "poison kills."

Ricordi smiled. "Only when it is swallowed, Giuseppe, only when it is swallowed. We shall ignore our reviewers. We shall move ahead with our *Bohème* and make them choke on their own toxins."

"The audience agreed with them," Puccini muttered.

"Do not be morose, Giacomo," Ricordi countered. "You are an artist. Artists lead; the world follows – *always*! The day will yet be yours."

After a half-hour of performance dissection, Ricordi ended their meeting on an optimistic note. He accompanied Puccini and his librettists to the door and sent them away in a final shower of encouraging words: "*La Bohème* will not die, gentlemen. Be assured, I shall never permit that to happen."

Ricordi's optimism was not bravado. The publisher was not new to critical resentments. Unlike his artistic clients, he had developed a cool immunity to harsh words. Reviewers were unavoidable nuisances that's all, sometimes useful, often destructive, rarely insightful. He believed unshakably in the beauty of *La Bohème*. Its reviews were only words to be erased by counter measures.

The next day, while still in Turin, Giulio Ricordi began a publicity and promotion campaign that set the entire opera community buzzing. He was not averse to spending money to prove his point. Huge advertisements appeared in all of Turin's newspapers. His colorful posters were hung throughout the city. The blindness of reviewers was made evident in a string of articles that stressed their grievous errors in previous judgments. And, finally, the stamp of *Scapigliatura* endorsement came from Arrigo Boito, who called the opera "*perfect* verismo *with real people living the truth of love, expressing poetic thoughts to the strains of exquisitely conceived music.*"

The results were exactly as Ricordi had anticipated. *La Bohème* did not suffer at the box office. Ticket sales increased daily. Houses sold out. And the Teatro Regio run was extended to twenty-four performances. Word spread to other cities: *La Bohème* was a hit; audiences loved it. Requests came in quickly for production rights from opera houses throughout Italy. Critics may have tried to obliterate this tender tale, they may have scorned its enchanting music, but they were defeated by Giulio Ricordi's favorite slogan: "Damn the reviewers! Audiences make successes, not critics!"

He was right.

Audiences became uniformly ecstatic in their reactions. *La Bohème* flourished. More clearly than anything he had previously composed, it became the centerpiece of Giacomo Puccini's virtuoso life.

- 27 -

As Turin's *La Bohème* grew into a resounding success, Giacomo and Elvira returned to Milan. However, instead of being completely satisfied with its full houses, Puccini continued to be plagued by its opening night failure. He couldn't stop asking himself: Why should that audience have responded so dismally to the same music and story that was exciting everyone who was presently buying tickets?

Only Giulio Ricord would be able to answer his question.

They met and sat in one of the publisher's favorite little restaurants, Milan's *Café Zabaione.* An unexpected cold spell had attacked the city overnight and piles of snow glutted the streets, preventing them from sitting outdoors. Their table was close to the café's warm, pot-bellied stove, and they were relaxing with large mugs of hot *zabaione* in their hands. *Café Zabaione*'s signature beverage was noted for its sweet, silky flavor; Ricordi, the cosmopolitan gentleman, knew precisely how it was to be enjoyed.

"To be fully appreciated," he advised, "this *zabaione* must be permitted to linger on the tongue. It is to be sipped, mouthed, and allowed to trickle down the throat. It must never be swallowed immediately."

He demonstrated.

Giacomo watched closely and imitated him. He grinned and nodded strong agreement. "This is truly excellent!" he said wide-eyed when he could speak again.

Ricordi smiled. "Surely you have had eggnog before."

"Elvira makes it, but it is never like *this*."

"Despite the failing," Ricordi joked, "your wife is an extraordinary woman."

"In what way?"

"Strong, determined, confident, decisive. I like her."

"I shall tell her that. But Elvira is not the reason I asked to see you alone."

"I am listening."

Earnestly, and as quickly as he could, Puccini explained the full nature of his opening night concern. And after Giacomo asked his troubling question, Ricordi said, "You did not fail, Giacomo. Never think that. There are two possible explanations for our opening night experience. Number one: It was a wealthy, jaded audience, too deeply immersed in its own judgments to understand what we are offering. Number two: Six weeks prior to our opening, Teatro Regio presented a huge production of Wagner's *Götterdämmerung*."

"I know," Giacomo said. "But what has that to do with *La Bohème*?"

"Fire, raging storms, love potions, a magic ring, treachery, betrayal, murder...that opera is a monster of gigantic effects. It is overblown theatricality with bombastic music and exhausting symbolism. I detest it. But audiences, apparently, disagree with me. It is an enormous success wherever it is presented. *La Bohème,* in comparison, is a gentler, more meaningful work of art, as deliciously sweet and delicate as the *zabaione* you and I are presently savoring."

"Then you believe we were too sweet for the tastes of our opening night audience?" Puccini asked.

"Who can say? We are certainly not too sweet for current audiences. We are filling the theater now every night, Giacomo. Applause is deafening. Curtain calls abound. *La Bohème* will make you wealthy and establish you among the masters of Italian opera. I predict that, and I am rarely wrong in my predictions."

Puccini left *Café Zabaione* fully satisfied. He smiled in the chilling air and hummed Rodolfo's Act I aria *Che gelida manina!* (*What a cold little hand!*) Ricordi had likened *Bohème* to the flavor of *Zabaione*, and to Puccini the comparison was apt and complimentary. He chuckled and shook his original concern from his mind, but when he did, something far more worrisome replaced it. It was the opening of Leoncavallo's *La Bohème*! Another successful *Bohème*, he suddenly feared, might seriously affect his own royalties, and life would once again become a horrible struggle.

As he entered his apartment, Elvira saw uneasiness in the tight set of his mouth.

"What is it?" she asked. "You look distressed again. Did it not go well with Signor Recordi?"

"It went well."

"Then why are you making that terrible face?"

"Am I?"

"I am in no mood for your evasions, Giacomo," she warned. "What happened?"

Wanting to avoid another of her tantrums, Giacomo told Elvira everything that had been said in *Café Zabaione*, ending with Ricordi's radiant estimation of her.

Elvira smiled. "Signor Ricordi is a wise and wonderful man. What he told you should not make you grim." Suddenly, she turned caustic and serious. "But there is more that you are not revealing. What is it?"

It was either silence and anger or revelation and reproach. He chose reproach. He explained his concerns about Leoncavallo and then waited for her rebuke. She didn't disappoint him. "If you had not wasted your time," she said, "if you had applied yourself to your work, instead of fishing and hunting and dallying in your godforsaken *Club La Bohème,* you would have completed your opera a year ago, and Leoncavallo would have been forced to abandon his effort. But no, you preferred to enjoy yourself and risk placing us two steps from poverty again. I cannot face that, Giacomo, I simply cannot!"

"Perhaps you should leave me, Elvira." He couldn't believe he had said that. It had come from him quietly, resignedly.

The suggestion inflamed her. "And where would I go?" she demanded. "Torre del Lago is my home. Perhaps you should leave *me*! This is unendurable, Giacomo. I cannot bear to be near you. I am going home...*now*!"

Elvira stormed from the room. She packed her bag and headed for the door. "If you return when your opera closes," she stopped to throw at him, "we shall find some way to share the house. If you do not return, be certain to provide enough money to save your family from starvation!"

Giacomo hadn't thought of apologizing. He'd only sat silently while she spat censure. But as the door slammed behind Elvira, the poetic truth of a *La Bohème* line flashed in Giacomo Puccini's mind. "*Love, once dead, can never be revived*."

Oddly, Puccini felt no regret, no sense of loss, and he wondered about this. *Why do I feel so buoyant? Why am I not in tears?*

Reality and acceptance had entered his heart. And surprisingly, they brought him an unexpected sense of freedom. He breathed in deeply. He smiled and stretched, but the smile disappeared quickly. "All right," he said aloud, "what do I do now?"

For the next nineteen days, until the end of *La Bohème*'s run at Teatro Regio, Puccini refrained from writing to Elvira. The rapidly growing popularity of the opera took possession of him. He had returned to Turin, where he attended every performance. He marveled at the audiences' fervor. Curtain calls increased in number so quickly they left him breathless. Again, as with the success of *Manon Lescaut*, he was approached and congratulated as he walked the city's streets. He accepted luncheon invitations. He attended receptions in his honor. And he reveled in the recognition and adoration being showered upon him.

Happy with *La Bohème*'s apparent success, Ricordi, Illica, and Giacosa had left Turin after the first week of performances. They would have stayed longer, but other matters required their attention.

Giacomo never missed them.

His worries regarding Leoncavallo's *La Bohème* dimmed to faint concern. The controversy was still being fueled by the press, but he felt his rival's *La Bohème* would never achieve the popularity of his own, especially if it did not première soon. Time proved him correct in this assessment, because Leoncavallo took another fifteen months before he believed his opera was ready. Premièring in Venice on May 5, 1897, it was only fairly received. Reviewers compared it to the Puccini/Illica/Giacosa *La Bohème* and not favorably. Though it had some fine moments, they said, it lacked the grace of Puccini's music, the cohesiveness of Illica's story and the beauty of Giacosa's verse. Leoncavallo's *Bohème* was quickly forgotten. Giacomo wallowed in the wave of *schadenfreude* that washed over him, and he laughed at his opponent's defeat.

When the curtains closed on *La Bohème*'s final performance, it no longer mattered to Puccini why opening night had failed. Taking his final bow, he smiled as if a light were shining behind his eyes. He thought: *Signor Giulio understands the world of opera as no one else: It is as he said, "Damn the reviewers! Audiences make successes, not critics!"*

Giulio Ricordi returned to Turin for *Bohème's* closing night. At a tumultuous cast celebration, he took Puccini aside. He grinned and said, "Now, you are famous, Giacomo. I am happy for you. I think I shall have to call you *Doge* from now on. Like the Doge of Venice, who was the lord of all he surveyed, you are the lord of opera."

Doge, Puccini thought. *I like that.*

"But you must not rest on your laurels," Ricordi continued. "Fame is a ravenous mistress. She will flee if she has to wait another three years to be fed. Find another story quickly, one that fires your passions, and she will be yours forever."

Puccini grinned at his publisher's urging. He asked, "Do we not deserve a respite? A little fishing? Some hunting?"

"Indeed; however, while you keep your eye on your gunsight, you must always have your mind on your music. Go home, enjoy your hunting. Regenerate, but *never* stop searching for that story. I have a request to make of you."

"Anything."

"Someday, I shall have to retire."

Puccini's brows creased at the thought. "Do not say that."

Ricordi smiled. "It is inevitable. The years are advancing, not retreating. But someday – let us hope it does not arrive for many years – my son Tito will have to assume control of Casa Ricordi. In preparation for that eventuality, I should like him to accompany you on some of your travels, to experience the premières of productions. Are you amenable to my request?"

Puccini answered without hesitation. "Of course, Signor Giulio. It is a small thing you ask of me. Tito and I shall have many wonderful days together, I am sure."

Ricordi's smile broadened. "Thank you, Giacomo. Of course, such excursions will be met in full for both of you by the treasury of Casa Ricordi."

In the past, Puccini had paid for most trips to see his operas. Now, he smiled and thanked his publisher profusely.

"Are you in need of money?" Ricordi asked.

"Always," Puccini responded shyly.

"To show my faith in *La Bohème* I shall advance you two thousand lire against royalties I am certain you will earn. Will that be of help to you?"

"Immensely. Thank you, thank you, Signor Giulio."

The very next morning, Giacomo returned home. The distance from Turin to Torre del Lago is only 200 miles. Unexpectedly 2,000 lire richer, he boarded the fastest, most comfortable train. But every inch of the journey tortured him with images of Elvira's angry departure. He saw her ferocity. He heard her vitriol. Thoughts of their living in the same house together made him close his eyes and shudder. He would have to see her daily. Proximity was bound to produce friction. Tirades were sure to follow. *Perhaps*, he thought, *I should find another house somewhere, put distance between us.* But then again – the house was his. It was where he was most comfortable. And there were his children. He loved Fosca and Tonio dearly. Though he didn't see them as often as he liked, they warmed his life and made him eager to return to Torre del Lago each time he was away. The problem tormented him. Miles passed steadily under the train's clacking wheels. Home drew closer, and

Giacomo Puccini grew increasingly uncomfortable with each noisy clack.

"Torre del Lago," the conductor finally announced.

Puccini gathered his belongings and stepped from the carriage's warmth into the snow of a Torre del Lago winter.

He could have sent a telegram, informing Elvira of his decision to return. But after careful consideration, he had chosen not to do that. It would have given her time to prepare another berating he was certain she would throw at him.

Sixteen years of age, Fosca was now becoming a beautiful young woman. Tonio, at ten, was losing his childish softness. When Giacomo approached his house, both were in the front yard laughing at the snowman they were fashioning. Tonio saw his father first. He dropped the handful of snow he was ready to pack on the snowman's round body. "Papa!" he shouted happily, running into Puccini's open arms.

Equally joyous, Fosca greeted him with a warm, but mature, embrace. "It is so good to have you home again, Papa!" she said.

Giacomo's soul expanded. He hugged them. He allowed the happiness of their reunion to fill his heart. Then when all three had fully expressed their joy, he cleared his throat and asked, "Where is your mother?"

"Inside," Fosca offered. "She will be happy to see you."

Puccini doubted that, but he disengaged himself from their embraces. ""I want to speak with your mother," he told them. "Join us when you finish your snowman."

"All right," Fosca agreed.

He advanced toward the house. His heart pounded.

Standing at a window and watching Fosca and Tonio playing in the snow, Elvira felt her own heart pound when Giacomo appeared on the scene. She pulled away from the window to catch her breath and plan the words she would use when he entered the house. Once she was in control of herself again, she straightened her dress, smoothed her hair, bit her bottom lip, and stood five feet from the door, waiting for it to be opened.

Giacomo entered his house uncertainly. Seeing Elvira, her arms straight and hands clasped, her face expressionless, he sensed a major battle was about to take place. *All right*, he told himself, *better now than later*. He put his bag on the floor. He straightened and looked directly at Elvira. However, her steady gaze flustered him. He coughed. He looked away. He bent to retrieve his bag, and while he did, he managed to grumble, "I am home, Elvira."

"And I am happy you decided not to abandon us," Elvira responded. Her voice was flat, unemotional.

Was she welcoming him? He straightened. He walked three steps toward her. "And I am staying," he said gruffly, as if it were a challenge.

Elvira suddenly smiled. "Good. I have been hoping you would say that."

Giacomo stared at her, unable to move.

"Come," she said, still smiling, "you must be tired from your trip."

The front door flew open. Fosca and Tonio burst into the room.

"Fosca, take Papa's bag to his room, while I make him something to eat, will you, please?"

"Yes, Mama." Fosca grabbed Giacomo's bag and disappeared, with Tonio laughing and trailing behind.

Elvira turned again to Giacomo, who stood as if he'd been turned to stone. "You must relax," she said, "while I prepare a little something for you to eat. And then you must tell me everything about *La Bohème*'s great success."

"It was poorly received while you were in Turin," he said. "How do you know it became a great success?"

Her smile widened. "Signor Ricordi sent me a telegram. I told you: He is a wise and wonderful man." Then she took Puccini by an elbow and guided him toward the living room. Dazed, he settled onto his favorite chair, where he was told to remain until his repast was ready.

At the dining room table, Giacomo nibbled on the snack she had prepared. Elvira did most of the talking. She offered trivialities about the children, the weather, shopping, and one of his friends, who had visited wanting to know when he would be home. Her demeanor confused Puccini. Elvira behaved as if nothing upsetting had occurred between them, as if no ultimatum had been hurled at him. He responded to her tidbits of information with small sounds of surprise or interest, but all the while he wondered what was truly on her mind.

He didn't have to wait long for that to be revealed. They faced each other from opposite sides of the table. She leaned forward, crossed her arms on the soft table cover and watched silently as he placed the last morsel of food into his mouth. Then the moment he washed the food down with the last drops of Chianti in his wine glass, Elvira pounced.

"I hope you found that satisfying," she said. She was no longer smiling.

"Very. I thank you."

"That pleases me. I want you to feel free to tell me when something does not satisfy you." She waited for a reply.

Giacomo squirmed. He felt he was being manipulated.

"Well?" she asked when the silence had lasted long enough.

Her question deepened his confusion. "Well, what?"

"Will you let me know when something does not satisfy you?"

"Yes...yes, of course, if that is what you want."

"That is what I want. I believe it will be essential. We must be truthful with each other, Giacomo, if we are to share this house. You will tell me what satisfies you, and I shall tell you what satisfies me. Agreed?"

Where is she going with this?

"Do you agree?" she repeated, her tone stiffening when he failed to respond.

"Yes...yes, I agree."

"All right, I shall start. First, you will satisfy me, Giacomo, by demonstrating some appreciation for what I am doing to provide you with a comfortable home. Next, I shall be a more congenial mate when you prefer your family's company to that of your friends.

Next, everyone will be happier – and that includes Signor Ricordi, who has given you every opportunity to prove yourself – if you devote yourself more industriously to the work for which you were born than to the meaningless pleasures that seem to dominate your thoughts and interests."

She stopped. She watched him. She waited. She hadn't spoken viciously, but she had established her rules for cohabitation with an insistence that made him think.

Puccini nodded his head slowly. He ran a thumb and forefinger across his mustache and around his mouth. A faint smile pulled at his lips. "Apparently," he said, "you have given much thought to this, Elvira."

"I have."

"Is there anything else you should like to add?"

"There will be more, but that is sufficient for now."

"Very well, now it is my turn."

Suddenly, Puccini felt more confident. She had expressed her desire for a fair exchange of needs. Very well, he would comply. He was certain there would be tension. But if he approached this properly, this moment could lead to a more tranquil home environment, something for which he had always desperately longed. *Is it possible? Or is she setting another of her devious traps?* He didn't know. But trap or honest invitation, he would have to proceed with his own articles of behavior and see where they would take him. *Just be careful, Giacomo,* he told himself. *Just be careful.*

"I do not ask much, Elvira," he started. "I respect all that you have said, and I shall do everything in my power to honor your needs. I give you my word on that."

Her eyes widened.

"My own needs are very limited," he continued. "First, I need you to be more patient with me. Verdi and others may draw their music from the ether. I cannot do that. I need inspiration. I cannot define inspiration, what it is or how it works, but without it, I find myself in quicksand. Notes will appear on the page, but they are not from my soul, and only music from my soul is worth the enormous effort that goes into composing. I should like you to understand that, Elvira, and understanding it, to be more patient with me."

He had expressed himself gently, almost as a plea. He stopped and waited for a reply. Nothing came. She watched him blankly, as if she were measuring a response. A full thirty seconds of this silence passed before Elvira inhaled deeply and said, "Please continue." Just two words, but the way they were uttered suggested the fury he'd anticipated earlier. For one moment, Puccini believed it would be fruitless to continue. But the next moment, moved by a sudden flush of fearlessness, he plunged ahead. If she could not be reached with earnestness, so be it. Nothing would be lost in a more direct approach.

"Next," he said, "I should like you to accept my recreations without judgment. Fishing and fowl hunting have been part of my life since they were introduced to me many years ago by my first music teacher, Carlo Angeloni. I love them. They are important to me. Important experiences contain memories, and good memories should never be erased. This is true for my other means of relaxation, as well. I am a man, and periodically men need the company of other men. Women may not appreciate our drinking and raucous behavior, but such indulgences are an occasional necessity. I should like you to be different from these intolerant women, women who deride their men for being men, and to appreciate this reality."

He blinked once very slowly to indicate he'd had his say. Now it was her turn again. *Let it come,* he thought. *I am ready for her bile. I am only sorry the children will have to hear our final wrangle, for after we have said everything I shall leave this woman and never never return.*

Elvira had held her chin in solemn thought as she listened to him. When he was through, she leveled her gaze and asked, "Is there anything else you should like to add?"

He recognized the words. They formed the same question he had asked. Was this a game? If so, he would play this game with her. He shook his head slowly. Using her exact words, he replied, "There will be more, but that is sufficient for now."

Elvira Gemignani was no fool. She understood immediately what he was doing. Her expression hardened. "I have described conditions that should allow us to share this house," she said with an ominous edge to her voice. "You agreed, saying you respect them. Then you counter and ignore them."

"That is not accurate," he replied. "I am merely asking that you respect my terms as you wish me to respect yours." Giacomo could feel his throat tighten again. He waited, preparing himself for the vituperation that customarily followed any opposition to Elvira's wishes.

Elvira surprised him once again.

"I am not like other women," she said. "I respect your masculine needs. If you wish to engage in your male activities, I can be more sympathetic and accepting of them. I ask only that you do not use them to avoid me or your responsibilities with Tonio and Fosca."

Giacomo blinked his surprise. "You want me to be at home more often?" he said.

"Is that too much to ask?"

"Not at all. I love this house. I love being here. I can easily restrict some activities that take me from it."

She smiled. "That will please me."

His expression changed. It became noticeably grave. His voice dropped an octave. "It will be easier, also, if you allow me to work without the added pressure of your expectations."

"I wish only for your continued success." The edge had returned.

"I know," he answered. "But I have Signor Giulio to guide me on that path."

She studied him. "Very well," she said after a few moments. "I shall try to curb my criticisms, but I must demand one more thing of you."

"What is that?"

Elvira became more serious than Giacomo had ever before witnessed. Her gaze held firm. But her voice veered into a warning. "You must never – and I stress the word never – you must *never* do anything that will bring shame upon me or make me look the fool. Can you agree to that?"

He matched her sharpness. "With no difficulty at all."

Elvira sat back on her chair. She sighed. Her stern expression melted into a smile. "Good!" she said and slapped the edge of the table once with both hands.

That brought a grin to Giacomo's face. He sighed so loudly it sounded comical in the aftermath of the thick tension that had filled the room. It caused both of them to chuckle in relief. An unanticipated compromise had been reached.

Life in Torre del Lago settled into a comfortable routine. Giacomo made a serious effort to adhere to the terms of their agreement. He continued to hunt with friends, and he continued his relaxed and bawdy behavior with them at *Club La Bohème*. However, he did curb the frequency with which he'd formerly engaged in these activities. Instead, he went with Tonio to Lucca to visit Ramelde and his other sisters. He celebrated birthdays and holidays. He wrote numerous letters, especially to Giulio Ricordi, reassuring his publisher constantly that his mind was still on music. He stayed home where, in grungy clothes with an ever-present cigarette in his mouth, he sat at the kitchen table and played cards with Elvira, Fosca and Tonio. And he read extensively, searching for that singular story, the one that would fire his passions and lead him to his next operatic undertaking.

One day, re-reading a drama by French playwright Victorien Sardou, he decided suddenly that *La Tosca* should be it. He hurried to Milan to tell Ricordi, "I considered it when I first read the play, but now, after reading it again, I am certain it should be an opera, one perfectly suit the magnificent imagination and genius of Illica and Giacosa!"

Ricordi couldn't have been happier. Nothing pleased him more than to see his favorite composer ready and willing to work. "This is excellent!" he said. "I shall have to read Sardou's drama."

"It is sure to excite you as much as it excites me," Puccini gushed.

"Briefly, please, tell me its story."

Puccini needed no further prompting. "There are three main characters," he began, leaning forward. "The soprano is a beautiful and famous opera singer – she is Floria Tosca. Her tenor lover, Mario Cavaradossi, is an artist. And Baron Vitellio Scarpia, Rome's Regent of Police, is the baritone villain. Scarpia falls so desperately in love with Tosca's voice he believes he must possess the woman. However, Cavaradossi is in his way. He hounds Tosca's lover and imprisons him on false charges that sentence him to death. Tosca pleads for his life, and Scarpia tells her he will release Cavaradossi if she will surrender to him. To save the man she loves, Tosca gives herself to Scarpia. However, Scarpia has lied. The next morning, Tosca discovers Cavaradossi is dead, killed by the Police Regent's firing squad. Tricked, humiliated, and grief-stricken by the loss of her true love, Tosca murders Scarpia and then leaps from the Regent's castle wall to her own death."

Nodding slowly, his eyes squinting in thought, Giulio Ricordi said. "It is a lurid tale, but, yes...as you, I can see its theatrical possibilities."

"It is a wonderful story," Puccini gushed. "It has decorative spectacle that suggests ample opportunity for musical expression. I urge you to obtain permission from the playwright. The great French actress Sarah Bernhardt is to perform the Tosca role soon. Elvira and I shall go to Paris to see her do it."

Ricordi assured Puccini he would investigate the availability of *La Tosca* immediately and encouraged him to see the play in Paris without delay. "Take Tito with you. I should like his opinion as well. All expenses will, of course, be met by Casa Ricordi."

This was an unexpected windfall. Puccini agreed readily. "I feel certain," he said, "that Tito will agree with me, and *Tosca* will become our next venture."

"I may encounter some difficulty in obtaining opera permission," Ricordi said. "I know *Tosca* has already been given to composer Alberto Franchetti. He is sure to become irate at any suggestion to relinquish his right to you. But do not fear, my dear Doge, for I shall never allow a little matter like professional pique to thwart what is clearly your carefully considered decision. Oh, Doge, Doge, it is so good to see you eager to thrill the world again with the resplendence of your musical genius!"

Ricordi had not misjudged Alberto Franchetti, who had just begun his composition of a libretto. He resisted Ricordi's request. However, when Giacosa expressed his willingness to join Illica and Puccini, Franchetti's resistance crumbled before the collective power of Ricordi and the *La Bohème* team.

"I promised *Tosca* would be yours, my dear Doge," Ricordi told Puccini gleefully. "It is now as I have promised. Illica and Giacosa will have the first act ready for you soon. Until then, continue to enjoy your respite. Go to Paris. Take your Elvira and Tito. See Sarah Bernhardt's *Tosca,* and come back to us with godlike music filling your head."

Giacomo Puccini seemed to be living on a cloud, above dissension, removed from reality. All through 1897 and 1898, occasionally accompanied by Tito Ricordi, he visited one city after another to see or to participate in *Manon* and *Bohème* premières. Berlin. London. Paris. Buenos Aires. Vienna. Even the medieval coastal city of Livorno, which is only twenty-three miles from Torre del Lago. Some productions satisfied him; others generated scorn. In time he grew tired of travel and wanted only to remain at home. However, in June of 1899, while in Torre del Lago, Puccini had another of his fortuitous encounters.

He'd already met and become friends with young, gifted Arturo Toscanini. Now another young man entered his life to stun him with gifted talent. Appearing at Torre del Lago unannounced, the intruder declared his desire to sing the role of Rodolfo in the upcoming Livorno production of *Bohème*. His visitor's audacity amused Puccini. He invited him into the house and, after a few words, accompanied him in an impromptu audition of Rodolfo's Act I aria *Che gelida manina*. Puccini's eyes widened in disbelief as the aria progressed. And when the tenor's fearless and clear high C faded to silence, Puccini was so moved by what he'd heard, he looked at the intruder and whispered, "Who sent you to me? God?"

That young man was Enrico Caruso, who won the role of Rodolfo and went on to become Puccini's friend and one of the greatest tenors in the entire history of opera.

Indeed, life had become extraordinarily comfortable for Puccini, and Elvira was content with how he was honoring their truce. She still conducted herself imperiously, but she smiled more, the gruffness in her speech vanished, and she requested assistance more often than she commanded it. The 2,000 lire advance that Ricordi had given Giacomo pleased her enormously. It confirmed her opening night estimation of *La Bohème*'s merit.

Royalty income increased and came from every city on the Italian peninsula that could boast an opera theater. But of all the productions that were bringing Giacomo Puccini wealth and fame, two in particular lifted him to heavenly heights. They occurred in the distant opera-loving city of Palermo and in the nearby Puccini-loving city of Lucca.

In Palermo, the Sicilian premiere night audience terrified *La Boheme*'s conductor. Prolonged foot-stamping and catcalls erupted when the curtain failed to open on time. Intensifying with each passing minute, the audience's frenzy continued for a full half-hour. Restlessness was turning into anger, and anger was threatening a successful opening night. But that changed swiftly when the curtains finally parted and Puccini's music filled the auditorium. A stillness of unparalleled attention settled over the house. It wasn't simple silence; it was rapture. And when Mimi and Rodolfo sang their first arias, the silence exploded in a burst of joy so profound it shook the theater's rafters. Curtain call after curtain call prevented a continuation of the action. The first aria and all arias thereafter had to be repeated. The audience could not be satisfied. It was a madness of cheers and endless curtain calls that extended the performance a full hour beyond its normal length! And after Mimi's heartbreaking death, the Palermo audience was so deeply moved it would not leave the theater. *More! More!* It called for more! So intense was this reaction that cast members were brought back to the stage in their street clothes. Half the orchestra had gone home, but conductor Leopoldo Mugnone felt compelled to repeat the entire last scene with the soprano and tenor appearing as ordinary singers and not as Mimi and Rodolfo.

It made no difference. The music… the music… it was Puccini who had filled their hearts and souls not the wigs, costumes, or stage make-up. Giacomo Puccini, the Doge of Opera…honored now in Palermo with another ovation that would live forever in the legends of theatrical receptions.

Only the Lucca production of *La Bohème* would bring Puccini greater happiness. Word came from Giulio Ricordi: Lucca's authorities intended to conduct a two-day Puccini Festival in honor of their Favorite Son. The celebration would end with a lavish production of his brilliant new opera. Would the publisher please convey to Maestro Puccini their devout wish that he would attend the festivities and be their distinguished Guest of Honor?

Giacomo smiled when he received Ricordi's letter. At one time, the Lucca city council had refused him a grant to continue his Conservatorio studies. Now he was a Favorite Son? He laughed, remembering something his friend Fontana had told him after the success of their *Le Villi*. They had just escaped a throng of enthusiastic well-wishers. "Someday," Ferdi had predicted, "you will be celebrated far beyond this minor distraction, and you will be forgiven all sins. When that happens, think of celebrity as a magnet. Everyone will be drawn to you. Everyone will want to speak with you, to touch you, to know you. It can become quite oppressive but, then again…" Fontana had looked slyly at Puccini, "beautiful women will also be part of that 'everyone,' and beautiful women are never oppressive, Giaco – only perilously desirable."

Later, the great success of *Manon Lescaut* proved the truth of Fontana's words. People did badger him, and they did become oppressive. But beautiful women also appeared everywhere, willing lovers for discreet evenings of secret pleasure. Alone and away from home, Puccini invited them often into his hotel room and found most of them far more agreeable than bothersome. Now, Giacomo Puccini had been transformed into a prodigious magnet with an entire city begging for his presence. *A two-day Puccini Festival*. His smile broadened. Why not? Yes, he would like that. It would be a triumphant return to the city that had turned against him. After reading Ricordi's letter to the family at the dinner table, he asked Elvira, "Would you care to accompany me?"

"Not at all," she replied. She frowned and shook her head as though something foul had been forced into her mind. "Lucca spurned me; therefore, I shall forever spurn Lucca."

"I should like to go with you, Papa!" Fosca piped up eagerly.

"I want to go to Lucca, too!" Tonio added.

Giacomo glanced at Elvira. "What do you say?"

"When is the festival?"

"In June."

Elvira faced Fosca and Tonio. "I am sorry. You will still be in school."

They groaned and sank on their chairs.

"It will be on a Saturday and Sunday," Giacomo offered quickly, winking at Fosca. "They will miss only Monday."

"Please, Mama, *please*."

Elvira looked at Giacomo. The prospect of having an entire weekend entirely to herself was much too enticing to ignore. "If you will not mind the responsibility...."

"Ramelde will enjoy watching Tonio, and I shall enjoy introducing Fosca to all of my Lucca friends and family."

"If it is what you wish, then I shall not object."

Fosca's and Tonio's happy shrieks could have been heard in Lucca.

Two months later, the Puccini Festival became an experience so profound it left a memory in Puccini, Fosca, and Tonio that remained detail sharp through the rest of their lives. Family and friends welcomed the three Torre del Lagoans. Their love was outstripped only by the city's proud recognition of its honored composer. Parades wound their way through Lucca streets for hours. Music and cheers filled the air. Colorful decorations adorned buildings. Vendors hawked memorabilia and delicious foods. Musicians stood on street corners and in piazzas, playing and singing Puccini arias. Puppets performed scenes from *Le Villi* and *Manon Lescaut*. Speakers praised Puccini as if he were a god come to Earth. And the Sunday première performance of *La Bohème,* in the newly renovated Teatro Comunale del Giglio, brought cheers, curtain calls and cries of *Bravo! Bravissimo!* that rivaled those of Palermo.

The celebrants returned to Torre del Lago like victorious soldiers who had just been knighted by Italy's king and queen.

"Did you enjoy yourselves?" Elvira asked.

"There were puppets, Mama, and they were singing, and everyone was singing with them!" Tonio said breathlessly. "Fosca did not like them as much as I."

Elvira looked at Fosca. "Why did you not like the puppets?"

"I liked them, Mama," Fosca explained, her eyes shining with happiness. "I liked everything about the festival. But Papa's opera... oh, Mama, it was so beautiful I cried for hours when it ended!"

"She especially loved the tenor," Giacomo said with a teasing smile.

"Who was he?" Elvira asked.

"He is new to me. However, I believe he was a perfect Rodolfo. About twenty-three, handsome, sensitive –"

"With the voice of an angel, Mama. He made me shiver. His name is Salvatore Leonardi. I shall never forget him!"

"She almost swooned when I introduced her and he kissed her hand."

"Ohhh, Papa...."

Giacomo suppressed his laughter.

"Well," Elvira said, "It pleases me that you enjoyed yourselves."

"And you, Elvira," Giacomo asked, "did you enjoy yourself while we were away?"

"Not really."

"What did you do?"

"I visited my sister. She is a sad woman. I should have stayed here."

Giacomo had expected an unhappy answer. It didn't distress him. Their truce had ended the marital war that twisted their lives.

Except for a moment when he was about to turn forty and he felt age settling upon him, Puccini believed his life was complete.

And in truth, from 1897 through 1899, he was a fulfilled man. He went everywhere he wanted to go and did everything he wanted to do without condemnation from Elvira. Totally relaxed, he began work in earnest on Act I of *Tosca* immediately upon receiving it from Ricordi "It will be easier to complete than *La Bohème,*" he told him. "Unlike Mürger's mélange of scenes for *Bohème*, Sardou's *Tosca* already has a fully developed tale. I am excited by it. *Tosca* has everything an opera requires for strong audience approval."

Ricordi could not have been happier.

However, *Tosca* did not progress as smoothly as Ricordi had hoped. Almost immediately, Puccini reverted to form, causing Illica to storm once more: "No! I will not continue with that man! He picks and cavils at words, phrases, sentences, *everything*. *Tosca* may ultimately find its way to the stage, but I shall never be its librettist!"

Calmly, carefully, Giulio Ricordi countered each of Illica's objections. And slowly, inch by inch, everything Ricordi offered weakened the librettist's position. Finally, Ricordi concluded, "I am sure, dear Illica, you will agree that it would be folly to discard everything you have achieved when even greater success is within your reach."

Grudgingly, Illica relented and work progressed on *Tosca*, but slowly – exceedingly slowly. The reason? Puccini's propensity for diversion pulled him easily from his piano and led him into lengthy periods of indolence and pleasure.

Illica and Giacosa took their concerns to Giulio Ricordi. "There is something going on," Illica said. "He has had the first two acts for months now and we have not received a single note of music!"

"Is he ill?" Giacosa asked. "Have you heard from him?

Ricordi frowned. "I know nothing more than you. I have written to him, and he has promised to give us *Tosca* when he feels it worthy to be heard."

"He is dallying again," Illica grumbled. "I can feel it. I know the man. I have said it before, I say it again: He will look for any opportunity to avoid work."

"What shall I do?" Giacosa asked. "Shall I continue with Act Three?"

"Yes, by all means, Giuseppe," Ricordi answered quickly. "Do not let this delay discourage you."

"He is tormenting us. I could be writing my own—"

"I know...I know," Ricordi cut him short. "Please, gentlemen, *Tosca* is too important for us to contemplate anything but its completion. We have formed a perfect team. We must not quarrel or quibble over creative idiosyncrasies. I shall goad him."

Prodded constantly by Ricordi, Puccini managed to complete the music for *Tosca* on September 29, 1899, *one-and-a-half years after he had begun his first passages!* He was proud of his accomplishment. He believed his music was ideally suited to the story, a perfect enhancement of his librettists' words.

Unfortunately, his publisher did not see the work as he did. To Giulio Ricordi, Puccini had created an abomination. He was so distressed he kept the music from Illica and Giacosa and wrote a lengthy letter to Puccini, in which he called *Tosca* *"a serious error in conception and execution with only fragmentary and modest melody. Production in its present form will not only be disastrous to the financial well-being of my company, but ruinous as well to your good name and artistic stature."*

Puccini was crushed. He couldn't believe what he was reading. The following day, calmly and as composed as he could be, he wrote an equally strong letter to Ricordi, explaining in great detail where and how the publisher had failed to see the opera clearly. He refused to surrender to Ricordi's analysis. *"If you look at it again,"* he concluded, *"I am certain you will change your opinion."*

Their disagreements continued heatedly for two months. Minor changes did take place. But, in the main, *Tosca* remained as Puccini intended it to be. Now only a production could prove who was right, adamant composer or worried publisher. Ricordi surrendered and a date for *Tosca*'s opening was set.

January 14, 1900.... 8:00 PM.... The Teatro Costanzi in Rome.

The city had been wracked by riots for days. A summer draught had made wheat scarce, and a new tax on what was available made tempers flare. Violence raged in the streets. Anarchists were also on a rampage bombing government buildings, attempting to assassinate high officials. Fear had a tight grip on the city. Nevertheless, there could not have been a more illustrious audience flooding into Teatro Costanzi that evening.

Queen Margherita was there, though an earlier engagement had forced her to miss Act I. The Prime Minister and his cabinet ministers were among the first to arrive. High members of the Catholic Church entered regally in their clerical robes. Noted musicians, the culturally elite, and correspondents came from all over Italy. No seat in this enormous 2,212 seat theater was empty. Everyone wanted to hear what Giacomo Puccini's labors had produced this time.

Conductor Mugnone's heart pounded when the police arrived to announce a bomb threat, which proved to be false. Then his hands shook when a commotion of latecomers in the house made him think the threat was real. Cast members felt their throats tighten. No one was comfortable waiting for the curtains to part.

Giacomo Puccini was, as usual, among the most fearful. Aside from the very real danger of violence and a warning from a gang of unsympathetic, rival musicians that the performance was to be disrupted, he had another good reason to be afraid. He had reached a level of success that invited disparagement. He had learned how fame works: First there is discovery, encouragement, a strong desire to see the fledgling fly. Then, once the bird is airborne and gliding gracefully in a friendly sky, there is the irresistible need to shoot it down. The audience at the *Tosca* première was filled with opera lovers carrying powerful critical guns.

And they used them.

Puccini could feel the weight of their skepticism that night. He could hear the screech of restlessness. Why were they talking when they should be silent and attentive? He felt the ache of failure throbbing in his body again. He bit his lips. *It will become better,* he told himself. *It must become better.* The acts continued, but despite his desperate wishes the audience remained stunningly unresponsive. There were a few encores and some curtain calls. They were tepid at best. He couldn't understand what had happened. He had been so certain of his music. How could he have been wrong? He thrashed in torment. Now he could only hope the morning newspapers would offer reviews that understood *Tosca* as he did.

They didn't.

One critic branded *Tosca* "*a shabby little shocker,*" and Puccini's music "*second rate stuff,*" adding his belief that the composer had abandoned talent for pretentiousness. Other reviewers complained about the story, saying it overwhelmed the music and that, unlike *La Bohème* which was rich in character, *Tosca* had too much nervous action, too many sensational events, making it more melodrama than true opera.

A few reviewers found some merit in Puccini's score, praising his imagination, identifying particular passages to prove their points. But, in general, *Tosca* had failed to offer them the grandeur they'd hoped to experience from the soul of a maestro who had charmed them so thoroughly in the past.

A shattered Giacomo wrote to Elvira. "*I cannot comprehend what happened. I am certain of my music. I know it to be good.* Tosca*'s weaknesses, therefore, must lie in its libretto! I should have been more uncompromising in my suggestions! I am devastated. There is nothing more I can do. I shall return home after I have spoken with Signor Giulio.*"

If he hoped for consolation, Puccini didn't get it from Ricordi. "Give up this self-pity," the publisher said firmly. "You are an artist. You suffer because your skin is as thin as tissue paper!"

Then Giulio Ricordi demonstrated his keen knowledge of the opera stage once again. Despite his reservations, despite the negative critical reviews, he shaped a promotion campaign that sent ticket sales skyrocketing. Less pretentious than première patrons, new audiences responded quite differently. They loved *Tosca*. Cheers and curtain calls abounded. Word spread. After only three uncertain evenings, Teatro Costanzi filled completely. Giulio Ricordi extended the run to twenty performances. And the House of Ricordi began to receive requests for production rights even before Puccini left Rome for his return to Torre del Lago.

Smiling as he said goodbye to his protégé, Giulio Ricordi intoned, "A lesson learned, my Doge, must never be forgotten. The lesson *I* have learned is never to doubt my Doge's creative instincts. If ticket sales are the measurement of success, apparently you were right about *Tosca*, and I was wrong."

Puccini beamed. This man was the father he never had. "Thank you, Papa Giulio," he said, extending a hand. "Thank you for restoring my confidence."

Ricordi grasped Giacomo's hand and laughed. "Now think of our next opera, yes?"

"That is what you always say."

"And that is what I shall continue to say until I am no longer able to say it."

Puccini arrived home with his spirit flying as if it wore the wings of Mercury. He was ready to relax with his family. And he did. He slept late. He read. He hunted. He puttered contentedly around the house. He even began an enlargement of the family's simple house into a grand villa. However, though he was extremely happy, he knew he would have to supply his publisher with suggestions for their next project. Strangely and fortuitously, work and pleasure merged for him on a visit to London.

He made the journey with Elvira in July of 1900 to see a production of *Tosca* at Covent Garden, England's international Royal Opera House. He and Elvira were wined and dined by society and lionized by an esteemed group of London opera lovers. England won their hearts. Wanting to experience more of London culture before returning to Torre del Lago, they accepted the theater manager's suggestion and went to see a play being presented by the famed

American impresario and director David Belasco. Though it was in English and he understood little of what was being said, Puccini was struck by the charm and intensity of the drama. "This may be what I am searching for," he whispered to Elvira as the action unfolded, and by the end of the tragedy he was certain he had found it.

Through the latter part of the 19th and into the 20th century, Japanese traditions could be found in all artistic forms of Western expression. It was called *Japonisme*, and painters like Van Gogh, Lautrec, Degas, Manet were quick to incorporate it in their individual developments of Impressionism. On the stage, Gilbert and Sullivan presented *Japonisme* in their triumphant *Mikado*, and David Belasco offered it in his equally successful *Madame Butterfly.*

It was *Madame Butterfly* that took Puccini's breath away that evening. He could not forget the sadness of Butterfly's love and death. Upon returning to Torre del Lago, he wrote and rhapsodized to Ricordi. *"It is beautiful theater, exotic, tender and touching. It has pathos, anger, and a tragic element that lives in the heart. I urge you to contact its American author and director David Belasco to explore the possibility of obtaining the drama's production rights for me."*

"I shall look into this at once," Ricordi responded immediately by telegram.

Ricordi obtained a copy of the play, and liking the drama he began negotiations immediately with David Belasco. The foremost impresario in American theater, Belasco was not an easy man to deal with. It took many months but finally Puccini received a letter from Ricordi telling him: *"Madame Butterfly is now yours, my Doge! I shall speak to Illica and Giacosa about its libretto. I am sure you will have the first acts in your hands shortly."*

Puccini clapped his hands excitedly. "I cannot express how eager I am to begin work on this opera," he told Elvira at the dinner table.

She shared his happiness with a warm smile.

Yes, 1900 was on its way to becoming a good year for the Puccinis – especially for daughter Fosca.

In 1900, Fosca was twenty years old and still living at home with her parents. Darkly attractive and electrifyingly vivacious, she had a number of suitors none of whom struck a spark of love in her heart.

Elvira was worried. “She will surely be a withered spinster,” she told Giacomo. “No man interests her. She prefers to be with us, she tells me, than to suffer the fatuous boasting of men her age.”

“She will meet someone, Elvira,” Giacomo said. “Personally, I do not look forward to the day she will leave us.”

“Of course. You love the way she dotes on you. You would have her live with us forever.”

“If it is what she desires.”

“Then we shall never have a grandchild. Is that what you would like?”

“This is a foolish conversation. I shall have no more of it.”

Closing the book he’d been reading when Elvira introduced the subject, Giacomo rose from his chair and promptly left the room.

Fosca’s reluctance to marry continued to nettle her mother. Elvira worried about her and badgered her with threats of spinsterhood. Dissension developed. Fosca threatened to run away and never see her mother again. But one day, a visitor appeared unannounced at the Puccini home in Torre del Lago, and everything changed.

When she opened the door at the sound of its rapper, Fosca felt her breath catch and her heart begin to race.

“Signorina Fosca?” he asked.

“Yes.”

“I doubt if you will remember me, but we met at the production of *La Bohème* in Lucca.”

“I remember, Signor Leonardi. You sang Rodolfo.”

His smile broadened. “You remember? I am honored and surprised. I was not very good.”

Her smile broadened. “I thought you were marvelous.”

“Thank you, Signorina. Is the Maestro at home?”

“Yes...yes...come in...come in. I shall tell him you are here.”

Salvatore Leonardi had appeared surprisingly to ask Puccini if he would be kind enough to audition him for Lucca’s planned production of *Tosca*. "I know I am being audacious in appearing this way without invitation, Maestro," he said with an ingratiating smile. "But I have read how the tactic worked well for Enrico Caruso, and I am hoping it will work as well for me."

"Listen to him, Papa," Fosca urged excitedly. "We loved him in *Bohème*, remember? That alone should warrant your interest."

"Yes, Papa, let us hear him," Tonio agreed.

"Please," Fosca entreated.

Both Giacomo and Elvira smiled at Fosca's fervor.

After a light repast, during which Elvira questioned Leonardi about his background and aspirations, everyone moved to the sitting room. There Giacomo sat at the piano and accompanied the young man in *E lucevan le stelle*, the difficult aria of Tosca's lover. It was evident immediately that the vocal demands of the character were far beyond the limited range of their guest.

And Leonardi recognized that, too. "I apologize for my boldness," he said sheepishly when the aria ended. "I see I am not yet ready for *Tosca*."

The gentle sincerity of his apology charmed the entire Puccini family, especially the daughter. Salvatore Leonardi may not have been ready for *Tosca*, but Fosca was clearly ready for him. After he thanked everyone for the graciousness with which he had been received, she invited him to visit whenever he would be in Torre del Lago and to write to her when he was not.

Elvira quickly endorsed the invitation.

And thus began a steamy romance that would lead Fosca quickly to marriage.

Giacomo and Elvira discussed Fosca's love often during Salvatore's courtship of their daughter. "I do not know if he is the right man for her," Puccini worried. "He is a tenor...and not a great one. Engagements will be few and far between."

"You say that only because you do not want to lose her," Elvira said. "We are becoming wealthy. We shan't let them starve."

"That is not what I fear. A man must have a path to self-sufficiency for the sake of pride."

"As you did, he will find his way. Giacomo, this must not be discouraged!"

Puccini accepted the inevitable. When Salvatore Leonardi nervously asked him for Fosca's hand in marriage, an elbow jab from Elvira ended his seconds of hesitancy. He smiled and welcomed Leonardi into the Puccini family.

The wedding took place three months later in Torre del Lago. Giacomo objected to its suddenness. "Do you think she is pregnant?" he asked Elvira.

"It makes no difference," she replied. "If she is pregnant, the wedding is necessary now. If she is not, it is best to have it before she becomes pregnant. I do not want her experiencing what I have had to endure."

It was a grand affair in early June of 1901. Celebrants came from distant cities, all prepared to enjoy themselves in the Maestro's home. There was abundant food, and oceans of wine, lively music and wild dancing.

Elvira smiled more that afternoon than she had ever smiled in her lifetime.

But Giacomo's eyes teared at the close of festivities when the happy, newly married couple said their goodbyes and then left for Milan and a life that would soon make Giacomo and Elvira loving grandparents.

It had all started with Salvatore Leonardi's surprise appearance in Torre del Lago, but 1900 also became the year when Giacomo Puccini's life was upended by another unexpected meeting.

Sitting comfortably in their living room one evening, Puccini took a deep breath and announced to Elvira, "While I wait for Signor Giulio to send me Giacosa's versifications, I believe I shall find some innocent form of entertainment to pass the time of day."

"What do you have in mind?" she asked.

"Nothing at this time, but it will come to me."

Regrettably, in March of 1900, it did come to him, but it was definitely not an innocent form of entertainment to pass the time of day.

- 28 -

Looking down at him, she introduced herself on a train going to Turin. "Maestro Puccini?" Her voice was soft and warm.

He looked up from the newspaper he was holding.

"I am sorry to interrupt your reading, Maestro, but I simply have to tell you how much I loved *La Bohème* when I saw it at Teatro Regio."

His curiosity was stirred immediately. Not by her love of *La Bohème,* though that made him smile, but by her eyes. They were wide, unusually bright green, and they looked at him with unguarded friendliness and interest. "Thank you for your kind words," he said. "It is always pleasant to know my work has affected someone so positively."

"I must conclude, then," she replied, "that you live an extremely pleasant life, for I was not the only member of the audience that night who was deeply moved by your music."

He liked the response. It had come quickly and with a hint of wit that made her instantly appealing.

"Yes, audiences have been as kind as you."

She had smooth, unblemished skin, a pert, little nose, high cheekbones, a delicate forehead with cleanly arched brows, black hair carefully bunned at the nape of her neck, and a perky pancake hat sitting on the top of her head. Her lips were full and inviting, showing perfectly aligned white teeth in the gleam of an enchanting smile.

It was impossible for him not to be charmed. He folded his newspaper and placed it on his lap. "Would you care to join me?" he asked.

Her green eyes flashed. Her voice lilted musically. "Nothing would please me more." She sat quickly on the opposite seat and straightened her stylish dress. Then, looking directly into his eyes, she said, "I am excited, Maestro. I never anticipated this good fortune."

He heard more musical notes.

She was no giddy child. She spoke calmly and appeared to be genuinely honored.

He guessed her age to be around twenty-four. *Spirited,* he thought. *And utterly captivating.* "Now that we are no longer strangers," he said lightly, "what would you care to talk about?"

"*La Bohème?*" she shot back quickly."

He grinned. "Of course. What would you like to know about it?"

"I have a theory about art." Her expression became serious.

"And what would that be?"

"I believe great art can come only from great pain. *La Bohème* is great art, Maestro Puccini, oh so very great! I should love to know something about the pain that produced it."

Giacomo Puccini went speechless. He stared at her as if he couldn't believe what she'd just said.

"Oh, my...oh, my...I hope I have not offended you, Maestro. That was surely not my intent."

Puccini shook his head. "No, no...you have not offended me. It is only that one never expects such depth from a young woman as attractive and spirited as you."

"Oh?"

"Now I have offended *you.* Please forgive me. That was quite chauvinistic, and I am not really that way."

She laughed and brought her hands prayerfully to her lips. "Maestro, Maestro, after hearing the exquisite music you created for Mimi and Musetta, I could never, *ever* accuse you of chauvinism."

He laughed. "I thank you again."

"No, I thank you. Are you acquainted with the origin of the word?"

"Chauvinism?"

"Yes."

"I must confess ignorance."

"Nicolas Chauvin – an extremely zealous supporter of Napoleon Bonaparte."

Puccini laughed heartily. "Marvelous! I thank you for the enlightenment. Where on earth did you learn that?"

"I am a schoolteacher. I love books." It was said demurely, quietly.

"Splendid! Now enlighten me further. Tell me your name, will you please?"

"Oh, my...I am also a dunce. I should have told you. Forgive me. It is Corinna...Corinna –"

"No, no...." He stopped her with a raised finger. "Corinna is enough. I prefer to know you only as Corinna. It is lovely name, lovely enough to stand solely by itself."

"Thank you, Maestro."

"You say you love books?"

"Oh, yes."

"Do you know the meaning of the word corinne?"

"Delicate and gentle. Is that correct?

"Exactly. But do you know how it came to be your name?

She shook her head. "Enlighten *me* now."

"The Roman poet Ovid turned corinne into Corinna."

She laughed her delight. "I shall remember that."

"And I shall always remember you as Corinna."

This trip to Turin became the most entertaining train ride Giacomo Puccini had ever experienced. They talked endlessly. They laughed. They were animated and so mutually agreeable it was as if they had been friends for years. When the conductor's announcement declared their arrival in Turin, it produced soft sighs of sadness. She extended a hand. He took it in his. "Maestro," she said with a smile warm enough to melt glaciers, "this has been unforgettable. It truly pains me to say goodbye."

He didn't want to release her. "I echo the sentiment. But there is no need for goodbye. I shall be staying at the Hotel Artisti on Via Bertola. Will you join me for dinner?"

Her green eyes twinkled. "I was hoping you would ask."

"Bravo! Is seven o'clock satisfactory for you?"

"It is not only satisfactory, it is perfect."

"I must say, today has been unexpectedly pleasant, and you are a perfect delight, Corinna. I look forward to this evening."

She appeared at the Hotel Artisti's dining room promptly at seven, dressed fashionably in subtle colors that accentuated the green of her eyes. He rose quickly from his seat and greeted her with a kiss on her extended hand. He wore a doubled-breasted grey suit with a handkerchief folded neatly in the jacket pocket. A black bowtie touched-off the formality of his white shirt, and spats covered the tops of his black and white shoes. He was freshly shaved, his hair was neatly combed, and he carried the faint scent of cologne. After delicious apèritifs, they were served a luscious dinner that ended exactly at nine. They remained in the dining room until ten-thirty. They talked. They laughed. They sipped after-dinner wine. By eleven, they were naked and in his bed, where they remained through the entire night.

Giacomo awoke before she did. He sat on a chair near the bed and studied her sweet face and the contours of her youthful body. He smiled. For the first time in many years, he felt thoroughly, happily, sexually sated. *She is a gift from heaven,* he thought. *Intelligent. Informed. Witty. Vivacious. Modern. Passionate. Beautiful. She is everything Elvira is not. And I am lost. I shall never allow this lovely creature to escape me.*

From the moment he made that decision Puccini, Composer in the World of Opera, became Puccini, Juggler in the Circus of Life. Attempting to keep four objects in the air, he swayed precariously over a huge tank of barracuda. The objects were: Corinna, Elvira, Ricordi, and *Madame Butterfly*. The barracuda were: agony and death.

Corinna quickly took precedence over the other three, causing him to become distracted, to lose his balance and to fall headlong into the tank. His fondness for Corinna quickly became love. Puccini became so enamored of this young woman that separation became torture. Unable to bear the pain, he purchased a small a house in the forested hills of Viareggio, a seaside town only seven miles from Torre del Lago. There they met often, and he romped like a young stud.

Corinna's fascination with Puccini deepened steadily. She found him to be everything she had ever fantasized about the perfect man. Kind. Sensitive. Sensual. Considerate. And constantly stimulating. Their discussions covered everything: music, history, religion, world events. She came to believe she had found her perfect mate. When she was not with him, she felt only half-alive. She confessed her love and said she could not bear their separations. Eventually, she stopped teaching altogether and moved to Viareggio.

Giacomo, in love, became a different man. His step was livelier. He smiled and laughed at a thought. He burst into song for apparently no reason. Corinna gave him life. She brightened his days. She made him welcome his tomorrows.

Elvira could not understand this new buoyancy. She wondered about its source. When she questioned him, he laughed and threw his arms wide. "I am happy," he said. "I have everything I want in life. Is it a terrible thing to be happy?"

Flustered, she could only frown and accept his words.

When Ricordi sent him the first act of *Madame Butterfly,* he attacked it like a hungry bear. He read it repeatedly, searching for that mysterious link to his soul. Then, believing he'd found it, he rushed to his piano and struggled there for hours to turn vague linkage into compelling musical themes.

His efforts quelled Elvira's suspicions. He was working. She heard music. If he felt life was now good, she could accept that. As long as he was at his piano, let him laugh. Let him sing. She would benefit from all of it.

Enjoying each other periodically in their isolated house, Giacomo and Corinna kept their idyll secret for more than two years! Illica and Giacosa sent *Butterfly* scenes to him as soon as they deemed them ready for music. Then he would rush to Milan to battle with them for changes that he said were absolutely necessary. To Giulio Ricordi, his demands were often admirable. To Illica, they were unfounded and niggling. "Where does he find these nonsensical ideas?" he complained bitterly. "His head is in the clouds!" Had he known of Corinna, Luigi Illica would have erupted with a violence to shame Vesuvius.

Puccini maneuvered blithely around these discordant bumps. He was in love. Life was exciting, and nothing could make him unhappy.

Or so he thought.

On January 13, 1901, Giacomo Puccini received word that sixty-seven-year-old Carlo Angeloni, his beloved teacher and friend, had died after a prolonged struggle with pneumonia. They had remained in frequent correspondence with each other, but the news was shocking. Puccini hurried to Lucca for Angeloni's funeral. "My mentor, my friend," he murmured over the casket, "I should have been with you. You needed me, and I was not here for you."

Then, before he could recover from this loss, Puccini learned only eight days later that the great Giuseppe Verdi had suffered a massive stroke and now lay in a coma, hovering between life and death.

Puccini raced to Milan.

All of Italy was shaken by Verdi's condition. No one seemed to know what to do. To soften noise, straw was placed on the street outside the Grand Hotel where he lived. Conductors refrained from sounding their trolley bells. Crowds stood in silence, waiting for news. It was all in vain; Verdi never regained consciousness. He died on January 27th, and the shock of his passing turned quickly into weeks of national mourning. Shops closed. La Scala suspended operations. Parliament identified him as "one of the highest expressions of national genius." Over 300,000 people lined the streets as his hearse, pulled by six horses, made its way to Cimitero Monumentale. And four days later, a memorial service took place at La Scala, where Arturo Toscanini conducted a chorus of 800, singing *"Va, pensiero, sull' ali dorate"* (Fly, thought, on wings of gold) from his opera *Nabucco*.

Giacomo Puccini and Giulio Ricordi were among the mourners at the memorial. As the chorus voices rose in this magnificent homage, Ricordi tapped Puccini's arm. "Now, Giacomo," he whispered, "you are truly the Doge. There is no one else to wear great Verdi's mantle."

Puccini shuddered. He sank in his seat. The weight of that pronouncement became heavier, he felt, than he would ever be able to carry. Yes, he enjoyed fame. And yes, he loved the adoration and money it brought him. But he wanted nothing to do with its accompanying responsibility. All he wanted was peace, freedom and harmony, not the formidable task of fulfilling lofty expectations. Ricordi's memorial assignment made him want to run away, to escape what had now become his destiny.

At the first opportunity, Puccini left Milan for Torre del Lago to bury his fears in *Madame Butterfly.* The need to complete the opera overwhelmed him and kept him at his piano daily, a routine broken only when a more desperate need possessed him. At these times he fled to the arms of his waiting mistress.

Puccini and Corinna's presence was not unknown in Viareggio. Believing Corinna was Signora Puccini, the town's mayor and wife even had them to their home for dinner. However, secret love can rarely go undiscovered forever. Eventually, someone will uncover it, especially when the lovers are careless. This occurred in the summer of 1902. A friend of a Puccini sister saw him and his paramour, laughing and strolling arm-in-arm in town, recklessly indifferent to the danger of discovery. The sighting was reported by the friend to the sister, who then informed the entire family of Giacomo's indiscretion. Vexed by their brother's behavior, his sisters conspired to make their disapproval known to him.

And somehow the family's ire reached Elvira. When it did, she went utterly berserk. At first, disbelief merely unnerved her. It couldn't be true, she told herself. Giacomo would never betray her. They had an agreement. Their life together had become placid, comfortable, at times even enjoyable. He had everything he wanted at home. Why should he ever look at another woman? She observed him more closely. Yes, there was something different in the way he was conducting himself. A jauntiness that wasn't simple happiness. There was something different about it – something out of character. And he satisfied her simplest requests now with an liveliness that wasn't there before. Why? *Why?* Her suspicions grew and pained her every time she looked at him. The pain became unbearable. She knew she could not continue this way. But she had to be certain about the gossip's truth before she could confront him. She made a dangerous decision.

When Giacomo was not at home in Torre del Lago, Elvira donned her favorite dress, pinned her best hat to her pile of hair, selected her most attractive purse, and boarded an early morning coach to Viareggio. She had no idea how she would test the veracity of the gossip that was tormenting her, but she knew her seething resentment would lead her to the truth.

In the main piazza of Viareggio, sipping coffee at a prominent café, Elvira engaged the restaurant's manager in pleasant conversation. Steering the subjects artfully to music, she posed a simple question: "Are you familiar with the operas of our great maestro Giacomo Puccini?"

"Oh, yes," came the rapturous response. "I saw *La Bohème* in Lucca during the Puccini Festival. I adore his music." Then he added proudly, "Maestro Puccini even dines here with Signora Puccini. They have a home in Viareggio, you know."

Elvira's anger almost stopped her heart. She fumbled with her spoon and rattled her coffee cup.

"Are you all right, Signora?" the concerned manager asked.

"Yes...yes...I am fine." She closed her eyes and breathed deeply, regaining her composure. Forcing a smiling, she said, "How fortunate for Viareggio to have so illustrious a citizen and his wife. Do you know where they live?"

"No, Signora. And if I did, I would never divulge that information. The Maestro, I am sure, would not appreciate admiring strangers intruding upon his privacy. I know I should not if I were as grand a figure as he."

"Yes...yes, you are quite right," Elvira muttered.

She left the café, her thoughts boiling in a cauldron of bitterness and rage. At first she felt compelled to ask about town for the location of their secret home. But she struggled with the idea and finally rejected it. She knew enough, and investigation in the heat of fury might not be to her advantage. It would be better to return to Torre del Lago where she could fashion an attack that would reduce him to ashes. Trembling, Elvira boarded a coach, and with images of Giacomo and another woman flooding her mind, she suffered insanely through the entire seven-mile trip home.

In the three days she waited for Giacomo to arrive, Elvira could think of nothing but revenge. Her loathing strengthened with every passing minute. Tonio sensed something was wrong. He could see tension in every movement of Elvira's body. He took special pains not to annoy her or to quicken her anger, and he avoided her whenever possible. But he watched her quietly and waited for his father's return. By the time Puccini entered the house, contented and exuberant, Elvira had worked herself into frenzy. She charged at him. She was a hurricane of malevolence, her face twisted into a grotesque mask. "*Where were you?*" she screamed. "Turin? Turin? You disgusting liar! Did you think I would never find out? Do you think I am an idiot? *You* are the idiot, you and your filthy slut! You deceive me! You deceive me! You tell me you are going to Turin, *but I learn you are rutting like a pig in Viareggio*!"

Puccini's smile disappeared. The day had come. He'd thought about it, feared it, but lost in the joy of love he'd always put it aside. Now it was here, and he was totally unprepared. "Wh...what are you talking about?" he stammered, retreating from her attack. "I...I was in Turin."

"Lies! Lies! You stink from her, and you continue to lie! I went to Viareggio! I found the truth!"

"Calm yourself...Elvira...calm yourself...." He backed into a table.

"I warned you never to shame me!" She kept advancing. "You promised!"

"I...I...."

"You think you can make a fool of me and never suffer?" Spittle flew from her mouth. "*You and your whore?*"

"I...I told you," he muttered lamely, "a...a man has needs."

"So does a dog!" she screeched and lunged at him.

His hands flew up. But not fast enough. Sharp nails raked his head, his face and neck before he could defend himself. Skin ripped. Blood ran from the wounds.

"Stop it! Stop it!" he shouted, grabbing her wrists. But she wrenched free and pounded him with fists, howling disgust and threats.

"Animal! Animal! God will curse you! You will suffer for this! I swear it! I swear it! You will suffer!"

He pushed her away. She tripped and fell to the floor. He looked down at her in disbelief, stunned by the violence of the attack. "I am...I am sorry, Elvira...I am sorry." He rushed to her and offered a hand.

She spat at it. Sobbing hysterically, she shrieked," *Get out of my house! Get out of my sight! Get out of my life!"*

Shaken to the core, Giacomo Puccini grabbed his travel bag and raced from the house with Elvira's wrath ringing in his ears. *"I hate you! I hate you!"*

His bewilderment paralyzed him. He stood at the edge of his property, looking back at the house, not knowing what he should do next.

"Papa, are you all right?" It was Tonio looking at him with bewilderment in his eyes.

The violence had been so sudden, so intense, he hadn't realized his son had been in the room's doorway witnessing the entire, terrible scene. "Yes... yes...I am all right," he said shakily. Tonio's presence and question made him aware again of his surroundings. "Go inside...tend to your mother. She will need you."

"You need attention, too," Tonio said. "Your face, your neck... you are bleeding."

Puccini ran a hand over his face. He pulled it away and looked at it. He saw the blood and gasped. No one had ever struck him. In his entire life no one had ever made him suffer physically for anything he had done. This was beyond his understanding. "Go inside," he repeated. "Go inside."

"Are you leaving us, Papa?" Tonio asked.

"No...no...I shall never leave you."

"But you are going away?"

"For a little while."

"Where to?"

"I do not know...I do not know. Go inside. See to your mother."

He kissed his son and hugged him tightly. Then looking sadly at him one last time, Puccini turned and hurried into town for the first transportation he could find to Viareggio.

He needed to see Corinna again, to hold her, to be comforted by her, to tell her of the insane experience he'd just had in Torre del Lago. However, instead of providing consolation, his welcome in Viareggio devolved into a scene almost as upsetting as the one from which he had fled. Seeing him, Corinna gasped. Her hands flew to her mouth. "Oh, my ...oh, my..." she cried, "what happened to you? What happened?"

He looked broken. The ride from Torre del Lago had not helped his appearance. His clothes were disheveled; his hair, unkempt. The claw marks on face and neck were bloody and raw. His head hung and his eyes appeared forlorn and glazed.

Corinna put an arm around his shoulders and guided him to an armchair in the house's small living room. "Here...sit...sit, my beloved."

He eased himself into the chair.

She rushed for a damp handkerchief, with which she gently cleaned the dried blood from his face and neck.

Puccini allowed her to tend his wounds. He didn't move. He said nothing as he tried to gather his thoughts.

She knelt before him. "Tell me," she pleaded. "Tell me what happened to you."

With great effort, the entire story came out.

She questioned him until she understood everything. "All right," she said with a note of finality, "we shall leave here. We shall be married and live far away where she will never be able to trouble us again."

"She will find us." Puccini rejected the suggestion with a wave of a hand. "But you are right We *must* leave here. She was insane... and she has my guns in the house."

Fear suddenly made Corinna blanch. "What...what are you saying? Do you believe she would...?"

"Now I would not doubt anything of her. You must go back to Turin."

"When?"

"Tonight."

"Will you not come with me?"

"She must not find us together."

"What will you do? Where will you go?"

"I do not know. But I shan't stay here."

"Come with me. We shall be married."

"Not now...not now, Corinna, for God's sake, not now!"

"You promised –"

"I know I promised, and we *shall* be married. But I need some time to make sense of everything that has happened."

Her voice became soft, suspicious, slightly threatening. "Giacomo, do not do this to me. I have left everything to be with you...my home, my teaching. I have nothing but you now, and I want nothing but you. Please, tell me you are not trying to discard me."

He took her in his arms. "Discard you? *Amore mio*, do not think that. I shall never discard you. You are everything in this world to me, even more than my music. But you must do as I say. You must leave for Turin tonight. I shall come to you when I can, and we shall be married. I promise you that, I promise."

Corinna was forced to agree. "I shall be with a friend," she said in tears. "Here is where you will find me." She wrote an address on a slip of paper and gave it to him with a shaking hand. They kissed, and she left Viareggio for Turin that very evening.

The next morning, still muddled but determined, Giacomo Puccini purchased an express train ticket for Milan and the seclusion of his business apartment. He believed he would be safe there, far enough from Elvira to consider his next move.

Distance was no safeguard. While he was aboard the train

traveling to Milan, Elvira sat at her kitchen table in Torre del Lago venting her rage in letter after letter to those who had shown personal or business interest in her common law husband. Illica. Giacosa. Ricordi. Ramelde. All were to receive condemnatory descriptions of Puccini's unfaithfulness. All were to learn how he betrayed a trusting, loyal wife, a woman who wanted nothing more than respect from the man for whom she had maintained a happy home. She had created a palace for him where he could create his music and rise to heights of greatness. She did not deserve his perfidy. She did not deserve to be replaced by a slut, a common whore. The words poured from her. She had sworn vengeance. She had promised he would suffer. *This*, she thought, gritting her teeth as she wrote, *is only the beginning*.

- 29 -

Opening the letters, all four recipients became instantly and deeply dismayed.

Ramelde's eyes widened as she read Elvira's vitriol. *This had to happen,* she thought. *The woman has always been disturbed. But this time she has good cause. My brother is a fool!*

Illica snorted and shook his head. "I knew it! I knew it!" he grunted. "There had to be something. A whore! My God, a whore! No wonder we are not receiving music from him!"

Giacosa closed his eyes and breathed: "A brilliant fool. He should know better than this. Why do I waste my precious time with him?"

Ricordi had to sit down as he read Elvira's letter. His hands shook. He snorted disapproval at each sentence. Giulio Ricordi was a traditionalist in all respects. He deplored disruptive changes in all aspects of life, from the atonal operas of Richard Wagner to the licentiousness of philandering husbands. And now he was being told that his protégé, the man in whom he had placed his faith, on whom he had bestowed his kindness, the heir to the great Verdi's crown – this man was violating everything in which he believed. *How can he be such a fool?* Ricordi thought. *How can he jeopardize everything we have worked so hard to achieve, his success, his future, his place in history? For what? For a prostitute?!*

Ricordi liked Elvira. He had told Puccini of his admiration. To see her being treated in this fashion – cruelly, immorally, degradingly – made him gasp in anger and exasperation. He sat at his desk immediately and wrote a letter to her, expressing his shock and regret. He didn't know what else he could do. But he was certain of one thing: if Puccini were with him at that moment, his head would have rattled from the berating words he would have heard.

Confused and suffering in his Milan apartment, Giacomo wrote twice to Ricordi to tell him he was in Milan and to request a meeting. But he received no answer from the irate publisher.

Luigi Illica, meanwhile, had sent a note to Ricordi. *"The man does not deserve your kindness, Signor Giulio,"* he wrote. *"Now we know for a certainty why his composing has been so erratic."*

Ricordi responded with sad agreement. *"Yes, he is preparing his moral decay. It is sure to affect him physically, and in that state of deterioration, he will no longer have the energy or spirit to proceed with* Madame Butterfly."

"You must tell him so, Signor Giulio, you must!"

Ricordi acted upon Illica's urging. He wrote to Giacomo and demanded a meeting. Puccini was greatly relieved. They met at Casa Ricordi where the publisher was stricken at once by Puccini's despondent and uncertain demeanor, both of which confirmed his belief of moral decay.

Learning of the letters Elvira had sent to Ricordi and Illica, Puccini tried to describe the ugliness of her attack. He pointed to the wounds on his face and neck. He repeated her words of hate. "She was a madwoman," he said, pleading for empathy. "She charged at me like a fiend from hell."

Ricordi looked at him steadily. "You struck her," he said.

"What?"

"She wrote you struck her. You knocked her to the floor."

"No, no. I pushed her away. She tripped on the carpet."

"You must have pushed her violently enough to cause the fall."

"She was attacking me!"

"And this woman, whom you have chosen to disgrace her, is justification for your violence?"

Puccini pleaded, "Signor Giulio, you do not understand – "

But Ricordi flared, "It is *you* who does not understand! You are consorting with a woman of low character and jeopardizing everything dear and meaningful in your life. It is my deep affection for you that compels me to insist upon an immediate termination of this impermissible affair. Until you end it, I do not wish to speak with you again."

He dismissed Puccini by quickly turning away from him.

The movement shattered Puccini's last shred of composure. Totally lost, dazed as never before, he stood and looked at his father-figure's back. There was nothing more he could say. Like a wounded animal, he left the Casa Ricordi offices and returned to the loneliness of his apartment.

The confrontation was not to end there. Ricordi reported his words to Illica and urged him to "emulate my position until our dear friend has come to his senses."

However, the librettist didn't do as Ricordi had advised. Instead, he immersed himself in the problem, attracted perhaps by its dramatic complexity. He corresponded with Elvira and Puccini's sisters, and then conveyed their sentiments to Puccini. "Everyone is distressed," he said. "And there is *Butterfly* to be considered. I am in agreement with Signor Giulio that your work is suffering because of this liaison. Set yourself free, Giacomo, set yourself free."

The advice was easier offered than followed. Giacomo was certain of his love for Corinna. He had sworn his faith and would not abandon her. Since Milan was not the friendly place he had hoped it would be, he left for Turin to find peace in her arms. Being with her intoxicated him. He felt attached again, connected to a nurturing spirit. The only thing that made their togetherness difficult was her constant plea for marriage.

"You are not married to the witch," she begged. "You are free. There is no reason why we cannot wed."

He couldn't dispute the soundness of her claim. He knew only that he could not break his ties with Elvira, despite the discord and absence of love in their relationship.

He rationalized his inability to leave her with vapid responses: "There is Tonio," he said. I cannot leave him alone with her. And Fosca –"

"For God's sake, Giacomo, your son is no longer a child, and

Fosca is her husband's responsibility now. There is no reason we cannot marry."

"We shall...we shall, *amore*...but I must first put an end to this difficulty. If I do not, she will make our lives impossible. I know Elvira. She *will*!"

His argument didn't satisfy Corinna. Her pleas for marriage continued until Puccini, harassed by them, found it necessary to leave Turin. Believing Lucca would offer him some solace, he flew from Corinna's harping and found himself instead in a nest of sibling hornets. His sisters Ramelde, Iginia, and Tomaide gave him no relief.

"My brother," his favorite sister Ramelde said sternly, "if you are looking for comfort here, you have come to the wrong house. You cannot expect sympathy while you are disgracing yourself and the woman who has sacrificed her life for you. Elvira does not deserve this treatment. She has been loyal to you and exceedingly patient. And you would cast her aside for a whore? You shame the Puccini name. You must give up this trollop, you must!"

Iginia, who had become a nun now known as Sister Giulia Enrichetta, agreed with religious conviction: "Giacomo, God will surely damn your immortal soul to the fires of Hell if you don't."

"You do not know Corinna," he said with annoyance. "She is not as you portray her. She is kind and gentle and loving."

"Loving, no doubt," Ramelde snapped. "How long did it take her to find her way to your bed? Weeks, months, or *hours*?"

The question shook Puccini beyond anything that had previously been said.

"And how long did you pursue her...or did she pursue you?" Tomaide asked quickly.

He frowned and shook his head. His sisters' questions had unraveled him.

"I...I...have to leave you now," he stammered. "There...there are things I must do."

He rose quickly from the chair on which he had been sitting and turned to leave.

"What you must do," Ramelde said gently, "is very clear,

Giacomo. You must separate yourself from this conniving woman. She has attached herself to you because you can offer her security and the excitement of a fascinating life. You are Maestro Puccini, a shining light of Italian opera! She does not love you, Giacomo; she loves only what you represent."

With a heavy, aching heart, Puccini left Lucca and his sisters that very evening.

- 30 -

Weeks stretched into months. Giacomo, alone in his Milan apartment, became a recluse, going nowhere, seeing no one, nursing his dilemma in waves of self-pity. Ricordi refrained from contacting him. His sisters remained silent. Giacosa would not permit himself to be drawn into this quagmire. Illica kept Puccini in touch with reality. But always insisting upon a separation from Corinna and a return to work, Illica's observations failed to alleviate Giacomo's pain. "I love her," he told Illica. "Life with her has meaning. Elvira offers nothing but castigation and vilification. I try to work but I am drowning in a sea of sadness. I feel no one cares. I should be with my love. Only she understands me."

Illica responded. "You are not in love. You know nothing about her. You are only enchanted by youth, vitality and copulation. She is using you."

Such observations only roiled his already troubled mind. *"They are all wrong,"* he insisted to himself. *"No one knows her as I do."*

However, despite his unwillingness to accept any negative opinion of Corinna, the seeds of doubt had been planted. Illica's words lacerated his spirit. His sisters' words haunted him. It was true that she had pursued him. It was true that she had shared his bed on the first night of their meeting. And it was true that he knew nothing of her background beyond what she had told him.

The final blow came in a furious, six-page letter from Giulio Ricordi. It professed great love for Giacomo, a love that permitted him to write the harsh truth. Then it accused him of violating sacrosanct promises to his art. It claimed his success had made him a spoiled little boy, stubbornly unwilling to listen to worldly advice. It charged him with mistaking his friends as enemies, and with being blinded by a "*meretricious, vulgar, and unworthy woman*." It said he, Puccini, did not understand the difference between love and "*a filthy obscenity that destroys morals and physical vigor*." It accused Corinna of being a low, corrupt, vile creature, a whore who had made him her toy "*by means of obscene sensual pleasures*." And it begged him to break the chain of lewd excitement that had removed him from nobler and higher ideals.

Ricordi's letter traumatized Giacomo Puccini. Tears flowed as he read the six pages of moral condemnation and passionate entreaty for a return to sanity. He shook with bewilderment. He choked on resentment. He languished for days before he was able to respond. And when he did, he wrote instead to Illica. "*Signor Giulio*," he concluded, "*has been most ungenerous. He judges too harshly and without evidence*."

Evidence. Yes, evidence. That is what he, Puccini, needed! If he had evidence of his love's honesty, of her gentleness, of the depth of her goodness, he would be able to end this nightmare of misunderstanding for all time. He thought about this for days and, finally, he knew what he had to do. He found a detective in Milan who was willing to go to Turin to follow Corinna and to provide him with a report of his findings.

The detective returned in two weeks with information that shook Giacomo Puccini to the core of his being. "The lady in question was seen on four different occasions to consort with strangers whom she met in hotel restaurants and with whom she remained overnight. It can be assumed that money exchanged hands in these encounters."

It was as if he had been bitten by a poisonous snake. Puccini gasped. His body shook. He dropped the report to his bedroom floor and fell back upon his pillow. An arm came up and covered his eyes, and he groaned as if he were in mourning. *I have been deceived*, he thought. *She only poses her goodness and purity. I loved her...I loved her as I have never loved before. Oh, God.... why has she done this to me... why...why?*

He suffered with this question for days. And each day's pain transmuted his love a bit more into resentment. He felt shamed for having been duped. He was wretched for the anguish he had caused friends and family with his defense of her honor. *They were all caring*, he thought, *and I reproached them for their love*.

Unable to rest until he could make his anger known to Corinna, he finally sat at his desk and wrote a scalding letter in which he described the detective's report and the agony he had been suffering since receiving it. *"I gave you my love,"* he concluded, *"and you have given me deceit, depravity, and prostitution in return! You are a slut, and I want nothing more to do with you!"*

The letter took the ground from under Corinna's feet. She dropped into an abyss of heartache so profound she became bedridden for weeks. She refused food. She refused comfort. She wept each day until she passed out in despair. "I love him," she sobbed. "I love him...how can he not see I love him?"

When she was able to write to Puccini, her first letter vehemently denied his accusations of prostitution, and she begged to see him. He didn't respond. Subsequent letters expressed her deep, eternal love and her desperate need to be with him. Still, he refused to reply.

Finally, she wrote, *"You promised to marry me. I have your word in your letters. Now you do not even answer mine. You have forced me to this, Giacomo. I am currently seeing a lawyer, who has advised me to sue you for breach of promise. I pray that public recognition of your infamy will repay you for the callous way you have been treating me."*

Puccini responded.

He said he was astounded that she would consider such a drastic step. Their relationship was dead, he insisted, and nothing could revive it, but he wanted her to return his letters, and he was certain he and she could reach an accord in respect to them.

Negotiations with Corinna and her lawyer continued for almost a full year. By the end of 1903, matters were settled to everyone's satisfaction. Corinna received a sizable financial settlement, the letters were returned, and the one-time lovers never saw each other again.

In the course of that year, though, Giacomo Puccini, a broken man, struggled to regain esteem in the eyes of family and friends. He lived months of *mea culpa*. And when victorious Elvira insisted upon his return to Torre del Lago, he went back to her like a timid poodle. There he immersed himself in *Madame Butterfly*. He chain-smoked as many as seventy cigarettes a day. And to escape Elvira's smug glances, he toured around Torre del Lago and travelled as far away as Lucca in a new 25 horsepower 1903 *Clément-Bayard* automobile.

It was in the evening of February 25, 1903, that tragedy struck.

Puccini's throat had been bothering him with a persistent cough and soreness, and he had gone to Lucca for an afternoon examination by a prominent specialist. Elvira and Antonio accompanied him. Assured the throat problem was nothing serious, they prolonged their stay with dinner at a local restaurant before proceeding on to Torre del Lago. It was a foggy winter night when they were back on the road again, and a thin film of ice coated the bumpy road. Giacomo and Elvira were seated in the rear of the car. Tonio sat in the front section with their experienced chauffeur.

"I am happy we have seen the doctor," Elvira said. "Your health is of primary importance to us."

"Yes, Papa, very important to us," Tonio agreed.

"Thank you," Giacomo answered. "Frankly, I was worried, but the doctor's diagnosis has eased my concern."

Only four miles outside Lucca, the *Clément-Bayard* hit a long slick of ice and went into a dangerous skid. The chauffeur fought for control. The car fish-tailed crazily and veered to the edge of the road. Elvira screamed. Tonio held his breath. Giacomo grunted fear. Nothing could prevent the inevitable. Pitching wildly, the car slipped over the road's edge and careened down a rocky hill. It plowed through ruts into a snowy field thirty feet below and then struck a boulder violently and flipped completely upside down.

Elvira and Tonio pulled themselves from the wreckage shaken

and bruised. They had miraculously escaped serious injury. The driver slouched behind the steering wheel gravely injured. But Giacomo was nowhere to be found. Tonio called his name. No answer. Desperation escalated. In the darkness, Tonio was helpless. He scrambled around the smashed vehicle, searching frantically, shouting for his father. He found nothing. He heard nothing.

Rescuers appeared on the scene as if by magic. They had lanterns. The search widened. And then, when it seemed as if Puccini had mysteriously disappeared, someone detected his hand beneath the overturned vehicle. Carefully, they removed a section of the back seat, and they saw him. He lay unconscious and crammed in a ditch beneath the overturned car and a shattered tree. Slowly, painstakingly, they extracted him, fearful at the same time that gasoline fumes might burst suddenly into flame and kill him before he could be pulled free.

In a stroke of good fortune that defies explanation, a Doctor Sbragia lived near the scene. He had heard the screams, the crash, the shouts, and he'd hurried to the site. Puccini was carried, still unconscious, to the doctor's house. There he was examined and found to have suffered a fractured right tibia and numerous cuts and bruises. Not satisfied with the diagnosis, Tonio summoned a distinguished surgeon in Lucca. Learning the identity of the patient, the surgeon rushed to Doctor Sbragia's house where he confirmed the diagnosis, set the break, and bandaged the leg. Giacomo, in excruciating pain, was then transported to Torre del Lago where a third doctor, this one from Florence, reset the broken bone and announced solemnly, "Be prepared to endure a long recovery."

The gravity of these words settled a shroud of gloom upon Elvira that was lifted only when she learned of Narciso Gemignani's death. Her legal husband had passed away suddenly in Lucca on February 26, 1903, the day after Puccini's horrendous accident. *A gift for all my suffering,* she told herself. *Now Giacomo and I will be married as soon as he has recovered.*

Word of Puccini's accident and injury spread quickly throughout the world. Hundreds of cables and letters flooded the villa in Torre del Lago. They came from Ricordi, Illica and Giacosa, from the parliament of Italy, from fellow composers, from opera houses, from foreign dignitaries, and from his adoring public.

They heartened the stricken maestro and he needed them, especially when his leg was placed in a cast and he was told he could expect to be incapacitated for more than a year.

"I do not know how I shall survive," he wailed to Elvira. "I shan't be able to work. It is the end of *Madame Butterfly*, the end of my career, the end of everything."

"Blackness," she scoffed. "That is all you ever see. You survived, did you not? What you are suffering is terrible, but it is not the 'end of everything.' Two of your sisters will be here soon to help me take care of you. Visitors are arriving to cheer you. You will have everything you need to make you comfortable. And you will heal faster than you believe. Your opera *will* be completed. You told me Signor Giulio always says, 'I shall have it no other way!' and I hereby echo his certitude!" Then she tossed her head in a rare display of lightheartedness.

Puccini snorted at Elvira's playfulness and mumbled, "Continue to remind me of that when you see my despair for surely there are black days ahead."

There were indeed dark days, but the months passed with fewer spells of depression than he had anticipated. A means of propping him at his piano was devised, and a delighted Puccini returned to *Madame Butterfly* with the energy of a child at play.

Ricordi, Illica and Giacosa were thrilled by this. The librettists quickly provided him with a finished libretto. It was delivered personally by Tito Ricordi with his father's promise to visit within weeks. In time, the flood of letters became a stream, the stream became a trickle, and visitors no longer crowded the Puccini villa. With more time to devote to *Madame Butterfly*, Puccini threw himself into the opera. Progress continued smoothly and satisfactorily until his two sisters had to return to their homes and families. Left alone to care for Puccini, Elvira grumbled about the weight of responsibility she was carrying. "I have the house to clean, clothes to wash, cooking every day, and your needs. It is too much...*too much!*"

"There is no reason to carry the burden alone," Giacomo said. "Hire someone to help you."

"Yes, you are right!"

The suggestion was acted upon immediately. After a few days of searching, Elvira brought a charming, sixteen-year-old girl to Giacomo while he sat at his piano. "Giacomo," she said, "stop your work."

He looked up at his intruders.

"This is Doria Manfredi. She will be at your call for your everyday needs. She will also be assisting me when she is not helping you. Say hello to the maestro, Doria."

"I am pleased to meet you, Maestro," the young girl said with an open smile and a soft, gentle voice.

Giacomo cocked his head and studied her for a moment. "And I, you. Did you say Doria?" he asked Elvira.

"Yes. Doria Manfredi."

"Very good. All right, Doria, I shall call when I need you by ringing this little bell." Elvira had supplied him with a small bell to summon his sisters. He lifted it from the piano and shook a delicate, jingling sound from it.

"When you hear that," Elvira said sternly, "you must stop whatever you are doing and answer the maestro's call immediately, do you understand?"

"Yes, Signora."

"Good. Now let us leave Signor Puccini to his work. Come and help me with dinner."

In the days ahead, Doria Manfredi became an indispensable part of the Puccini household. She did everything Elvira asked without complaint, and she answered every call from Giacomo with alacrity and a smile. Her eagerness to please soon softened Elvira's forbidding manner enough for her to tell Giacomo, "Thank you. Hiring help is the best suggestion you have made in the past ten years."

Immersed in his work on *Madame Butterfly*, Giacomo Puccini

gave little thought to the outside world. But he caught Elvira watching him occasionally with a sly and calculating smile. *Her mind is on her face,* he thought. *There is no love in her glance. She is the animal trainer, and I am the subdued beast.* It was at these times that his mind took him back to Viareggio and Corinna. He heard her lilting laughter. He felt her softness, the thrill of her touch, her sensual excitement. He would relive their evening strolls along Viareggio's sandy beach. They had held hands, admiring the streak of moonlight limning the sea's placid water. And they had stopped their walking for an occasional embrace and a sweet kiss. His memories stirred deep longing. He wondered if he had been unfair to Corinna. Had he allowed everyone's opinion to force him into the termination of a love that had brought him incomparable happiness? Then he would sigh and dim the unsettling thoughts by attacking *Madame Butterfly* again. Passion drove him, and he was able to announce on December 29, 1903, only ten months after his accident, "It is finished. *Butterfly* is now ready to take wing and flutter to Milan and the La Scala stage."

The Corinna affair and accident delays had stretched completion time to slightly more than three years. But listening to a pianist play the full score, Giulio Ricordi could not have been happier. "*Bravo, my Doge! You have done it again!*" he wrote. "*Despite the adversity with which you have been plagued, despite the limitations of incapacitation, you have forged ahead and given the world another brilliant expression of your genius. I salute you, and I thank you for a* Butterfly *that will fit beautifully into our repertoire and make your name long remembered*!"

Illica and Giacosa concurred with Ricordi. "*My dear Giacomo,*" Illica wrote, "*Butterfly has settled on my heartstrings and made them vibrate with love and tears. You have made all of our waiting worthwhile!*"

Giacosa the Buddha responded with equal fervor. "*Great accomplishment,*" he wrote, "Butterfly *will lift you onto the Pedestal of Immortality.*"

Despite this praise, the opera suffered through two months of angry altercations. Puccini lapsed again into his galling insistence upon libretto changes. He was like a painter who never knows when to stop applying one last dab of color. Giacosa complained to Ricordi, "His willingness to unbalance perfect scenes displays an odious ignorance of lyrical equilibrium. *Butterfly* will never float on the turbulent winds of irresponsible demands. I pray I am wrong, but I see ignominious defeat where once I saw sublime victory."

Illica was no less condemning. "I cannot in good conscience accede to everything the composer demands," he said. "If he were in heaven, he would want changes in the perfection of God. *Butterfly* must not go on indefinitely like this. Production should take place now!"

Giulio Ricordi agreed with the librettists' positions. He, too, wanted an immediate production of *Madame Butterfly.* He believed the opera to be a memorable example of creative brilliance. "*Butterfly* will be exalted long after all four of us have passed on," he predicted.

He set its 1904 première for Saturday, the 17th of February, at the La Scala opera house in Milan.

- 31 -

Pleased that Giacomo had finally completed *Madame Butterfly*, Elvira directed her energies to a plan she had formulated only one week after their terrible automobile accident. Giacomo's recovery, however, had precluded any action. Now, though, with Puccini well enough to hobble about on a cane, Elvira believed the time was ripe. She started with a simple statement: "You have completed *Madame Butterfly*, and I am happy for you. I promised myself I would not mention this until you were free. It is time now, Giacomo."

Puccini closed his eyes and inhaled deeply. He could not imagine what she had in mind, but her tone had him dreading the subject. "Please, Elvira," he said wearily, "I need rest. We can talk another time."

"No. I have been extremely patient. We shall talk now."

There was no escape. *Whatever this is, it must be faced,* he thought. *It might as well be now.* He placed the book he was reading on the lamp stand at his side. "Very well," he said, "we shall talk, but do not expect me to act on anything. I am not prepared to act."

Elvira's eyes narrowed. Her lips drew into a smirk. Then, without saying another word, she turned away and left him alone.

Puccini blinked in surprise. He wondered what her narrowed eyes and smirk could possibly have meant. He muttered, "She is plotting something. I know she is plotting something."

He was right. Elvira was plotting something. And since he was being resistant to discussing anything, she could either wait until he was more amenable, or she could put her second option immediately to work. Confident that the tactic she had used in disposing of Corinna would work once more, Elvira decided not to wait. Without mentioning the subject to him again, she began another letter campaign to family and friends.

Elvira suffered the indignity of illicitness every day while her husband Narciso Gemignani was alive. Being Catholic, she saw the impossibility of divorce, and annulment would have made Fosca illegitimate in Church law and Italian society. Elvira had always contemplated marriage to Giacomo. She was a hungry wolf waiting for the perfect moment to pounce upon its prey. That moment had arrived. Italian law dictated a one year waiting period for all widows before the woman could marry again. Secretly, Elvira had obtained a two-month dispensation, and her ten-month waiting period had just expired. She was ready.

She sent out a stream of plaintive letters. They went to Giacomo's sisters, to Giulio Ricordi, to Illica and Giacosa. They begged assistance in bringing understanding to Giacomo, this time to correct the status of their relationship and the illegitimacy of their son Antonio.

Ramelde reacted immediately. She convened a family council where all of Puccini's sisters (especially Iginia who was now a church Mother Superior) embraced Elvira's plea without hesitation. Their brother had to marry Elvira. Failure to do so, they agreed, was unthinkable, and for them to believe otherwise would be as immoral and sinful as his refusal. They sent letters to Giacomo, urging him harshly to save his soul by accepting God's will. *"By taking Narciso to His heart, the Lord has given you an opportunity to erase a long-standing sin,"* Iginia argued. *"I beg you, dear brother, do not ignore Him. Correct Antonio's illegitimacy. Bring peace to Elvira. Marry the deserving woman. Become a righteous, honorable man!"*

Illica and Giacosa were no less insistent.

But Giulio Ricordi was the most forceful of all. His warm sentiments about Elvira and his own moral precepts made him shudder when he received her letter. *Why is he hesitating?* he wondered. *She has been his true companion and support through years of struggle and uncertainty, and now when he can atone for the pain he has caused her, he compels her to demean herself this way. What is wrong with that man?!* Elvira's letter was a torch thrown into the tinderbox of his morality. Aflame, he considered it carefully, and every thought intensified the disappointment he had come to feel in his protégé. When he could bear it no longer, he sat at his desk at the close of a day's work and vented his dismay:

My dear Doge,

I have always been concerned about your penchant for self-destructiveness. I attempted to guide you from your unhealthy affair with a prostitute, and now I urge you toward a healthy act that can bring you only joy and stability. I am referring to your relationship with dear, honest Elvira. You must marry this exceptional woman, who has given you a family, a home and her life! If you remain unwilling to be honorable with her, I fear the damage you will be doing to your creative soul. Do not disappoint all who love you. Consider what I am writing and act with the purity of your moral conscience. I offer these thoughts with love and a passionate wish that they will not be ignored.

The letter came as a complete surprise, and it caused a fierce argument when Puccini waved it before Elvira's face. Defiantly she held her ground. And thereafter, she missed no opportunity to unsettle him with her demand for marriage. It didn't take long. Puccini's defenses collapsed in the weight of collective pressure.

He surrendered on January 3, 1904. The wedding was a civil affair, conducted in their home. However it was followed later by a brief Catholic ceremony in Torre del Lago's parish church. Only two witnesses were allowed to attend, and marriage banns were never posted. Elvira smiled through both proceedings. Though he wore a brave face, Giacomo Puccini was not a happy groom. The next morning he wrote a splenetic letter to his sister Ramelde in which he grumbled: *"Are you satisfied now? I am sure Iginia is happy, though I am not!"*

Then one hour later he left for Milan, more to escape Elvira than to prepare *Madame Butterfly* for its La Scala première.

Elvira wrote to her supporters to inform them of her marriage and to thank them for their assistance. In Milan, though, Puccini accepted all congratulations with a distinct absence of warmth.

Giulio Ricordi pulled him aside and told him with a severe frown, "Smile, Doge. You have been honorable, and honor brings respect and reverence from moral admirers everywhere."

Illica offered a more mundane observation: "Now you are safe from the hopeful illusions of other female predators."

Somehow, Illica's words comforted Puccini more than Ricordi's, and he faced Tito's *Butterfly* preparations with a lighter heart.

Tito Ricordi had become the opera's producer, and he spared no money to prove himself. A renowned set designer was imported from Paris. Gifted singers and an eminent conductor were found. Promotional plans were easily formulated. There was little discord, and the dress rehearsal ended with the entire cast, stagehands and orchestra standing in rousing cheers for the composer and librettists.

Madame Butterfly's premiere, however, became a disaster of monumental proportions. Foot stamping, screams, hisses, bird whistling and obscene shouts punctuated every action. At one point, the soprano's kimono opened accidentally, causing raucous laughter and derisive shouts: *"Look, look, she's pregnant! How can a Butterfly be pregnant?! She's been doing the dirty, that's how!"*

At the final curtain, the audience howled with hoots and catcalls. No one called for author bows. The patrons had treated its Japanese delicacy as a ridiculous piece of entertainment, more suited to the comic stage than operatic theater.

And most reviewers agreed. They condemned Puccini for what they perceived to be his *"lack of originality"* and his *"desire to offer us a hastily conceived opera."*

With feverish agreement from *Butterfly*'s composer and librettists, Tito canceled all further performances. "However," he told the trio, "this does not end *Madame Butterfly*. It is evidently beyond the ability of our present audiences to appreciate its foreign subtleties. We continue to believe in its grandeur, and we shall find a way to lift plebian tastes to new heights."

Puccini was crushed. In his mind *Butterfly* offered some of the finest music he had so far composed. No changes could improve it. Wounded and defeated by the savagery of an ignorant public, he returned to Torre del Lago.

As usual, Giacomo brooded. He stared through his villa's windows for hours on end. He spoke little. He ate listlessly.

Elvira lashed at him. "You shame yourself! The behavior of rowdies and the words of insensitive reviewers have reduced you to pathetic lifelessness. You are Maestro Puccini! Never forget that. *Maestro Puccini!* And not one of those who demean you can boast accomplishment equal to yours! Arouse yourself! Go to your piano! Compose another opera! Show the fools how wrong they are in their assessment! Do something! I cannot accept your indolence and despondency another day!"

Haranguing rarely moved Puccini to action. He needed sympathetic stroking in times of distress something Elvira was incapable of providing.

However, sweet, solicitous Doria Manfredi, now seventeen years old, was still available to comfort him with kind words and thoughtful attention. She was the only one who could move him to wan smiles.

What moved him to action was a telegram from Tito Ricordi:

RETURN TO MILAN IMMEDIATELY. STOP. BARBARIANS MAY NOT DICTATE TO ART. STOP. WE HAVE WORK TO DO.

TITO

This was not a request. Tito rarely requested. Unlike his father, who was temperate in all his dealings, Tito Ricordi was acerbic in speech and abrupt in manner. He cared little for niceties, and he often antagonized friends and strangers with abrasive opinions.

Association with him had never been easy for Giacomo, despite their having shared lodgings while attending productions in their visits to other cities. Now, Tito's telegram puzzled Puccini.

"What does it say?" Elvira asked, seeing his frown.

He mumbled as he offered the message to her waiting hand, "I have no work to do in Milan. Why does he bother me?"

She read the telegram and tossed it back at him. "We shall never know until you go back to Milan, shall we?" The tone of her voice told Puccini that remaining in Torre del Lago was not an option he could enjoy.

"All right," he agreed with a sigh, "I shall leave tomorrow."

Elvira smiled. "Excellent," she said. "Now you are behaving like an adult."

Giacomo was on the first morning express train to Milan. He had telegrammed Tito to inform him of his arrival. Elvira had made certain of that. Also, she'd had Doria prepare sandwiches and cookies for him, and while he nibbled on them during the trip, he mused: *Yes, she can be considerate, but such thoughtfulness can never substitute for love.* The moment he entered the offices of Casa Ricordi, Tito approached him unsmilingly with only an outstretched hand in greeting. Giacomo shook his hand and looked around the office. "Where is your father?" he asked.

"He is unable to be with us. Come, let us sit. There is much to discuss."

Once they were seated, Tito Ricordi launched into a stunning pronouncement. "My father has assigned all future Puccini considerations to me. It is I who shall make production decisions for you from now on."

It was as if Giacomo had received a blow to his head. He jerked in his chair. A hand flew to his chest. His jaw dropped. "Is...is...he removing himself from all my efforts?" he stammered.

"Not entirely. He will always be available when he is needed. But you have nothing to fear. I shall have your welfare at heart as seriously as does my father. And the first matter I want to discuss with you is another production of *Madame Butterfly,* this one to take place three months from now in Brescia. The city has a small theatre, one far more conducive to the intimate character of *Butterfly* than La Scala. And its opera audience has not been poisoned as yet by the boorishness that infects our Milanese attendees. What say you, Giacomo, are you ready to work?"

Puccini was speechless. He had considered *Butterfly* a dead opera, interest in it not to be revived for years to come. "But your father –."

"This is my decision. As I said in my telegram, 'Barbarians may not dictate to art.' I believe in *Madame Butterfly*. I say unequivocally, it *will* succeed. A Brescia production in a smaller theater will prove me correct."

A smaller theater. A city other than Milan. A more receptive audience. Doubt about Tito's leadership abilities softened. Puccini looked at him with shade of respect. He had no idea what Tito expected of him, but *Butterfly* was being afforded a second chance to be seen as he felt and heard it, and he was suddenly ready to begin.

"We have only two months in which to revise our *Butterfly*," Tito explained. "I want to start rehearsals in April and open on May the 28th at the Teatro Grande in Brescia. I repeat, Giacomo, are you ready to work?"

"I am ready, Tito," Puccini said.

Tito grinned for the first time, and the two men sealed their new association with a vigorous handshake.

They met again the next day. Tito's persuasiveness had convinced Illica and Giacosa to join them. It was easy; neither man wanted to see his past efforts wasted when an opportunity to save them was being afforded. Also the prospect of working only two months appealed mightily to both of them.

Instead of indicating Casa Ricordi's plush armchairs Tito directed them to the office's conference table. No cigars were passed around. No wine was made available. Tito looked at them with only the faintest sign of warmth. "I am extremely pleased to see you here," he said. "Your commitment to another *Butterfly* is laudable and a portent of the great success it will certainly enjoy."

This was a distinctly different approach from that of his father. Cooler. Crisper. More professional. The contrast didn't seem to bother Illica or Giacosa, but it made Giacomo feel uncomfortable.

Tito continued: "I have already received assurances from Zanatello to sing Pinkerton once more, from Campanini to conduct again, and from a new soprano to sing *Butterfly*'s Cio-Cio San ...if she meets with your approval, gentlemen."

"What is her name?" Illica asked uncertainly, as Giacosa and Puccini scowled.

"Solomea Krusceniski."

Giacomo jerked upright in his chair. "Yes!" he said excitedly. "I know her. She is the wife of Viareggio's mayor. I have heard her sing. Her voice is clear and strong. She will make an excellent Cio-Cio San!"

Giacomo's enthusiastic endorsement changed the temper of the meeting entirely. Everyone suddenly smiled. A refreshing spirit of cooperation took hold, one that prevailed through two months of drastic libretto/music revisions and strenuous rehearsals. The result of this synergy was everything for which Puccini and his librettists could have wished.

Brescia's Teatro Grande was packed on May 28, 1904, with an enthusiastic audience. Critics came from everywhere prepared to find fault again. Would this be another catastrophic evening, another damning display of critical displeasure? The audience didn't wait long to make its feelings known. Puccini's music touched all hearts. Appreciation punctuated everything. Arias were rewarded with resounding applause. Comedy with loud laughter. Suffering with empathic silence. Unlike the La Scala response to *Butterfly,* the Brescia reaction was totally positive. Even the orchestra and conductor were cheered. That evening, *Madame Butterfly* commanded thirty-four curtain calls, and ten of them belonged to a stupendously gratified and vindicated Giacomo Puccini.

Behind the final curtain, composer, librettists and producer congratulated each other and embraced like victorious teammates after an exhausting game. They had proved the Milan judgments insane! The next morning's reviews supported their happiness. Little fault had been found. Predictions of a long life for Cio-Cio San assured the opera's future. It was identified as a delicate tragedy, not the usual confrontational tale. It was a tender story, the journey of a young girl from naiveté to love, to disillusionment, to death. Its Japanese setting was exotic. Its costumes and makeup striking. It was different. Puccini's music had once again masterfully captured the nuances, the passion and pathos of meaningful opera verismo. Word of *Madame Butterfly*'s beauty spread swiftly. Requests flooded the House of Ricordi. And productions were speedily mounted around the world, the first foreign staging taking place in Buenos Aires, where Arturo Toscanini conducted the orchestra to rousing approval.

With four supremely successful operas to his credit now, Giacomo Puccini returned to Torre del Lago, glowing and hoping to enjoy a brief period of comfort and pleasure. It was a beautiful afternoon in early June. Sunlight washed the landscape. Birds drifted on gentle air currents over the lake. Serenity reigned. Nevertheless, Puccini approached his handsome villa with trepidation. He never knew how Elvira would receive him. This time, she welcomed him with smiles. "The conquering warrior returns," she said. "I am proud. Welcome home, my victorious husband. *Madame Butterfly* triumphs!"

The warmth of her reception surprised Giacomo. He breathed easier, and even grinned at her effusive greeting. "Thank you, Elvira" he replied. "Yes, Cio-Cio San lives."

"It is no surprise, Giacomo. I have more faith in you than you have in yourself. Come, relax. Are you hungry? I shall have Doria prepare something for you to eat."

Now that she had achieved legal respectability, Elvira seemed less distressed, more accepting of life's irregularities. Her customary severity softened, and she engaged more amiably with Giacomo, with servants, and even with some townspeople. Days passed into months of pleasant conciliation. Puccini fished. He hunted.

He bought things: bicycles; foreign cigars and cigarettes; a new motorboat for fishing and racing around Lake Massaciuccoli; clothes from London and Paris; and another car that he drove everywhere in speed competitions.

Elvira was contented. Free of money problems, she hired additional help. She purchased fashionable clothes. She assumed the role of respected Signora Puccini with the ease and authority of a benevolent despot. She not only had her husband legitimately now, she owned him. With uncharacteristic finesse, she even convinced him to accept her company on trips abroad. One such excursion occurred in October of 1904. It was a trip to England, and it involved another beautiful and vivacious woman, one who breathed unexpected excitement into Giacomo Puccini's turbulent life.

- 32 -

Her name was Sybil Seligman. She was thirty-six when they met, ten years younger than Giacomo. She was wealthy, sophisticated, well-educated, and extremely intelligent. She was also Jewish, happily married, and the mother of two bright and appealing children. Her husband David was an American banker. Sybil's fluency in Italian endeared her to the artists in London's Italian community. It also allowed her to sing popular Italian songs alluringly in a delightful, sweet voice. As patrons of artists, Sybil and David were active members of London's high society. They were seen often in fashionable drawing rooms and salons. And it was at one of these gatherings that they were introduced to Giacomo and Elvira Puccini. This meeting had been orchestrated by expatriate songwriter Francesco Paolo Tosti. Tosti had invited his compatriots to enhance his own already formidable social standing. (After all, bringing Maestro Giacomo Puccini to a social gathering of affluent patrons would surely be a coup of newsworthy importance!) But he was interested also in benefiting Giacomo professionally in all of his British endeavors. Tosti made the introductions happily and graciously.

"Maestro Puccini," Sybil said after conveying her pleasure to Elvira, "I am delighted to finally meet you. When Francesco told David and me he would bring you and your charming wife to his little soirée, I believed he was teasing us. But now we owe him a debt of gratitude. Welcome, welcome, I hope the evening proves to be worthy of your time." She turned to Francesco Tosti. "Francesco, may I have the honor of introducing Maestro and Signora Puccini to your other guests?"

Tosti responded with a slight bow. "Sybil, you honor me with your request. By all means, do."

Giacomo and Elvira were charmed at once by Sybil's command of Italian and by her warmth and graciousness.

"Thank you, Madame Seligman," Elvira said. "You make us feel at home."

"Please, not Madame Seligman. Sybil will do. And may I call you Elvira?"

"That would please me."

Giacomo said little as they entered the main room. He allowed his smile to speak for him. But in the course of the evening, he found himself in deep conversation with Sybil about *La Bohéme.* She had initiated the discussion, and in it she expressed a keen awareness of musical subtleties that impressed him mightily. She spoke knowingly and articulately about the opera's delicate balance of music, story, character, and vocal virtuosity. They sat in a corner of the room where Giacomo was utterly taken by her controlled yet passionate discourse. It reminded him of discussions he'd had with Corinna, only this was far more insightful, far more enthralling. Here was another woman who could stir his interests beyond the mundane. And he never noticed the worried glances coming from the opposite side of the room where Elvira was engaged in casual talk with two female guests from Argentina.

At the close of the evening, as Francesco Tosti thanked them for coming to his home, Sybil approached and offered her hand to Elvira. Elvira took it in hers. "I am so happy to have met you," Sybil said, "but I am afraid I spent too much time with your husband. It prevented me from knowing you better. I should dearly love to have lunch with you before you leave London. Just the two of us, Elvira. Would you be willing?"

Elvira nodded. "I should like that."

"*Wonderful!* Tomorrow?"

Elvira grinned. "Yes."

They agreed to meet at an elegant tea garden that Sybil

recommended, where the "Cornish fish cake and custard pudding will take your breath away."

The Puccinis remained in London through the month of October. In that time, they were feted and lionized by British society like visiting royalty. Elvira and Sybil met once a week, and Elvira's earlier suspicions about her new English friend soon disappeared entirely. It had been a thoroughly gratifying month away from home. As Elvira and Giacomo prepared to return to Torre del Lago, they dined with Sybil and her husband David one last time, after which Giacomo kissed Sybil's hand as they said goodbye and asked, "Would you be averse to a correspondence with me?"

"Averse? No...no. I should be delighted, Giacomo," she answered.

Returning to Torre del Lago, Elvira was pleased for months with memories of their London experience. She smiled faintly whenever one came to mind, and occasionally she even hummed a bit of song. Life with her became endurable for Giacomo, sometimes actually pleasant.

Temporarily relieved of Elvira's volatility, Giacomo felt more inclined than ever to compose. Only the absence of a libretto prevented him from attacking his piano. He wrote to Tito Ricordi: *"I am searching for my next opera. I have several stories in mind, but nothing as yet inspires me."*

Tito wrote in return, *"I am eager to hear your thoughts. Come to Milan. We shall discuss them, and you can sign your contract for the opera while you are here."*

The response troubled Puccini. He had never signed a contract before seeing and approving the libretto. His next letter to Tito explained his reluctance to do that now. But Tito was insistent. *"I know my father allowed that procedure. However, I manage affairs differently. It will be better this way. Casa Ricordi will know you are at work on a score, and you will be assured of its production."*

Puccini protested. *"No, Tito. A contract now, before we have a libretto, will put demands upon me that I may not be able to meet. I must feel free of time to create. I cannot be inspired when I am expected to submit a completed opera by a contracted date. Be secure in the honor of my word. When the opera is completed, Casa Ricordi will be its publisher."*

Tito had to accept Puccini's adamant stance, but it displeased him enormously.

Giacomo described his dilemma to Sybil Seligman in a long letter that bemoaned the loss of freedom he always faced in the pursuit of his art. She soothed him with an astute observation about creative sensibilities and the artist's need to resist the boors who place obstacles in his way. *"Ignore them, Giacomo,"* she advised. *"Never allow your genius to be shackled. Find your next opera. Compose sublime music for it and elevate the world again!"*

Giacomo was deeply moved by her reply. *She understands,* he thought. *Her soul is synchronous with mine. God has smiled at me again. She is the muse for whom I have been searching.* With his complaint validated, Puccini plunged into a story search for his next opera. He read books, plays, poetry, writings old and new, but nothing stirred his imagination. He didn't know what he wanted. As always, it was "something different," a nebulous demand that continued to drive Illica to distraction. At one point, he believed he was tired of serious stories and said he wanted a comedy, a scintillating operetta "that will make this very sad world laugh." At another, he longed for something heroic, in the order of grand opera "that will stir the heart and soul to majesty." In truth, Giacomo Puccini was supremely adept at self-delusion. What he truly wanted was to be free of the expectations that his great success had placed upon him. Consequently, he traveled extensively after *Madame Butterfly,* ostensibly to help in productions everywhere in the world. In reality, he wanted only to escape the discomfort of hard work for the pleasure of adulation. He was a glutton for praise and honors, but a man who also complained about the burden of celebrity. Each season saw the production of his operas everywhere in the world. He found it almost impossible not to be present – especially when monetary incentives were extended to him. Though he no longer needed money, when he was offered 50,000 pesos and accommodations aboard a luxurious ocean liner, he went all the way to Argentina with Elvira for a Puccini season of *all* his operas, including *Edgar.* The newspaper *La Prensa* had organized the entire summer of 1905 to delight and honor him for his *"immortal contributions to the glory of music."* And he loved every minute of it. Budapest, Paris, Buenos Aires, London, Bologna, Milan, New York – anywhere one of his operas was being produced, Giacomo could be found waiting anxiously for the applause and curtain calls that would pull him to the stage.

Puccini was a tormented man whose principal longing was for freedom. However, to satisfy Tito's persistent inquiries he mentioned some sources he intended to consider for his next opera. He identified stories by Pierre Louÿs, Oscar Wilde, Edgar Allen Poe, Tolstoy, and Maxim Gorky as strong possibilities.

Tito complained to his father. "He reads, he considers, he names possibilities, but he reaches no decisions. Meanwhile, weeks become months, and we do nothing but wait."

The elder Ricordi agreed with his son. The Corinna affair and Elvira's entreaties had permanently damaged his faith in Giacomo. He saw him now in an entirely different light. Now, Puccini's indecisiveness added to Giulio's disappointment. "He is your problem, Tito," he said. "I am done with him."

Freed of concern that he would distress his father, Tito Ricordi became firm with Puccini. "You are being forgotten by the public," he told him sternly. "Your value to Casa Ricordi is diminished with each day that you fail to supply us with another opera. How much longer are you willing to jeopardize our relationship?"

This new tone unsettled Puccini. "I should like to work on a story by the French novelist Pierre Louÿs," he responded quickly. "I discovered it in 1903, and it has fascinated me ever since. It is called *Le Femme et le Pantin,* The Woman and the Puppet. The more I consider it, the more my imagination is excited by its promise. However, I do not like the title, and I should prefer to call it *Conchita,* after its principal character."

"What is it about?" Tito asked.

"A beautiful Spanish virgin who enslaves a lusting man and

drives him mad by simulating a sexual act with a younger man. The older man then ravages her, arousing in her an appreciation of his passion and making her *his* slave."

"Are you sure of this?" Giulio asked.

"I can hear music even as we speak. Lofty, sweeping sounds, arias of raging intensity, moments of gentle beauty. It will be magnificent!"

"Very well," Tito said. "I shall read the story and, liking it, engage Illica to begin work on its libretto."

The meeting ended with handshakes. At last, Puccini was enthusiastic about a subject. At last he was eager to work!

Tito obtained an Italian translation of *La Femme et al Patin*. It intrigued him. He notified Illica, who read the story at once and agreed heartily with Puccini about its dramatic possibilities. He began work on its libretto immediately.

While he waited for the libretto, Puccini wrote frequently to Sybil Seligman. He described his experiences in detail and entreated her sympathies. She responded swiftly with unqualified support. And their relationship strengthened. In time, he suggested a meeting away from London. She agreed. They met in Paris where physical intimacies were attempted. These failed so miserably that one morning Sybil took his hand and explained gently, "This is not right, Giacomo. It must end. I should like to continue our friendship, but in more Platonic terms. I am extremely uncomfortable with what we are doing. A clandestine affair is too dangerous to the safety of my marriage and certainly inconsistent with my character. Can we not, instead, be friends who will share each other's life and always cherish the beauty of that bond?"

Puccini looked at her with deep appreciation. "I shall be with you anything you wish, dear Sybil, and I shall cherish your honesty always as I cherish it now." His voice was husky with emotion. "Yes, you and I shall be friends, the very best of friends, and that is more than this lowly composer ever hoped for or deserves."

Meanwhile, Illica wrote and Puccini waited. And while he waited, he visited Ramelde in Lucca, he traveled with Elvira to see

Fosca, he read, and he loafed. However, his serenity ended abruptly on September 1, 1906, when wonderful Giuseppe Giacosa died suddenly and unexpectedly. The news had Puccini wandering about his house like a lost soul. Giacosa had been the Buddha, the gentle, all-encompassing voice of reason and lyrical artistry. His death would be a grievous loss to Italy's literary and musical cultures. With a heavy-heart, Giacomo left for Milan and a very sad burial.

Believing in the *Conchita* story, Illica continued to write feverishly, and shortly after Giacosa's death, Puccini received his libretto. He read it hungrily and then circumvented Tito with a surprising letter to Giulio Ricordi: *"Illica does not understand this story. His libretto is a disaster. I must have a new librettist, someone who can see my vision."*

Giulio Ricordi gasped. What was he saying? *Discard Illica?* End their relationship? They had just lost their poet, and now he wants to lose Illica? Is he mad? He took paper instantly from his desk drawer and wrote a scathing reply to his Doge: *"What in heaven's name are you thinking? You astonish me sometimes with your fears and foolishness! Work on* Conchita *must continue with Illica! Your constant harping is surely affecting my health! I have always believed that most artists constitute a brigade of idiots! I see you joining the brigade!*

It was too late. Puccini had lost interest in *Conchita,* and nothing could reignite it.

On learning of Giacomo's change of heart, Illica became furious. "He is as I have always said, a man who does not know his own mind! I am finished with him!"

Thereafter, though he continued to be friendly, Luigi Illica would have no further artistic connection with Giacomo Puccini.

The year 1906 ended on this sad and appalling note of dissension.

- 33 -

Giacomo Puccini left Italy quickly. The Metropolitan Opera House had invited him for a six-week stay in New York to direct productions of *Manon Lescaut* and *Madame Butterfly*. This provided Giacomo with the perfect excuse to escape the repercussions of his actions. He and Elvira boarded the huge S.S. Kaiserin Auguste Victoria on January 18, 1907, a liner with every modern convenience imaginable. However, nothing could calm the rough seas during the ten-day voyage, and Elvira rarely left their luxurious stateroom. Except for one difficult moment of queasiness, Giacomo found the Atlantic crossing rather pleasant. As usual, he was idolized by his fellow passengers, who gathered around him at every opportunity. He dressed immaculately for the dining room, and as he walked the outer deck with his hat tipped jauntily, his hands deep in his winter overcoat pockets, and a cigarette dangling from a corner of his mouth, he never failed to attract attention. The very few times Elvira was able to leave their stateroom, she watched grimly and distrustfully as women flattered and fawned over him.

Elvira challenged him coldly: "Must you always welcome the advances of women?"

"I can do nothing to stop them," he replied. "Women are little gardens always offering themselves for cultivation."

Elvira's expression hardened. "Truly? Then I must caution you, Giacomo, never to become their gardener."

This warning stirred images of Corinna's duplicity and Elvira's rage, and he was mindful to be more restrained through their entire stay in New York. Caution with women, however, didn't prevent him from enjoying the city's sights and hospitality. The

Astor Hotel, where they were staying, provided the Puccinis with an ideal location to experience the city's vibrancy. The Metropolitan Opera house was only five short blocks away. The theater district, only two blocks away. Pedestrians crowded the sidewalks. Horse drawn carriages and bell-clanging trolley cars snaked over the cobblestones, and electric streetlamps kept the area alive long past midnight.

Giacomo found the energy and continuous activity stimulating. Elvira found it boring. Though she preferred to remain in the hotel, Puccini managed to coax her at times into the city's life. He and Elvira walked the Brooklyn Bridge over the East River. They visited Wall Street. They dined in Chinatown and Little Italy, they viewed the Statue of Liberty, and marveled at a thirty-story skyscraper when its elevator took them to the very top. Despite her persistent apathy, Elvira had to admit she found some things about New York "quite enjoyable."

Needing someone to share his enthusiasm, Giacomo made his thoughts and feelings known to Sybil Seligman in a steady stream of letters, all written while Elvira slept. He wrote also to Giulio and Tito Ricordi, his words a feeble attempt to re-establish their earlier opinion of him. "Manon *and* Butterfly *have been magnificently received,"* he told them. *"Caruso is Caruso -- wonderful and lazy. Geraldine Farrar has a small voice and she is difficult. Nevertheless, audiences demand many curtain calls! I continue my search for something that will be our next opera. I hope for a story that will surpass all that we have done together."*

To that end, Giacomo and Elvira attended a few plays, and one of them stirred his interest. It had been written, produced and directed by David Belasco. Puccini had heard of Belasco's new play, and he decided now to see a performance at the Belasco Theater. Tickets to this spectacle, *The Girl of the Golden West,* were virtually unobtainable. But *Madame Butterfly* had brought playwright Belasco and composer Puccini together successfully, and now Belasco was delighted to invite Giacomo and Elvira to his new play.

From 1850 until 1910, the United States frontier was known as the Wild West. Journalists traveled the gritty countryside recording stories of desperate struggle and gory violence. These tales, plus *The Great Train Robbery* (the world's first narrative motion picture) fascinated American easterners and Europeans alike. Giacomo Puccini was not ignorant of the stories or the movie. Consequently, as he watched the inventively staged production of *The Girl of the Golden West*, he found himself drawn to the fire of its love and the menace of its conflict though he couldn't understand a word being said. *Interesting...very interesting,* he thought. *The woman has Tosca's strength, the devotion of Cio-Cio San, Mimi's vulnerability, and the defiance of Manon – all four of my heroines in one body. Also, it has action, strong emotion, an exotic setting, and, best of all, the impact of reality and truth. Verismo, pure Verismo. Hmmm, I shall have to consider this more carefully.* He was particularly impressed by the play's astonishing stage effects: moving curtains to replicate California's shifting clouds; the voices of minstrels singing authentic old songs; and, best of all, a raging, hair-raising blizzard.

The audience left the theater in a clamor of satisfied comments. Giacomo wished he could understand what he was hearing. *Someday,* he thought, *I shall have to learn this English.* In the ornate lobby, he saw Belasco waiting for him and Elvira amidst a cluster of enthusiastic patrons. Belasco saw them, touched the arm of a tall man, and excused himself from the group. Both David Belasco and the tall man approached the Puccinis with warm smiles. "Maestro...Madame Puccini..." the impresario said, "I hope our little presentation tonight did not disappoint you." Then he erased their blank expressions with an introduction. "May I present Signor Francesco Bascone? Mister Bascone is a dear friend who speaks your beautiful language and will be our translator this evening."

Giacomo shook the extended hand. And the Puccini faces brightened with huge smiles as Francesco Bascone went into a lovely flow of cultured Italian.

From that moment on, the evening could not have been more enjoyable if it had been designed in heaven. Bundled against the cold, they rode down to the end of Manhattan in Belasco's brand new, 60 HP, 1907 Hewitt Limousine, a drive that thrilled the Puccinis and had Giacomo questioning Belasco about the vehicle every mile along the way.

"Signor Bascone, where are we going?" Elvira asked.

"Delmonico's," Bascone answered. "It is a restaurant where the steaks melt in one's mouth. They have a small steak, which you must try. It is called the Hamburger."

It was a convivial foursome. Animated conversation. Laughter. Warmhearted flattery. Plus Delmonico's food and wine, which were all that Giacomo and Elvira had been promised. As the evening drew to a close, Elvira excused herself to use the powder room, and the three men lit their after-dinner cigars. Their conversation turned to Puccini's interest in *The Girl of the Golden West*.

"An opera, hmm," Belasco mused. "That's intriguing. I've never imagined it as such."

"I tend to think in musical terms," Giacomo replied, drawing nods and chuckles from the two men. "That is not to say I guarantee great success, but I believe it would be different and that alone makes it a subject for opera consideration."

Belasco squinted in thought. He murmured. "*The Girl* as an opera...interesting. I'd never thought of *Madame Butterfly* as an opera either, and look what you did with it. Yes, Maestro...I believe I would be open to further discussion about this."

"It may be worth pursuing. I shall speak with my producer and promoter about it," Giacomo said. "Let us see what their thoughts may be."

"Very well," Belasco replied. They shook hands warmly, both knowing they were far from any final agreement.

Later, back in their suite at the Astor Hotel, Puccini waited for Elvira to fall asleep before writing a long letter to Sybil Seligman. It was late, but the entire day had been so thoroughly exhilarating that sleep was impossible. After chronicling impressions of New York, he detailed his discussion with David Belasco. *"I am considering* The Girl *for my next project. I should like to write something with an American setting. This may be it, dear Sybil, this may be it."*

By the middle of March, both Giacomo and Elvira were ready to return to the quiet of Torre del Lago. They boarded the *S.S. La Provence* and settled-in for a relaxing voyage home. Again, Elvira spent more time in the stateroom's vomitorium than in the ship's lovely dining room. This gave Giacomo ample time to think more seriously about *The Girl of the Golden West.* And the more he considered the western drama, the more it piqued his interest. Finally, when he was once again comfortably settled in his Torre del Lago villa, he wrote to David Belasco. *"I have been giving much thought to your play, David, and I believe it could become an inspiring opera. Please send me a manuscript. I will have it translated into Italian. That way I will be able to study it carefully and give you a more definitive perception."*

Belasco responded quickly. Puccini forwarded the play at once to Sybil, asking her to translate it for him. She was delighted with the assignment.

Tito Ricordi, however, was not so easily pleased. He attributed Puccini's interest in *The Girl of the Golden West* to the stimulation of New York, and he doubted any genuine commitment on his part to anything anymore. Time proved him wise in his assessment. Giacomo Puccini allowed many months to pass while he considered other dramatic possibilities and traveled extensively (even to Egypt) to see more productions of his work.

Also, his search for a librettist to replace the disaffected Illica took him down several ridiculous roads. One of them involved lengthy, time consuming negotiations with a strange man named Gabriele D'Annunzio. D'Annunzio was a prolific, but arrogant, writer with an ego the size of a continent. His bombast and tireless self-promotion had convinced much of Italy that he was the country's greatest novelist, dramatist, and poet. Puccini was one who accepted D'Annunzio's puffery. Believing he needed a libretto with Giacosa's lyricism, he discussed story possibilities with D'Annunzio for many months. But, finally, he concluded that swaggering D'Annunzio had nothing to offer, and he turned again to the Belasco play. Meanwhile, as the search for a librettist continued, Tito Ricordi shook his head and waited for a decision.

It was Sybil Seligman who helped to rescue Giacomo from his dilemma. In one of her many letters, she wrote: *"I should like to suggest another look at* The Girl of the Golden West. *Its American character is alien to most of the world. Consequently, it would be fresh and delicious to audiences everywhere."*

Puccini placed great store in Sybil's intelligence and in her breadth of culture. He went back to the Italian translation of *The Girl* that he'd requested of her. And he liked what he read. After repeated readings he wrote a happy note to Sybil Seligman on July 12th, 1907, in which he told her: *"Yes,* The Girl of the Golden West *will surely be my next opera! I thank you, dear Sybil. You have become an integral part of my creative life*."

Now he would concentrate on finding a satisfactory librettist. The search did not prove difficult. Tito Ricordi directed him to an Italian poet whose mother just happened to be an American from Colorado. His name was Carlo Zangarini. He was fifteen years younger than Puccini and, as a respected professor at the *Conservatorio Liceo Musicale* in Bologna, he was well-acquainted with opera. He wrote librettos, and he deeply admired Puccini's music. Accepting Tito's suggestion, Giacomo met with Zangarini and came away from their meeting deeply impressed.

The Puccini-Zangarini collaboration began on the highest plane of optimism. Zangarini began his work on *The Girl* the moment he received the Italian manuscript and quickly presented Act I to him. Stirred by the librettist's eagerness, Puccini told Tito in September of 1907, "I am in a fever over this. I can think of nothing else. I am certain *The Girl* will be another *Bohéme*!"

Then, in the second week of October, he expressed his enthusiasm to Sybil, telling her Zangarini had finished the First Act, and was working on Act II. He wrote: *"I love my heroine Minnie, and I am hungry to put her to music. This will be a marvelous libretto. Zangarini is a true poet."*

By the end of November, Zangarini was losing favor. "*He is taking too many liberties*," Puccini wailed. "*He is losing western character and the truth of cowboy language. He is a pig! I may have to find another librettist to complete his work!"*

Fortunately, Zangarini's American mother came to the rescue. As a teacher of English she was versed in American literature and able to supply her son's libretto with the western flavor Puccini felt was lacking. As 1907 drew to a close Giacomo once again believed *The Girl of the Golden West* would be another glowing masterpiece.

But Puccini could never sustain happiness. He was a depressive, which turned him into a constant doubter. In one of his letters to Sybil, he confessed feelings of incapacitating despair, of dark moods from which he was unable to extricate himself. *"Why is there not something to help me from debilitating desolation?"* he wrote. *"It is an insurmountable obstacle in my work."*

In response Sybil sent him a popular elixir and guaranteed him results. It was one of those early 20th century remedies that promised cures for everything from gout to baldness. Giacomo drank the liquid and, in true placebo reaction, he told Sybil it had been enormously helpful but distressingly short-lived. He could not escape his depression, and virtually everyone (except Sybil Seligman) suffered. Inevitably, the luster of Carlo Zangarini dimmed to impatience and contempt. *He cannot do this,* Giacomo fumed to himself. *He is incapable of understanding me. His writing lacks lyricism! I must find someone to help him!*

The suggestion of a collaborator distressed Zangarini. He rejected it so vehemently Puccini had to threaten legal action to force agreement. He met with Tito Ricordi in Milan and begged for another librettist. And it was in this meeting that Giacomo Puccini experienced the first unmistakable indication of fortune reversal with the House of Ricordi. "You appear reluctant to help me in this matter," he told Tito. "I cannot accept that. Your father always appreciated the complexities of collaboration and never failed to find a solution to its problems. Zangarini has become a problem. The solution is another poet!"

"My father has always been too concerned with your sensibilities," Tito replied. "I do not have time for them. Carlo

Zangarini is an excellent poet. That is why I brought him to your attention. Perhaps your differences lie merely in your inability to communicate your needs."

Giacomo could not believe what he was hearing. Earlier complaints had always generated productive concern. Now, Tito's insulting resistance bewildered him. Puccini compressed his lips and swallowed hard. "I shall have to discuss this with Signor Ricordi," he said quietly.

Tito smiled faintly. "I am sure you have noticed that my father is aging," he said. "He is contemplating the peace and comfort of retirement. Control of Casa Ricordi is being passed on to me."

"Where is Signor Giulio? I informed him of my desire to see him."

"Unfortunately, he had to be in Naples for a new production of *Otello*."

"Please contact him and tell him of my predicament."

"I should not like to bother him. Instead, I shall give some thought to another poet for you. Now, if you will excuse me, Maestro, I have a luncheon engagement with another client. It would be discourteous of me to keep him waiting."

Stupefied and feeling he'd suddenly been dislodged from his lofty position with Casa Ricordi, Puccini only muttered, "All right, Tito. I shall be waiting to hear from you."

Outside the office building, he tried to gather his scrambled thoughts. What had just happened? Was he no longer important to the Ricordis? After twenty-five years how could this be? He was Giacomo Puccini. He was Italy's opera idol. How could he be treated in this cavalier manner? He felt helpless, alone. *I cannot depend on Tito*, he thought, *I shall have to find another librettist myself.*

But Tito Ricordi surprised him again. Before Pucini could initiate his own search, he was informed that a copy of *The Girl* had been sent to Guelfo Civinini, a poet and novelist in Livorno. Civinini had read it, liked it, and was eager to begin further versification of Zangarini's libretto.

Puccini didn't know what to do. He had virtually separated himself from Casa Ricordi and now he was being offered a collaborator. He decided to correspond with Civinini. To his surprise he found the poet not only amiable but open as well to all his suggestions. Mutually satisfied, the collaborators immediately attacked their western opera. In May of 1908, Giacomo was able to tell Sybil *"He is everything I have ever wanted. He has already sent me Acts One and Two. Finally, I am able to start composing again."*

However, scars from his treatment by Tito remained. His association with Casa Ricordi would thereafter be tenuous at best. He admitted this concern to Sybil, whereupon she advised him to be patient. *"Once you have completed* The Girl," she predicted, *"its brilliance will cause Tito Ricordi to regret his pettiness."*

Letters with such encouragement came continually from Sybil. They buoyed Puccini's spirit. They brought smiles of pleasure to his lips. They also brought scowls of resentment to Elvira's face. "What is she writing that makes you so happy?" she felt compelled to ask him one day.

"Nothing of importance," he replied. "She writes to you also, does she not? And I have seen you smile when reading her letters."

His tactful answer prevented further inquiry, but it failed to satisfy Elvira. If her husband would not be explicit, if he could not be honest with her, she would find out what Sybil Seligman was writing to him by herself. She waited for her opportunity. It came when he was away from Torre del Lago, supervising another Lucca production of *La Bohéme.* Searching carefully through his belongings, Elvira found the hidden cache of letters underneath a stack of Puccini's shirts. She read them – *all* of them – and though there was nothing erotic in any of them, the strong affection they expressed provoked another tempest of irrational behavior. With anger escalating each day, she waited for Giacomo to return to Torre del Lago. Amazingly, she restrained herself until he was comfortably settled in the living room after dinner. Then, with deceptive gentleness, she said, "Two more letters arrived from Sybil."

Giacomo's face brightened. He took the letters from her hand. "Thank you, Elvira," he said.

"May I read them?" she asked.

"They would not interest you."

"Everything about you interests me, Giacomo. I can read one while you read the other."

"No...but you may see them after I have read both."

"And that is because they may contain something you do not wish me to see, is it not?"

Puccini was too familiar with Elvira's jealousies. He closed his eyes and inhaled deeply. Then, with lips compressed, he offered both envelopes. "Here," he said. "If it matters that much, you may read them first. They are merely letters from a dear friend."

Suddenly losing all control, Elvira shouted: "A dear friend who has all your confidence, a dear friend who knows your darkest secrets, a dear friend who steals your affections from a wife who loves and protects you!"

Giacomo rose from his chair. He looked directly into her eyes and said with the solemnity of a judge, "I have said this before; I say it again: You are insane, Elvira. You are blind to everything decent because you are insane!"

And quickly to escape her wrath he hurried to the safety of his bedroom with Elvira's anger trailing him in screaming accusation: *"You* are the one who is insane, not I! It is insanity to pursue women the way you do! *It is insanity to forsake the decency of your home for the obscenity of lecherous pleasure!"*

Alone in his bedroom, behind a locked door, Giacomo Puccini held his head in both hands. He muttered, "I must leave her. I cannot go on this way. I *must* leave her!"

But he didn't.

Once again, Puccini found it impossible to separate himself from Elvira. Again, he found ways to placate her. And again, life in Torre del Lago resumed a strained but placid pace, enabling him to focus his energies on *The Girl of the Golden West.*

Of course, once again, Giacomo had misjudged his ameliorating skills. Everything should have been splendid for him. Tonio had recently returned from schooling at an exclusive academy in Switzerland. Fosca was now pregnant with his second grandchild.

Productions of his operas were taking place all over the world (for 1908 alone, he would be able to boast more than 200 productions!). Royalty money poured into his bank accounts. And music lovers everywhere clamored for information about his *Wild West* enterprise. However, while Puccini struggled to complete *The Girl* as quickly as possible, Elvira continued to be erratic. And now she directed her frustrations toward those of the domestic help who strove to keep her husband contented and healthy enough to work.

Principal among her targets was Doria Manfredi, the youngest of Elvira's three servants.

Doria came from a family of two older brothers and a widowed mother. She had joined the Puccinis in 1903 when she was sixteen years old, an industrious girl who worked tirelessly to aid Giacomo through his automobile accident recovery. Though Elvira's harshness with servants usually made their tenures short-lived, Doria's employment survived for eight years. At twenty-four she was a conscientious young woman with an attractive figure and a pleasant disposition. However, though Giacomo noted her growth into womanhood, he never saw her as anything more than a dutiful servant. Nevertheless, in October of 1908, Elvira suddenly, and for no apparent reason, turned her irrational suspicions upon Doria. "I have been watching you," she snapped one day. "You believe you are clever. You smile. You pretend loyalty. But I see through your affectations. I know you for what you are...a *baldracca*!"

Astounded at being called a slut, Doria could only stammer, "S...S...Signora...Signora...I...I... do not know what...what...."

"Do not lie to me! I see the way you look at Signor Puccini! The Smiles! The ingratiating mannerism! Do you think I am a fool? Do you think you can hide your foul behavior from me? You have been sleeping with my husband, you filthy *prostituta*!"

Tears flooded Doria's eyes. She pleaded, "S...S...Signora... Signora...."

"And you prove it now with tears of guilt! I want you out of my house! Do you hear me? Out! Out! This instant! Now! Get out! *Get out!*"

Bewildered beyond control, Doria fled before Elvira's screams like a child before a snarling dog.

"Run! Run! You slut! You whore! You will never escape me! The entire village will learn of your filthy treachery!"

Hearing Elvira's rage, Giacomo hurried from his piano. He arrived in time to see Doria fleeing the house. "What happened?" he asked. "What did she do?"

Elvira turned her frenzy upon him. "Do not play the innocent with me! Do you think you could fornicate with your slut and I would never discover your perfidy?!"

"What are you saying?"

"I warned you! *I warned you!"*

"Is that why she raced from the house? You accused that innocent soul of being my mistress? This is too much, Elvira. It is the limit of my endurance!"

Without saying another word, Puccini returned to his piano while Elvira stormed about the kitchen, throwing pots and utensils at the walls in her fury. Muttering to himself, he gathered his music notes, closed the piano lid, and hurried to his bedroom. There, he packed a suitcase, snapped it shut, and grabbed a coat before rushing from the villa. He said no goodbyes. He didn't look back. He slipped into his newest car and sped away.

Elvira heard him leaving the house. She raced to the door. "Where are you going?" she screamed. "Come back here! We must talk about this!"

But Giacomo did not return. He drove to Viareggio, to the house he had purchased years ago for his trysts with Corinna, a house he still owned.

His absence in the following days bewildered Elvira and served to deepen her frenzy. She went into the village to find him and, failing there, she accused Doria publicly and vociferously of stealing and hiding her husband. "I caught them in their illicit act!" she ranted to any villager who would listen. Her behavior precipitated a fiery scandal that lasted for months.

Ramelde and Puccini's other sisters attacked him: "First

Corinna and now this! Will you never be a faithful husband?" Tonio opposed his father and sided with his mother: "She has been a faithful wife, and for that she is made to suffer!" Villagers took sides. Some doubted the rectitude of their honored Maestro. "He is guilty," they declared. "The richer they are the looser their morals!" Others defended the Manfredis: "We have known them for years," they argued, "and never has there been a hint of immorality!" Doria continued tearfully to profess her innocence. *"I have done nothing wrong! I have done nothing wrong!"* Her enraged brothers threatened Elvira with bodily harm. But nothing would stop her. Elvira hunted the girl. She waited for Doria outside her house. She followed and berated her in the streets, spitting curses and hurling wild accusations for all to hear.

In Viareggio, Giacomo learned of Elvira's persistent persecution.

He had promised the Ricordis a completed opera, and he had been working on it diligently. However, news of Elvira's vitriol reached him, and he found himself too overwhelmed by it to continue. He wrote to Sybil: "I *am helpless. Elvira demands my return, and I lack the courage to stay away. Elvira is unapproachable. She never listens. She screams. She is destroying the poor girl. I fear something terrible will come of this."*

Puccini struggled with his dilemma. He felt Doria's distress. But when it came to Elvira he was a self-admitted coward. Not knowing how to stop his wife's frantic, uncontrollable behavior, he avoided confrontation by running farther away, this time to Paris. From there he wrote to Sybil and whined: *"I am alone....My success should make me happy, but I suffer too much....I think of putting a bullet in my brain, but I lack the courage to do it...."*

He wrote also to the Manfredis. He pleaded Doria's innocence and swore himself not guilty of Elvira's charges. *"I have always been fond of Doria,"* he admitted, *"but I swear to you there is no truth in the vile way she is being maligned! Lies! All lies, and I suffer with her!"*

The Girl of the Golden West also suffered. Work on the opera came to a halt. Puccini did nothing but fret his days away. Confused and beaten, he told Sybil, *"Elvira has been unrelenting. I have returned to Torre del Lago. However, my brain is muddled. I am unable to feel inspiration. I am desolate. My opera languishes, and I do too."*

Elvira's victimization of Doria intensified. Seeing the girl in Torre del Lago's marketplace, she rushed at her screaming, "You whore! If you do not stop meeting my husband in the dark of night, you will one day be drowned in the lake! I swear it – I will drown you!"

At another time, dressed in Giacomo's clothes, Elvira waited near the Manfredi house, hoping to trap Doria in a meeting that would prove all accusations.

Villagers began to look at Doria questioningly. Some shunned her. Others spat at the ground when she greeted them. It all became more than the poor girl could bear. On January 23, 1909, Doria Manfredi exchanged one pain for another. She swallowed a terrible poison and suffered for five days and nights before she died.

Her suicide shocked Torre del Lago to its foundations. A cruel rumor flared overnight and spread through the village like fire in dry grass: "Doria Manfredi did not commit suicide. She died, instead, during an abortion of Giacomo Puccini's child!"

Infuriated, Doria's brothers demanded an autopsy. The demand could not be ignored. It was performed at once with several authorities in attendance. After his careful examination, the performing doctor looked up from the body and announced solemnly, "The young lady did not have an abortion. She was a virgin when she died."

The autopsy results were printed in the local newspaper. Instantly, public opinion reversed itself. Doria and Puccini were vindicated. Giacomo was greeted everywhere again with respect. Ramelde sent her apologies. Tonio faced him with downcast eyes. And Elvira became the village's scapegoat. Fury at having been duped turned everyone against her. She was openly reviled, cursed and threatened. It was made clear that she was no longer wanted in Torre del Lago and that everyone would be much happier if she lived elsewhere.

Elvira fled to Milan in terror, but she could not escape.

Doria's brothers wanted blood. Avoiding Elvira directly, they consulted two lawyers and filed a suit against her, claiming her vicious lies had defamed and killed their innocent sister. They didn't ask for financial reparation -- they demanded punishment.

Giacomo, meanwhile, consulted his own lawyers. He said he had suffered enough with Elvira, and that he wanted a legal separation.

Receiving the separation papers from Puccini's attorneys, Elvira wrote a scorching letter to Giacomo in which she accused him of merciless abandonment at a time of her enormous distress. *"You are evil incarnate! You live only for the pain you can cause me! You think only of yourself. It is you who should be facing action for all your deceit and heartless entanglements. Selfish! Selfish! I regret the day we met!"*

Puccini's hands trembled as he read Elvira's words. A giant wave of confusion and guilt washed over him. He thought, *"She has brought this upon herself, but I must accept some responsibility."* That afternoon, he went to the Manfredis. He begged them to withdraw their charges. He offered them money. They scorned him. Their unshakable refusal guaranteed litigation and the possibility of imprisonment for Elvira. He wrote to her, *"They are adamant. I shall find some excellent attorneys for you."*

"I do not need nor do I want your assistance," she shot back. *"I have attorneys of my own!"*

The case went to trial on July 6, 1909, and it became an international sensation. From the start, it was evident that Elvira's lawyers were incompetent fools who knew little if anything about legal defense. Their primary argument was absurd: "The accused has been unjustly blamed for the death of someone she barely knew. There is no evidence that our client defamed the deceased, and we shall present proof that the charges leveled against her are the malicious imaginings of less fortunate members of her community."

The prosecution destroyed this ridiculous defense with little difficulty. The verdict came in quickly and harshly. It found Elvira guilty of slander. It said she was guilty of character defamation and of being a menace to honest members of society. She was ordered to pay a fine of 700 lire and to pay all court costs. But most shocking of all – *she was sentenced to spend five months and five days in prison!*

The verdict traumatized Elvira. "I cannot go to prison," she wailed at Giacomo. "If I had courage, I would throw myself from a window and kill myself! Do you see what you have brought me to? You are the cause of my grief, and now you gloat at my misery!"

Puccini reacted to her crazed accusation as if *he* had been sentenced. He agonized. He squirmed. Only Elvira's freedom could release him from the torment of his guilt. He ran to his lawyers. "She cannot go to prison," he implored. "There must be a way to save her."

"It is too late," he was told. "The court's judgment is irreversible. We can appeal the decision, but that will take months."

In desperation, he turned again to the Manfredis. "What can I do to have you retract your charges?" he begged.

"Nothing," they told him emphatically. "She killed our sister with her lies as surely as if she had plunged a dagger into her sweet heart. She must be punished!"

"But revenge will not satisfy the loving spirit of Doria. I understood your sister. She was dear. She was gentle and forgiving. She would never seek my wife's imprisonment."

The exchange continued. Giacomo persisted doggedly, and slowly his pleas penetrated the Manfredi resolve. Agreement was finally reached. He would guarantee Elvira's permanent banishment from Torre del Lago, and for withdrawal of their charges the Manfredi family would accept his offer of 12,000 lire to help them through their grief. The complaint was withdrawn, the verdict cancelled, and the entire case expunged from official records.

Giacomo was greatly relieved.

Elvira was not. "If you were not pernicious, this would never have happened. You have destroyed my reputation," she argued. As for Giacomo's agreement with the Manfredis, she accepted her banishment from Torre del Lago at once. "I never want to see that village again," she fumed. "Its people are all perjurers and hypocrites!"

She even quibbled over the 12,000 lire settlement. And though it was completely irrelevant to her verdict, she demanded the cancellation of Puccini's petition for a legal separation. "You are my husband," she avowed. "I shall never sign your papers. No matter what you have done to hurt me, you will always be my husband. But I am forgiving. I shall even accept you back into my life if you are willing to apologize for your cruelty."

"Apologize?!" Puccini exploded. "You expect me to humiliate myself for the death and pain *you* have caused? There is a ghost between us, Elvira. I swear it: We shall never again be together!"

"Returning to her is out of the question," he wrote to Sybil Seligman. *"I shall live alone and peacefully in my beloved Torre del Lago. I am a wounded man, wretched, sad, a pathetic figure. I may never compose again."*

Puccini may have considered never composing again, but that sentiment was unacceptable to Casa Ricordi. Too much money had already been spent on *The Girl of the Golden West* for Tito to calmly accept the loss.

- 34 -

COME TO MILAN. STOP. IMPORTANT NEW DEVELOPMENT. STOP. DISCUSSION IMPERATIVE.

TITO RICORDI

The telegram unsettled Puccini. It seemed like an order. *I am in no condition to travel,* he thought, *especially to speak with Tito.*

He ignored the telegram.

A second message from Tito followed immediately.

CRITICAL. STOP. MUST SEE YOU.

TITO RICORDI

Puccini sighed deeply. "It is most likely about *The Girl*," he mumbled. "Tito...Tito...why will you not leave me in peace?"

But Giacomo knew how persistent and implacable Tito Ricordi could be. So, he groaned, pulled himself together, and boarded the next morning's train to Milan. He was not happy about this, but a question nagged at him through the entire trip: *What can this critical development be that makes discussion so imperative?*

When they met at Casa Ricordi, Tito's first words were: "You look terrible."

"I need rest."

"There will be ample time for that after you complete your new opera. I have news for you. The New York Metropolitan wants to première *Girl of the Golden West* as soon as it is ready. When do you estimate that will be?"

"I have no idea."

"I must be brutally candid with you, Giacomo. This latest scandal may have tarnished your name internationally, and interest in all your operas may suffer. To offset that possibility I have successfully obtained a Metropolitan commitment for *The Girl*'s première. Now I must be able to tell them when they can expect that to take place. When do you estimate that will be?"

Puccini was stunned. He did not appreciate Tito's businesslike demeanor. "I do not compose under pressure, Tito," he replied with equal coldness. "Music comes from the soul. When my soul is ready, it will release it."

"The soul can be a lazy thing, Giacomo. Without prompting, it may never respond."

Puccini stared at his publisher. "If that is to be, so be it, Tito."

Tito stared back at him. "And that can destroy a lifetime of work, leaving a sad legacy of questionable accomplishment."

Puccini had no answer. He left Milan that same evening thinking of his musical legacy. He had never considered the possibility of permanent damage to his name. He'd hoped the sordidness through which he had just passed would eventually fade and disappear into the indifference of time. But now...well, Tito had compelled him to think of the future.

Back in Torre del Lago, Puccini sat at his piano and forced himself to feel music for *The Girl of the Golden West.* At first nothing happened. But in the days ahead his original enthusiasm resurfaced slowly and pulled him evermore deeply into the excitement of invention. He began to hear snatches of musical passage. A refrain here. A hint of aria there. He jotted them onto a composition page, and the very act of seeing them on paper stimulated him into a full day of creativity.

That evening he wrote exuberantly to Sybil, "The Girl *is alive. I work again! Fortitude has the power to encourage inspiration. Despair no longer strangles me. My soul sings!"*

By the end of 1909 he reported the completion of Acts I and II to Tito Ricordi. And he promised the third act by the summer of 1910. Tito immediately resumed negotiations with the New York Metropolitan Opera House. A tentative date for *The Girl of the Golden West*'s world première was set for December 10, 1910, that same year.

Meanwhile, Giacomo responded to a plea from Elvira to visit with her and Tonio in Milan. He had told Tonio he would never see Elvira again if she continued to blame him for her unhappiness and all their suffering. However, satisfaction with his work softened his resolve, and after repeated pleas, he finally acquiesced to Elvira's entreaties.

They met on neutral ground, not in her Milan apartment as she had suggested. A café, Giacomo hoped, would discourage another outburst of rage and recrimination. Tonio assumed the role of mediator the moment they were seated. He was twenty-four now, a young man who longed for only one thing – the end of his parents' discord. "Father," he began, "Mother wants you to know she is grateful that you have agreed to this meeting."

Giacomo looked at Elvira.

She was watching him with a pained expression and nodding slowly.

Tonio continued: "She also wishes you to know how sincerely she prays for an end to your differences."

Giacomo frowned.

"And she is willing to –"

Elvira touched Tonio's hand and stopped him in mid-sentence. She addressed Giacomo quietly and pleadingly. "We miss you, Giacomo," she said. "Terribly. Life has little meaning when a family is torn by dissension. "

Puccini glanced from one to the other.

"We are not whole without you," Elvira continued. "Please let us come home to you. Let us be a loving family again, with no more vile denunciations. Let us help each other, instead, through whatever difficulties that are placed in our paths."

"Please, Father," Tonio said.

The gentleness of their pleas disarmed Puccini completely. "I...I have never wanted more than love and harmony for us," he said. "I have always wanted us to be a blessed family."

It seemed to be a moment of honesty for the Puccinis. Earnestness replaced the emotional outbursts that all three hoped to avoid, and the meeting settled into an agreeable exchange of thoughts and feelings.

Five days later, Puccini wrote to Sybil: *"Tonio and Elvira have returned to Torre del Lago. She is chastened. Fear of the townspeople keeps her close to home, and she is decidedly more attentive to my needs. Consequently, work on* The Girl *progresses smoothly. If all continues to go this well, I shall have my opera finished by this summer!"*

Everything did continue to go well. A slight problem developed over the opera's title, which in Italian was too unwieldy for Puccini – *La Fanciulla dell'Occidente d'Oro*. But Sybil solved it with a simple suggestion to delete the word `golden,' to make it *La Fanciulla dell'Occidente*. Puccini liked that. It translated easily from Italian as *The Girl of the West*. Thereafter, his opera became known by no other title. True to his word, Puccini delivered a completed score to Tito Ricordi on July 10, 1910, with his usual assertion, "I know you will agree that *La Fanciulla* is the best work I have ever done!"

Preparations for the Metropolitan's world première proceeded. Contracts were signed by David Belasco to direct the opera, by Enrico Caruso to sing the tenor role of Johnson, by Emmy Destinn for the soprano heroine Minnie, and by Arturo Toscanini to conduct. Puccini was offered 20,000 dollars for a four week stay in America, plus luxurious stateroom accommodations for two on the massive ocean liner S.S. George Washington, plus a New York hotel suite, plus all food and taxi expenses. Promotion and advertising began and gathered momentum with each passing day. Reviewers filled their columns with every tidbit of information they could glean about Puccini and *La Fanciulla del West.* Blasé New York became a crystal glass of opera with excitement, like vintage champagne, bubbling to the brim.

Ecstatically, Tito Ricordi kept track of every bubble.

Nervously, Puccini counted days to the start of rehearsals.

Quietly, Elvira waited for an invitation to accompany him to New York.

"How would you like to be with me in New York?" Puccini asked one morning at breakfast. The question was directed at Tonio, not Elvira.

"Really?" Tonio replied. "New York?"

"You could help me during rehearsals."

"I would love to go with you!" Tonio exploded.

"Excellent! We shall leave the first week in November!"

Elvira waited for her invitation. It never came. That evening, grim and unable to restrain herself, she challenged him with, "You invite the son but you ignore the wife and mother?"

Giacomo answered, "You said you hate New York. You lived in the vomitorium both ways, and you felt ignored because I had to be at rehearsals. Have you forgotten your misery?"

"That is not the issue. You should invite. It is my choice to accept or refuse."

Giacomo snorted. "Very well, would you like to be with us in New York?"

"No!" Then turning quickly she left him and went directly to her room.

November arrived on the wings of Chronos. Puccini thought: *Yes, time does fly*. Aboard the S.S. George Washington, he, Tonio and Tito Ricordi enjoyed a calm and thoroughly entertaining voyage. *"This ship,"* he wrote to Sybil, *"is bigger than the pyramids of Egypt!"*

And the treatment he received made him feel like a pharaoh.

New York's reception reinforced that feeling tenfold. He was received like royalty. His hotel suite eclipsed every accommodation he had ever enjoyed. Reporters wouldn't let him out of their sight. His picture appeared in every newspaper almost every day. Two aides were assigned by the Met to satisfy his every need. He could not have been happier. Well, that's not entirely accurate. He worried. As always, fear of failure lay behind his every smile. Having been lifted to the Pinnacle of Expectation, was he now to be dashed into the Pit of Anticlimax? *Dear God,* he prayed, *please allow* La Fanciulla *to succeed …please allow* La Fanciulla *to succeed….*

Rehearsals proceeded extraordinarily well. Belasco directed his actors tirelessly, and he achieved a form of reality with them that surpassed anything Puccini had ever witnessed. Opera singers became actors. Instead of standing like sticks that sing directly to their audience, they interrelated excitingly. Caruso's voice sounded like the voice of an angel. Destinn, who had been a magnificent Cio-Cio San in *Butterfly*, promised now to be an even better Minnie, and Toscanini was shaping his orchestra to perfection! Puccini could have asked for nothing more. On December 10, 1910, the Metropolitan Opera House was filled to capacity. Tickets sold-out one hour after the box office opened. Scalpers were asking and getting *thirty* times the box office ticket price! Anyone of musical, social, or political importance was in the audience.

Seated alone in the private box of the Met's general manager, Puccini waited for his opera to begin. Finally, the house lights dimmed. Audience conversation softened to silence. Toscanini raised and lowered his baton. The music started. The curtains parted. And the world's first performance of *The Girl of the West* entered musical history.

Ten minutes into Act I Giacomo Puccini felt the palms of his hands begin to sweat. What was wrong? Everything on the stage sounded right to him. Why wasn't the audience responding? His breath quickened. Fear gripped him again. He sensed disaster and slouched in his seat. However, everything changed when the curtains closed on the act. Suddenly, a monumental wave of applause crashed through the house and straightened his back. Approval reverberated like thunder in a canyon. He couldn't believe what he was hearing. He looked about. People were standing, cheering, shouting *Bravisimo!* They looked up at his box. The opera would not continue until he stood, all smiles, and bowed his appreciation. From that moment on, pandemonium reigned at the Met. The evening became a continuum of curtain calls – *fifty-two,* in all. Performers glowed. Toscanini bowed. Puccini and Belasco were called to the stage numerous times, and at the end of Act II an elaborate silver wreath was placed ceremoniously upon Puccini's head. Then, Act III, as it is said in theater, "tore down the house." Applause continued for fifteen minutes at the final curtain. This was another hysterical ovation for Giacomo Puccini, one that exceeded, by far, anything he had experienced in the past.

The next morning, newspaper and magazine reviewers confirmed the magnitude of *The Girl's* success. They said it was brilliant, powerful, grand, a triumph, and that Giacomo Puccini had conquered America. Only three reviewers expressed reservations. The success, they contended, lay more with Belasco than Puccini. "*Signor Puccini's music is not American,*" one wrote. "*And being Italian, it does not capture the color of our West.*"

And all three predicted the opera would fall out of favor and soon be withdrawn from the Met's repertory.

These few negative comments were no more than insignificant gnat bites to Puccini. Applause, praise, veneration continued through the opera's entire Metropolitan run and into productions that followed around the world. Unfortunately, however, one of those gnat bites proved to be painfully and mystifyingly prophetic. Audience interest in *The Girl of the West* faded steadily, and after only three seasons the opera was removed from the Met's annual selections.

While in New York, though, Puccini had no idea this would occur, and he reveled in his victory. He wrote to Elvira and described the city's acceptance in detail. She answered with impatience to see him and Tonio again and with happiness for his great success.

On December 28, 1910, Giacomo, Tonio, and Tito Ricordi left New York for home on the fabulous S.S. Lusitania. Three nights later, above the din of the New Year's Eve celebration, he shouted wearily at Tonio, "I am exhausted. I think I shall go to our stateroom away from this noise."

"Stay, Papa," Tonio urged. "The night is young. You will miss all the merriment."

Puccini smiled at his son's youthful exuberance. "I am now fifty-two years old, Tonio. I have everything for which I have ever yearned. I cannot imagine what else life could offer me now."

Tito Ricordi would soon reveal some of his future to him, and Giacomo would not be pleased by the revelation.

- 35 -

Through all of 1911 and into 1914, Giacomo Puccini traveled everywhere a production of *La Fanciulla* could bring him kudos. City after city, country after country hailed the opera and heaped honors upon him. Kings praised it. Audiences cheered it.

Only critics found fault. Some said Puccini's music lacked his customary lyricism and melody. Others, like their New York counterparts, predicted: "*...it is not an opera for the ages*."

Tito Ricordi agreed with the prophets of doom. To Tito, the importance of a production lay solely in its revenue, not in the cheers and honors it generated for the composer. *La Fanciulla*'s receipts, he noticed, continued to weaken with each passing year. Opera houses were scheduling fewer performances. Fewer performances meant loss of interest. Loss of interest augured problems for Casa Ricordi. Once again he summoned Puccini to Milan.

"Traveling everywhere you are no doubt enjoying your fame," he told him bluntly, "but I am not enjoying the reports of our treasurer. Your opera is not the great success you are being misled to believe."

Giacomo Puccini creased his brows and waited for more. His intense dislike of Tito's crass demeanor had made all meetings with him irritating experiences.

"You do not seem to appreciate the importance to Casa Ricordi of continuous creativity," Tito added. "We rely on new operas to meet the costs of supporting our clients. It grieves me to say this, Maestro, but your catalogue no longer produces its earlier income."

"Are these your words, Tito," Puccini asked, "or are you conveying the thoughts of Signor Giulio?"

Tito bristled. "I am not a messenger, Maestro."

"Certainly not. Nevertheless, I should like to hear your estimation of my value to Casa Ricordi from Signor Giulio himself."

"That is not possible. My father is not well, and he has removed himself from the company."

"Not well? It is not serious, I hope."

"I am not at liberty to say."

Deeply troubled by the suggestion that his friend and mentor's health might be failing, Puccini wanted only to end this encounter and to escape his antagonist.

"Now," Tito asked, "when may I expect a decision from you on your next undertaking?" Tito's tone made it more demand than request.

Puccini had had enough of his brashness. He replied curtly, "As soon as I make it." And then he added sardonically, "If you will excuse me, I have some possibilities to consider."

Away from Tito, Giacomo pondered the unsettling implications of this meeting. Working with Tito had become impossible. He, Puccini, could not be rushed into decisions. And he could not tolerate Tito's condescension. What would he do, though, without Giulio Ricordi? To whom could he turn? Did this foretell the end of his opera career?

No, but it did add another twist to Puccini uncertainties.

"I may be getting too old for this," he thought. *"I tire easily now and find myself saddened by the changes I detect around me."*

At this juncture in life, Giacomo Puccini was more than ever a profusion of conflicting emotions. Adding to his eternal despair, his favorite sister Ramelde died on April 8, 1912. Elvira accompanied him to Lucca for Ramelde's funeral. She stayed with him constantly, tending to his needs, quietly comforting him in the depth of his sorrow. She sat with him in a corner of his sister's living room, holding his hand as he wept, thanking visitors and relatives for their expressions of regret, protecting him from all who would attempt lengthy conversations.

On their return to Torre del Lago, Giacomo acknowledged her help. He leaned close. He whispered, "I shall never forget your thoughtfulness, Elvira. You were my voice, my stalwart shield."

"As I shall always be, Giacomo," she said. "We are husband and wife. We belong to each other." She took his arm and held it tightly.

Then Puccini's last link to artistic stability was shattered when Giulio Ricordi died on June 12th. Another mentor, another father, had been taken from him. He packed at once and left for Milan and Giulio Ricordi's funeral. Unfortunately, Elvira had contracted a terrible, incapacitating cold and was unable to accompany him. He could have used her shield, particularly when Tito approached the group of mourners of which Puccini was a member. "Maestro," Tito said, interrupting their quiet conversation. "I should like a few words with you, please."

Giacomo allowed himself to be led from the group.

"With my father's passing," Tito told him when they were apart from everyone, "you must understand that Casa Ricordi has passed entirely into my hands."

Puccini closed his eyes and slowly shook his head.

"I think it proper to inform you that certain changes will be made in the way business is conducted at the company."

"Tito," Puccini murmured, "this is neither the time nor place for such matters."

"On the contrary, Maestro. I determine time and place for Casa Ricordi affairs now, and I should like you to know that I expect a commitment from you for a new opera within a month, or...."

Giacomo stared at him. *"Or...?"*

"Or we shall have to reconsider our relationship." Then Tito turned away abruptly to join another group of mourners.

Puccini's eyes widened. His breath caught. He had just been given an ultimatum! How dare this upstart, this arrogant nonentity, whose status was achieved only through the good fortune of inheritance, speak to him this way?

"Are you all right?" he was asked when he rejoined his group. The question came from Pietro Mascagni, his friend from conservatorio days. "You look shaken."

Puccini smoldered in silence.

Sitting next to Giacomo during the funeral proceedings, Mascagni watched him carefully. *Something terrible has happened,* he thought. He had to know what Tito had said. He poked Puccini's thigh for attention. Giacomo turned his head. "Whatever it is," Mascagni whispered, "Tito is a pig."

Puccini nodded and tried to smile.

"Coffee when this is over?" Mascagni asked.

"Yes."

"You look ready to explode."

"Let us leave quickly."

"As you wish, Giaco."

Both waited impatiently for the service to end. When it did, they left without speaking to anyone.

They chose Cucina Milano in the Palazzo Marino near the La Scala opera house. Facing each other across the table, Mascagni said, "Before coffee, before anything, tell me what happened between you and The Pig."

Puccini inhaled deeply. Then as calmly as he could, he related every detail of his alarming encounter with Tito Ricordi. When he was through, Mascagni cursed, "That shit! That bastard! He should die all alone and rot in the Gobi Desert! You do know why he is treating you this way, do you not?"

Giacomo looked at Pietro questioningly.

"It is because he believes he must establish his own authority at all costs. Despite his bravado, Tito Ricordi is a weak and fearful man. He is not his father, and he knows it. You are not alone. He is treating me and others the way he is treating you, Giaco."

"Why? What does he hope to gain from such insolence?"

"A new Casa Ricordi, one that embraces a new wave of opera... new composers, new librettists, new music. Tito believes you and I are the past. Our music, he has said, is too sentimental, too romantic. He wants young artists, a fresh catalogue of unnatural reality and unappealing dissonance. Then he will not live in the shadow of a genuinely great man, his illustrious father, Signor Giulio."

Puccini had absorbed his friend's explanation without interruption. Now, he spat, "He is a fool! I have made millions for Casa Ricordi, and he would dispense with me?!"

"To Tito, you, I, Bieto, and the entire body of *Scapigliatura Milanese* are yesterday. The future of opera, he believes, lies in the minds of composers like Riccardo Zandonai, D'Annunzio and their gang."

"I have asked D'Annunzio several times to write a libretto for me," Puccini mused.

"What happened?"

"Agreement with him was impossible. He is in a world of his own."

"A strange man."

"Very."

"Zandonai is little better. He is brilliant but difficult. I know. I was his teacher at the Pesaro Conservatorio."

"And these are the future of Italian opera?"

"If Tito has his way. He believes Zandonai is heir to Puccini the way you were heir to Verdi."

"Why has he not made this known to me?" It was a rhetorical question, a thought muttered in perplexity and not meant for an answer. Nonetheless, Mascagni answered. "It has always been there for you to know, Giaco, but perhaps you have been too busy with success to have heard about it. Simply stated, Tito believes a new age in Italian opera is dawning, and we are not part of it."

The statement was startling. Like an incessant bell it jangled in Puccini's mind all the way back to Torre del Lago. *My music is old? Too sentimental? Too romantic?* He recalled how, many years ago, the *Scapigliatura* had said the same thing about Verdi, how they had denounced him and relegated him to museum status. *And now Tito is saying the same about me.*

Elvira saw his distress the moment Puccini entered their house. Though her cold had her coughing, sneezing and teary-eyed, she said sympathetically, "I am sorry I could not have been with you. You look so sad."

"I am," was all he said, letting her believe he was grieving over the loss of Giulio Ricordi.

Through all of 1912 and 1913, Giacomo Puccini searched for a subject that would release his musical genii and prove Tito Ricordi wrong. He considered over thirty different stories but leaped from one to the next like an agitated grasshopper. And his desperation grew with each futile leap. *I need something with love and despair, something that will make people laugh and weep,* he thought. *My next opera must have tremendous force. It must abandon the old ways but still be enduring.*

Then, confuting his own desires, he agreed to compose eight or ten melodies for a witty Viennese operetta. The incredible sum of 400,000 Austrian crowns and 50% of the box office receipts was simply too much to reject. But once again he lost interest, and this too faded into nothingness. As it disappeared, though, it gave birth to another Vienna agreement: He would compose a full operetta to be called *La Rondine* (The Swallow). With resentment still boiling against Tito Ricordi he brokered the entire contract himself.

A young playwright named Giuseppe Adami became Giacomo's eager librettist. He began work immediately on September 4, 1914. Six weeks later Puccini was back in his pattern of hopelessness, cursing *Rondine* and the day he had signed the contract to write its music. *It is nothing but trash! I am going to kill myself. Better to die than to suffer the ignominy of La Rondine!*

He didn't have to kill himself. He didn't have to die. Giuseppe Adami supplied a revised version of the operetta that surprised and pleased Puccini immensely.

Composing began again, and it continued steadily until the operetta was completed eighteen months later – despite a political convulsion that shook the entire globe.

Hatred had been fermenting for months. The royal families of Europe were intoxicated by it. Opposing alliances had formed. Nations were flexing their military muscles. Passions were boiling, and conflict was inevitable. It came suddenly on June 28, 1914 with the assassination of Austro-Hungarian Archduke Franz Ferdinand.

Exactly one month later on July 28th, World War I began and the world went mad.

Puccini considered himself apolitical. Current events rarely interested him. Music was all that mattered....music and now *La Rondine.* Unable to tolerate the sight of Tito Ricordi any longer, Giacomo signed a contract with the Sonzagno Publishing Company, Casa Ricordi's archrival. He laughed as he wrote his name; gratification tickled him.

Edoardo Sonzagno was delighted to have Puccini as a client. He despised Tito's abrasive business attitude as much as Giacomo hated it. "We shall make *La Rondine* an experience that opera *cognoscenti* will honor for decades to come," he pronounced.

Giacomo beamed. He shook his new publisher's hand. He felt unchained, free of Tito's objectionable behavior forever.

Told of Sonzagno's intention to make *La Rondine* an operatic sensation, Tito feigned indifference. "It is of no consequence to Casa Ricordi," he responded. "Puccini no longer matters. I doubt if he will ever compose something of significance again."

Giacomo heard about this and seethed. Now engaged in a deadly feud with Tito Ricordi, he believed an outstanding production of *La Rondine* had become imperative.

But most of the world had more important things to consider than opera. Detailed war news and shocking photographs alarmed civilians everywhere. Puccini was no exception. He suffered with everyone. "War is the ultimate evil," he said. "I want nothing to do with it!"

His neutrality, however, was unacceptable. Global war fever brought him vilification everywhere, and his reputation collapsed in a tidal wave of opprobrium. Even his close friend Arturo Toscanini turned against him in a blistering denunciation that almost produced blows. "I am an artist," Giacomo cried, "not a warrior! Why must I be drawn into something so hideous, something I deplore?"

On May 5, 1915 Puccini was given the answer to that question. Italy entered World War I on the side of the Allies and, like it or not, he was compelled to choose. The side he chose, of course, was that of his country. Quickly, he made his position known, and he strove to restore his reputation with concrete actions. He declared his allegiance to Italy and her cause. He contributed money to war relief. And most telling of all, he sent his only son to war.

"I have enlisted in the army," Tonio announced one evening at the Torre del Lago dinner table.

"*What?*" Elvira cried.

"I cannot sit by idly while others fight my war."

Giacomo said nothing. A faint smile touched his lips.

Antonio Puccini was now twenty-nine years old. He had become a handsome, early-20th century playboy. The knowledge he'd acquired in his Swiss Academy schooling meant absolutely nothing to him. He avoided any kind of work. Only women, speed, and good times interested him. When Puccini gave him a new Bobber motorcycle for his twenty-second birthday, Tonio joined a bike club and became a reckless wonder on Italian racetracks. Sometimes he would disappear for weeks to party and race around the countryside with other enthusiasts. Giacomo had expressed disappointment in his son's carefree behavior. But now that Tonio had joined the army to fight for Italy, Puccini felt a sudden flush of pride.

Not so Elvira. "How could you have done that?" she demanded. "War is not one of your escapades! Thousands are dying on the battlefields every day! You may never return!"

Tonio grinned at her anguish. "I shall return, Mama," he said. "I promise. I shall return." And he embraced his mother and wiped her tears with a handkerchief.

"When do you leave?" Giacomo asked.

"In ten days."

"Will you be in the infantry?"

"No. I have been accepted as a motorcycle courier."

"Then you will not be in the trenches?"

"No, Mama."

"*Grazie a Dio! Grazie a Dio!*" Elvira cried in relief as she threw her arms around her son and covered his face with kisses.

True to his promise, Antonio Puccini brought great joy and relief to his anxious parents when he returned safely three years later.

The conflict had convulsed Italian life. Travel had become

limited. Few friends visited Torre del Lago. The Puccini's were alone. Giacomo avoided his piano, and the inactivity choked him. Throughout the country nothing had mattered more than victory. Opera had become an event of marginal importance with almost no productions taking place.

Despite these circumstances, Edoardo Sonzagno managed to première *La Rondine* on March 27, 1917. It took place in Monte Carlo, and it was a huge success. It earned cheers, twenty curtain calls, and an award for Puccini from Prince Albert I of Monaco. Strangely, the operetta's success foretold its failure. Learning it had been contracted originally for a Vienna production, disgruntled French officials denounced it as being sympathetic to Germany. The resultant uproar discouraged further productions, and *La Rondine*'s luster faded rapidly. Puccini loved his operetta. He believed the story was simple, touching and perfect: A beautiful woman falls madly in love with a handsome, penniless poet. She leaves her older lover for him. Sadly, she is forced to return to the older man when the poet's mother requires virginity as a prerequisite for her son's marriage.

Puccini's music enhanced the simple story; it gave the tale all the uplifting brightness and gripping sadness it required. He told Elvira, "It is not grand opera. It is a little thing, but it is a perfect little thing."

However, the French denunciation sent him into another of his suffocating tailspins.

In addition to this suffering, he experienced another crippling blow. In 1918, Arrigo Boito last of the *Scapigliatura Milanese*, died after a horrible year of illness. *"Boito was a giant,"* Giacomo wrote to Sybil. *"He championed the best of Italian music. I see the end of opera in the hands of our new artists. I am an alien in today's music world, dear Sybil, but I must continue to compose if I hope to retain my sanity."*

In desperation, Puccini reconsidered an idea he'd had years earlier: three short, unrelated operas, all to be performed in one evening, all to be a mixture of darkness, light, and cleverness.

He would call it *Il Trittico* (The Triptych). He explained the idea to Adami, who liked it and then responded positively to a suggestion that another young librettist would be of infinite value to them. One was found quickly. Giovacchino Forzano joined the team. Working harmoniously, they completed *Il Trittico* five months before the Great War's Armistice papers were signed in France's Palace of Versailles.

The last shots of the *War to End All Wars* were fired on November 11, 1918. It had lasted four brutal, harrowing years. Sixteen million men had been killed. Twenty-one million more became grim casualties. But as soon as the war ended, old ways struggled to regain their former respectability. City lights invited activity once more. Restaurant dining became popular, and full seasons of opera returned everywhere.

Learning of *Il Trittico,* the general manager of New York's Metropolitan Opera House cabled Puccini at once with an offer to hold the trilogy's world première in New York. Giacomo was thrilled. All the glory, all the excitement of his American *La Fanciulla* experience rushed back upon him. He accepted the proposal without hesitation.

A production of *Il Trittico* opened on December 14, 1918. Puccini did not attend, but he waited anxiously for word of its success. Once more, the maestro was crushingly disappointed. *Il Trittico* failed miserably. The first two operas, *Il Tabarro* and *Suor Angelica,* stirred no favorable interest at all. Only the third, *Gianni Schicchi,* was accepted enthusiastically, with some reviewers even calling it another masterpiece. "If I had been there," Puccini told Elvira sadly, "I would have made all three successful."

In a newspaper interview, Tito Ricordi appraised Giacomo smugly, "I suspected *Il Trittico* would be received this way. It is sad, but Maestro Puccini has never been a good judge of his own work." Tito Ricordi seemed to enjoy making him look foolish to the world.

The huge Brescia success of *Madame Butterfly* had taken place a long time ago, sixteen years to be exact. *La Fanciulla*'s popularity had been short-lived. *La Rondine,* and now *Il Trittico,* did absolutely nothing to guard Puccini's reputation or to improve his state of mind. "Have you lost your creativity?" he asked his mirror image one morning. "Can Tito be right about you? Has your time of glory passed? You have gray hairs now, Giacomo, and coughing starts your days. You are growing old... Yes, sadly, you are growing old."

He stared at himself. Finally, he sighed and murmured, "Tito be damned. I shall compose something to astound the world again, and I shall silence that fool forever."

However, Puccini did not have to complete another opera to silence Tito Ricordi forever. Casa Ricordi's board of directors did that for him. In the spring of 1919, incensed by Tito's failure to further the company's fiscal standing, Casa Ricordi's directors voted unanimously to relieve Tito Ricordi of his producing responsibilities. Enraged by what he interpreted to be a humiliating insult to his integrity, Tito then resigned from all positions of authority and left the company and Milan.

Puccini learned of Tito's demotion and departure while casually reading a Viareggio newspaper. He sat up straight. He could not believe his eyes. He gripped the paper and burst into a roaring laugh. Leaping to his feet, he did a wild little dance around a table.

Elvira rushed into the room. "What is it? What happened?" she demanded. In all their years together, she had never seen Giacomo display this degree of joy. He was beside himself with happiness. He was jubilant.

"Look! Look!" he shouted. "Read this!"

He thrust the newspaper into Elvira's hands and jabbed his finger repeatedly at the affecting article.

A smile spread across Elvira's face as she read. When she finished the report, she nodded her head and whispered, "Yes, God is just." She looked at Giacomo and grinned with him. "I am happy for you," she said. "Now, you have nothing to darken your days. The future looks bright."

And the next four years were, indeed, a bright period in Giacomo Puccini's life. Casa Ricordi's directors begged him to return. When he agreed, they assigned their new publisher to him, Carlo Clausetti, a young man who believed Giacomo to be the greatest composer in the long history of music. He introduced himself to his idol with the words, "Maestro, it will be the joy of my life to work with you and to assist you every way to your satisfaction."

Puccini beamed. "Thank you, Carlo. You and I shall become good friends. I look forward to many years of happy association."

It was as if he were a bird, liberated suddenly from a cage in which he had been denied food for body and soul. He hummed tunes. He laughed frequently. The jaunty tilt of his hat became a little more pronounced. Instead of wallowing in gloom, he hungered now for things to do.

"We must move," he told Elvira one afternoon, the idea coming from nowhere.

"Move? I love our home."

"You will love the next one even more."

"You love Torre del Lago."

"I did, but the new peat plant is too near our home, and the smell is nauseating."

"Where would you care to live if not here?"

"Viareggio. The sea air is clear there and the view is magnificent. We can build a house that will have in it everything you could desire, the palace of your dreams."

Elvira frowned and mumbled, "This is insanity." But how could she reject a dream palace?

Construction of their Viareggio home began in 1919. While they waited for its completion, Giacomo was again overwhelmed by death. Leoncavallo died on August 9, 1919, and Luigi Illica followed him four months later, on December 19th. He attended Leoncavallo's funeral out of simple respect, but he could not attend Illica's. To see his old friend being lowered into a grave would have been more than he could bear. Puccini stayed in Torre del Lago and grieved. More and more he was being isolated in the new world of opera music.

The Puccini home in Viareggio was completed in 1921. It was a huge house, furnished eventually with everything a wealthy and happy composer could possibly want. Giacomo, Elvira and Tonio settled-in with a measure of happiness that allowed them comfortable cohabitation. Their relationship had now become a matter of custom and routine, free of strife.

Puccini gathered friends around him – artists, musicians, writers – and they established a version of Torre del Lago's *Club La Bohéme* in the Viareggio hills. They christened the building the *New Gianni Schicchi Club*, after the successful third act of *Il Trittico.* Like its predecessor, it was a place of laxity and gaiety, the mottos being: **"LIVE AND LET LIVE!!"** and "**NO POLITICS HERE!!**"

Months passed in the pursuit of pleasurable interests. Finally, sated with self-indulgence, Puccini breathed deeply one morning and announced to Elvira: "I am ready to work again."

And to Sybil Seligman, he wrote: "*I am on fire. If I do not find an opera subject soon, I shall be consumed by the flame of my passion*!"

He met with Giuseppe Adami, his *Rondine* librettist. "*Caro* Adami," he said, "put your brilliant mind to the task of a new opera. Give me something that will startle and soothe, something of sorrow and joy, something simple and grand, a libretto that will endure forever. It is a small request. I know you can do it, Adami, for your genius knows no bounds. But hurry. I tremble in fear that my passion to compose may falter and fade before I see you again."

He pleaded with friends, playwrights, fellow musicians: "Help me if you love me!"

But what followed was the habitual rejection of countless suggestions until....

Renato Simoni, a noted literary figure of the day, rescued him with a suggestion. "There is a story," he said one afternoon in casual conversation. "It is an ancient Chinese fable called *A Thousand and One Nights.* Based upon it, a play was written by Carlo Gozzi in 1761 –"

"You are referring to *Turandot*?" Puccini interrupted.

"You know of it?"

"Of course. It was an extremely popular play."

"It would make a thrilling opera."

"*Hmmm*....that is something to consider."

"I suggest you look at it, Maestro. It has everything for which you have been searching. Pageantry. Oriental splendor. Crowds. Mystery. Conflict. And a cold, cruel princess who despises love but is brought to her knees by a handsome young man whose cleverness and passions are overwhelming."

Simoni's statement reignited Puccini's interest in *Turandot*. The Gozzi play was among the numerous books that constituted his personal library. He searched for it, found it, and reread it as soon as he and Renato Simoni parted that day.

Yes, he thought, *this could indeed be my next opera.*

He couldn't stop thinking about the play. He read Gozzi's play again and again. He saw scenes. He heard music. And each passing week intensified his excitement. Finally, on March 18, 1920, he could avoid his decision no longer. He wrote to Adami, "*Turandot is our elusive treasure, caro Adamino. We have found it! Here is my copy of Gozzi's play. Read it. I am certain it will charm you as it has charmed me. I bless Renato Simoni for bringing it to my attention! Now we must move forward quickly. Simoni will join us in our work. Your collaborative libretto will be a modern variant of an old story, a beautiful and fascinating explosion of imagination. Let me have a detailed outline, but not necessarily of the entire play. The first act will do. Do not keep me waiting, Adami, my piano must not be allowed to gather dust. I burn to begin!*"

Giuseppe Adami, Renato Simoni and Giacomo Puccini met in the first of many meetings. The three artists complemented each other in a blend of creative spirit unlike anything Giacomo had previously experienced. There were no endless arguments, no demands, no impatient conflicts of temperament and ego. Everything progressed smoothly, excitingly.

The libretto of Act I was presented to Puccini in January of 1921. He was not entirely satisfied with it. Suggestions for changes were agreeably received by Adami and Simoni, and they returned a few weeks later with an act that pleased Puccini enormously. Working feverishly on it, Giacomo played the act's music for his rapturous librettists that summer, and for his arduous work he was presented Act II.

This process of discussion and change proceeded with only one major dispute. Puccini wanted to make the libretto a two-act opera by shortening and squeezing Act III into Act II. Adami and Simoni believed the demand was ridiculous. They held their ground and after weeks of squabbling, Puccini relented and grudgingly accepted their strong arguments.

Work on *Turandot* continued for *three* years! Why so long? Giacomo Puccini reverted periodically to his abhorrence of work whenever the beam of inspiration wasn't lighting his way, his fits of melancholy draining him and leaving him weak and despairing for months at a time.

One day, seeing her husband in one of these moods, Elvira stood before him with hands on hips and upbraided him into action. "You sit in that chair every day and do nothing but smoke and stare into space. You make me want to scream."

Giacomo looked up at her mournfully.

"I cannot bear your indolence another day!" she said before a sudden thought brightened her face. "You told me La Scala is planning another presentation of *Manon Lescaut*. I want to see it."

Puccini's inclination to attend his operas had been choked by the depth of his depression. "*Manon* does not interest me," he said. "I am too anxious about *Turandot*."

"This must not continue, Giacomo. You need stimulation. You need diversion. Evidently, you need more than Viareggio or your Schicchi Club can offer. Milan. I want to go to Milan!"

Every day for the next few days, Elvira stood before him and made the same demand with ever-increasing finality. It was more than Puccini could bear. "All right," he eventually conceded. "I surrender. We shall go to Milan."

It became a supremely gratifying decision.

On February 1, 1923, La Scala's exquisite production of *Manon Lescaut* repaired an old, damaged friendship. Arturo Toscanini conducted the La Scala orchestra with an understanding of Puccini's intent that transcended all other productions the composer had ever attended. Toscanini brought tears of exultation to Giacomo's eyes. Overcome with emotion, Puccini rushed to him when the cheers and endless curtain calls stopped. "Arturo...*Arturo*!" he cried, embracing the startled conductor. "*Grazie...grazie*! I have waited thirty years for an orchestra to play *Manon* as I hear it in my head! You are an angel from heaven! *Grazie, my dear friend, grazie!*"

Grateful for the reconciliation, Toscanini laughed happily with his friend.

The gala reception that evening added to Puccini's joy. Hundreds of attendees honored him, toasted him, presented him with gifts, hailed him as Italy's beloved. He reveled in his evening of glory. He glowed in the recognition of his work.

All the while, Elvira stood silently at his side with a faint and knowing smile on her face.

Returning to Viareggio, and still charged with the visit's excitement, Giacomo faced his wife. "You have saved me again, Elvira," he said emotionally. "I shall be eternally grateful."

"I want only your happiness."

Puccini clapped his hands once. He stood taller, as if an enormous weight had been lifted from his shoulders. "I am ready for *Turandot* again," he said. "And I shall persist until I have written its final notes. Nothing will deter me from completing it. *Nothing!*"

If he could have seen into the future, Puccini would never have uttered those fateful words.

- 36 -

Work on *Turandot* recommenced with verve and determination. Act II progressed slowly, each musical passage emerging painfully like an infant in birth. Unlike his past behavior, when he ranted and demanded action, Puccini's responses now became gentler, more subdued. Now he did not demand. Instead, he begged his librettists for help. "I am getting old," he told them. "I require the fire of your imagination. Please, Adamino, Simonino, I implore you, give me words that will set me ablaze. I am lost without them. Give me the words, and I shall give you the music that will secure our names forever in the annals of opera. I promise you that. I promise. Just give me the words."

While Adami and Simoni strove desperately to supply the poetry that would satisfy him, Puccini continued to fret, filling ashtrays with cigarettes butts of dismay.

Elvira warned, "Your anxiety will kill you. You know Adami and Simoni will not fail you. Take your mind off them. Do something refreshing. I cannot stand to see you this way. Do something that will pull you from this house!"

He tried. He hunted. He fished. He went sailing with Tonio. But his mind was always on *Turandot*.

Act III came from Adami and Simoni. There were elements in it he found exciting. He went to work again enthusiastically, energetically. But his vigor soon left him. Something was wrong, and he didn't know what it was. In May of 1924, he complained to Sybil, *"I cannot understand what is happening to me. I sit at my piano and stare. I have no desire to work."*

Nevertheless, Puccini persisted doggedly until he was able to tell Simoni, "Except for the final trio, I have completed *Turandot*'s score. The end is in sight."

How ironic!

Two weeks later the nagging cough that started his days erupted in a spasm so violent it had him gagging and gasping for breath as if he were dying. A terrified Elvira rushed into the room. "Are you all right? What can I do? What can I do?" she implored.

He continued to cough.

She stood near him, wringing her hands.

In time the choking abated. Breathless, Puccini fell back in his chair. Tears streamed down his cheeks. Mucus ran from his nose. His hands lay limp in his lap.

"I have told you to see a doctor about your coughing," Elvira said. "Do you need more than this episode to prove it is necessary?"

With eyes closed, Giacomo shook his head slowly. "I shall do that tomorrow," he whispered. "Tomorrow."

Tomorrow arrived, and Puccini sneaked away from his Viareggio home to visit a local physician. The diagnosis of his ailment was heartening. "You have a slight inflammation. Its cure lies in the purifying waters of a health resort."

Enormously relieved, he told Elvira and Tonio the good news and left the next day for the Salsomaggiore Health Resort near Parma. The drive was delightful, the July air perfect. The resort relaxed him completely. He stayed for a week, and in that time he was freed of his debilitating cough.

He wrote to Adami: *"All that remains are the third act love duet and the finale. My dear Adami, our journey is almost over. I thank you from the depths of my being for your endless patience."*

However, Puccini continued to smoke his cigars and cigarettes, and the soreness in his throat returned. This time, it persisted. It tormented him. And it stopped all work on *Turandot*.

"I cannot understand why this pain will not abate, he told Sybil in a brief letter. *"I can barely swallow. I must go to Florence to see a highly recommended throat specialist."*

The next morning, without telling Tonio or Elvira where he was going, Giacomo Puccini slipped away from Viareggio. His concern deepened during this trip with each troublesome swallow of saliva. And there was good reason. In Florence, he learned that a growth deep in his throat was the source of all his pain and discomfort.

On his return to Viareggio, he informed his son Tonio of the diagnosis and asked him to discover the meaning of some medical terms the doctor had used. Tonio complied immediately. He communicated with the doctor in Florence and soon learned the horrible truth: "Your father has a throat cancer too advanced for surgery."

The diagnosis was stunning. It suggested death. Tonio did not tell Puccini or Elvira what he had learned. Instead, he fabricated a lie and arranged to have Giacomo examined by a series of esteemed throat specialists. All came to Viareggio from distant cities at different times. To keep Elvira ignorant of his fears, he had the examinations take place in a Viareggio hotel room.

All examinations confirmed the Florence physician's conclusions: throat cancer; treatment impossible.

The shattering truth could no longer be denied. However, well aware of Elvira's emotional proclivities, father and son feared her unmanageable outbursts and contrived to keep the shocking news a secret as long as possible.

Giacomo and Tonio sat silently in the living room of their Viareggio home. They had just discussed a plan of action: They would slip away to Brussels, to the Institut de la Couronne. In his research, Tonio had learned that a gifted physician, Doctor Ledoux, was performing cancer miracles there with specialized X-ray treatments.

Puccini seemed befuddled by the swiftness of events. Yesterday, he had only a bad cough and a sore throat. Today, he faced death.

In pain and deeply troubled, he left for Brussels with Tonio in early November. Learning of Puccini's condition from Tonio, Fosca left husband and children and joined them in Brussels. But Elvira, still ignorant of the gravity of Giacomo's condition, was encouraged to remain at home.

At the Institut de la Couronne, Puccini faced a three-pronged treatment. It consisted of a series of radium throat injections, a radium collar, and a troublesome tracheotomy, which allowed him to breathe but prevented him from speaking and eating.

Seven radium needles were inserted directly into the cancer. The procedure lasted more than three hours and was accomplished while he lay awake under local anesthesia. For the next few days Puccini endured excruciating pain and the terrible discomfort of being fed through a nasal tube. However, Doctor Ledoux was quite optimistic. "Your father," he told Fosca and Tonio, "has remarkable stamina. Everything looks quite promising."

Two days later, Giacomo Puccini slipped into a deep coma.

The radium needles were removed quickly, and he was injected with a heart stimulant. He failed to respond. Elvira was notified; she rushed to Brussels. A priest was summoned. Last rites were administered. Notices were sent to all waiting newspapers, and the entire world of opera waited anxiously for one of its greatest composers to recover or to die.

Tonio, Fosca and Elvira sat at Puccini's bedside. Fosca held Giacomo's hand, stroking it lightly. Tears wet her cheeks as she murmured loving words. Tonio watched his father grimly and wordlessly. Elvira sat at the other side of the bed, one hand on Giacomo's arm, the other wiping her steady flow of tears. Fear and weariness lined all three faces.

Uncertainty ended abruptly. On November 29, 1924 Giacomo Puccini exhaled a final shuddering breath and sent the nation into a paroxysm of mourning that lasted for weeks. Though a funeral ceremony was held in Brussels, the true service took place in Milan four days later, on the third of December.

Puccini's body was transferred to Milan by train. After a somber ceremony, it was conveyed to the Cimitero Monumentale. Mobs of mourners lined the streets. Sobs and cries of lamentation punctuated the entire procession. Even heaven mourned the nation's loss; torrential rain poured from a dark sky as the horse-drawn hearse made its way slowly down the city's streets. At the cemetery, Puccini's body was placed in Arturo Toscanini's family tomb, where it awaited transfer to a mausoleum that Tonio would have constructed in Torre del Lago.

The death of father and husband weighed heavily on the family for years. Fosca, sometimes weeping for no apparent reason, immersed herself in her own family's needs. Tonio, somber and unusually pensive, struggled with subsequent legal matters. And Elvira withdrew into a cocoon of self-pity from which she found it impossible to free herself. In time, however, the collective suffering eased, and a semblance of normality returned to all three.

One day, Tonio told Elvira "I have received word that Toscanini would like to have *Turandot* completed for presentation at La Scala."

"It would then not be your father's opera," she protested.

"Toscanini assures us it will always be his."

"How can he guarantee that?"

"I trust him, Mama. *Turandot* was not meant to languish and die on a shelf. Papa would not want it so, and Toscanini is the only maestro to whom I would entrust it."

Elvira finally relented, though she remained deeply troubled by the prospect of having another composer's name added to the opera. Tonio informed Toscanini of his mother's approval, even sending the conductor thirty pages of Giacomo's notes for the opera's ending.

Assured of the family's approval, Arturo Toscanini was galvanized to action. He searched and quickly found a young, gifted composer whom he could easily control. His name was Franco Alfano, and he was thrilled to be part of this august undertaking. Work began at once and continued without interruption until Toscanini was satisfied that *Turandot* had been completed to Puccini's specifications.

On April 25, 1925, a year and a half after Puccini's death, *Turandot* was presented to the world at Milan's La Scala opera house. A grand audience of Italy's notables filled the theater. Murmurs of eagerness, of curiosity, of apprehension rippled through the auditorium. What had the master left as his final creation? Another memorable masterpiece? Or another unforgivable disappointment.

Instrument tuning faded to silence. A hush of expectancy filled the theater. Arturo Toscanini appeared. He bowed to welcoming applause and then faced his orchestra. His baton tapped the music stand before him. Silence settled over everything like a velvet cloak. The baton rose, waited a moment, and then came down. Overture music filled the theater. It entranced the audience and brought resounding applause at its conclusion. Then Toscanini tapped his music stand again. The audience waited. His baton poked the air. The curtain parted. And everyone was transported to the noisy activity of a Peking, China, market place.

Applause filled La Scala theater for the exotic splendor of the scene, and later, repeatedly, for the glory of Puccini's music. In Act III, *Nessun Dorma*, the tenor's brilliant aria, brought a response so reverberating it demanded performer and conductor bows. Toscanini complied, but he despised interruptions, and he hurried back to the pit and his orchestra. The performance continued. The audience was enthralled until....

Near the end of Act III and immediately after the touching aria of Liu the slave girl, Arturo Toscanini suddenly slashed the air with his baton and brought his orchestra to an abrupt and complete silence.

La Scala's patrons waited. Murmurs of puzzlement rippled through the theater.

The great conductor turned and faced his audience. He paused. He scanned the house. Then in a voice that trembled with emotion, Arturo Toscanini announced: "At this point, our beloved maestro, Giacomo Puccini, was unable to continue his work. Death deprived us of his genius."

After that brief statement, he placed his baton on his music stand and with head bowed swiftly left his orchestra.

Turandot's auspicious audience buzzed in surprise. However, as the curtains closed slowly to a rustle of applause, someone shouted: "Puccini lives. *Puccini lives!* ***Viva Puccini!***" and the rustle exploded into thunderous waves of agreement.

This abbreviated performance was Toscanini's homage to Giacomo Puccini, his dear friend and fellow artist. It recognized the end of a brilliant career, one that continues to thrill lovers of music everywhere.

There are opera houses in all cultured countries of the world today. More than 25,000 performances take place in them annually. Many of those performances are of Giacomo Puccini's greatest operas, and they never fail to stir its deeply appreciative audiences to cheers and tumultuous reactions. It is safe to say such appreciation will continue until opera itself is no longer an important form of music artistry.

Indeed, Puccini lives. *Puccini lives!* ***Viva Puccini!***

REFERENCES

Novels about historical figures require information that can be obtained only from factual sources. These most often are the biographies written by other authors. For readers who have had their interest in Giacomo Puccini piqued by ***VIVA PUCCINI!*** to the point of further investigation into the life of this astounding composer, I recommend most heartily the following books:

- Giacomo Puccini - The Man and His Work by Richard Specht and Catherine Alison Phillips
- Puccini by Julian Budden
- Giacomo Puccini by Conrad Wilson
- Giacomo Puccini and His World by Emanuele Senici (Edited by Arman Schwartz)
- Puccini - A Critical Biography by Mosco Carner
- Puccini - A Biography by Mary Jane Phillips-Matz
- Puccini and His Operas by Stanley Sadie
- The Life of Giacomo Puccini by Stanley Jackson
- Puccini by Howard Greenfeld
- Puccini Without Excuses by William Berger
- The Puccini Companion - Edited by William Weaver and Simonetta Puccini
- Letters of Giacomo Puccini - Edited by Giuseppe Adami (Translated from Italian by Ena Makin)

OTHER TITLES BY MEL WEISER

FICTION

On 174th Street - The World of Willie Mittleman
The Trespasser a psychic thriller*
Within the Web an action thriller*

NONFICTION

Nick Nolte - Caught in the Act
(Award: Best Celebrity Book of 1999
Book Publicists of Southern California)

PLAYS

A Tiny Piece of Land (co-written with Joni Browne-Walders)
Merci, Mercer!
Cry, Tiger!
Check Your Worries
Stop, You're Killing Me!
Plenty of Money

CHILDREN'S STORY

The Devilish, Dastardly, Criminal Crime